PRAISE

'Ryan is a freaking good storyteller, what a brain!'
— Ron Davis, author of *Disadvantage Line*

'A ripping good yarn, well told.'
— Capt. Martin Knight-Willis MC Rtd.
Formerly New Zealand SAS and Rhodesian SAS

'Ryan is that rare breed of thriller writer,
a craftsman and an artist.'
— Lee Jackson, author of *Redemption*

THE FIELD OF
BLACKBIRDS

ALSO BY THOMAS RYAN

Short Stories

THE FIELD OF BLACKBIRDS

Thomas Ryan

THOMAS & MERCER

Published by Thomas & Mercer, Seattle

Amazon, the Amazon logo and Thomas & Mercer are trademarks of Amazon.com, Inc., or its affiliates.

www.apub.com

ISBN-13: 9781477830093
ISBN-10: 147783009X

Cover design by bürosüd° München, www.buerosued.de

Library of Congress Control Number: 2014958627

Printed in the United States of America

For Meg,
my muse,
my friend,
my perfect wife,
with all my love.

1.

rben Shala. Get your passport out of that hotel. Get the hell out of Kosovo.

The imperatives flashed in Arben's mind like neon signs.

But he knew the more immediate threat might well be hypothermia. Released from the detention centre without gloves or hat, he asked to be driven to his hotel. The police had laughed. Their response: leave or go back to the cell. His choice: ankle deep snow or another night in prison. The snow won.

Arben's arms rose to beat at his chest. But this threw him off balance. Precious strength went to save his stocky frame from crashing to the icy boulevard. Steaming billows of breath disappeared into the night in rapid succession. He knew he must resemble an arthritis-ridden old man. Would he be attracting unwelcome attention? Stinging eyes cast side to side for evidence of it. None.

A screech above his head.

Arben stumbled. His heart thumped like a hammer.

More screeching.

The crows had arrived. He'd seen them at the end of each day when temperatures plummeted. They swooped across the Prishtina rooftops like a black cloud, settling on sagging power lines, television aerials and the fractured clay guttering that edged dilapidated apartment buildings. Silhouetted against a darkening sky, they would perch, watching the activities below like an army massing for an attack.

Out of the dusk emerged the bronze statue of Mother Teresa. Arben's hand reached to find the solidity of its base. He stopped there, chest heaving. A fit of coughing half-doubled him. He wiped his mouth. Icicles forming in days-old stubble fell away in his fingers.

An unsteady step forward. Then another. His eyes encountered those of two women entering a nearby shop. He noted the frown lines. Lifting a hand, he gestured he was okay. They hesitated. The one closest to the door said something. The other nodded and they disappeared inside.

Arben rubbed his hands together in a vain attempt to keep the circulation going. Wrapping his jacket tighter around himself, he pressed on. The lights of the Grand Hotel were now in sight.

Along the busier part of the boulevard nervous drivers blasted car horns at motorists and pedestrians alike. The defining line between pavement and carriageway had become lost beneath two feet of snow. Light from shops splashed colours out of a child's paintbox across the snow and sludge. Through shop-front windows Arben could see cheerful faces flushed with the warmth of central heating. He dismissed any thought of joining them, even for just a moment.

Away from cover, the more hardy vendors stood alongside small iron cookers filled with hot embers. Arben's mouth watered as aromas of roasting chestnuts and maize cobs assaulted his nostrils. The growl in his stomach reminded him that he had refused to eat for two days. A symbolic and largely futile protest, it was true, but one that at least had served to boost his spirits. He would eat later. No time now.

As he crossed the top of the lane flanking one side of the Grand, he caught a glimpse of the multi-storey UN headquarters building barely visible through the falling snow. Had he a machine gun he would have emptied the magazine at it. Arben was not a violent man, but the UN had known he was in prison. And it wouldn't have escaped them that the circumstances of the crime of which he stood accused were so unlikely, so bizarre for a man with his profile, that almost certainly official corruption must have been lurking around somewhere. Yet they did nothing. Working saliva into a dry mouth, Arben spat in the direction of the building. It disappeared into the snow on the pavement.

He looked over his shoulder to search the shadows. No one in sight. But he knew they'd be there. Watching.

6∼9

At first glance Arben's hotel room looked just as tidy as he had left it. Despite the housemaid's best efforts, the smell of air-freshener and bathroom cleaner failed to mask the background odours of damp carpet and mildew. Arben drew open the door of the wardrobe. His coat was still there. He laid it on the bed and ran his fingers over the satin lining. When he felt the package he whispered an elated 'Yes'. He dragged the serrated brass teeth of the door key across the cotton threads holding the seam. The stitches parted. Inserting thumb and forefinger into the gap, he clamped onto the edge of an envelope and pulled it out. Two thousand euros and his New Zealand passport were inside it. The police had confiscated the Serbian passport he had used to enter Kosovo. The corrupt bastards could keep it for all he cared.

On the bedside table a silver photo frame lay face down. He extended the plastic flap at the back and stood it up in the space next to the telephone. There was no resisting an urge to reach out and run a finger across the images of his wife and children behind the protective glass.

'I'll be home soon,' he whispered. 'I love you.'

He kicked off his shoes. The malodorous clothes he had worn the past week followed. When he was naked, he dumped the filthy pile into the plastic bin by the door. He sank into the downy duvet on the bed. It would be so easy to collapse there and sleep.

'Keep moving, Arben, don't stop now,' he muttered.

In the bathroom, he turned on the basin's tap and scooped water over his head. The haggard unshaven face looking back at him through the mist on the mirror shocked him. He wiped the glass and leaned closer. Eyes had puffed up. Skin looked bruised with fatigue.

He soaped his face. None too gently, he dragged the razor across his stubble.

'Dammit.'

He ripped off a piece of toilet paper and dabbed away fresh blood.

'Damn. Damn. Damn.'

The headache that had plagued him all day returned. Dropping the bloodied paper to the floor he massaged his forehead. It had no effect. He needed painkillers. A search through his toilet bag proved fruitless. He slammed his fist against the wall, then leaned on the basin and closed his eyes. His mind drifted back to the days of his youth, of hunting with his father and grandfather in the mountains on the border with Macedonia. Freezing winds had howled through the rocky crevices, chilling his bones until he thought they might snap. The pain had made him cry. But never had he experienced such misery as now.

Shaving done, he stepped into the shower. Water sprayed over him in erratic bursts. At least it was hot. Frozen limbs began to thaw.

The hot shower and a change of clothes lifted Arben's spirits. As he trundled his bag across to reception new vitality returned to his step. The sense of freedom, now so close, had beaten off fatigue for the moment. A squeaky suitcase wheel alerted the duty manager of his approach.

'Mr Shala. We haven't seen you for some days.'

Arben's response was little more than a curl of the lips. Not quite a smile but it would do.

'Have you been travelling?'

Arben knew that nothing happened in Kosovo hotels that managers did not know about. And that hotel staff had no qualms supplementing their meagre incomes by spying for anyone prepared to pay them. This conversation was a reminder that he still needed to be on his guard.

'May I have my bill?' asked Arben.

'You are leaving Kosovo?'

A shake of the head. 'I've met a friend. From the old days. He has an apartment near Kaminice. I'm going to stay with him.'

'How nice for you.' The stocky manager's greying head dropped as he thumbed through a stack of documents. An invoice came to light. 'Here it is. Would you like the hotel driver to drop you somewhere? The bus station perhaps?'

Arben hadn't anticipated this offer. 'Um. My friend's waiting at a cafe. A short walk from here.'

'Wonderful.'

Arben gave the invoice a quick scan then dumped a handful of euros onto the counter. Pocketing the receipt, he grabbed the handle of his bag and wheeled it towards the door.

'Please come again,' the duty manager called after him.

Arben didn't bother to reply.

At the door a pair of gloves and woollen hat came out of his overcoat pocket. He pulled the hat down over his ears. Gloved and warm, Arben stepped out into the cold with his bag trailing behind him.

The snowfall had become heavier.

A street seller at the bottom of the lane was keeping himself warm by swinging his arms like propellers. Arben bought a phone card from him. The intrepid entrepreneur withheld Arben's change. He lifted a cloth covering a small wooden crate to reveal a stack of cigarettes and a dozen chocolate bars. Arben licked his lips. He counted off another ten euros and bought all the chocolate bars. By the time he reached the public phone a few metres away he had devoured one bar and was partway through another.

The phone attached to a metal pole had only a sheet of Perspex as overhead cover. Arben hunched under it and removed a glove. He had decided against calling his home. Kimie would know from the tone of his voice something was wrong and he had no time for explanations. He pushed the card into the slot and dialled a number he knew as well as his own.

Two rings.

'Hi. You've reached the number of Jeff Bradley. Please leave a message.'

'Dammit, Jeff. It's Benny. I'm in a lot of trouble. I'm leaving Kosovo tonight. I'll ring you tomorrow from Macedonia.'

He rang off and crossed the street to the three taxis lined up outside the shopping mall. Only one cabbie was prepared to venture outside his vehicle. Arben eyed him.

'I need to go to the Macedonian border.'

The driver looked to the heavens with a world-encompassing sweep of an arm.

'The road conditions are very bad. Even if I was prepared to take you to the border it'd take twice as long as usual and I would never get a return fare. Not at this time of night. For sixty euros it's just not worth my while.'

Arben was in no mood for bartering. He reached into his pocket, pulled out a handful of notes and counted some off.

'How about three hundred?'

Fanned out like a poker hand, six fifty-euro notes appeared before the cabbie's eyes. He plucked them from Arben's fingers.

With a sense of deep relief, Arben threw his bag onto the back seat and climbed in after it. As the vehicle pulled away he felt he could relax. But only a little. He would not feel truly safe until he crossed the border.

⁍

The man in the passenger seat of the black Mercedes lit a cigarette. He lowered the window and flicked the match into the darkness. A blast of cold air swept across the front seat.

'Shut the fucking window,' the driver moaned.

'Stop complaining. At least we're moving.'

But with a shiver the passenger rolled up the window.

The car followed Arben's taxi. When it took a left-hand turn at the central bus depot, the passenger pulled out his mobile phone and punched in a number.

'Tell me,' said a voice.

'He's in a taxi on the road to the Macedonian border.'

'He might be visiting friends like he told the hotel manager. But if he's not, make sure he doesn't cross the border.'

'Will do.' The passenger snapped his phone shut and slipped it into his pocket. 'We're to follow. If he tries to cross the border, we're to stop him.'

The driver's face pressed almost against the windscreen as he manipulated the steering wheel to take the car through the blizzard.

'We need to get ahead. It'll be impossible to pass in these conditions.'

'Don't worry. Our chance will come.'

ᴄ∾ᴏ

His money had bought a drive to the border as far as Arben was aware, not a racetrack trial. A shout at the driver to slow down earned him a grunt followed by an accelerated burst out of the next corner. Arben got the message. The cabbie would drive his car any way he damn well liked. To steady his nerves Arben preoccupied himself with checking to see if he was being followed. It proved a futile exercise at best. Through the grimy rear window all car shapes were lost in a haze of bobbing headlights.

When the taxi finally reached the border town of Kaminice, Arben unclenched his hands and rubbed the tops of his thighs. His muscles, taut from tension and cold, threatened to cramp. He had a sudden vision of his legs collapsing just metres short of the border crossing, and him being bundled into an ambulance and driven back to Prishtina. He shuddered at the thought. Massaging his legs was having the desired effect. Warmth was returning.

Cafes and small shops lined the right-hand side of the long main street. In Kaminice at night, as Arben knew was the tradition in all the towns of Kosovo, the locals left the comfort of their homes to gather in small groups. So there they were, chatting with friends and warming their hands over coal-fired stoves. A few curious eyes glanced at the taxi, but no particular interest came his way.

The taxi stopped two hundred metres short of the border control.

'I can go no further. You have to walk from here.'

With a cursory nod Arben climbed out and plodded forward, dragging his suitcase behind him. He barely glanced at the car easing past. But when it stopped a few metres ahead and the doors opened, his gut turned.

'Oh fuck. No.'

THE FIELD OF BLACKBIRDS

Two men, braced for the cold in long woollen overcoats, climbed out of the Mercedes and picked their way through the dirt-streaked tyre-churned snow towards him. They displayed no obvious urgency. Arben cast around in panic. His eyes focused on the shadowy figures inside the control booths two hundred metres away. But he knew very well that the border guards would not intervene to help him. Even if they bothered to notice that the occupants of the black car were acting in a suspicious manner, the heavy snowfall and sub-zero temperatures would prove persuasion enough for underpaid border guards to look the other way.

Arben's shoulders sagged.

He offered no resistance as the men pushed him to their vehicle. All he could do was pray to God that Jeff Bradley had got his message.

2.

'Holy shit, Jeff. Take it easy.'

The task of Manny the trainer was to steady the punching bag from behind. It was normally a cakewalk. But on this occasion the need to unwind and release pent-up aggression was powering Jeff's fists.

'You're the trainer, Manny. You know I don't hold back.'

'What's got you so pissed this morning?'

Like dew on a windscreen, drops of perspiration merged into rivulets running over the chiselled pecs and six-pack of the upper body that Jeff took pride in sustaining. Another duck, another weave and he let fly with a right cross. The leather glove sank into the canvas hard enough to jolt Manny backwards. Jeff followed with a left hook. The bag elevated, throwing Manny completely off balance and sending him crashing onto his rump. Jeff reached out a mitt to help pull him to his feet.

'Come on, old man. I'll buy you a fruit juice.'

'How about you take me next door and buy me breakfast?'

'Not today. I'm off to see my lawyer.'

'Ah. Explains the workout. Is that bitch you were married to trying to steal more of your money?'

A furrow formed on Jeff's brow.

'Have a little respect, Manny.'

'Sure, man. No offence.'

Manny took a position on the bench-press seat, elbows on knees, catching his breath.

Jeff understood the reason for Manny's hostility towards women. Three divorces had cost him dearly. What he didn't understand was why Manny, approaching sixty, balding and paunchy, still went clubbing most nights trawling for wife number four.

The trainer reached for the hand towel draped across a stack of bar bells and tossed it. Jeff used it like a dish cloth to wipe sweat from his face and arms. The sight of his profile in a floor-to-ceiling mirror caught his attention. He straightened and patted his abs. Manny chuckled.

'Admiring yourself again?'

'Just checking for fat.'

'There isn't an ounce of fat on that physique of yours. But don't worry. With hard work and training, one day you too could have a gut just like mine.'

'When that day comes I'll shoot myself.' Jeff tossed the hand towel back. 'I'm going to take a shower. See you, Manny.'

'Okay. Good luck with the lawyer.'

ᏋᎷᏉ

Jeff couldn't help shaking his head when he saw Quentin Douglas and Associates in shiny gold leaf lettering on Quentin's new oak door. Associates? What mischief was his friend up to now? In all the years Jeff had known him, Quentin had never had a partner. He hated the idea. His uninceremonious dumping from one of Auckland's premier law firms had turned him off the idea of ever again working for or with someone else.

Jeff pushed through the door just as Quentin's receptionist, her back to him, was leaning forward to water one of two leafy rubber plants. Jeff smiled. He had long admired Mary's well-formed derrière and shapely legs and here they were on display like jewellery in a glass case. Fortune had decreed that this international tri-athlete would escape the athlete's curse: tree stumps for legs.

Quentin was quite unbegrudging in allowing Mary time off for training. In return he had gained an Olympic medallist to staff his front desk. It was good for his practice, and it was a bonus that Mary held a law degree. Jeff fancied her. But Quentin had made him promise to keep his distance.

'Mary is the best secretary I've ever had, so hands off,' Quentin had ordered. But to Jeff it had sounded more like begging than a warning. So he continued with mild flirtation, more to wind up his friend than out of any serious intention of seduction.

A blond ponytail flicked across Mary's shoulder as she looked up.

'Were you looking at my arse?'

A smile robbed the question of any edge.

'Of course I was. If you put it out there I'm going to look.'

Mary leaned over the second plant and emptied her copper watering can.

'Pervert. Did you go to the pool this morning?'

'Fifty lengths. Then the gym.'

'Why don't you come when I'm there? We could train together.'

'I couldn't cope with being shown up by a woman, especially one with such a cute butt.'

Mary snorted.

'How can you find little old me intimidating? I thought you were a Green Beret or something.'

'Firstly, the Green Berets are American. I was in the SAS. Special Air Service. And secondly,' he leaned closer, 'you are one very scary woman.'

This earned him a kiss on the cheek and a hug.

'Thank you for the gift, I love it.'

'You're welcome.'

The watering can came in for a fond pat before disappearing under Mary's desk. Jeff had found her the polished hammered antique at the Ponsonby Market. 'For your treasured "babies", he had written on the card.

'The boss didn't even remember my birthday.'

As she spoke, Jeff noted Quentin Douglas's dark-suited form appearing in the doorway.

'That's because he's mean-spirited.'

With a good-natured harrumph, Quentin gave Jeff the once-over.

'Shit, Jeff. Jeans and a T-shirt? I told you to dress up.'

'They're my best faded jeans and these running shoes cost three hundred dollars.'

'Add ten percent to his bill for refusing to take advice, will you?' Quentin said to Mary.

'What's with the sign on the door, Quentin? Since when have you ever had an associate?'

Quentin chuckled.

'Image. You've heard of marketing, haven't you? My new clients gain great comfort believing that somewhere behind these closed doors lurk dozens of lawyers poring over piles of books, beavering away and doing their bidding. Anyway, come on through. They're waiting for us.'

'Rebecca's here already?'

Jeff heaved a sigh. The thought of confronting his ex-wife raised his hackles. Quentin grinned.

'And not alone. She's brought company. The sharks are circling. They can smell blood, my friend. Your blood.'

'Yeah, and I have a feeling her lawyers probably have real associates.'

'Fret not. You're in good hands.'

The first thing Jeff noted about his ex-wife when he and Quentin entered the conference room was her uncharacteristic stiff-backed stance. He sensed the polite smile she bestowed on him was somehow detached.

'Morning, Rebecca.'

Jeff's tone sounded more formal than he'd intended. His ex-wife's smile quickly faded. She'd cut her hair short so it showed off her long neck. He had always liked her neck. He noticed it was also nicely tanned, no doubt from lying in the sun, plotting ways to milk him of more money.

Two men Jeff didn't recognise sat either side of Rebecca. He picked her lawyer as the one wearing a carbon copy of Quentin's suit. But the other had him guessing: a study in unshaven chic and dressed in casual slacks, T-shirt and a chocolate corduroy jacket.

'Right, let's get down to it,' Quentin said. 'Jeff, Rebecca and I talked a little before you arrived. Everything is pretty much agreed, except for the vineyard.'

'You don't agree to be paid out?'

Jeff addressed Rebecca, but it was the lawyer who replied. 'My client has some concerns. There are discrepancies between the valuations offered by real-estate agencies and what appears to be an achievable price if the property went to auction. Mrs Bradley feels she might lose out on many thousands of dollars.'

It irritated Jeff that his wife was still using his name. 'That vineyard was left to me by my grandparents.'

'Just a minute, Jeff.' Quentin's voice cautioned calm. 'Does Mrs Bradley have a figure in mind?'

'Not as such. What she wants is for the property to go to auction.'

'Rebecca, we had an agreement.' Although he fought to keep an unflustered demeanour, Jeff was aware that the muscle on his right forearm would be flexing with the clenching of his fist.

Rebecca looked away. The man alongside touched her arm. By the familiarity of the gesture, Jeff realised that he must be the new boyfriend. He'd heard tell of some computer geek from Christchurch. But why had she brought him to the meeting? The man raised his eyes and looked at Jeff. Was that smugness he saw? It took a lot of willpower for Jeff not to reach across and smack it off his face.

'Be that as it may,' Rebecca's lawyer continued, 'Mrs Bradley is convinced this is the best course of action.'

'That property will not be sold.' The words flew from Jeff's lips. A scrape as his chair pushed back and he rose to stand. Quentin caught Jeff's arm and pulled him back down.

The geek leaned closer to whisper something in Rebecca's ear. It was followed by a smirk at Jeff. There could be no doubt in Jeff's mind: the geek was behind this.

The geek leaned forward. 'Rebecca wants what's hers.'

Jeff's finger stabbed in his direction like a knife.

'You keep out of this. It's none of your business.'

The man recoiled. Under the table Jeff felt Quentin's fingers tap on his thigh. Rebecca's lawyer raised a hand.

'I think that Mrs Bradley has made clear her intentions. If an auction is not agreed to, we shall seek a court order.'

Jeff remained in the meeting room while Quentin saw the trio off the premises. When he returned, Mary followed with coffees. She laid out cups on the table and a plate of biscuits. Quentin looked at them.

'Rice crackers? Where are my chocolate fingers?'

'Orders from your wife. No more choccie biccies.'

With the waggle of a finger and a smile she departed. Quentin pulled a chocolate bar from his suit pocket.

'Can they do that?' Jeff asked. 'Force me to put the vineyard up for sale?'

'A court can order it, yes.' Quentin removed the wrapper and chewed off a piece of the confection. 'But don't worry. It won't happen today.'

'And that's supposed to comfort me? You don't seem to be taking this very seriously.'

'Of course I am. But Jesus, Jeff, for the moment there's not a hell of a lot I can do. The next move is theirs to make. I think they're bluffing. I'll get back in touch with Rebecca's lawyer in a few days.'

'I don't think he's the problem. It's that scruffy germ she's hooked herself up with.'

The chocolate bar finished, Quentin licked his fingers. 'Look. How about we do lunch?'

'Sorry. Not today. I need to get out to the vineyard. Arben Shala left a strange message on my answering machine two days ago and I need to speak with Kimie. If she's heard from him then I'll stop fretting but if she hasn't . . . then I'm worried.'

'Phone her,' Quentin said, pushing his mobile across the table.

Jeff pushed it back. 'These types of conversations need to be face-to-face.' A thought struck him. 'And that's another thing. Where would the Shalas go if the property was sold?'

'Not your responsibility.'

This brought a grimace out of Jeff. 'That's easy for you to say, Quentin. I was the one who sent Benny to Kosovo. If something were to happen to him, the Shalas would become very much my responsibility.'

3.

The usual twenty-five minute trip to the end of the Western Motorway had only taken fifteen. Traffic had been light. At the Kentucky Fried Chicken roundabout, Jeff made a left turn, then hung a right. Within metres the urban sprawl gave way to rural green.

The drive to the village of Kumeu and the Boundary Fence Vineyard gave Jeff the feeling of coming home. He'd been raised on a farm, and even though he had left rural life behind years before, whenever he drove in the country, memories of log fires and freshly baked bread made him smile. But the boundaries of a city's development never rested. Jeff harboured quiet regret that Greater Auckland was slowly eating into the landscape: farmland was losing out to subdivisions and lifestyle blocks.

He slowed, passing the green manicured lawns on the front boundary of Soljan's Winery. A glance took in the sprawling cream building that housed a restaurant and wine shop. Palm trees lined the entranceway and led to a white gravelled car park beyond. This historic family vineyard had long been an inspiration to him. Jeff sighed. It would be a wonderful day if Boundary Fence could ever become a serious competitor to Soljan's. But matching their kind of success would require a lifetime of commitment. And as much as he loved the country and his grandparents' vineyard, in his heart he doubted he was up to the challenge. He lacked the Soljan clan's dedication to winegrowing.

Loose gravel scrunched beneath the BMW's tyres. Small pebbles and dust sprayed out in a scything arc as Jeff slewed into his vineyard's driveway. Of course, he should have slowed down. But he was still irritated after his meeting with Rebecca.

He pulled up next to the company's silver Toyota Land Cruiser and eyed the splatters of dried mud along the side. Marko had been off-roading in it again, and as usual he hadn't bothered to clean it. Jeff knew Arben would have had his son's hide for that. And Jeff would have given Marko a bollocking himself had he not been the bearer of disquieting news about the kid's father.

Easing his six-foot frame out of the car, Jeff stretched his back then stood with hands on hips and kicked at the ground. It was a stall and he knew it. Jeff had replayed Arben's phone message several times, listening for any possible hints in the phrasing, the tone, the background noise, that might lead him to believe there was no need to worry. Now, with no further contact after two days, he had to assume the worst. And Kimie was bound to demand why he hadn't told her earlier. What could he say?

His eyes swept across the vineyard. The vines looked lush and green with a new season's canopy of growth. It was as if the hailstorm that ruined the last season's crop had never happened. He walked across to the first row. No evidence now of the ruined grapes that had hung in shreds on the vines or of the residue of those scattered across the ground.

Kneeling, Jeff scooped up a handful of soil and rubbed it into his palm. Before his inner eye the face of his manager, friend and mentor appeared.

'Nature can be a good friend and an equally cruel mistress,' Arben had once said. 'But never forget that we must always be thankful for what she provides. When she curses us, and from time to time she will, you must caress her gently in the palm of your hand to show you still love her.'

At the time Jeff had laughed off what he considered to be a melodramatic veneration of Mother Nature. But after the first year of digging ditches and pruning vines, he too began ritually rubbing soil in his hands whenever he came to Boundary Fence.

'Hey, Jeff. Where've you been hiding?'

The head of Marko Shala popped around the corner of a storage shed. He ambled across. Jeff tried to raise a smile.

'So. You missed me?'

'Yeah, man. Like I miss my appendix.'

Despite the twenty-year-old's Auckland bro-vocabulary, his accent still bore a trace of his native Albanian.

Jeff opened the boot of his car and pulled out a damp towel to wipe his hands clean. 'Marko. Why have you been chucking mud over the Land Cruiser?'

Marko hesitated, then delivered one of his disarming aw-shucks teenager grins. 'I'll wash it later. Promise.'

'Later might be sooner than you think. You do know where the hose and cleaning rags are kept?'

'Uh-huh.'

Jeff flicked the towel at him. Marko recoiled with a laugh. 'Hey, man. I could lose an eye, you know?'

Jeff finished wiping the dirt from his hands and threw the towel back in the boot. 'Just clean the vehicle. You know your dad wouldn't be happy if he saw it like that.'

Marko's eyes brightened. 'Have you heard from him? From Dad? Mum's been worried.'

'He left a message a couple of days ago.'

'Really? What did he say? Did we get the wine?'

Jeff looked towards the old house shaded from the morning sun by a giant jacaranda tree. 'Is your mother in?'

'Yeah, she's there. What did my father say? When's he coming home? Come on, Jeff. Tell me what Dad said, I have a right to know.'

Marko bounced from one foot to the other, impatience growing.

'Yes, you do,' Jeff said. 'Let's go up to the house and see your mother.'

⌖

Even in baggy black pants, a shapeless deep-purple T-shirt and a sunhat that resembled a Mexican sombrero, Kimie Shala looked elegant. Her flawless complexion belied her forty-plus years. And her figure held no hint she had borne two children. Kimie approached life with such passion and energy that she often left the super-fit Jeff feeling breathless. It was easy to understand why Arben worshipped his wife.

He had once boasted that Kimie was a violinist of some note.

'She studied at the Belgrade School of Music,' he had informed Jeff in tones of respect tinged with pride.

One day sitting in the shade of the jacaranda, Jeff had casually asked Kimie if she still played. She excused herself and disappeared into the house. Perplexed, Jeff looked to Arben for an explanation.

'The violin reminds her of home. Of her family. Of all she has lost. These memories are still too painful. Maybe one day she will play again, but for now it is a part of the life she has left behind her.'

Now here he was, bringing even more bad news from the country Kimie needed to forget.

Decking ran the length of the eighty-year-old kauri villa. Leaning on the railing, Kimie waited. That she hadn't waved a welcome filled him with apprehension. She must have suspected something was up.

Bending forward Jeff allowed Kimie to hug him and kiss his cheeks three times in the custom of many Eastern Europeans.

'Morning, Kimie.'

'Jeff. You're just in time for lunch.'

'Not today.'

'Coffee, then?'

Jeff nodded.

'Take off your boots, son,' Kimie growled at Marko. He ducked as she reached a hand to tidy her fingers through his dark mop of hair.

'Mum. Don't do that. I'm not a kid.'

Jeff considered her manner a touch mechanical. Normally when she showed affection to her son there was playful banter between the two. Not today. He assumed it was because of the anxiety that must have been eating away at her since Arben had left.

The aroma of hot meat and fresh mint wafted along the hallway. A roast lamb would be in the oven. His stomach rumbled, but he'd decided to make do with the fruit juice he'd had at the gym. No way could he sit and eat with Kimie and Marko after what he was about to tell them.

'How have you been, Jeff? We've not seen you for a week.'

'Busy with my lawyer, Kimie.'

She nodded. The Shala family knew what 'busy with my lawyer' meant for Jeff. He'd have been dealing with his marital problems. They would never question him about it.

Six chairs were neatly pushed in around the dining table. Jeff sat in the place long ago regarded as his, at Arben's right hand and next to their daughter, Drita. In the early days, the cute child with the mop of blond hair that bounced whenever she ran could be found anywhere Jeff happened to be, following him like a puppy. But now, at the ripe old age of thirteen, her former crush on Jeff had transferred itself to high school boys. Today the precocious and loveable teenager was in school.

On the bench a cafetière sat brewing on a silver tray. Kimie placed espresso coffee cups and saucers round it. A pack of biscuits followed. Kimie tore open one end and jiggled a few onto a small white side plate. All this while her back was turned to Jeff and Marko. The son kept fidgeting on his chair and aiming expectant glances at Jeff.

Jeff waited until Kimie placed the tray on the table. 'Benny left a message on my answer phone two days ago.'

Kimie sank into a chair. Her eyes focused on a spot on the back of her left hand. A distracted finger rubbed over it. 'Oh?'

'I'm sorry, Kimie. The message wasn't good news.'

'Two days,' Kimie whispered, her head drooping. 'Two days. Jeff, you know how worried we've been.'

Jeff shifted position in his seat. 'I wanted to be certain.' He turned to Marko. 'Your father said he was in trouble. He was on his way to Macedonia the night he left the message. He said he would phone me once he got there.'

Kimie's hazel eyes rose to seek Jeff's. Her expression revealed a mixture of resignation and fear and a hint of the rebuke that he knew he deserved. 'I take it he hasn't telephoned?'

Jeff shook his head. 'No. Not yet.'

Marko's elbows dropped onto the table. He looked at Jeff. 'That doesn't mean anything, does it? Maybe he couldn't phone. Maybe he got to Macedonia and lost his money. He doesn't know anyone there.'

Jeff caught Kimie's glance. He knew they shared the same thought: *Arben would have found a way.*

'I think if your father hasn't called it's because he's unable to do so. Not because of money.'

'That's what I think, too,' Jeff said. 'My guess is he's still in Kosovo.'

Cups rattled as Marko's fist slammed the table. 'If my father is in trouble then I'm going to Kosovo to look for him. Will you buy me a ticket, Jeff? And lend me some spending money? Please. I'll pay you back. You know I will.'

Jeff found himself suppressing a smile at the display of youthful impetuosity. 'Not on your life. You're staying right here, Marko. I need you to look after the business. And your father would want you here looking out for your mother and sister.'

'Jeff is right,' Kimie nodded. 'Your place is with me and Drita.'

Marko stood, knocking his chair backwards. 'Look. If something's happened to Dad, I have to go find him. It's my duty to go. If you won't let me have the money, I'll find it somewhere else . . .'

'Forget it, Marko. You're not going. I'm going.'

The words had blurted from Jeff's lips before he had time to think. But once spoken, the adrenaline rush that followed surprised him. Cleared his senses. At the same instant, he realised how much he'd missed the SAS. Here was an opportunity to do what he did best in the service of a friend.

Kimie's eyes widened. 'You would do this?'

Jeff sucked in a deep breath. Kimie held his gaze.

The conversation they'd had before Arben left for Kosovo had been haunting him for two days. Kimie had begged Jeff not to let Arben go. 'You don't know what it is like there,' she had pleaded. 'The country is overrun with criminals. It is too dangerous. Something will happen to him, I know it will.'

Kimie would never openly blame him if things did turn out as she feared. Jeff knew her well enough to know this. But he also knew that in her eyes he would always see the unspoken accusation.

'Yes, of course I'll go.'

Marko was now at his side. 'You can't go alone, Jeff. You don't speak the language. I do. How would you find your way round? How would you know who to trust? Kosovo is full of bad guys. You must take me with you. Tell him, Mum.' Kimie reached out to stroke her son's arm. Marko yanked it away. 'It's not fair.'

It looked as if he wanted to say something more. Instead he turned and raced out of the room. Jeff suspected he must have been close to tears.

'There is a man who was a close friend to my father.' Kimie's voice was calm. 'I'll phone and ask him to have his son, Sulla, meet you at the airport. He used to have his own business, importing household products from Macedonia, I think, maybe to Serbia. But something happened, I do not know what, but Sulla no longer does this business. So he has time. He can look after you. Be your driver.'

Jeff nodded over a sip of coffee. Even then his military brain was beginning to formulate a strategy.

4.

Halam Akbar smiled to himself at the beginning of a lovely winter's day.

The rays of the early morning sun glinted through dew clinging to the leaves of drooping willow branches, creating tiny rainbows. Against the opposite bank, a long glass-topped boat bobbed at its mooring. Creepers along the riverbank bloomed with flowers – purples, reds and whites. His eyes rose to take in the three-storey apartment buildings behind. The colours on the bank were reflected in flowerpots in almost every window.

Good to be alive.

Crisp temperatures hadn't forced Halam inside the cafe. He chose instead a table against the metre-high stone wall that banked the Ljubljana River. There he sat and sipped his espresso. Italian, the waiter had said it was. It tasted Moroccan to Halam. Ripping the top off a sugar sachet, he upended the contents into his cup then stirred while contemplating the day ahead.

Across the river, athletes were gathering in the town square. As part of their limbering up, men and women had been jogging past him for the past half-hour. A few had smiled and offered morning greetings. Halam had responded with nods of acknowledgement. Supporters milled about, watching the warm-up routines and seeking out the best vantage points for the start of the marathon. It pleased him to see such a growing crowd of spectators.

At his back, a row of trestle tables stretched to the end of the street. The Sunday market was further incentive for citizens to leave their centrally heated apartments and take the opportunity to haggle over an assortment of war medals, paintings, flags, old coins, new coins made to look old, and household bric-a-brac from second-hand garden tools to fake stained-glass lampshades. To Halam it was all junk. But what did he know? He had no wife to discuss such things with. Nor a home to hang paintings in. Nor a garden to dig with second-hand tools.

In the foreground, three bridges less than fifty metres apart spanned the river. Beyond the bridges were the fish and vegetable markets. For the past few days while reconnoitring the Ljubljana inner city, Halam had seen these markets teeming with shoppers. But today they had closed. Halam mused how sometimes people just got lucky.

Magazines described Slovenia as a fairy-tale land and Halam had to agree it was true. He had enjoyed his stay. A night at a world-class ski resort and a walk along the shores of a lake with a castle in the middle of it had been a joy. Picture postcard villages snuggled into forested slopes. And up in the mountains too he had found a peace he had not experienced for as long as he could remember.

He stirred his coffee.

He was satisfied that the placement of the bombs would achieve maximum effect. Now it was time to move on. In his world it was always time to move on. To any passer-by he might easily be mistaken for a resident from one of the nearby apartments: a man without a care in the world.

$\sim$

Only he and his baby brother had survived the Israeli bombing raid that had destroyed his family home and killed his parents. Forced to live on the streets, their miserable experience had fuelled Halam's hatred and fed a desire to exact revenge. He and his brother's history did not differ greatly from that of thousands of bitter young men trapped in the war zones of the Middle East. Hamas had duly offered Halam martyrdom, but becoming a suicide bomber held no appeal. His family, devout Muslims, had taught their sons well. Although barely out of puberty and filled with the naivety of youth, he was not stupid. Halam had no interest in killing himself and he did not believe seventy virgins awaited him if he did. The Koran was very clear: martyrdom rewarded soldiers killed defending or fighting the enemies of Allah. It said nothing about innocent women and children. Luckily for Halam there was no shortage of alternative opportunities.

Hamas found him other work. Halam discovered he had a talent for bomb making. In his hands explosives became sophisticated masterpieces used to create maximum damage on buses and trains, and in city centres. Codenames protected his true identity but his bombs became as recognisable as a fingerprint. But with each explosion his hatred blurred. Having revenged his family many times over, his youthful zealotry waned with maturity and the onset of middle age. His younger brother, Zahar – barely out of his teens and too young to even remember the attack that had orphaned him – still burned with the fire of idealism. Halam knew it would eventually get the boy killed. So, establishing a new and different kind of life for them both had become a priority. Occasionally, he would daydream about finding a wife and starting a family to carry on his father's name.

But Israeli agents had infiltrated parts of the organisation. When they came for him, his group's counter-intelligence unit had received advance warning. With his brother in tow he just managed to escape to southern Lebanon.

Hezbollah welcomed the brothers and soon found work for Halam's unique set of skills. But the Israelis were persistent. They wanted Halam Akbar and they would destroy anyone standing in their way to get him. Even for Hezbollah, Halam had become a dangerous liability. He and his brother were supplied with new identification documents and smuggled into Italy, dropped off at a seedy hotel and left to their own devices. A new employer would make contact, Halam was told. So he kept his head down, kept his brother pacified and waited.

It surprised Halam that when the contact finally came, it came from Kosovo. From that day on he discarded his old life and identity as thoroughly as a desert lizard sheds its skin. He became a contract bomber available to anyone prepared to pay the price for his services. It amused him to think of himself as no better than a high-priced whore pimped out to the highest bidder by his intermediary contact in Kosovo.

What he was mattered little to him.

Halam's new life of five-star hotels and first-class travel was a welcome change from hiding in rubble and sharing food with sewer rats. Hiding in plain sight had its merits. But Halam entertained no dreamy illusions. Eventually it would end.

Then a letter arrived. An old acquaintance from his Hezbollah days was offering them a new life in a village in northern Iran – for a considerable amount of money. The village elder had two daughters he was willing to offer as brides in exchange for half a million US dollars each. The letter had enclosed photos of the two girls, both barely teenagers. They were not unattractive.

Halam had agreed. Paying for new identities, the purchase of two houses and the dowries well exceeded their current cash reserves. However, the reward for completing the job that currently occupied him and his brother would set them up nicely. After this they could put violence behind them. Village life might well prove too sedate for them after the cities and towns of Europe, but he did not care. It would be nice just to sit in the shade of a tree and enjoy a sunset with a young wife resting her head on his shoulder and children playing at his feet. He knew Zahar had a different future in his head. Village life held no appeal. It was for goatherders, not for men of substance, Zahar argued. His young head lacked wisdom but when the time came he would obey.

⌒◎

On the opposite bank in front of the pharmacy, Halam observed that two athletes involved in a stretching routine had blocked Zahar's progress. One of the runners eventually noticed him and stood aside. Zahar gave a bow and continued on his way. Halam smiled. Zahar played the cooperative citizen so well.

When Zahar reached Dragon Bridge, the furthest of the three bridges, he turned towards Halam, lifted his baseball cap and ran his fingers through his hair – the signal that it was time to leave.

The square had filled with athletes. More runners were spilling into the surrounding streets. Those marathon runners who hadn't yet stripped out of their tracksuits did so now. Others finished loosening up and began to gather near the start line.

Police paced back and forth inside barriers erected earlier to keep spectators away from the competitors. The well-behaved crowd needed little supervision. The officers smiled and exchanged pleasantries with them. When the race started the runners would cross the first bridge, run through the barriers, between the buildings and out of sight onto the course proper. Halam checked his watch.

Twenty minutes to start time.

He dropped a handful of euros on to the table, including a large tip, and waved to the waiter before moving off. The explosives in the two refuse bins – one in the square in front of the old Franciscan Church of the Annunciation and the other in front of the antique shop a few metres ahead of him – were now covered by drink cans and other rubbish.

Two excited young girls darted in front of Halam as he approached the police barrier. The parents offered an apologetic smile which Halam returned. The children climbed onto the refuse bin. Their parents scolded them to get down but the children would not move. The couple looked back at Halam and shrugged. The children, happy they had won the day, turned their attention back to the festivities. Halam hesitated, but only for a moment.

He gestured to a police officer that he needed to cross. The officer pulled a barrier segment aside to let him through then placed it back into position. In the middle of Dragon Bridge he stopped to survey the scene. Spectators occupied every vantage point on the ground. Overhead onlookers leaned out through apartment windows.

Satisfied that today would be a good day's work, Halam walked on.

Halfway up the sloping street that led away from the square to where their car waited, Zahar materialised and fell into step beside him. Patrons of the adjacent McDonald's hamburger restaurant had ventured out onto the terracing and sat round tables munching on the breakfast menu. They looked down on the activity fifty metres away. Halam and his brother exchanged nods. They both knew it was well within the planned blast zone.

Halam tossed Zahar the keys.

'You drive.'

They climbed in. As Halam buckled his seat belt, he noticed his brother had not done the same.

'Zahar, seat belt. Don't forget to turn on the headlights, you know that it is the law in Slovenia. And keep to the speed limit.'

He wanted the drive to the Italian border to be without incident.

5.

Pushed into a cell, the door slamming behind him, Arben sat on a bed with his head in his hands. Then he stood and paced awhile before leaning against the wall. He scratched his arm, but stopped when he realised it was bleeding. The stench of vomit and urine was overpowering. He tried breathing through his mouth. After a few quick breaths his head spun and he gave up. Mercifully, fatigue and depression took its toll. He collapsed onto the bed, curled into a ball like a child and fell asleep.

He awoke disorientated. All perception of time had departed. Staring at the light bulb overhead he trawled his brain for recall. Then memories came flooding back and with it his depression.

He knew he was in the basement of the Central Police Station in Prishtina. The police who had brought him back had marched him through the main entrance then pushed him down the stairs. He had fallen at the bottom and smashed his knee on the cement floor but had refused to cry out. To his befuddled mind, by not crying out he had been putting one over them. Thinking it through now, he wanted to laugh at the silliness of his bravado. Who would have cared? Who would even know?

The policemen had hauled him to his feet and dragged him along a narrow corridor to a small room next to the shower block. Behind a wooden bench were two overweight middle-aged female police officers, both in uniforms too small for them. Their breasts threatened to burst the buttons, and the trousers on the one with short black hair had ridden up into her crotch. They looked him up and down and dismissed him as if he were little more than a bug. Answers to personal questions were written down on a form attached to a clipboard. The form and his watch and other valuables went into a brown envelope. The woman with the short black hair tossed it into a tray sitting on shelving bracketed to the wall. Arben had protested at the treatment of his valuables and both women had turned on him, snarling like trapped ferrets.

A prison guard took over from the police and pushed him into the cell. There was no toilet. The guard instructed him to bang on the door if he needed to relieve himself.

That was hours ago.

He swung his legs to the floor and sat up. Wiping the sleep from his eyes, he scanned his new environment. Four beds were lined up against the right-hand wall, each covered with a quilted duvet. Arben pulled back the duvet on the bed he'd selected. The sheets looked brownish. The state of the other beds was much the same. He picked up the pillow. It was lumpy and grimy. Imagining a succession of prisoners drooling saliva over the spot where he had just laid his head caused him to gag. He dropped it, rubbing his fingers across the front of his shirt like a man who had just shaken hands with a leper.

A small window high on the rear wall proved to be only for show. A single light dangled from the ceiling on the end of a strand of wire. A plastic bottle filled with water stood on the floor beside the bed. He was thirsty. Holding the bottle to the light he determined that no strange creatures were swimming in it. He screwed off the top and took a swig. It tasted refreshing enough. He gulped down a third of the contents.

No cellmates. Isolation might be a form of punishment. If it was, Arben thought it was probably for the best. Sharing with others might make his already unbearable predicament a lot worse.

He needed to pee. He banged on the door. Nothing.

He bashed on the door again, harder this time.

For an hour he sat legs crossed. The door finally opened.

'Toilet,' Arben cried.

The guard nodded and Arben raced past him.

༺⚬༻

Hours passed. Arben lost track of how many.

A cockroach crawled across the floor. This one must have escaped the heel of his shoe. He decided it would become his ally. An unlikely companion to help him cope with the solitude. When he paced back and forth in the few metres of space available, he was careful not to tread on his little friend.

The cell door swung open. A guard entered. 'Advocate,' he grunted.

'For me? Are you sure?'

'Advocate,' the guard repeated. 'Come with me.'

Without a belt or laces, Arben had to hold on to his trousers to prevent them from falling down. His shoes flip-flopped as he walked. He was led to a room only a few metres from his cell, the only furniture a table and two chairs. His lawyer was sitting on one of the chairs, waiting for him. A friendly face should have been a welcome sight, but Arben had learned to his cost that this smartly dressed man was not to be trusted.

'How are you, Arben?' Tomi Mema pointed to the seat opposite.

Arben slumped into the chair. The guard turned his back, a gesture to imply privacy, but Arben had no doubts the man would be listening to every word.

'How do you think I am, Tomi? You know I haven't done anything wrong. You know this is bullshit.' Arben leaned forward and lowered his voice. 'Why can't you just have the charges dismissed?'

'You know it is not that simple. Only the courts can release you. You were out on bail and you tried to run. Why did you do this? Where was your head? This is very bad for you.'

'I don't need you to tell me that. I'm the one in a filthy, stinking cell.'

Mema gave the guard a quick glance. 'The people I represent are not happy. They gave you an opportunity to make everything right, but instead you decided to be foolish.' He rolled his eyes to emphasise the level of disbelief he entertained. 'What made you think you could escape these people? I warned you of the consequences if you tried.'

'All right, all right. I've got the message. Tell them I understand. I'll play ball. Just get me out of here.'

'It will not be so easy this time. Now they don't trust you. They think if you are released that you will only try to flee again. You may even cause them trouble when you are out of the country.'

Arben gave the bridge of his nose a vigorous rub.

'How can I cause trouble, Tomi? I don't even know who they are. But now that I think about it, who is doing this to me?'

Mema shook his head. 'This is exactly why they worry. Don't ask this question.'

'And your best legal advice is that I cannot win?'

Mema nodded. 'You know you cannot win.'

'Okay. Okay.'

Arben hadn't the strength or the will to fight an invisible enemy. All he wanted was to see his wife and children again. To hold Kimie in his arms, talk to his son, kiss his daughter. The money, the family farm didn't matter – whatever they wanted they could have. He was at the point of no longer caring.

'Tell them they have nothing to fear from me. I will sign whatever they want me to sign and no one will hear from me again.'

Mema nodded once more. 'In the morning you will be taken to court and maybe I can arrange for you to be released. But remember, if this happens you must organise the money and sign over the documents or they will have you sent back here.'

'Just organise it, Tomi. I'll do whatever they ask.'

'I will pass on the message.'

❧

Back in his cell, Arben sat on the bed and watched the cockroach crawling up the wall. To relieve the boredom he made small wagers with himself as to which direction it would take next. The guard brought in a mug of lukewarm tea and a stale crusty bun filled with mushy tomato and a brown lettuce leaf. He ripped off a piece of crust and tossed it onto the floor.

A banquet for his six-legged friend.

Falling back on the bed, Arben's thoughts turned from his family to Jeff Bradley. Jeff would have received his message by now. But, realistically, what could Jeff do? He didn't expect him to jump on a plane and come to Kosovo. And even if he did, Jeff would have no idea where to start looking for him. All he could hope for was that by tomorrow it would be over and he would be free.

He closed his eyes. It was time to sleep.

He conjured up an image of Kimie.

She was working in the vegetable garden at the rear of the house. He remembered she had badgered him for days until he had dug it over for her. She reached out and snapped off a parsley stem next to bushes of mint. He could almost smell it. How he loved it when she sprinkled mint over new potatoes. He walked closer to her, ever so slowly. She heard his approach and looked up. The joy in her smile melted his heart. He pulled her to her feet and took her in his arms, caressing her face and whispering her name over and over, until he drifted off to sleep.

6.

Jeff gave the other aircraft the once over as the Austrian airliner taxied past on its way to the terminal building. An American Air Force VC-25 that looked a lot like Air Force One sat parked on an offshoot of tarmac isolated from civilian air traffic. Within spitting distance of the Air Force Boeing VC-25 were two Apache helicopters acting as sentinels. Behind them was a sandbagged radar unit.

Jeff had surfed the Internet before leaving New Zealand. He discovered that after NATO had chased the Serbian army out of Kosovo, the province came under the governance of the UN. NATO troops remained but with a new role: keeping the ethnic Albanian and Serbian civilians from killing each other. Somewhere near the Macedonian border, the Americans had built a military base.

Jeff gave an involuntary shiver as he stepped out of the warm cabin onto the mobile stairs and into sub-zero temperatures. With cheerful insistence, a young woman in a charcoal ankle-length coat and bright red scarf directed the disembarking travellers towards the arrivals processing area. Jeff was in no hurry. The bags still needed offloading and the handlers were nowhere in sight. The sun hovering in a cloudless sky did little to thaw the chilly breeze sweeping across the exposed surroundings. His hands had already turned a chapped blue.

Inside the terminal, three Indian soldiers looked on as passengers formed shuffling queues in front of the four immigration control booths. When his turn came, Jeff handed his passport across to a Nigerian police officer. The man gave him a quick scrutiny before placing the travel document under a blue light. Satisfied it was not a forgery, he put it to one side and typed some information into a computer.

'What brings you to Kosovo, Mr Bradley?'

The Nigerian officer's English was impeccable.

'I'm here on business.'

'Are you staying long?'

'No longer than two weeks, I shouldn't think.'

The Nigerian banged a stamp onto a middle page and slapped the passport back onto the counter.

Ten minutes later, Jeff retrieved his bag from the carousel and followed the arrows to the exit. Outside, crowds waiting for family members swarmed the exit and the attempts by police to keep a clear pathway appeared to be a losing battle. As passengers descended the sloping ramp, welcome-home groups engulfed them. Jeff stood at the top of the ramp and scanned over the mass of bobbing heads. He caught sight of a sign written in tortured English: Welcum Geeff Baddley. It was being held aloft by a tall, solidly built man dressed in black trousers, black shirt and black leather jacket. Kimie had assured Jeff that her friend was a good man from a good family, and therefore his son would be a man who could be trusted. Jeff was far too sceptical to accept anyone from this part of the world at face value, but for Arben's sake he would give Sulla the benefit of the doubt until proven otherwise.

He shouldered his way through the crowd.

'I'm Jeff Bradley.'

The man smiled.

'Good to meet you, Jeff Bradley. I am Sulla Bogdani, a friend of the family of Arben Shala. Welcome to Kosovo.'

Sulla was close to the same height as Jeff, equally broad-shouldered and pretty much the same age. Thick black hair curled over the top of the man's jacket collar. The disarming smile and movie star looks had Jeff wondering if Sulla might fancy himself as a Kosovon Don Juan.

Sulla reached down and took hold of Jeff's suitcase.

'No worries, Sulla. I can carry my own bag.'

'You are my guest. Please, allow me this honour,' Sulla said, pulling on the luggage strap.

Jeff decided to humour the man. He released his hold.

Sulla, bag in hand, walked off. 'My car is in the car park. Not far.'

Taxi drivers called out in anticipation of a fare to the city. But Sulla shook his head and waggled his finger like a teacher admonishing a child. The disappointed cabbies directed their attentions elsewhere.

When they reached the car, Sulla popped open the lid of the older-model silver Mercedes and tossed Jeff's bag inside.

'You had a good flight?' Sulla asked as he drove out of the airport car park.

'As good as it gets in an airplane.'

'How long is the flying time from New Zealand?'

'Close to thirty hours.'

Sulla expelled an exaggerated puff of air. 'That is much too long. You have been to Kosovo before?'

'No, this is my first time.'

'Ah. Then maybe you will be disappointed. Kosovo is a poor country. The airport is good. The main roads are good. The UN has spent much money. NATO has repaired bridges. It is good they have done this. But it is a facade. Behind the walls it is third world.

In the minds of the people it is third world. The war destroyed everything. Many people died. Many people left. Some came back. Most did not. How can a country grow when it has lost so much?'

Sulla turned onto a highway.

'Why didn't you leave?' Jeff asked.

'I did for a short time when the NATO bombardment started. But as you can see, I came back.' Sulla honked at a car that had cut in front of him. 'Idiot. Sorry, Jeff. Getting a licence in Kosovo is too easy.'

Jeff laughed.

'And what do you do, Sulla, as a job, I mean?'

'Like everyone else in Kosovo I must do a little of everything. Right now I am a driver. When you are gone I will sell goods. Simple products. Washing powders, cooking oils. It is very difficult to import goods. I have my contacts. So, it is a good business for me.'

'And you live in Prishtina?'

'Yes, I live in Prishtina.'

'Have you heard from Benny?'

'Benny?'

'Arben.'

'Ah, Benny is nickname. Very good. No, I am sorry but I must tell you I have heard nothing.'

'You know Arben well?'

'Not so much. My father is an old friend of the Shala family. He lives in Peje now. Arben and his wife were students at the university in Prishtina. My father was Arben's professor. In Kosovo, the student never leaves the teacher. They are like father and son. This is how it was with Arben and my father.'

Hand pressed on horn, Sulla accelerated past a car. Jeff held onto the dashboard, knuckles whitening as the car barely missed an oncoming truck.

'Is that why Kimie Shala contacted you and not a relative?' asked Jeff.

'There is no one else. Sadly, the Shala family and all the relatives are no more. Killed during the war.' Sulla's voice lacked any discernible expression. 'The whole village. Massacred.'

'Jesus.'

Now Jeff's memory of Kimie, Drita and Marko huddled together at the airport – three pairs of eyes pleading with him to find their father and husband and bring him home safely – held far more significance. Kimie had insisted they see him off. She had fussed over him, brushing cat hair from his jacket lapel and squatting to wipe a smudge from his shoe. There had been no point in protesting. Jeff knew this was her way of coping. Nothing was said, but Jeff could see in their faces that they held him responsible for Arben's disappearance. Only when he returned Arben to them would they forgive him.

'You haven't forgotten anything?' Kimie had asked.

'No, Kimie. I have travelled before.'

'I know. I know. Socks. Have you packed extra pairs of socks? It's winter in Kosovo. Very cold this time of the year.'

'I've got plenty of socks. If I need more I'll find a market.'

'Yes. There are markets.'

When the loudspeaker announced his boarding call, Jeff had caught Marko's eye and they exchanged nods. Marko had tried hard to adopt a macho attitude, but the tears were welling in his eyes. Drita said nothing, but clung to her mother's arm. Kimie slipped her hand around Jeff's neck and pulled him down to her. She touched his cheek with her own.

'Bring my husband home,' she whispered.

'I will.' Jeff gave her hand a squeeze.

Kimie mumbled something in Albanian. A prayer, Jeff assumed. Whatever trouble Arben was in, Jeff fervently hoped he hadn't made a promise that had already passed its use-by date.

'We are on the outskirts of Prishtina,' Sulla announced, breaking in on his reverie.

A sign perched on top of a three-metre-high fence read 'UN Administration'. Behind the fence Jeff could see a Legoland city made up of twenty- and forty-foot shipping containers. The specially designed containers held offices, generators and anything else an administration centre might need. Jeff assumed Legoland would go with the UN the day they left.

'The UN. You're glad they're here, Sulla?'

Sulla shrugged. 'The Americans and NATO rescued us and the UN is trying to make us a nation. They try hard to make everyone happy, but you cannot make everyone happy. They do good things and they do bad things. All the time they make promises and still no one knows for certain what is the future.' Sulla offered a cheeky smile. 'The UN has money and they spend it, so not everything is bad.'

He turned left at a set of traffic lights. 'Here we are. The Grand Hotel. This is where you will stay. It is old but it is the best accommodation in Prishtina. All foreigners stay here. This is where Arben Shala stayed.'

The sprawling twenty-storey brown-and-grey building dominated the skyline. On the roof huge letters in white suspended on wires spelled out H-O-T-E-L with five stars perched above the letters.

When the car stopped no doorman rushed out to greet them.

Jeff tensed the way he used to in his SAS days just before a mission was about to start. 'Before we go in there's something we need to discuss.'

Sulla turned off the engine and fixed his attention on Jeff. 'What is it?'

'What exactly did Kimie Shala tell your father?'

'Not much. Only that she had not heard from Arben and she was worried.'

Jeff nodded. He was weighing up a decision. Could he trust Sulla? He decided he had little choice. He needed the Kosovon's help.

'Benny left a message on my answer phone. He said he was in trouble and he was leaving for Macedonia and would call from there.'

Sulla raised an eyebrow. 'And of course this did not happen?'

'Correct. Now I'm assuming the worst. Also, whoever was causing him trouble will be on their guard. My cover story is that I met Arben in New Zealand and he invited me to Kosovo to look at a business opportunity. And now that I've come such a distance I'm keen to locate him.'

Sulla grinned. 'Okay, I can play this game. So now you have a reason for asking questions.'

When they left the car, once again Sulla carried Jeff's bags for him. This time Jeff didn't bother protesting. The expansive hotel lobby confirmed that in its heyday the Grand might indeed have been grand and deserving of the five stars it still proudly displayed. But now the white ceiling tiles had yellowed and flakes of pink paint, faded almost to white, had peeled away from the plaster walls. The marble floor tiles, although polished, were cracked. The dimmed lighting failed to hide the fact that the shining jewel that once might have been the gathering place of the Prishtina glitterati was now simply seedy.

Sulla stood back and watched Jeff check in.

'One question,' Jeff said to the concierge.

'Yes, sir?'

'Can you tell me if a Mr Arben Shala is staying at the hotel?'

'Shala. Let me see. It is a name I remember.' The concierge flicked through the registration book. 'Ah, yes. Here he is. Yes. Mr Shala was our guest. He checked out more than a week ago. Are you a friend of Mr Shala?'

'I know him from New Zealand. I had arranged to meet him here. A business matter.'

The concierge conceded a polite smile. 'I am so sorry you have missed him. But please enjoy your stay.'

Sulla walked Jeff to the elevator. 'Now it is in the open, you must be careful, Jeff,' Sulla said. He looked back at the concierge. 'Trust no one.'

'You don't have to worry on that score.'

'You are on the third floor. I will leave you to rest. Tomorrow we will meet and decide the next step.' Sulla took a card from his pocket. 'If you need me, phone my mobile number. And remember: watch your back.'

Jeff nodded and stepped into the elevator. As the doors closed he glanced back at reception. The concierge was speaking into the telephone. His eyes didn't leave Jeff.

7.

Jeff's bag bounced on the end of the bed. The wardrobe door opened at a pull. Inside, a selection of wire and plastic hangers dangled from a dowelling rod slotted into the V of crossed nails either side. The curtains looked to be in need of laundering, and from the pervading mustiness Jeff guessed it had been a long time since a window had been opened to welcome fresh air into the place. Several prods of the mattress encountered no lumps, although Jeff would have preferred it firmer.

Shirts and jeans went onto the hangers and the empty bag went on top of the wardrobe. The white tiles covering the floor and walls in the bathroom looked to be free of grime and mildew. A hint of pine needles and ammonia irritated his nostrils. He flicked on the extractor fan and arranged his toiletries on the shelf above the basin.

Taking up a position on the bed, Jeff placed the hotel phone on his lap and opened his notebook to the page with the information Kimie had given him at the airport. Before he disappeared Arben had phoned each night and given Kimie details of his progress. In his last phone call he told Kimie he had met with a lawyer named Tomi Mema. Arben had given her Mema's contact details. Jeff decided the lawyer was as good a place as any to start. A laminated card pinned to the wall above the bedside table instructed him to dial 0 for reception and 1 for an outside line. Upon hearing the click that indicated a free line, Jeff dialled the number Kimie had jotted down next to Mema's name.

A man's voice answered. Jeff guessed the language to be Albanian.

'Do you speak English?'

'Yes, of course. I am Tomi Mema. How may I help you?'

'Mr Mema, my name is Jeff Bradley. I understand Mr Arben Shala is a client of yours?'

A pause.

'May I ask how you came by my private number?'

'Arben's wife gave it to me. I've just arrived in Kosovo from New Zealand.'

'I see. What can I do for you, Mr Bradley?'

Jeff's military-honed instincts had caused him to think hard about how he would explain himself to this lawyer. In a hostile environment he'd learned to treat everyone as an enemy until proven otherwise. Mema might be the best lawyer in Kosovo, but he was not a member of the New Zealand Law Society. Jeff doubted there was even such a thing as a code of legal ethics in Kosovo. And in his experience lawyers could be very tricky customers.

'I met Arben in New Zealand. He invited me to Kosovo to look at a property he wanted to sell. A vineyard. The trouble is I arrived today and Mr Shala seems to have disappeared. The hotel manager said he left a week ago.'

'I see. I have not heard from Mr Shala recently. If I hear from him, I'll be sure to ask him to contact you at your hotel. Where are you staying?'

'At the Grand. Mr Mema, I've come a long way. Shala isn't really that necessary in the scheme of things. I just want to look at a vineyard and find some bulk wine. Maybe you could help me?'

'I am very busy Mr Bradley. You might like to talk to a real-estate agent.'

'Yes, I guess I could.' The disappointment in Jeff's voice was genuine. This lawyer was the only firm link he had to Benny. But he had a strong hunch that Mema, like most lawyers, would prefer to avoid messy hassles. 'Come to think of it, I suppose I could go talk to the UN police. Arben is a New Zealand citizen. They might help me find him . . .'

Jeff's hanging pause achieved its purpose.

'Very well, Mr Bradley. You have come a great distance, as you say. I will meet you in the hotel lobby at eight thirty tomorrow morning.'

Jeff dropped the phone back onto the receiver and reached to switch on the television. Static but no picture. He pressed the off button. Stretching his legs seemed like a good idea. He didn't want to spend any more time in the room than necessary.

༒

Only a few minutes out in the elements and Jeff's knuckles ached. He breathed into his hands and rubbed them together until they warmed up. He knew full well it was never a great strategy to wander about in hostile territory without the right kit. In the morning he would find the markets and buy gloves. Hands plunged deep into the wool-lined pockets of his parka, Jeff set off on what he now resolved would be but a short walk around the block.

The hardy citizens of Prishtina were out en masse. But unlike Jeff they had dressed for the conditions. Seated at tables lined up against the wall of the hotel, groups of men in heavy coats and woollen hats chain-smoked cigarettes and drank coffee and cognac. Family groups out for evening strolls cut across the courtyard at the rear of the hotel and disappeared down a lane.

Jeff decided to follow.

The lane looked as if it might have once been a through-road that had since been reduced to just a few metres of useable pavement. To his left a three-metre-high iron fence topped with razor wire ran the entire length as far as a lower boulevard. The fenced-off section of road acted as car park for neat rows of white Toyota Land Cruisers with large black UN transfers on the doors. In the background stood the imposing multi-storey United Nations headquarters.

Wooden shelving strung onto the UN fence displayed a variety of CDs and DVDs. On top of upended fruit crates street vendors had arranged cigarettes, tissues, biscuits and confectionery in tidy stacks. They hailed the strollers and haggled for sales. To Jeff's right, the entrepreneurial-minded had turned ground-floor apartments into restaurants and cafes. These were all busy.

The distinctive shape of Gurkha knives painted on a board over the entrance of a bar called the Kukri caught Jeff's attention. Peering through the window he thought it had the look of an ex-pat watering hole. Every third-world country had one, in his experience. A quick drink before returning to the hotel struck him as more inviting than hazarding cracked pavements and cigarette salesmen. He decided his walk could wait for another time.

Inside he found the bar packed and noisy. Chinese, Indians, Africans and Europeans crowded shoulder to shoulder. Some wore uniforms: mostly police. Jeff recognised insignias from South Africa, Italy and the USA. The ratio of men to women was about fifty-fifty. He chuckled at this evidence of equal opportunity policies in an institution such as the UN. Even in a war zone.

Television sets hung from wall brackets, all tuned into English sports channels. Waiters wended back and forth carrying handles of beer, and at least three more staff behind the bar kept them supplied. An assortment of paraphernalia adorned the back wall. Jeff spotted international football jerseys, berets and hats, and photos of UN and NATO personnel. The aroma of cooked chicken and French fries did battle with a blanket of cigarette smoke.

Jeff elbowed his way through the crowd to the bar. A barman was bellowing orders to his staff in a regional English accent. The burly man eyed Jeff as he approached.

'What'll it be, mate?' he yelled.

'I'll have a beer.'

'What brand?'

'Anything that tastes good. I'll leave it up to you.'

'Ah ha. Just arrived, have you?'

Jeff nodded.

'Where're you from?'

'New Zealand.'

'Another bloody Kiwi.' The man's tone and hearty laugh belied his disapproval. He swung a glass under a tap and yanked the lever. 'What's your name?'

'Jeff Bradley.'

'Call me John.' He deposited the handle of beer on the counter. Froth erupted down its sides. 'First one's on the house.' John turned and yelled to a man standing at the end of the bar. 'Hey, Barry. Another one of your compatriots has just landed.'

The man called Barry waved an acknowledgement and made his way towards Jeff. 'How yer goin', mate. I'm Barry Briggs.' The accent was definitely Australian.

'Jeff Bradley. I did tell him I was a New Zealander.'

Barry snorted derisively. 'No problems. Ignorant Pommie bastard thinks Australia and New Zealand are the same country. Come on down and join us.'

Before Jeff could answer, Barry had snatched the beer from under his nose and walked off. There was little choice but to follow. Barry nodded at his two drinking companions.

'These two arseholes are countrymen of yours. Bruce from Wellington. Gary from the Waikato. I'm from Sydney. Manly. The northern beaches. Maybe you've been there?'

'I know Manly.'

Jeff scrutinised his three companions. Gary looked a bit woozy. His hands gripped the bar like it was a lifeline. Bruce attempted a smile of sorts, but there was little discernible warmth behind it. And no verbal comment either. This big man appeared to be the type who kept to himself. Barry, on the other hand, was the open book of the three. Friendly, chatty. And honest, Jeff judged. He felt he was a man he might be able to trust. In a pinch. His life had often depended upon forming quick judgements like this.

'What brings you to this shithole?'

Gary's voice slurred. A fringe of hair fell across his face.

'Business.'

Gary's jaw dropped. 'Christ, you gotta be bloody joking. Don't waste your bloody time. You can't trust any of these thieving bastards. Want my advice? Take the next plane home.'

Jeff offered a polite smile. 'I wish it was that simple.'

'Well, don't say you weren't warned. Tell him, Barry.'

'Gary's pretty much on the money, Jeff. If you're looking to do business here, at least be careful.'

Gary waved to one of the bar staff for another round of drinks. He glanced across at Jeff with what looked like contempt. Gary had obviously decided Jeff was a fool, and he was far too drunk to be convinced otherwise.

'How long have you guys been in Kosovo?' Jeff asked Barry.

Gary butted in: 'Two years too bloody long, mate. Thass how we know about these shitheads.'

At this point Gary saw someone else he preferred to talk to. He turned his back on Jeff and wobbled unsteadily into the crowd.

'Don't mind Gary,' Barry said. 'He's been away from home too long and makes up for it with the booze. Hell, we all do, except Gary's an ass when he drinks too much. I'm with the UN. Maintenance. Gary's a driver and Bruce here's a liaison officer. God knows what the hell that is. Truth be known, mate, I think he hides in a corner all day and hopes no one finds him.'

Bruce smiled again, sipped on his beer, but kept looking straight ahead of him.

'How did you come to be here, Barry?' asked Jeff.

'I'm a carpenter by trade. Me and a mate went to the UK for a working holiday. One night I met this bird in the pub who worked for UN recruitment. She told me the UN was looking for carpenters and asked if I'd be interested in going to Kosovo. Good money. I'd had a few too many so said sure, why not. I didn't remember giving her my number and by Sunday had forgotten all about it. Monday morning she phones and tells me to come into her office and bring my passport. Two days later I was on a plane to Kosovo. And I'm still bloody here.'

Bruce chuckled at his story.

'How stable is Kosovo? Anything I need worry about?' asked Jeff.

'For now it's peaceful enough. On the surface, anyway. The Albanians and the Serbs hate each other, but the Albanians are in the majority so they have the upper hand. The KFOR troops – that's NATO if you didn't know – try to keep a lid on it. Every now and then they beat each other up. Nothing too horrendous. You can walk the streets without getting hit over the head if that's what's worrying you.'

As the evening progressed, the crowd grew noisier. The numbers of drinkers ebbed and flowed. Jeff remained in his position leaning on the bar but paced his alcohol consumption. He could learn a lot from those who didn't. Even Gary's drivel had assisted in building an overall picture of life in Kosovo.

Gary returned in a worse state. At first he mumbled what could have been abuse to anyone who would bother listening. But finally his head inclined onto the top of the bar and that's where it stayed.

Two burly men joined the conversation, with accents Jeff recognised as South African.

'Jeff, meet the two most useless bloody cops in Kosovo,' Barry said.

The South Africans laughed and bought a round of drinks.

'You are an Aussie?' asked the South African who had been introduced as Hansie.

'He wishes,' Barry butted in. 'He's a bloody Kiwi.'

The conversation turned to rugby and soon Barry and the South Africans were deep in discussion about the chances of their national teams that year. At eleven o'clock Jeff roused himself to stand.

'Barry, I'm leaving. Thanks for the heads up and the hospitality.'

'No problem, mate. You know where to find us. We're right here every night.'

Jeff bought a final round of drinks for everyone and left.

The brisk night air was a welcome respite from the smoke-filled bar.

෴

When Jeff turned on the tap in the bathroom no water came out. He phoned the desk. The night manager told him with a touch of tartness that the city's water supply was turned off every night at midnight. It would come on again at six in the morning.

'You should have bought some bottled water.'

Jeff slammed down the phone, resisting the urge to go downstairs and wring the man's neck. He took a glass from the bedside table into the bathroom and dipped it into the toilet cistern. It'd quench his thirst at least. With luck it would be as clean as anything likely to exude from the hotel's plumbing system.

Jeff fell back on the bed and burst out laughing. His SAS mates would give him hell if they heard him whingeing over a glass of rusty water. He had drunk worse from Iraqi swamps. He hoped he would not be paying for it in the morning.

Tomorrow, the lawyer. Then the hunt for Benny would begin in earnest.

Welcome sleep could claim him now.

8.

The travel magazine on his lap lay open at an article about fishing in Lake Ohrid. Jeff had read the first paragraph a number of times but the aroma of freshly ground coffee beans kept distracting him. He was desperate for a caffeine fix. Breakfast in the hotel basement had consisted of a choice of cold meats, cold eggs, cold tea, and worst of all, cold coffee. He had settled for a bun and fruit juice.

The foyer buzzed with activity. Guests and new arrivals waited as the manager and his assistants tended to requests and filled out paperwork. Knots of men and women, mostly UN personnel, milled about engaged in noisy conversations and sipped coffee that could never have come from the basement.

In his peripheral vision Jeff saw a figure approaching.

'Mr Bradley?'

'That's me.' Jeff dropped the travel magazine onto the coffee table and stood.

'I am Tomi Mema.'

Mema's handshake and manner reminded Jeff of Quentin Douglas, though his divorce lawyer had a firmer grip.

'If you like we can talk over coffee,' Mema said.

'If it's hot and fresh I won't say no.'

'Ah ha. You have tried the Grand Hotel breakfast menu. Come. I will take you to a cafe where the beverages are drinkable.'

Mema's neatly clipped jet-black hair, not a strand out of place, matched the manicured nails and hands that had never dug a hole or chopped a piece of wood. He had a small scar above his right eye, spoiling an otherwise immaculate appearance. Jeff recognised the Armani suit. He'd had to buy one for himself when Rebecca dragged him back into Civvy Street and tried to turn him into a corporate executive. He'd never worn it. Mema's shoes looked Italian quality. Jeff's guess was that the shirt and yellow silk tie came from a similar home. If the fortyish Tomi Mema was anything to go by, Kosovon lawyers made good money – and the care and attention Mema devoted to his appearance left Jeff thinking he might earn more than most.

With a light touch to Jeff's elbow, Mema led him down the same lane he had walked through the previous evening. By night, neon lighting had added a sparkle to small pockets of the street, but failed to illuminate much of the dominant red-brick buildings and grey concrete. Now, the dreary scene came into full view. Deciduous trees lined the roadways, their naked branches adding little charm to the all-round drabness. The early morning sun could do nothing to dispel the city's bleakness.

The Kukri bar stood open, but empty. Staff in green aprons were cleaning and preparing for another night. Vendor calls and general clatter filled the air. The night before, Jeff hadn't made it as far as the bottom of the lane. Now, as he and Mema continued further, security guards at the entrance of the UN compound watched their movements – until two young women in tight-fitting jeans grabbed their attention instead.

Mema stopped on the kerb. Jeff guessed they were heading for the complex on the other side of the road. Cars, bumper to bumper, honked along the muddied carriageway. Citizens wrapped in greatcoats, scarves and boots dodged the odd tsunami thrown up by tyres that had discovered concealed potholes. Apart from the pervading sense of dampness, Prishtina looked like any other city newly awake to a working day.

'It snows in Prishtina through the winter,' Mema explained as they walked towards a huge concrete edifice. 'Sometimes the outside temperature can drop below minus ten, very cold. This building is a shopping mall, just as they have in America. It is centrally heated and inside very warm. Today the sun is shining and it is not so cold. Shall we sit outside?'

'Outside's fine by me.'

Jeff blew into his hands. It reminded him of his resolve to buy gloves.

Mema pointed to a table then called to a waiter to bring coffee. He pulled a tissue from his pocket and dried off Jeff's seat then did the same to his own. He shrugged. 'The waiters are paid very little. Please, sit. You said on the telephone you are acquainted with the Shala family?'

Jeff nodded. 'A mutual friend introduced us. I'm interested in purchasing bulk wine and possibly investing in a vineyard. Mr Shala said he could offer both. I arranged to meet with him here. But when I booked into the hotel last night I was told he left more than a week ago. So I telephoned his wife who gave me your contact details. She said you were his lawyer.'

A second or so of thought, then Mema took a sip of his coffee. 'It is true that Mr Shala came to see me. His family owned a property in a region near the city of Gjakova. It had been sold by his father and Mr Shala had not been told of the sale. He did not believe such a thing would have occurred without his father telling him. This is why he came to see me – to dispute the legitimacy of the new ownership. He showed me his documents and I made some enquires on his behalf. Then he stopped coming. I thought nothing of it. My fees are high. I assumed he found a new lawyer.'

'You've heard nothing from him since?'

'Not at all.'

'Had Arben visited the property?'

'Yes, of course. As you can imagine it was very upsetting for him. Two brothers, the Xhihas, are the new owners. They expressed an interest to sell to Mr Shala, but he was adamant that he was already the legal owner. He wanted back what he considered rightfully his.'

Jeff screwed up his face into a pissed-off expression he hoped looked convincing to Mema. 'I don't mind telling you I feel let down. I've travelled a long way and I don't want it to be a wasted trip. You said these owners are keen to sell? I'd like to meet with the brothers if possible. Give it the once over. Can you arrange it? I'll pay for your time.'

Mema continued to sip his coffee, eyes cool as stone. 'Yes, I can arrange it. When would be convenient for you?'

'Today. This afternoon, if possible?'

'I will make a phone call.' Mema stood and pulled a mobile phone from his jacket. He squinted at it and held it up above shoulder height. 'The signal is very bad right here. I need to make the call away from the building. Will you excuse me a minute?'

'Sure. Go ahead.'

Jeff turned his attention to the comings and goings of the people around him. Young boys moved between tables offering cigarettes, watches and phone cards. When they looked in his direction he waved them away. Jeff took up his teaspoon and tapped the side of his cup. He gazed across at Mema. The lawyer stood on the pavement some distance away. His back and forth pacing looked somewhat agitated. Jeff tried not to be too obvious as he observed the lawyer's actions. Mema's free hand found constant release in gesticulation. His voice had risen too, although he was too far away for Jeff to make out what was being said. He assumed it would be in Albanian anyway.

Minutes later Mema returned all smiles. 'That's all set, Mr Bradley. The owners will meet you at the Pastriku Hotel in Gjakova and take you to the vineyard. I will ask the hotel manager to make the introductions.' He took out a small notebook and scribbled down directions, then ripped out the page and passed it to Jeff. 'Now if you will excuse me, I must get to court. Please, stay and finish your coffee. I have taken care of the bill. Good luck for the rest of your stay.'

Jeff watched Mema until he disappeared from sight. To his mind the man appeared professional enough, but the circumstances of that phone call bothered him. Was the raised voice only about Mema being heard over the traffic noise? Or was there more going on?

He'd worry about it later. Right now he needed to get back to the hotel and ask Sulla to drive him to Gjakova.

9.

ourt. You must hurry.'

Arben raised his head. Bleary eyes stared with little comprehension at the guard. 'What?'

A hand shook Arben's foot. 'Court. You must go to court.
Hurry.'

'Okay, okay.'

Arben rolled his legs over the side of the bed and bent to pull
on his shoes. 'Toilet?' he said, looking up at the guard. The guard
nodded and hurried him through to the toilet block.

Bladder emptied, Arben shuffled across to the stainless steel
basin. No mirror. Fingers rasped across days of stubble. From the
time of his arrest he had had no change of clothes. No shower. Now
he was on his way to court. Should his appearance be a concern?
Despite Mema's promise that he'd be released, Arben fretted that
once the judge viewed the smelly, scruffy man before him, he would
order him locked up and the key tossed away.

He splashed water onto his hair and face and rubbed a finger
across his teeth. No way of telling if any of this made a difference.
And his teeth still felt furry. After his release he'd book into a hotel
and spend an hour under a hot shower and use up a tube of tooth-
paste.

He nodded that he was ready and two guards walked him to the waiting vehicle.

Thirty-odd people crowded round the entrance to the two-storey Municipal Court. When the police vehicle stopped, curious eyes turned Arben's way. He was helped onto the pavement where a court officer took charge of his arm and guided him forward. Another walked ahead, pushing a passage through the throng. A big man, similarly unshaven and dressed in dirty trousers and a long grey overcoat, turned and yelled abuse as he was elbowed aside. The officer scowled and levelled his face to within centimetres of the protestor's. The man hesitated then backed away. His wife, emaciated and possessed of a leathery face that attested to a lifetime of hoeing cornfields, glared back at the officers. She flicked her head towards them, hissing like a viper through pencil-thin lips.

Inside the courthouse, police, court staff and Prishtina citizens stood in lines or walked about with pieces of paper and busy expressions. Arben's escorts moved him quickly across the foyer and up a flight of stairs and along a corridor. The courtroom was the second door on the left.

Tomi Mema sat at a table, an empty chair beside him. With sore wrists relieved of handcuffs, Arben took the vacant seat.

Mema patted him on the knee. 'Try to be positive. This won't take long.'

Arben's nod belied the apprehension he was feeling. He made an anxious sweep of the room. A woman clad in a severe business suit sat behind a desk on a dais at the far end, perusing a document. Black-framed glasses hovered on the end of her nose. Arben had imagined the judge would be in robes. Without them, she looked no more important than the clerk seated in front of her.

'Over there is the public prosecutor, Avni Leka.'

Mema nodded in the direction of a grey-haired, square-faced man attired with just a little less elegance than Mema himself. The steely eyed prosecutor displayed scant compassion when he glanced Arben's way. His assistant, a pretty young woman, looked like she should still be in school. She giggled when the prosecutor whispered in her ear. For some reason, Arben took an instant dislike to both of them.

The judge put her document aside. 'Mr Mema. Are you and your client ready to begin?'

'Yes, Your Honour.'

'Mr Prosecutor?'

'Yes, Your Honour.'

The court recorder, a woman in her fifties with bleached blonde hair gathered in a bun, asked Arben some personal details. There was a delay after each question as she typed his answers into a computer. She nodded to the judge when she had finished.

The judge glanced at Arben over the top of her glasses.

'Mr Shala, this is not a trial. It is a hearing to assess evidence and arguments to determine whether you should remain in custody. Do you understand?'

'Yes, ma'am.'

'Good. Mr Mema, you can start.'

Arben tried to concentrate as Mema presented his opening statement. Mema demanded that the charges be dismissed, arguing that the prosecutor had produced no evidence to show his client had knowingly obtained a stolen mobile phone.

'Mr Shala is now a resident of New Zealand and wishes to return to that country and his family as quickly as possible.'

Although it had not been with the greatest of passion, Mema had presented all the facts relevant to Arben's alleged crime – as far as Arben could ascertain. And Mema seemed on track in emphasising that no evidence had been presented to support a charge for the possession of stolen goods. Surely the judge must release him.

Prosecutor Avni Leka rose to speak. He looked directly at Arben. Something in the look caused Arben's hands to tremble. He squeezed them between his thighs to stop the shaking.

'Your Honour. The argument as to whether Mr Shala knowingly obtained a stolen mobile phone has no bearing here. A different set of protocols than those pertaining to this hearing will apply when that matter is finally dealt with by the court. The only argument possible today is whether or not Mr Shala broke the conditions of his bail. Mr Mema may have presented compelling evidence that his client is innocent of the mobile phone charges. However, in the matter of breaking the condition of his bail, which was that the defendant remains in Kosovo until the police finish their investigation, no evidence at all in exculpation has been adduced. Thus, the court has a right to conclude that when Mr Shala was arrested at the Macedonian border, carrying luggage, passport and money, his only intention could have been to escape the jurisdiction of this court. Because Mr Shala has a New Zealand passport he seems to believe that he can leave Kosovo without any concern for our legal processes. Mr Shala's actions prove beyond doubt that he is a flight risk. Your Honour, I seek an order that Mr Shala continue to be held in custody until the police investigation regarding the initial charge is completed.'

With a flourish the prosecutor flung his notes onto the desk before him. The theatrics drew a look of disapproval from the judge. Leka, unmoved, resumed his seat. All eyes turned towards the judge. She leaned forward to whisper something to the court recorder then straightened. The crack of her gavel split the silence.

'I will give you my decision in an hour. Hearing adjourned.'

One of the court officers gripped Arben's arm and hauled him upright. His eyes remained on the judge who was sitting back and speaking on a mobile phone. Perhaps sensing Arben watching her, she swivelled her chair away.

❦

As the cage-gate of the court's holding cell clanked closed behind him, Arben noticed there was no furniture but the wooden bench sitting on brackets bolted into the wall. A door at the rear of the cell was secured by heavy iron stays. A small window above it afforded a glimpse of the uneven and broken terracotta-tiled roofing of adjacent buildings. Vertical bars ran floor to ceiling along the front of the cell. A female court officer sat at a desk reading a book. Arben slumped on the floor in the corner farthest from her, leaned his head against the wall and shut his eyes. A flood of images of home filled his mind and hot tears spilled through eyelids squeezed tight.

A tap on the cell bars snapped Arben back to the present. The court officer was holding up a document and a pen and signalling him to come forward. Tomi Mema stood beside her. Arben shuffled towards them. He reached through the bars and took hold of the document and pen, then looked to Mema for an explanation.

'You need to sign the top copy.'

Arben scanned the top sheet. 'I don't understand this. What is it?'

'It is the court order.'

Mema pointed to a spot. Arben signed and passed the top slip back to the court officer, then looked at Mema for some kind of lead. But Mema's face disclosed no particular sign of reassurance.

'The judge ruled against us. You are to be held another fifteen days or until the investigation is completed, whichever is the sooner.'

Arben's eyes rounded like saucers. 'I . . . I have to go back to the police station?'

'It's out of my hands.' Mema glanced behind him. The court officer was out of earshot. 'You know what you have to do. The people you have upset want the money you promised and the original documents for your land signed over.'

Arben gripped the bars between them so hard that his wrists hurt. It all became clear to him now: Mema's inept defence, the judge's apathy. Everything had been orchestrated. Everyone was in on the swindle, including the police. If he could have reached far enough through the bars, he would have strangled this corrupt lawyer. His anger fuelled a last attempt at defiance.

'I will ask the UN to help,' he spat. 'Someone will listen.'

Mema shook his head with an expression Arben took to be of pity. 'This is the Municipal Court. The UN ceded control to the interim Kosovon government. However much you protest, they will not interfere. You have no other options, Arben. No one cares.'

'They can't hold me for ever. Eventually they'll have to release me. I'll find a way to get the UN to help. So fuck you, Tomi. I will keep my land.'

Mema leaned closer.

'Listen to me carefully. You are not going back to the police cells. They are taking you to the detention centre. You will be with other prisoners. I can do nothing to protect you in such an environment.' Mema's teeth bared in a semblance of a smile. 'When you change your mind, tell the guards to call for me.'

Arben held Mema's gaze for a matter of seconds, then turned away. Three slow steps took him back to the corner. He dropped to his knees. When he looked up again, Mema had gone.

10.

'Why should we go to them?' Sulla's voice had raised a decibel or two. 'Why could these people not come to Prishtina? It will take an hour and a half to drive to Gjakova. Three hours, the whole trip. Four hours with the meeting included. Maybe longer.'

The aggression in Sulla's attitude took Jeff by surprise. 'Money's no object. Name your price, for God's sake, Sulla.'

'Jeff. Please. I know you do not intend to insult me. This is not about money. What is money to me in this? It is a matter of principle.'

'Okay. Sorry, Sulla. I do understand. But I also do need to see the property.'

Sulla's hands spread palms-up to the heavens. 'What difference does that make? These sons of dogs are stealing Arben's land. We should not run around after them. They are peasants.'

Jeff's powers of persuasion were severely tested over the next ten minutes. But in the end Sulla finally agreed to drive him to Gjakova. And although he continued to complain from behind the wheel, Jeff just sat quietly and let him talk his frustration out. It was when they had passed the turnoff to the airport that Sulla finally tired of hearing his own voice and lapsed into silence. A grateful Jeff sat back and confined his comments to uncontentious remarks about the landscape.

An hour later, Sulla announced that the billboard in the distance that advertised a local construction company marked the turnoff to Gjakova. As they left the main road, Jeff caught sight of several bombed-out buildings. Charred roof-framing jutted into the sky like the steepled fingers of children at prayer.

'In this region it was very bad during the troubles.'

Sulla's tone sounded subdued. Jeff had certainly read the news reports. The NATO bombing raids had gone on for three months. Not a building, factory or bridge deemed strategically important was allowed to remain standing. He wondered how farm buildings fitted into the category of strategic. But his military training had taught him that the more comfort you can deny the enemy, the quicker he will collapse. Battles, he knew, were often won in the minds of armies before even the first shot was fired.

After another twenty minutes, they crossed the Bardhe River and entered wine country. Vineyards stretched across the rolling landscape for as far as Jeff could see. Vines in need of pruning sagged on wires no longer taut. The majority of wooden posts were unable to support the weight and had fallen. Plastic bags and paper wrappings blown down the rows by prevailing winds were wrapped round vine roots. Not even the cover of melting snow was enough to hide the signs of general neglect.

'Gjakova is round the next bend.'

Before Jeff's eyes a long, sloping road stretched down into the city. On either side women and children dressed in parkas and woollen hats manned makeshift stalls of wooden shelving and cardboard boxes. Waves and hopeful smiles greeted the approach of Sulla's car. Everything appeared to be for sale, from stolen hubcaps and motor oil to portable radios, fridges, televisions and bottles of Coca-Cola. As the road levelled out, Sulla steered his car onto a bridge over the bed of a stream. Broken glass glinted along the mudflats in the early afternoon sun. Plastic rubbish bags festooned the trees along the banks.

Into view came a sandbagged wall that encircled a compound opposite the bus station. Razor wire extended along the top.

'Italians,' Sulla said. At the next set of traffic lights he pointed towards a pyramid-shaped building. 'That's the Pastriku Hotel.'

Like the Grand Hotel in Prishtina, the Pastriku was a remnant of more opulent times. But even from a distance it was clearly a lot more dilapidated.

Jeff glanced at Sulla.

'It doesn't look busy.'

'Not any more, Jeff. Gjakova was once a major industrial town. Companies from all over Yugoslavia had factories here. It was very prosperous. During the war NATO bombed the factories and the Serbs burnt much of the rest of Gjakova to the ground. The old part of the city was totally destroyed. Many people were massacred. Now there is nothing. No work. No future. No one comes to Gjakova any more and no one comes to the hotel.'

Sulla pulled into a space in front of a Western Union office.

Once inside the hotel entrance it became clear there was no artificial lighting. The place made do with the sunlight that streamed through the door and skylights. There was no heating. Sulla appeared impervious to the chill. Jeff wrapped his arms across his chest and rubbed the tops of his arms.

'It's cold in here. Feels like the inside of a bloody freezer.'

'Electricity cut. Maybe they do not have a generator.'

A sign in English told guests to follow the arrow to the dining room. Bare wires looped through gaps where ceiling tiles were missing. Another sign announced that the basement boasted a swimming pool and a hairdresser. Jeff doubted anything existed in the basement other than damp walls and cobwebs.

A marble staircase flowed from the dingy heights down into the foyer like a glacier. The woman descending it had the unmistakable air of management. Prim black hair pinned back behind her ears and a dark-grey trouser suit. She approached Jeff with an outstretched hand.

'Mr Bradley? I am Aurora, the hotel manager.'

Jeff took her hand.

'Please call me Jeff. My associate, Sulla Bogdani.'

The woman's eyes flicked towards Sulla.

'Yes, I know of Mr Bogdani.'

The voice carried a hint of hostility.

Jeff glanced at Sulla. He appeared to have stiffened but his expression betrayed no emotion. They exchanged a few words in Albanian between them. The tone did not rise above strict formality. The lady shrugged then turned to Jeff.

'We are in darkness, as you can see.' To emphasise the point her arm arched through the air with the elegance of a ballerina. 'There is no electricity. We have a generator, but no guests. It is too expensive to turn on the big machine just to keep an empty hotel warm. Come. Let us go outside and enjoy the sun.'

A courtyard patio boasted tables and chairs bereft of patrons. It overlooked the river and parts of the city. Tufts of green grass struggled through cracked paving stones. Aurora pointed to a corner table then left to organise refreshments.

'You have a coffee with the manager,' Sulla said. 'I am going to stay by the car and make sure it does not get stolen. When the Xhiha brothers arrive, I will come back.'

Jeff didn't have to wait long before Aurora returned with a waiter in tow. Her eyebrows rose at Sulla's absence.

'In the car. Outside. Thinks it might get stolen.'

The waiter placed two espressos and two glasses of water on the table and looked at Aurora. She said a few words in Albanian. He left with the third coffee still on his tray.

'He'll take that out to your driver.'

Whatever Sulla's fame or infamy might be, it didn't appear heinous enough to warrant discourtesy.

'Kind of you. Thanks.'

'The Xhiha brothers are on their way. I think maybe thirty minutes.'

'Do you know these men?'

'I know them, but they are not friends. You are going to do business with these people?'

'I don't know. It's a possibility.'

'I see.'

Was there a warning in her intonation or was it just a matter of accent? Jeff wished Sulla had stayed with him.

'How long have you been in Kosovo, Mr Bradley?'

'Please call me Jeff. I arrived yesterday.'

'A very short time to form an opinion on Kosovo, I think. However, I have no doubt an opinion is forming all the same.'

Aurora's tone remained non-committal, but Jeff couldn't help but notice what he judged to be shrewdness behind the eyes. It occurred to him that she may well be forming her own opinion about him. Possibly along the lines that he was an idiot for wanting to do business in Kosovo.

'How long have you lived in Gjakova?' he asked.

'All my life. My house is down the end of that road beside the river.' Jeff looked in the direction she was pointing. 'It is not a luxury home such as you have in the West. But it is mine. My children and I are comfortable. This is all that matters.'

'And your husband?'

Aurora looked down at her coffee then back in the direction of her house. 'I do not know where my husband is. Dead, I think. No one knows for sure.'

A matter-of-fact statement.

Jeff leaned forward to stir his coffee. 'I'm so sorry.'

The lady's eyes settled back on Jeff. 'The Serbs stopped him one night when he was walking home with a friend. His friend escaped, but they made my husband climb into the back of a truck then it drove away. It was a long time ago. I have heard nothing of him since. Now the war is over. Milosevic has gone. There are no prisoners of war. He must be dead.'

Aurora lapsed into silence. Jeff guessed she had taken herself to the place she must go to whenever she talked of her missing husband. He found himself hoping that she would not become one of those war widows who wasted their lives mourning lost loved ones. Outwardly, she appeared to be strong and resilient, but he suspected just beneath the surface lay a well-hidden fragility. An image of Kimie came to mind, of her sitting at the kitchen table with the same faraway look. He dismissed the the thought. He would find Arben.

11.

The Xhiha brothers ambled across the courtyard twenty minutes late. When he saw them arrive Sulla left his car and dogged their every step. Upon invitation, the brothers slid into the chairs bedside Jeff. Sulla sat opposite. He crossed his arms and glared at them. Jeff suppressed a smile. Sulla's naked hostility would have been difficult to ignore.

The shorter brother mumbled something to Aurora. She didn't translate. There were apparently no apologies for their tardiness. It irritated Jeff, but he kept his mouth shut.

'Mr Bradley, this is Ahmed and Skender Xhiha,' Aurora said.

Sulla had referred to them as peasants. They certainly bore scars of the harsh existence that Jeff knew to be the life of country folk in Eastern Europe. Both men wore white felt *qelesche* hats shaped like cut-in-half eggshells on their shaven skulls. Both looked skeletally thin, sunken-chested and unshaven. They could have been anywhere between thirty and sixty. Jeff thought Skender and Ahmed would both qualify as models for an anti-TB poster campaign. He knew the disease was rampant in this part of the world.

'Skender has no English skills. Ahmed understands a little,' Aurora said. 'I suggest for the purposes of this meeting they speak in Albanian and I will translate.'

'That's fine by me.'

Sulla added a terse comment in Albanian. The brothers' heads spun towards him, rope-like veins bulging behind the leathery skin of their necks. Sulla leaned forward and fixed his eyes on them. Jeff stiffened. But the brothers turned their attention back to Aurora.

The shorter Ahmed claimed that he and his brother had inherited the property from an uncle. Neither had any experience with wine and they had employed a manager to oversee day-to-day operations. When Jeff asked how the uncle had come to own the land and how long he had owned it before that, Ahmed said he did not know. The Serbs had killed their uncle and it had come as a big surprise that they were his beneficiaries.

'Allah has blessed them with good fortune,' Aurora translated.

Ahmed bared an incomplete set of yellow teeth in the semblance of a grin at Jeff. The laugh that came out of Sulla sounded little short of scornful.

'These are fairy tales, Jeff.'

Ahmed hissed a sneer at Sulla. Sulla's chest heaved. The colour of his face and the way his eyes almost popped out of his head suggested to Jeff that at any moment he'd leap from his seat and grab Ahmed by the throat. There was little doubt in Jeff's mind either that the brothers were lying. However, he had to remind himself that he was not here to debate land ownership. He was here to find Arben. With a quick shake of the head he threw a warning glance at Sulla.

'Look. I came to Kosovo to buy a vineyard. The lawyer, Tomi Mema, told me these two wanted to sell their vineyard. I'd like to look over the property. Today, if possible.'

Aurora translated.

Ahmed turned to his brother. Skender shrugged and muttered something. Eyes flicked back and forth between Jeff and Sulla like a sparrow wary of a cat.

'Ahmed says he was told by the lawyer that you are a friend of a man named Arben Shala,' Aurora said.

Jeff shrugged in an effort to appear unconcerned. 'Mr Shala is an acquaintance. I met him in New Zealand. Have they seen Mr Shala?'

A brief exchange between Aurora and the brothers.

'Ahmed said he came to the vineyard and made some trouble and then went away. They have not seen him again.'

'Tell them I was given to understand the land belonged to Mr Shala,' Jeff said.

Another exchange. Two pairs of eyes shot at Jeff.

'The courts declared their ownership documents that are valid,' she reported. 'Ahmed says nothing else matters. They are the legal owners.'

'Would they know where Mr Shala might have gone?'

Jeff knew he was pushing his luck. The next exchange with Aurora left the brothers looking agitated. Both glared at Jeff.

'No, they say they don't. Ahmed wants to know why you are so curious about Mr Shala.'

'I'm a businessman. I like to know exactly what I'm dealing with when it comes to money. Mr Shala said he is the owner and now these men say they are the owners.'

Hardly had Aurora finished addressing the brothers when Ahmed spat a response at her.

'He says the court has confirmed them as the rightful owners.'

'They're definite about that?'

'They are most emphatic about it, Jeff.'

'Then would you please tell them that as far as Mr Shala is concerned there's nothing more to discuss. Ask them if I can see the vineyard today.'

After Aurora's translation the brothers turned aside, heads down, and mumbled to each other. Jeff looked at Sulla. He didn't react to whatever it was they said.

'They are not sure today is possible,' Aurora said.

'It has to be today. I'm only here for a few days and I have a lot of meetings to attend.' Jeff stood. 'If they aren't interested in selling, then I'll say goodbye.'

Following Aurora's translation, Ahmed looked across at Sulla then said something to his brother. Skender nodded.

'They agree for you to go today,' Aurora said.

Jeff nodded.

Sulla said, 'They drive. We follow.'

∽

Sulla followed the Xhiha brothers' battered red Toyota hatchback out of the city centre and onto the road to Prizren.

'Okay, Sulla. What the hell was that really all about back there?'

'These men are animals. Now you have seen them, maybe you believe me. In Kosovo, family is family. To my father, Arben is family. Because of this he is like a brother to me. An enemy of Arben is an enemy of mine. These sons of pigs are stealing his land. Maybe they have killed him.' Sulla glared through the streaked windscreen, knuckles showing white on the steering wheel. 'I should cut their throats and be done with it.'

Jeff speculated how much of Sulla's hostility was genuine and how much rhetoric. For the moment, he leaned towards genuine.

'We need to find out about Benny first, Sulla. Then you can do what you like.'

Sulla's smile reminded Jeff of a shark. 'It will give me great pleasure.'

'Hang on. What's that up ahead?'

'NATO checkpoint. Do not worry. They will hassle us a little then send us on our way.'

Rifle slung across shoulder, a helmeted soldier stepped out onto the road. He gestured Sulla into an unsealed lay-by. An officer in a greatcoat bearing distinctive German insignia on the lapels pointed to the spot he wanted Sulla to park. Standing in the turret of an armoured personnel carrier just metres away, a soldier leaned across the barrel of a .50 calibre machine gun pointing in their direction. Jeff doubted the weapon had a live round up the spout but would still have preferred it to point elsewhere. Six more soldiers stood next to the carrier. All wore flak-jackets. Three stepped forward and surrounded Sulla's car. The officer tapped on Sulla's window. He gestured Sulla and Jeff to get out.

'There are still problems in Kosovo, as you can see,' Sulla said, opening the door.

The officer confronted him. 'Documents.' He snapped out the order as if he was addressing a platoon.

Although the man's brusqueness irked Jeff, he took his passport from his jacket pocket and held it out, but not far enough. His small triumph was to observe the man having to stretch to collect it. Sulla leaned into the car and pulled a plastic bag from the glove box. The German studied Jeff's passport, then glanced up at him over the top of it.

'You're from New Zealand,' he said in English. 'What were you doing here in Gjakova?'

'I am here on business. This man is my driver.'

'What type of business?'

'That's confidential.'

'You will tell me what I want to know when I ask,' the German barked.

In the military Jeff had obeyed authority without question, but that was usually from men he respected. He was a civilian now and not about to give this arrogant bastard anything more than strictly necessary. He fixed his eyes on him and said nothing.

Sulla passed his papers across. The officer averted his gaze from Jeff and snatched the documents from Sulla's hand.

'Search the car,' he yelled.

Jeff noticed the Xhiha brothers had pulled their car over to the side of the road a hundred metres ahead. Ahmed had climbed out and was leaning on the roof watching.

After several minutes one of the soldiers yelled an all-clear. 'You may go now.'

The officer passed everything to Sulla, including Jeff's passport, then spun on his heel and walked off towards the next vehicle to be checked.

'This happen often?' Jeff asked as they drove away.

'All the time. Kosovo is Kosovo. KFOR, NATO, whatever you want to call them, they need to do something to fill their days so they stop motorists.'

'What are they looking for?'

'Guns, explosives, drugs, contraband, whatever they can find.'

'And do they find any?'

'Of course. All the time. Everybody has a gun. We are just like America. Except for the money and jobs.' Sulla laughed at his little joke. 'And like in America, someone is always getting shot.'

'Sounds like the Wild West.'

'This is the Balkans. There is no difference.'

༄

'May Allah cause the Xhiha brothers to die a thousand deaths.'

Sulla's voice came as a growl as he followed the brothers' Toyota across a muddy potholed field with pretensions of being a parking lot. The car lurched. Jeff bounced forward in his seat, banging his knee against the dashboard. Sulla breathed another curse and drew his car to a halt.

The windowless brick building they stopped behind was in need of plaster and paint and, from what Jeff could see, a new roof as well. A man wearing white overalls came out to greet them. The Xhiha brothers fell in behind him.

He spoke to Sulla in Albanian.

'This man is the manager,' Sulla said to Jeff. 'His name is Astrit. He speaks English.'

The manager beamed and shook Jeff's hand. 'Welcome. You're interested in buying into this vineyard?' he asked.

With some surprise Jeff thought he noticed a touch of London cockney accent. 'Your English is very good, Astrit.'

'I lived in London for two years. Then the authorities found me and sent me home.' He grinned. 'No visa.'

Jeff decided he liked Astrit. 'Yes, it's true that I am looking to invest.'

From a distance Jeff observed that the vines looked in much better shape than those he'd seen on the slopes as they entered Gja-kova. But certainly nowhere near the pristine condition of the vines at Boundary Fence.

'If you do decide to buy, don't worry about the staff and myself. We would work very hard for you. There are thirty hectares of vines, a processing plant and a house. There's fifty hectares more we could plant, but for the moment there's no point. The three hundred thousand bottles we produce each year is just for the local market. Unfortunately, Kosovo has a wine glut. If we could export, it would be different, but we cannot. Sending goods out of Kosovo is dif-ficult.'

'I wasn't aware of a blockade,' Jeff said.

'Not a blockade like they have in Africa or Cuba. No, it's dif-ferent here. Kosovo is a non-country. It has no trade agreements.

The Serbs use this as an excuse to not allow goods to cross their borders, unless of course it is something they want. This also applies to Macedonia and Montenegro. We can only ship goods through Albania but that is a road to nowhere. Bandits steal the trucks.'

Despite Jeff's earlier misgivings, it seemed Arben had been right. Kosovon wine could cover the losses from their crop failure. The Serbian province, once at the heart of the Yugoslavian wine industry, was awash with unsellable bulk product and Yugoslavian wine was readily accepted in the New Zealand market. Not that that mattered. The bulk wine would only be used for blending. But shipping the wine to New Zealand might prove more difficult than either of them had first thought.

Ahmed and Skender Xhiha grew bored with the discussions in a language neither fully comprehended. They left Astrit to show Jeff the vines and facilities. The vines needed feeding but they had been pruned competently. Up close, any disorder in the vines had more to do with the posts and wire than the plants themselves. Inside the factory, four men and two women in white overalls looked up as Jeff, Sulla and Astrit entered. Astrit yelled something in Albanian. Jeff received smiles all round, with an additional bow from the women's scarved heads. The women returned to pushing corks into the necks of filled bottles and passing them to the men for labelling and packing into cartons.

'What type of wines do you produce?' Jeff asked.

'Reds, mostly. Cabernet is our specialty. Would you like to taste?'

'Sure, why not?'

Astrit took a bottle from the line and poured some of the red liquid into a sherry copita. This amused Jeff. The building might be falling down around their ears, but the tasting glass was international standard. Astrit took a step back. The manual production line came to a halt as all the workers watched in anticipation. The tasting had clearly taken on more than casual significance. Jeff's verdict – whatever it might be – would affect all their futures. Now was not the time to mention he was far from an expert in wine differentiations.

He made sure to pick up the glass as Arben had taught him. Turning to the wall he tilted the glass against the white background. What had Arben said to look for? 'If it is red turning purplish it is young. Deep red and it is aged.'

The contents of this glass were approaching purplish, just as Jeff expected. He doubted the Xhiha brothers would allow wine to age for more than a season when it could be turned into cash. He swirled the glass and brought it to his nose, breathing in the newly released polyphenols. Jeff took a sizeable sip and let it swish and circulate to every part of his mouth. To Jeff's amateur palate it seemed to have what he'd describe as good body. He looked for a basin. There was none. He spat the wine back into the glass and put it on the table with a nod of the head. He adopted what he hoped would pass for a wise expression.

'Mmm. Young, yes. But better than I expected.'

Had he done it right? Was there any part of the process he'd got wrong?

Astrit's bright grin and thumbs up to the others reassured him he'd not made a complete dick of himself. The staff clapped then returned to the bottling with what looked like renewed enthusiasm.

'Astrit?' Jeff said cautiously. 'Has a man named Arben Shala visited the vineyard at any time in the last two weeks?'

'Yes, Mr Shala was here.' Astrit checked behind him then lowered his voice. 'He was with an American woman. They had a big argument with the brothers. I didn't overhear much of what was said, but he and the woman did not look happy when they left.'

'Really? An American woman? Do you know who she was?'

'When they first arrived she gave me a business card. I have it in the office. Come, I will find it for you.'

Jeff gave Sulla a quick glance.

'As they say in the movies,' Sulla said, 'this might be our lucky break.'

'A lead, at any rate, Sulla my friend. Sounds like a promising one too.'

❧

The sun hung low in the sky when Jeff and Sulla drove back into Prishtina. Jeff mulled over the bits and pieces of information he'd been gathering. The disagreement between Arben and the brothers had no doubt been when Arben confronted them over the ownership of the land. He looked at the woman's business card in his hand. What interest did she have in Arben Shala's affairs? Her name was Morgan Delaney and the card was embossed with the USAID logo.

Impatience tightened his shoulders. He wanted to get back to his hotel room and phone the number on the card.

12.

The trained eyes of Lee Caldwell scanned the blast zone. His steps needed to be slow and measured. Grid searching by a man of his experience was never rushed. Not if he expected to find clues that lesser professionals might miss.

A pause to check his bearings.

The cobbles of the narrow, sloping street, Čopova ulica ran from where he stood right into Prešeren Square, Ljubljana's city centre. To his left, tangled wires roped through the glassless window frames of McDonald's restaurant. The balcony had collapsed. Further down he noted a few store owners had covered shattered windows with plywood and canvas. But most gaped open. Caldwell looked into the burnt out interiors sodden by fire hoses. The stench of charred stock and timber filled his nostrils.

He paused at the entrance into the square. Beside him, a torn piece of yellow police tape, still attached to a length of mangled aluminium framing, fluttered in the breeze. The broken glass and debris he expected to see had already been swept up. But specks of blood splattered across the walls and cobblestones still waited to be washed away.

The gentle flap of tarpaulins draped over a handful of apartment buildings sounded like the wings of giant birds passing by. Wooden panels had been nailed over the doors and windows of the rest. The two buildings cornering the alley that the marathon runners were to have run through had collapsed into a mountain of rubble. The acrid smell of charred timbers was much stronger here. In three languages somebody had whitewashed on the wall that the Sunday morning bric-a-brac market would stay closed indefinitely.

Groups of the city's inhabitants huddled together in silence. Most held lighted candles as they continued the city's vigil for the 83 Slovenes killed and the 117 injured.

Head bowed in respect, Caldwell picked his way through the groups to the monument to Slovenia's greatest poet, France Prešeren. The residue of countless melted candles glued wreaths of brightly coloured flowers, framed photos and crucifixes around the statue's feet. Caldwell had seen scenes like this many times before. But as immune as he thought he had become to such bombings, the collection of teddy bears and small dolls reflecting the death of children filled him with renewed rage. This was barbaric cowardice, pure and simple. It disgusted him.

He knew the city would recover. In his experience, the effects of terrorist bombings were never long-lasting and whatever their political justification may have been was quickly forgotten. Suicide bombers died in vain. However, this time his trained eye told Caldwell those responsible for the wreckage in Presnov Square were not suicide bombers.

These ones were almost certainly still very much alive.

As always in such places, Lee Caldwell walked to a quiet spot. He closed his eyes and uttered a silent prayer to the dead, promising their ghosts that he would find those responsible and make them pay.

When he was finished, he walked back up Čopova ulica to his waiting car. He had a plane to catch.

13.

From the outside, the glass multi-storey OSCE building looked like a giant mirror. It reflected the light of the setting sun, sending shafts of burning orange light across the city. It didn't surprise Jeff to see that most motorists heading west had one arm raised to shield their eyes. Jaywalking would be hazardous in these conditions. For once Jeff would err on the side of caution and wait for the traffic lights to turn red before crossing the road.

The building had been easy enough to find but determining which was the entrance to the Land Registry Office proved more difficult. A security guard outside the Bank of Kosovo directed Jeff down a side street. It was a little after five and past office closing. Morgan Delaney had agreed to wait for him but, he suspected, with some reluctance.

An ID badge attached to his jacket lapel, Jeff made his way along a corridor to the last room on the left. He knocked twice on the open door and took half a step inside. A standing woman speaking on the telephone waved him in and pointed to a leather two-seater.

'I don't give a damn what the minister is saying, Ron, he's lying. The documentation is quite clear on this point and I don't want him to get away with it.'

Jeff took a seat. He judged Morgan Delaney to be in her late twenties, maybe early thirties. The charcoal trouser suit she wore fitted snugly over her tall, athletic physique. A neat chignon of thick, wavy red hair sat pinned at the nape of her neck. Green eyes glistened as she spoke. Her raised voice warned Jeff that she was angry about something.

'Yeah right, and a big to-hell-with-you as well, Ron.'

The hand piece met the receiver with a loud clatter. Then Jeff encountered a wide smile.

'Bureaucrats. Don't you just love them? You must be Jeff Bradley.' She thrust out a hand. Jeff stood to respond. 'Morgan Delaney.' She perched on the edge of her desk and waved him to resume his seat. 'How can I help you, Mr Bradley?'

'I got this yesterday.' Jeff fished the business card out of his pocket and handed it to her. 'It was given to me by the manager of a vineyard near Gjakova. He said you gave it to him when you visited with a man called Arben Shala.'

'Arben Shala. Yes, I remember Mr Shala very well. Nice man.'

'May I ask why he came to see you?'

Morgan's brow creased. Her eyes squinted at Jeff for several seconds. He was pretty certain she was not mentally undressing him, but it did look mighty close. Either way Jeff had the weird sensation he had just been put through some kind of washing machine.

'There are no privacy laws in Kosovo, but all the same I'm not prepared to discuss a client's business unless I'm certain it's in my client's best interests. So before we go any further, would you mind telling me your connection to Mr Shala?'

Jeff turned on a smile. 'Fair enough. I own a vineyard near Auckland. That's a city in New Zealand.'

Jeff noticed a tightening of Morgan's lips. 'I have heard of Auckland, Mr Bradley. And I do know where New Zealand is as it happens. Not all Americans are geographically challenged, you know.'

'Really?'

'Yes, really. Fact is I had a Kiwi penpal in Dargaville when I was ten years old. At that age I thought New Zealanders lived in grass huts. I was terribly disappointed when I found out they were actually quite civilised.'

'Some of us even wear shoes.'

To Jeff's relief, Ms Delaney's smile returned. 'Anyway, I met Arben through a mutual acquaintance. He told me he had a vineyard in Kosovo and was keen to sell. So here I am, an eager buyer, but no Arben. The hotel said he booked out a week ago. When I phoned his family they had not heard from him and they're worried. Does that qualify me to ask questions?'

'Okay, here's the deal. The US government funds our company and what we do is investigate property disputes. Mr Shala came to see me for that reason.' Morgan turned and shuffled through the documents spread across her desk. She held up a manila folder, opened it and withdrew some papers. 'Here it is. Two brothers by the surname of Xhiha claim they inherited the disputed property from their uncle.'

'Yes, I already know that much. I met with the Xhiha brothers earlier today. Is it possible that Arben could be wrong and the brothers really do own the property?'

'Mr Shala had an original deed of ownership.' Morgan held up a photocopy. 'Two legal documents for the same property is not uncommon in Kosovo.' She waved her hand over the desk. 'All these files tell a similar story to Mr Shala's.'

'I guess I have to ask the obvious question. How can there be two legal deeds of ownership for the same property?'

'That's the simple part. During the war, many Kosovons fled the country. Some came back. Many didn't. Anyway, someone, or a group of someones, or an organised gang – I don't know which for certain – have been moving in on the abandoned properties. In

Kosovo everyone is poor and in need of money, especially public servants. Pay the bribe and hey presto: new documents, all legally registered. Lately a number of the original owners have returned and, as you can see from the pile of files on my desk, there are an awful lot of disputes. Some are easily resolved, but most, as in the case of Mr Shala, are not. The difficulty is that during the war local council records went missing. There was never a central land registry in Kosovo.'

'I see.'

'Unfortunately, there are no easy solutions. Either one party gives up and walks away, or someone gets a gun and we end up with dead bodies.'

It occurred to Jeff that he now had the probable reason for Arben's phone message. He exhaled a deep breath.

'I hate to think that someone would kill Arben over a shitty piece of land.'

Morgan raised an eyebrow. 'Wars are usually fought over land.'

'Okay. Point taken,' Jeff said, allowing a sheepish grin to acknowledge the absurdity of his comment. 'And you don't know whether the false registrations are attributable to lone opportunists or organised gangs?'

'That's about where it sits, Mr Bradley. My investigations have turned up more questions than answers. But at the moment there is one red flag flying higher than the rest.'

'Which is . . . ?'

'More than eighty per cent of these disputes are concentrated in the Peje and Gjakova regions. It's too early to jump to conclusions, but I think I can safely say I smell a rat.'

'This is not good news for Arben Shala.' Jeff addressed this comment more to himself than to Morgan Delaney.

'No need for pessimism. He could have just gone into hiding. It happens.'

'Even if that were the case, I'm sure he would've found a way to get word to his family. Trouble is, after having met the Xhiha brothers, I have no difficulty believing they're capable of murder. But to successfully cover it up? No. I think they're far too stupid.'

Morgan tapped a pen on the table. 'Let's think about that. To arrange false documentation requires the cooperation of public servants and judges and, of course, lawyers to handle the lodging of the documents. I don't see the Xhihas having the aptitude for that either. I doubt they can even read. I'd be inclined to say that somebody else is pulling their strings.'

'You think Arben's claim is genuine then?'

'Oh, yes, I'm positive. Firstly, unlike many others, he did have the original documents. Secondly, he's now a New Zealand citizen with a family and a good job. So why bother coming back to Kosovo if the claim wasn't legit?' She shrugged. 'It just doesn't sit right when I look at it from either angle.'

'If you believe he is the real owner, what can your office do?'

Morgan shook her head. 'Not a lot. Our job is to determine the truth and pass the information to the courts. Then it's up to them.'

'Did he mention to you he was being harassed?'

'No, he didn't. But he was very angry. He might have tried to resolve the dispute in the typical Albanian way. But somehow I don't think so. Mr Shala didn't seem the violent type. However, there are some ruthless individuals out there. Intimidation and violence are a part of Kosovon daily life. The value of these disputed properties runs into millions of dollars. The average monthly wage here is a hundred dollars. Do the math, Mr Bradley. For a few measly bucks people like Mr Shala can be made to disappear.'

Jeff well understood the math. The bottom line chilled him. He stood up. For some reason his legs felt unsteady.

'Ms Delaney, thank you for your help. I guess I might revisit the vineyard and have another talk with the Xhiha brothers.'

'I'd be careful. I didn't like the look of those two any more than you did.' Morgan passed back her business card. 'If I can be of any further assistance, please call.'

Outside, Jeff stood on the pavement mulling over his conversation with Morgan Delaney. He refused to believe Arben was dead. He was not about to give up hope, not yet. But if Arben wasn't dead, then where the hell was he?

14.

Arben's eyes tracked the decline of the sun through the small wire-meshed window. Dusk crept across the Prishtina rooftops, sucking up the city's colours like leeches draining life from a drunk collapsed in a gutter. Silhouettes dimmed then disappeared into darkness, yet Arben found himself still in the court cell.

Hours of sitting on a wooden bench had numbed his rump. His calf muscles cramped from time to time. Pacing back and forth had helped, but it failed to ease his general discomfort. The bravado that had imbued him with the courage to confront Tomi Mema had withered into depression: a depression made worse by the realisation that Mema was right. There would be no compassion for him from the court. No hope of release.

Voices approached. American voices.

The clank of keys signalled the arrival of the court guard at his cell. She swung the gate open and beckoned him forward. Two brawny black UN policemen emerged from behind her and smiled at him.

'Arben Shala?' one asked. Arben nodded. 'Do you speak English?'

'Yes, yes I do. I live in New Zealand. I'm a New Zealand citizen.'

'That so.'

The American's voice betrayed little interest. The woman guard removed Arben's handcuffs. He felt a nudge in the back.

'Face the wall, Mr Shala.'

Arben did as he was told. The second American ran his hands quickly down his trunk and legs.

'Okay buddy. Turn around and hold out your hands.'

Arben found his hands confined by a new set of handcuffs. The policeman bent to look into his face.

'Is that okay? Not too tight?'

'No, not too tight. Look, officer. This is a mistake. I shouldn't be here. The people responsible are using the courts to steal money from me. I can't get a message to the UN to let the New Zealand government know I'm here. I need help.'

A frown crossed the brow of the policeman.

'Do you have a lawyer?'

Arben gave the man a vigorous nod. 'Yes. But he's part of the problem. I need international help.'

'Okay, I hear you. You need to talk to the director of the detention centre once you get there.'

It struck Arben that the director was an unknown quantity and that these men weren't. He hated the thought of pleading, but his position didn't leave a lot of room for pride.

'Can't you guys do something? This is desperate for me, officers.'

Both policemen shook their heads. 'Sorry, friend, no can do. We've got no authority here. We only drive the van. If you're unhappy with your lawyer, the director will bring in someone from the UN to help you. You're not alone. Really. Okay?'

Arben's flash of optimism disappeared into the cosmos. Mema had been right. No one cared. One of the policemen stepped into the corridor.

'Okay, let's go.'

The court had closed long ago and Arben saw the street outside was clear of onlookers. At least the walk to the police van would be less harrowing than his arrival.

'Sit anywhere. There won't be any other passengers. Try to relax. It's a short trip.'

Three rows of seating confronted Arben. He slumped into the nearest and rested his head against the window. As the streets went by he gazed at the locals going about their business. What was he to anyone in this city? He was just a shadowy figure who demanded less concern than a box of onions outside the minimarket.

Rap music blared out of the vehicle radio. Arben hated rap music. To see the two black Americans nodding to the beat added a ludicrous dimension to his Kafkaesque situation.

What would become of him in the detention centre?

15.

Arben had no idea the Prishtina Detention Centre was behind the Central Police Station, barely a hundred metres from its main entrance. Never having had to visit incarcerated family or friends here before, it astonished him that the entrance to the prison must be on the boulevard. It was just one of the many doors built into the facades of government buildings that stretched the length of the block. He had never seen the two-storey cell blocks. That did not surprise him. From the road they would be well hidden. However, like all Kosovons he had heard the stories. During the war, prisoners held in the detention centre had been tortured by the Serbs. Now here he was, about to experience the interior firsthand.

A day gone and he had barely moved a hundred metres.

The courtyard gates were opened by a section of Indian soldiers. After the van had driven through, they closed them again and gathered to peer through the window. Arben felt like a bear in a cage. He wondered if they were going to poke him with a stick. The American driver looked over his shoulder.

'Okay, buddy. Time to get out.'

Two metres away, a metal door set into solid concrete swung open. The two Americans led Arben through it into the processing area of the detention centre. It was as busy as the foyer of a hotel. American and Italian police officers stood in the background, smoking cigarettes and chatting and apparently supervising the Kosovon prison guards as they carried out their duties.

One of the American cops passed across Arben's documents to a guard then turned to leave.

'You take care, buddy.'

Without responding, Arben accepted the cop's smile and pat on his shoulder. But as the backs of both cops disappeared, the clunk of the metal door shutting behind them suggested the impenetrable solidness of a bank vault. Arben's spirits plummeted.

He stood motionless, as mesmerised by his surroundings as a deer in a spotlight. A guard behind a three-metre-long desk waved him forward. There were questions. Sounds emanated out of Arben's mouth in response, but the voice he didn't recognise as his own. He prayed that at any moment he would wake and this would all have been a nasty dream.

An Italian officer approached to observe the proceedings. He gave Arben the once-over then returned to the conversation with his companions at the rear of the room. Arben considered pleading his innocence. He decided against it. The long day had tired him. He didn't think he could take yet another rejection. He would gather some strength from the night and ask to see the director in the morning.

Paperwork finished, next came fingerprinting and a photograph. In a small room next to the holding cell he was subjected to a body search. He submitted in silence. When the processing had finished he was made to sign for a mattress and a plastic bag filled with blankets, toiletries and orange prison overalls. The plastic bag in one hand and the mattress under the other arm, Arben followed a guard down a curving corridor and up a winding metal staircase. At the top they had to wait for security gates to open. From there it was a short walk to cell thirteen.

The guard slipped a colour copy of the photograph taken downstairs into a Perspex holder on the wall next to the door. Arben found it hard to believe that the shaggy-haired unshaven bum in the photo could possibly be him. He barely glanced at the three other photographs on the wall. The cell door opened.

A shove in the back had Arben viewing his new cell from the inside. No particular thought had entered his head as to whether shared accommodation was a welcome state of affairs or not, until his gaze met those of his cellmates. Hands of cards before them, three men sitting around a moulded plastic table eyed their new companion. Arben's stomach turned. He swallowed hard and tried not to think about the possibility of throwing up.

The room was about twenty square metres. Graffiti scrawled across pink walls reminded Arben of the inside of a men's urinal. Two sets of bunks, four sets of drawers and the table and four chairs filled most of the available space. The sound of running water came from behind the one other door in the cell. A toilet, Arben guessed.

One of the men leaped from his chair and confronted the guard. 'Why are you bringing this man here? We have no room.' He glared at Arben. 'Take him somewhere else.'

A skull-grin from the guard and an insolent salute. The clang of the closing door echoed behind him.

'Bastard. A curse on your family,' the man yelled after him. Then he turned to Arben and pointed at a chair. 'Sit.'

Arben fought for breath. The tightness in his chest felt like his ribs were caving in. He gripped hold of his mattress like a drowning man.

'Sit,' the man said again. He took the mattress from Arben and placed it against the wall. The plastic bag followed. 'Sit.' Less belligerent this time.

Arben sank onto one of the plastic chairs. He tried to smile but his face felt as responsive as a mask. His head dropped.

'You want a coffee?'

Arben's head rose. He encountered a grin.

'I'm Imer. Don't worry. I'm not trying to make you feel unwelcome. But as you can see we don't have much room. When someone new comes we always complain. Maybe one day they'll listen.'

Imer laughed. The others joined in.

'What's your name?'

'Arben. Arben Shala.'

Imer reached across and took the court documents still clutched in Arben's left hand. He read through, shaking his head at times. When he finished he dropped the papers onto the table for the others to read. The young man sitting next to Arben scanned the top page with a scowl. He passed it on, strode to one of the bottom bunks and threw himself onto it.

'I'm Bedri,' the third man said, and pointed to the man on the bunk. 'That's Sabri. Not so friendly. But don't be afraid. Nothing will happen to you.'

Arben nodded, but not with a lot of conviction.

'Sugar and milk?'

'Er . . . Just sugar. Thank you.'

Imer took the bottom half of a plastic Coca-Cola bottle with string tied round the middle and disappeared into the toilet.

'We have no kettle,' Bedri said. 'We must improvise.'

He did not elaborate and Arben could not begin to imagine what Imer might be doing to make water boil in a Coca-Cola bottle.

'Where are you from?' Bedri asked.

'I grew up in a small village close to Gjakova. But now I live in New Zealand.'

Bedri's eyes widened.

'Really? I've seen that country. On television. A beautiful country. How long have you been there?'

'A number of years. I have full citizenship.'

'You're a lucky man. I too would love to get out of Kosovo. Anywhere would be better than this shithole.'

Arben looked across at Sabri still lying on his bunk, tattooed arms folded across his chest. The young man worried him. He could not help but hope that in this particular Kosovon shithole where he found himself, a comraderie formed from shared adversity with Imer and Bedri might offer some small assurance of protection.

Imer emerged from the toilet, steam rising from the Coke bottle. He poured the hot water into three paper cups.

'Would you like a cigarette, Arben?' Bedri asked.

'I don't smoke.'

'I don't either. Nor Imer. Only Sabri. When he does, we make him sit on the top bunk with the window open. Imer would beat him if he didn't. Imer is the boss of the cell.' Bedri laughed. 'Obvious, you'd think, eh? But don't worry. Imer's a good man. He's been here the longest. Three years.'

Three years? To Arben it seemed inconceivable that anyone could survive under such conditions for so long.

Imer placed the coffees on the table, then picked up Arben's mattress and threw it onto a top bunk. Arben made to rise but Bedri stopped him.

'Drink your coffee. Imer will do everything. Don't worry. Let him. It gives him something to do. Besides, he has no money. The rest of us buy from the prison shop. Coffee, Coca-Cola, biscuits. And we share with him. In return Imer runs the cell. He makes the coffee and keeps everything clean. He's the boss.'

Although Arben was contemplating that Imer might be more servant than boss, he nodded and sipped his coffee.

'Why are you here?' Bedri asked. 'What did you do? It doesn't say in the documents.'

'They said I stole a mobile phone. I told the police I bought it from a shop in the mall. I even had a receipt for it. But they didn't care. Now they say they're investigating. But of course the man who sold me the phone has disappeared. I've not even been indicted yet, but here I am anyway.'

'I'd say you've been set up,' Imer called out. He pulled two blankets from the plastic bag and began to arrange them on Arben's bunk. 'It's very common in Kosovo these days, you know?'

Arben breathed into his coffee. Pleasant aroma. Who'd have thought?

'All I want is for it to go away. But I don't know who's behind it, so I don't know how to stop it.'

Bedri and Imer burst out laughing. Arben raised eyebrows at them.

'Don't be offended,' Bedri said. 'We're not laughing at you. You've been in the West too long. Everyone in Kosovo's corrupt – the judges, the prosecutors, the police. Everyone. To buy your freedom you'll have to pay them all. They'll want a lot of money. Who's your lawyer?'

'Tomi Mema.'

Bedri and Imer exchanged glances and nodded. 'Tomi Mema is big time in Kosovo,' said Imer. 'He's always on television. And he's very expensive.'

'I can't argue with that.'

Arben heard the bitterness in his own voice.

'Imer is right,' Bedri said. 'The judges are jealous of him. He makes too much money representing rich people. Are you rich?'

'Hardly. I work for wages and live where I work.'

'Then this might not be so good for you. Maybe they think that because you live in New Zealand you have plenty. Why didn't you apply for bail?'

'I was given bail. I tried to get into Macedonia the same night.'

Bedri let out a long low whistle. 'Mema advised this?'

'No. But when I was caught and taken back to the judge he put little effort in arguing to keep me out of this place.'

'Hah. He makes more money the more trouble you get yourself into, my friend. Why did you choose him? Why not someone else?'

'I'd spoken with him on another matter. When this trouble came along, Mema just turned up. I was desperate so I agreed to accept his help.'

Bedri and Imer exchanged another glance. Bedri's brow creased in a frown.

'Just turned up, did he? Well, my friend. Maybe the mobile phone is not your only problem. Maybe the bigger problem is Tomi Mema.'

It was on the tip of Arben's tongue to say he already knew that the lawyer was in on the conspiracy against him. But the warning to him from that very same Tomi Mema about the dangers inherent in an open prison still rang in his ears. Had it also been a message for him to get wise and keep his mouth shut?

'The American police said I should ask to see the prison director. That he would get someone from the UN to help me . . .'

Imer and Bedri began laughing. A sneer came from Sabri on his bunk. Bedri centred his sights on Arben.

'My friend. To see the director you'll first need to apply for a request form. Maybe after a week you'll get one. More likely two. If you make a mistake on it, even a tiny one, you must apply for another request form. Another week. Maybe two. When it's ready you must turn it in to the guards to give to the director. They'll want money. And even if they do give it to him, it can take up to a month before you're called. And that's just to start.'

Arben's shoulders slumped. Bedri gave his arm a tap.

'Learn to eat shit, my friend. Get Tomi Mema in here to see you. Only a lawyer can help.'

'How do I get word to him?'

'No problem. For the lawyers, the guards carry the message straight away. The lawyers pay them. Now, my friend, you must be tired. Soon they will turn off the lights. Maybe you wish to use the toilet and wash a little?'

'Yes. I'd like to brush my teeth and wash my face. I would also like a shave and a shower.'

'We shower in the morning. We are lucky in Kosovo. The UN manages the prisons so they are just like in the West. We have hot showers, heating and good food.' Bedri seemed almost proud. 'Anything you need.'

Arben took his plastic bag into the toilet. The area was compact, but it was clean and had a basin. A small square of polished metal had been stuck to the wall for use as a mirror.

When he climbed onto the top bunk, Arben found he was too exhausted even to think. As soon as his eyes closed he was asleep.

16.

Jeff had a lot to think about: the meeting with Morgan Delaney and the phone calls he'd placed following that. But he needed to catch up on sleep. It was destined not to happen. After tossing and turning for nearly an hour, he gave up, showered, threw on a pair of jeans and a heavy sweater and headed for the Kukri bar.

The place was as busy as it had been the previous night. Big John proved to be the consummate publican. Through the crowd and bustling waiters he'd spotted Jeff's arrival. A handle of beer had landed on the bar for him before he even reached it.

Jeff spotted Barry occupying the same spot as last evening. There was no sign of the drunken Gary or his other drinking partner, Bruce. Beer in hand, Jeff moved in Barry's direction. But stalled. Barry was engaged in conversation with two women. One was Morgan Delaney, less formal in skirt and black polo-neck sweater, hair falling loose just above the shoulders. Tough soldier as he was, Jeff always suffered a degree of awkwardness in mixed company. As he debated with himself whether or not to proceed, Barry caught his eye.

'Hey, Jeff. Come and join us.'

Jeff jostled his way through a group of Austrian uniforms and placed his beer on the counter. For some reason he made a point of not looking Morgan Delaney in the eye.

'Jeff. Meet Bethany Bridge.' Barry indicated the woman leaning into his side. 'She's a Kiwi just like you, mate. You'll know that as soon as she opens her mouth.'

Bethany jabbed Barry's arm and smiled. 'Hi, Jeff.'

'Hi.'

'And this is Morgan Delaney. She's a Yank and you'll definitely know that when she opens her mouth.'

A pair of green eyes greeted Jeff's. 'Now, how about that? Mr Bradley and I have already met.'

'So we have, Ms Delaney. Hello again.'

A loud guffaw from Barry's direction. 'Hey. Drop that Mr Bradley, Ms Delaney shit you two. This isn't a bloody cocktail party. Kosovo's a small world, Jeff. You stay here long enough and you'll meet everyone. They all come to the Kukri.'

Jeff doubted one of them would have been Arben. Not this sort of place. He flashed a grin around the group. 'Can I buy everyone a drink?'

Barry emptied his handle and banged it on the counter. 'Damn right you can.'

Jeff caught the bartender's attention and signalled for another round of drinks. When he turned back, Barry and Bethany were speaking to someone standing behind them. He passed Morgan a glass of wine. 'Ms Delaney . . .'

'Morgan, please.'

'Morgan. After I left your office I went back to the hotel and phoned Arben Shala's lawyer. I've arranged to meet with the Xhiha brothers in his office tomorrow. I think they know more about Arben than they're letting on. If I push on the ownership issue, maybe I'll get confirmation one way or the other. If it's okay with you, I'll swing by your office in the morning and get a photocopy of Arben's ownership document. There isn't any confidentiality issue, is there?'

'If we were in the States I'd be sued. In Kosovo? Who cares? What time's your meeting?'

'Around eleven.'

'Drop by at ten thirty. Would you like me to come with you? I have background that you don't. I might come up with a question or two you might not think to ask.'

The offer took Jeff by surprise. 'I can't say no to that. Thank you. That's very generous.'

'Arben Shala is still a client. My organisation has an ongoing interest in him. Besides, someone with USAID connections might make them nervous. The body language could prove very interesting.'

Jeff nodded. 'Good idea, but I'll leave that for you to interpret. I don't do body language.'

'Really? You're not a man who notices bodies?' An involuntary exhalation of breath and Jeff found himself wiping froth from his nose. Morgan's face looked like she may have been suppressing a desire to laugh. She cleared her throat.

'Anyway, I must say Mr Shala's lucky to have found such an honest man.'

'Oh yes?'

She shrugged. 'Think about it, Jeff. If all you wanted was a vineyard, it would be quicker and easier to slip a few officials the required bribe, pay off the Xhiha brothers, and it could be yours. All legally registered. If Mr Shala was wealthy enough to challenge you, you might have a problem. But I get the impression he isn't. You probably know that.' A pause, then a steady look. 'So, my question is this. Why bother going to all this trouble if Mr Shala is just an acquaintance?'

How to answer that? Jeff took another sip of his beer while he thought. Barry saved the moment for him.

'Hey, you guys. Grab the drinks. There's a table come available in the corner.'

Jeff took the drink out of Morgan's hand and nodded that she should follow Barry. This gave him a view of her from quite a new vantage point. Thick red hair bounced with each step. Skirt just below the knee displayed shapely calves. With that kind of distraction in front of his eyes, moving through the crowd successfully proved a task Jeff was not quite up to. By the time he reached the table, the glasses were as wet on the outside as they were on the inside and beverage was dripping from his hands. He signalled for fresh drinks.

For the next ten minutes the foursome laughed at Barry's stories about a typical working day with the UN. One of the South African policemen from the night before, Hansie, joined the table. A heated argument began between Hansie, Barry and Bethany on the comparative sporting prowess of South Africa, Australia and New Zealand.

Jeff took the opportunity to talk again to Morgan. 'What brought you to Kosovo?'

'A friend established the NGO here that employs me. He knew I was good with languages, and offered me the job managing it. I needed to get away so I accepted. I'm glad I did. No day in Kosovo is ever dull.'

Jeff lifted his handle of beer. A stray elbow from the crowd nudged his arm. Beer sloshed onto the table.

'Bloody hell,' he said and looked up. The people around the table blocked any chance of attracting the attention of a waiter. Morgan opened her purse and pressed a tissue into his hand. The press lingered for just long enough that Jeff shot her a glance. He was treated to a smile.

'Thank you.' He returned the smile. Was his libido misreading things here? His eyes dropped to the task of wiping the bottom of his glass. Then the table. 'Um . . . So anyway. I'm guessing your work has an element of danger. Am I right?'

Morgan scanned the crowd for a second. Then she centred back on Jeff. 'There's always an element of danger in confrontation, I suppose. Maybe more so in Kosovo than most places. It's something I've learned to ride with. But I try to keep a low profile. Sometimes I have to kick butt to get things done, but most of the time I'm bashing my head against a brick wall. As you saw in my office.'

Jeff was thinking that maybe Morgan got more wins that she was letting on. She struck him as a woman who would never take no for an answer.

'What about family?'

'There isn't one.'

Morgan's voice sounded a bit sharper than he would have expected.

'Sorry, just making conversation. No offence?'

Her expression softened. 'None taken. This isn't the sort of job that leaves a lot of time for bending over a crib looking down at a third child.'

Jeff blinked. 'You have three children?'

A laugh. 'No. No children. No husband. At least, not any more. I was married. Then I came home one day and found my husband in bed with someone else.'

'Let me guess. Your best friend?'

'I wish. No, my brother.' Morgan's mouth widened in the pretence of a smile. 'It was a shock. Not about my husband. I'd started suspecting there was something amiss when he stopped sleeping with me two months after we were married. But to find him with my own brother? Geez. Now that was a mind-bender.'

'Did he work in government as well? Your husband?'

This earned Jeff a laugh. 'No. He was some sort of marketing guru in New York when I met him. Now he's a bartender.' She

sipped at her wine. 'I grew up in Los Angeles. You've heard of LA?'
The smile told Jeff she was teasing him.

'I might have. Somewhere in California. Mickey Mouse lives
there.'

'Full citizen. My family owns a pub-cum-restaurant in the
town. Mother's Italian American. Dad's Irish American. Both of
them good Catholics. The family business was always destined to
be either a pizzeria or an Irish pub. My dad's ancestors won out,
although we did end up making great pizzas in the restaurant. I
worked in the kitchen with my mother. My younger brother helped
Dad in the bar. My two older brothers said there wasn't enough
work for all of us in the pub and went off and opened their own
pizza parlours. One in Chicago, the other in Dallas. But I think that
was just an excuse. They wanted to do their own thing and get as far
away from my mother as they could. Italian women find it hard to
let go of their sons and tend to make the wives' lives miserable. It's a
stereotype, I know. But believe me, in our case it's all true.'

Jeff chuckled. 'My mother's parents came from Yugoslavia.
From the stories they told me of the old days, I think it was the
same for them. Luckily for me, when they came to New Zealand
they left the old ways behind.' An image of his grandmother pleading for him to resurrect the family vineyard suddenly popped into
his head. 'Most anyway.'

'I met my husband in New York on vacation. Whirlwind
romance and all that. I guess I married him hoping I could get away
from the pub like my brothers. But my mother wanted me close to
home, and my husband didn't put up much of a fight. So we left
New York and came to live in LA. He couldn't find a marketing job
so Dad put him to work helping out in the bar. Even paid for him
to go through bartending school. Right from the start, he and my
brother got on well. I was so proud of my new husband. He was
putting in such long hours and stayed on late to clean up when we

closed. My mother kept badgering me about babies. But he was always too tired by the time he got home at night. What could I say? He was working his arse off for the family. Stupid me. I felt guilty about it.'

'You tell a good story.'

'If only it weren't true.'

Jeff was enjoying Morgan's company. She had a ready laugh and he liked the way she touched his arm when making a point.

'If it sounds like I'm bitter and twisted, I am. Sure, I would love to have had kids and a house in the suburbs. And maybe a dog.' Morgan shrugged. 'But here I am in a bar in Kosovo, pouring my heart out to a guy I barely know.'

Barry and Bethany were now standing. The argument about sports supremacy had widened. Many voices were yelling to be heard. Jeff leaned closer to Morgan. 'What about your family. How did they react when they found out?'

'They never did. My parents idolise my baby brother. How could I tell them he was screwing my husband? It would break their hearts. So I left. Now I'm the bitch who ran off on her husband. But at least the family's happy.'

'And your husband?'

'He's still there, complaining how much it hurts that I abandoned him. My brother moved into our house. Tells my parents they're just sharing. My mother is convinced my brother's charity towards my ex-husband is almost saintly. My father would have him ordained if he wasn't such a good barman. And I get Christmas cards every year warning me I'm going to burn in hell. So that's my story. How about you?'

Jeff shrugged. 'Divorced.'

A pause. Morgan's eyebrows arched. 'That's it? Just . . . divorced?'

Barry's face materialised beside them with a broad wink.

'Bethany and I are going home. For . . . ah, dinner. Okay?'

Barry disappeared. Jeff turned back to Morgan. 'Lucky man. I've had bugger-all nourishment of any kind today. I hate eating alone.'

'Is that an invitation to dinner?'

'Could be. I take it there's better stuff out there than I'm getting at the Grand Hotel.'

'What do you like eating?'

'I'll eat anything.'

A slow smile came to Morgan's lips.

'I might know just the place.'

17.

Jeff had enjoyed the best meal of his trip so far with Morgan, though if he was honest that hadn't been down to the food. When he was back in his hotel room he found it hard not to think of her.

In the morning they met again at Toni Mema's office.

'Mr Bradley. Jeff. Welcome to my office.'

Tomi Mema was all smiles. This time the Armani suit was a grey pinstripe. However, Mema's expensive taste in clothes did not seem to extend to rental property. A twenty-foot shipping container dumped onto a vacant lot had been converted into his office.

Mema may have read his thoughts. 'There is a scarcity of commercial space in Prishtina. The international organisations have taken most of what was available and anything left is too expensive. The property owners want Kosovons to pay the same rates as internationals. Ridiculous. This place has worked quite well for me. It is convenient. I am across the road from the detention centre where most of my clients are and within walking distance of all the courts.'

The office furnishings bordered on austere: a desk for Mema, a smaller table for his secretary, an assortment of plastic chairs and a three-drawer filing cabinet. In the corner an ancient electric heater did little to warm the place. A plastic container on top of the filing cabinet might have once contained a plant but now only dozens of cigarette stubs half-buried in the dirt.

'Mr Mema. I'd like to introduce Morgan Delaney. Ms Delaney is with the Land Registry Office.'

'Ms Delaney, welcome. Are you a friend of Mr Bradley's or are you here in an official capacity?'

'As an advisor, Mr Mema.'

'Very well. Please, take a seat. I will order us some coffees.'

Mema sent his secretary to the cafe next door then sat behind his desk. Hands shuffled papers for no obvious purpose.

'I am sure Ms Delaney is an expert in America, Jeff. But when it comes to Kosovon law, you will need to use a Kosovon lawyer. I offer you my services. No offence to you, Ms Delaney.'

Mema flashed Morgan what he may have considered to be a winning smile.

Morgan's smile in response looked to Jeff to be just as winning. And just as unconvincing. Was there a game going on here?

'Oh, none taken. All Kosovo knows your reputation, Mr Mema.'

Mema's sharp glance into Morgan's face would have revealed to him nothing more than what Jeff saw as practised neutrality. It appeared that tacit ground rules were being established between the two. Jeff suppressed a chuckle and looked back at Mema.

'Mr Mema. Arben Shala made contact with Ms Delaney and asked for her to help get back his property. She went to the vineyard with Arben. I've asked her here to discuss the legitimacy of both sets of ownership documents. You'll understand that if I go ahead and purchase the vineyard, I'll want to be certain I'm buying from the rightful owners.'

Mema managed to drag his none-too-subtle scrutiny away from Morgan and back to Jeff.

'I see. And Ms Delaney, do you have an opinion as to who the rightful owners might be?'

The charm was back, but it looked to Jeff as if it might well be disguising a range of sentiments that did not include goodwill towards Morgan.

She nodded. 'I've verified Mr Shala's documents, Mr Mema. They're legitimate. The Xhiha brothers' documents are also in order. However, I can find no paper trail showing a legal change of ownership from Mr Shala's father to the Xhihas' uncle.'

Mema leaned back in his seat. 'That is easily explained. The Serbs destroyed all documents held by the Gjakova Regional Council during the war. Unfortunately this happened in a number of districts.'

'I'm aware of that, Mr Mema. I'm also aware that the Shala family lived on the property until the start of the war. I find it hard to believe that the land legally changed hands without Arben's father ever having informed his family.'

'Maybe his father needed the money to join his son in New Zealand, and would have told him after he arrived.'

'That's a possibility, sure. But there are very good grounds for doubting its probability.' Morgan leaned forward. Green eyes held Mema's. 'Mr Shala informed me that when he and his family fled Kosovo, he begged his parents to come with him. His father insisted on staying to protect the property. Now. Does that sound like the action of a man who had any intention of selling?'

Mema again shifted in his chair. 'Maybe so. Maybe not. However, I also had this conversation with Mr Shala. He admitted that the vineyard had never been signed over from his father to him. Under normal circumstances, if Arben had been in Kosovo at the time of his father's death – as would be expected of any dutiful son – the property would automatically have passed to him. However,'

Mema shrugged, 'Arben was in New Zealand. Maybe that changed things.'

'Mr Shala's father didn't simply die, Mr Mema.' Morgan's voice had taken on a chilly tone. 'The Serbs murdered him. Arben Shala's decision to leave the country almost certainly saved his life. He's lost his parents, most of his family, and many friends. Does it not seem unfair to you that he might now also lose the family property?'

'Most definitely unfair, I must agree.' Mema's palms spread on the desk as he leaned across it. 'But the courts are not interested in what is fair, only in what is legal. Unfortunately Mr Shala was not in Kosovo and has not been home for some time. The Xhiha brothers have now lived on the property a number of years.'

Jeff glanced at Morgan. Her eyes held Mema's. Jeff admired the way her silence appeared to put pressure on the lawyer. Mema's tongue licked at the corner of his mouth.

'Er . . . These Xhiha brothers. They have a legitimate legal document that says they own the land. And under these circumstances, as I told Mr Shala, I believe the court would rule that his father did indeed sell to the Xhiha brothers' uncle, just as they have claimed. The court will have good reason to believe that Mr Shala, who ran away and abandoned Kosovo for a better life in New Zealand, heard of the destruction of documents in Gjakova and returned to try and cheat the Xhihas out of a property that was rightfully theirs.'

Morgan's gaze on Mema never flinched. But Jeff noticed a slight increase in the colour of her cheeks.

'Look, Ms Delaney. As a lawyer I must deal with the facts, as must the courts. And as you've said yourself, the Xhiha documents are in order.'

At that second the secretary came in with a tray holding three espressos. 'Ah, good. Look. Our coffees have arrived.'

The lawyer took the tray from his secretary and put the cups on the table. Jeff watched him. Mema may have felt he was winning the exchange with Morgan, but for Jeff the discussion had only served to convince him that someone was indeed intent on stealing Arben's land. And it wasn't the Xhihas.

Morgan relaxed her concentration on Mema and reached for a coffee. 'You'll have to admit that there remains a lot of conjecture in what you say. Now, if we could speak with Mr Shala, he might be able to provide us with additional information. Something that could shed light on how all this has come about.' She turned eyes on Jeff. 'You agree with that, don't you, Mr Bradley?'

'Mr Mema, I don't suppose you would have any idea where Arben Shala might be, do you?' Jeff asked.

Tomi Mema's palms spread to the heavens. 'None whatsoever, I'm afraid. Perhaps he is already returning to New Zealand.' Mema's gaze suddenly focused somewhere over Jeff's shoulder. 'Ah. Come in, gentlemen.'

When Jeff turned he saw that the Xhiha brothers were already standing inside the office door. Ahmed whispered something to his brother. Skender gave Jeff a quick glance and nodded. The way the brothers' eyes flicked about made Jeff think how devious and guilty they looked. Guilty exactly of what, Jeff intended to determine. He needed to have another talk with the Xhiha brothers. However, the talk he planned to have could not take place in Mema's office.

18.

When the door opened, Avni Leka resisted the urge to look up. The Municipal Court's chief prosecutor knew it was Osman Gashi. But the pile of documents before him had been demanding his urgent attention for two days. Gashi could wait. Leka heard the leather chair in front of his desk creak as the fat man eased himself into it. Leka continued scanning his paperwork and initialling where needed. When he signed off the last page, his fingers riffled through the pile once again. Satisfied that all was in order, he lifted them in both hands and dumped them into his out tray.

'Okay, Gashi. I have an urgent meeting in ten minutes. What is it?'

Gashi smiled, teeth too white in his dark face. In Leka's view, Gashi wore good-quality clothes badly. He never quite managed to achieve the look of a successful businessman. No matter how hard he tried, he still looked every bit the slovenly pimp Leka knew him to be. His gut, the result of too much food and too many cognacs, threatened to burst the buttons off his waistcoat. The top of his shirt remained unbuttoned around his oversized neck.

Leka had long been aware that Gashi brought in girls from Moldova and Bulgaria to work as high-priced hookers for the thousands of UN and NATO personnel. Gashi fed the craving for illicit sex like a stoker shovelling coal into a furnace. He had brothels and strip clubs hidden in the suburbs of most Kosovon cities. To protect his illegal activities and escape the scrutiny of the law, Gashi paid out thousands of euros in bribes every month.

To those who did not know him the way Leka did, Gashi came across as a jovial bon vivant – if maybe a little slow witted. However, behind the affability and flab lurked the most dangerous man in Kosovo. Leka knew that Gashi was an unpredictable psychopath who was devoid of conscience. A money lord who protected his hard-won domain with ruthless efficiency, as many a policeman and politician had found to their cost.

'There's a problem?' Leka asked.

It was a rhetorical question. Leka knew very well that Gashi would not have come otherwise.

'Tomi Mema has had visitors. That man from New Zealand looking for Arben Shala and the American woman from the land office.'

'Do we have cause to be concerned?'

'No, I don't think so. Tomi said that once he explained how the court would certainly find the Xhiha documents legitimate, they did not argue and left. They have no idea where Shala is or what has happened to him. Tomi thinks that as long as they don't make contact with Shala, there will be no problems.'

Leka stood. Leaning his shoulder against the wall he gazed out of the window. His office was directly above the court entrance. Beyond the steps, he spied two gypsies pushing a cart down the street to collect discarded aluminium cans. He knew Gashi hated gypsies. Obsessed with his own dark complexion, Gashi feared that somewhere in his past lay Romany ancestry. The big man's view was that gypsies had crawled from the same gene pool as the sewer rat. Neither Leka nor anybody who knew Gashi well would ever dare joke about his suspected gypsy heritage. Gashi had been known to strangle men with his own hands for such disrespect. It was because of these savage tendencies that Leka had orchestrated the killer's release from prison. Kosovons had come to regard Osman Gashi as the incarnation of evil, and to a person they feared him. The situation couldn't have suited Avni Leka any better.

But from time to time he found it necessary to remind Gashi that he could have his parole revoked at a moment's notice. Handling a reptile as poisonous as Gashi had its risks, as Leka was aware, and he needed that kind of constraining influence over him.

'The Shala business worries me, Osman,' Leka said, returning to his seat. 'I've kept him in prison as you asked. But can you be certain he won't cause us trouble?'

Gashi shook his head and mopped his brow with a large yellow handkerchief. It intrigued Leka how Gashi managed to perspire continuously regardless of the weather.

'If the man's become a problem, then maybe it's better he never leaves,' Leka suggested.

'But he hasn't signed over the property yet . . .' Gashi caught the sudden frown on Leka's face. 'It's not important. I'll have it taken care of.'

'Let me know when it is done. And no mistakes this time.'

'There's something else.'

'Yes?'

The sharpness in Leka's tone indicated his impatience.

Gashi didn't appear to notice. 'The man from New Zealand is interested in buying the vineyard. He said that is why he came to Kosovo.'

'Tomi told you this?'

Gashi nodded.

Leka lifted a pen and tapped the paper pile for a second. 'This I don't like. First he comes to Kosovo from New Zealand looking for

Shala. Now he's interested in buying the Shala vineyard. I think it best you don't let him anywhere near it.'

Gashi grimaced. 'Too late for that.'

Leka's eyes narrowed.

'Oh? How's that?'

'Tomi arranged it. He thought he was doing the right thing.'

A frown of anger now turned on Gashi.

'It's not up to Tomi to make such decisions. Get a grip, Osman. Control your people.' A barely concealed smirk on Gashi's face angered Leka even more. 'Now get this straight, Osman. Make sure that man from New Zealand doesn't get anywhere near Shala. You understand?'

Gashi nodded.

Leka picked up another pile of documents and began flipping through them. The message didn't escape Gashi. He pulled himself out of the protesting chair and ambled from the office like a bear in search of a cave to hibernate in. Leka glared at the door left open in his wake. He knew it was a deliberate gesture. No matter what, Gashi would always let him know he was still his own man.

19.

L ee Caldwell grinned at the tall Greek.
'I'm honoured the head of airport security can find time to
take me by the hand through Customs and Passport Control.
Many thanks.'

'No problem, sir. Maybe twenty million tourists fly into Greece
every year. We can't have you being held up under the processing
overload.'

This level of cooperation impressed Caldwell. No doubt his
Greek counterpart Dimitris Tsakiris had organised it. He decided
he owed him one. The US embassy car sent to meet him was waiting in a no-parking zone. A uniformed airport official stood next to
it, shooing away parking wardens. Noticing his boss arrive with the
American, he pulled open the rear door. Caldwell tipped a salute
to his escort through customs and climbed into the back seat. He
directed a perfunctory smile at the two staffers in the front as the
door closed and then he retreated to his own thoughts.

It was a forty-minute drive from the airport to the ports.
Caldwell pulled out his mobile phone and checked for messages.
The Admiral had sent a text: *I wish you a happy birthday*. He chuckled at the code for *I hope all is well*. Like all professionals he didn't
particularly like such cryptic spy-speak; the non sequiturs and double entendres more often than not seemed quite pointless. But the

Admiral had a military mind, as well as being the man who paid the bills. So Caldwell played by his rules.

He could picture his boss well right then. The Admiral expected regular updates. So after no contact for more than a week, the square jaw would be jutting out like a bulldog's. And he'd be pacing, steely grey eyes constantly snapping towards the phone. Caldwell allowed himself a lopsided smile. His text in reply said: *I had chocolate cake*, which meant *Everything is okay*. The phone slipped back into his jacket.

As always his mission brief had lacked detail: 'Find whoever is setting off bombs in Europe and make them stop.' Caldwell's business card claimed he worked as a Technical and Management Advisor for Devon Securities. What it didn't show was that Devon Securities was a very minor subsidiary branch of Incubus, the world's second largest private-security company. The office headquarters, buried deep in the bowels of a Washington building, demanded the highest of security clearances for entry. Caldwell knew that not even the President of the United States was exempt.

The official role of Incubus was to ensure American citizens outside the United States came to no harm. Especially high-level government personnel. Incubus reported directly to the State Department. Devon Securities' role was to clean up. Seek out those who carried out the attacks on Americans with extreme prejudice. Take out the garbage, change the sheets, scrub the blood off the floors. Caldwell thought of himself as a janitor to the spook world: unseen, unappreciated, but very necessary.

The Admiral's department worked with a mix of government and private funding. Whenever an unpalatable circumstance arose that might embarrass the government, the money trail stopped at private funding bases. The simplicity of this had always appealed to Caldwell. He recruited from the ranks of disgruntled CIA operatives who relished the opportunity to continue doing the same kind of work without the irksome legal restrictions inhibiting government employees. The Admiral protected him from crusading politicians and, within reason, Caldwell had a free hand and access to any government agency he needed. Technically, the modus operandi was simple. It wasn't Caldwell's job to hunt down those masterminding the bombings – just get the guys who lit the fuses: the triggermen. There were better-funded and better-equipped agencies to deal with the top dogs. It was Caldwell's call to either terminate the bombers or call for a pick up.

Recently, however, a variation had arisen.

The US Ambassador to Belgium, along with his wife and two young sons, had died in a Brussels department-store bombing. The Admiral had taken the death of Jim Scott very personally. He and the Ambassador had served in the Navy together.

'His boys called me Uncle, for Christ's sake,' he had fumed. 'Find the bastards who did this. Then kill the sons of bitches. Screw intelligence interrogations. Forget about any goddamned fucking trials.'

Caldwell had seen close-up the misery that such killers could inflict. He had no qualms about sending any one of them to join their victims. But he was no arbitrary executioner, and certainly no murderer. He would allow perpetrators of such atrocities as befell the Ambassador to determine their own future. If they surrendered, he would hand them over. If not? Well, the consequences would have been no secret to them.

Idle eyes watched the traffic on the road. Caldwell's thoughts now focused on the way the Brussels bombers had slipped through his grasp and resurfaced in Slovenia. With horrendous results. He knew it was the same men. Interpol forensics had positively identified residue from the explosives in Brussels and Ljubljana as the same. It had been matched to a consignment passed into the UN arms-for-money programme in Kosovo by a former Kosovon

Liberation Army operative. It was as clear to Caldwell as anyone that not all the explosives under the deal had been turned in. Someone was still using them to make bombs.

It had lifted Caldwell's spirits that, after months of sleuth work by his colleagues, they'd managed to identify a lead. A Kosovon national had been detained at the Albanian–Greek border trying to smuggle a million euros into Greece. Caldwell had little doubt Dimitris and his people used some creative interrogation techniques on the hapless courier. The man claimed to be unable to provide information of any value. He said he had no idea the suitcase held such a large amount of money. And he did not know the intended recipient.

What did appear beyond dispute was that the money he carried was not drug money. This man's particular gang did not deal drugs – it was too risky in Kosovo with so many UN police and NATO checkpoints. But a million euros was a considerable sum to be coming out of Kosovo. It piqued Caldwell's interest even though he knew it was a huge leap to connect that money to explosives passed to the UN. But like most experienced law enforcement officers, Caldwell didn't believe in coincidences. The lead might be tenuous. But it was something. And it was all he had.

❧

At the gates of the Port of Piraeus, Caldwell ordered the driver to enter and pull into one of the bus parking spaces. Dimitris would be in one of the cafes a few hundred metres away on the wharf. He told the two staffers to wait with the car then climbed out.

Caldwell walked along the jetty's edge. In the calm waters beneath his feet he spotted the flash of small schools of fish near the surface. They would disappear, only to reappear a few metres further along. The salt air reminded him of childhood holidays in Santa Barbara. He made a mental note to phone his sister.

Dimitris Tsakiris waved when he saw Caldwell approach. The grin that lit up the Greek's face was genuine. The men had long since struck up a friendship outside their respective callings. Dimitris called to the waiter for more drinks.

'My friend. How has your life been since we last met? What? A year ago?'

'Give or take a month.' Caldwell's gaze dropped to Dimitris's belt line. 'Pleasant anyway. But nowhere near as pleasant as yours appears to have been, Dimitris.'

Dimitris laughed and patted his paunch. 'You're right, too much of the good life and not nearly enough running after criminals to keep me fit. My wife, she likes to cook. And I like to eat. A good marriage, but it will kill me in the end.'

Caldwell chuckled. 'I'm sure it won't.' A waiter placed two cold beers on the table. 'Now, what've you got for me?'

'My man masquerading as the courier is over there in the corner.' Dimitris indicated with a surreptitious flick of the eyes. 'He is wearing a yellow baseball cap and a light brown jacket. We are following the instructions left by the people he is to rendezvous with. First was to go to a post box in Athens. The courier had brought the key to open it with him from Prishtina. Inside the postbox were new instructions: to catch today's ferry to the island of Syros. That boat behind you. The big red one?'

Caldwell turned to see where Dimitris was indicating.

'A tracking device is in the suitcase. I have men everywhere. It won't be lost. The ship leaves at five thirty. The cruise to Syros will take four hours. So, you and I have time to kill.' Dimitris gulped down half his beer and smacked his lips. Caldwell hadn't touched his. 'This is good beer. Drink, my friend.'

Caldwell sighed inwardly. Dimitris was a good man but a lousy spy.

They had first met in France when Caldwell had been little more than a rookie in his first job for the Admiral. Caldwell and his team had netted two Greek citizens in a raid on a villa in suburban Paris. Fingerprint checks revealed the pair topped Greece's most-wanted list. Caldwell had suggested to the Admiral that the CIA collect them, but the Admiral had other ideas. He believed in building bridges. He told Caldwell it was a matter of banking favours: 'Payback time will come. Mark my words.'

So instead, the Greek Intelligence Service had been prevailed upon to take the pair into custody. And the Greeks never forgot how the Admiral had made sure they received credit for the capture.

An elated Dimitris and his men had flown to Paris. As a thank-you from the grateful Greeks, Caldwell had spent the evening drinking ouzo at the Athenais in the rue de la Victoire. The next day, Dimitris left with his prisoners and Caldwell was left with a hangover. He never again tried to match the Greek drink for drink.

Now payback time had arrived. The Greeks were coming through just as the Admiral had predicted. Caldwell glanced at his watch. Close to four thirty.

'I have a car waiting. I need to send it on its way. I'll be back in a few minutes.'

He left his beer untouched and walked back to the car. The two staffers were stretching their legs.

'Which one of you is in charge?' A quick exchange of glances between the two. He turned to the woman. 'Marion, right?'

'Yes, sir.'

'You'll do for the moment. I want you to go back to the embassy and arrange for a chopper to be waiting at Syros airport from nine tonight.'

'Yes, sir.'

A check of Caldwell's watch. An hour until the ferry left. Conscious that now was not the time to get into a drinking contest with Dimitris, he decided to take his time walking back to the cafe.

∽

A fly crawled across the table towards a crumb that had fallen from his croissant. Zahar swatted it with his plastic ticket holder then flicked the twitching insect onto the floor. A glance at his watch told him boarding would start soon. Not before time. He disliked surveillance, and the man in the periphery of his vision wearing the yellow baseball cap hadn't moved for the last hour. That made his job much easier but he was tired of sitting in the one spot and the coffee was awful. He stirred his espresso for lack of anything else to do. He had already decided it was undrinkable.

Praise to Allah for his brother, Halam, being forever cautious. Creating a paper trail for the courier to follow, and monitoring the postbox had been smart moves. Halam had considered the possibility of a tail on the courier and his intuition had paid off. Now, Zahar's own knack for sniffing out undercover operatives had borne fruit. The pudgy Greek was too sloppy. Spotting the pursuers had been absurdly easy. And now a fourth had joined their team. It did not matter. They would be no match for him and his brother.

Zahar flipped open his mobile phone. He needed to update Halam already on Syros. By the end of the day the suitcase would be in their hands and they would be on their way to a new life in Iran. He needed to find a way to make Halam listen and accept that he did not want the life Halam chose for himself.

∽

The lights of the ferry alerted those waiting on shore that the red boat had entered the mouth of the harbour. Halam Akbar sat in one of the many cafes lining the promenade, tapping a straw against the side of an aluminium drink can. Soon the cruise ship would slow and reverse into its docking position. He had ten, maybe fifteen minutes. Behind iron railings drivers sat in line in their vehicles with the engines turned off. When the ferry unloaded, they would drive aboard for the return trip to Athens. The fence that surrounded the berthing area also demarcated the car park. Security guards at the gates controlled the flow of vehicles, but pedestrian access remained unrestricted. Halam had twice walked through the gates – the first time without the bag, the second time with it. All was ready.

In summer Syros was a popular destination but Halam was thankful that the council of Ermouplis, the capital of the island, managed to maintain a festive atmosphere even though it was out of season. Despite the chill in the air, most of the tables outside the many cafes were full. With dusk now gone, the floodlit blue dome of Saint Nicolas on the hill dominated mansions and whitewashed houses gleaming in the moonlight. The town's waterfront drive buzzed with activity. Tourists strolled along the full length of the promenade from the Hermes Hotel to the airport turnoff. Locals sat on benches drinking coffees and ouzo.

Halam was just another nondescript tourist.

The distinctive Greek aromas of hot seafood, olive oil and herbs and spices reminded Halam he had not eaten all day. Those seated about him had spent the last few hours gorging themselves. Except for bottled water and two espressos, he had ordered nothing. At this stage of an operation a stomach full of food was a handicap, especially if something went wrong and he needed to run.

∽

The four-hour cruise to Syros convinced Lee Caldwell that Dimitris had lost his edge. He needed to retire. His men looked sharp enough, but their boss's carefree attitude was bound to influence their effectiveness. Dimitris's preoccupation with wine, food and relaxation was understandable. After all, this was Greece. But Caldwell knew well the type of men they were dealing with. He worried that Dimitris did not fully appreciate the danger.

He saw no sign of anyone tailing the Greek agent masquerading as the courier, but that meant nothing. The merry-go-round of instructions must have had a reason. It seemed pretty obvious to Lee that whoever was about to receive the million euros would ensure he was not also walking into a trap.

Dimitris hadn't entirely disagreed with Caldwell's analysis, but he was certain any tailing would occur on the island and not the boat.

'You are too paranoid, my friend. Rest assured: if we had a tail we would know. That's our job, isn't it?'

He roared with laughter and patted Caldwell on the shoulder. Caldwell waggled his head at Dimitris and kept scrutinising the passengers.

The ship lurched as it executed a one-eighty-degree turn. After a pause, its huge engines growled into reverse. Propellers spinning like giant eggbeaters churned the surrounding surface into froth. Slowly the vessel began moving sternwards. Friends and families on the dock jostled as they sought to catch glimpses of loved ones amongst the dozens of passengers leaning over the railings. Backpackers milled about near the top of the ramp posing for last-minute photos.

Caldwell swayed as a slight shudder ran through the deck signalling that the ferry had docked into its final position.

Passengers began to crowd the stern. Caldwell found himself pushed backwards. Already he could see it was going to be impossible to maintain a cover on the decoy courier. 'This is hopeless, Dimitris.'

Although Caldwell yelled, the din from the excited crowd made verbal communication next to impossible.

'Do not worry, my friend. I have two men guarding the case. They've been instructed to keep to the left-hand railing. If an approach is made, we will be ready for it.'

~

Halam watched as the boarding ramp settled onto the dock. Within minutes the passengers would begin disembarking. In his ear, on an open line, Halam could hear his brother's steady breathing. Halam's thumb was already caressing the detonator trigger in his pocket.

'Count to ten, then do it,' Zahar said, then rang off.

Halam counted down . . . five – four – three – two . . .

~

The boom from the explosion reverberated across the dock area just as Caldwell reached the top of the ramp. The sight that greeted him resembled nothing less than a volcanic eruption. Flames and sparks and shredded metal spewed skywards. A car flung into the air hurtled back onto the tops of waiting cars in a sickening crunch of metal and shattering of glass. Caldwell's ears rang. Inside the enclosed space of the ship the sound of the blast was deafening.

Passengers around Caldwell froze en masse. Eyes peered back and forth as brains struggled to cope with the phenomenon. No one moved.

'It's a bomb.'

The shout came from someone near the bottom of the ramp.

Caldwell watched as wide-eyed fear descended onto the faces of those closest to him.

'Jesus.' He knew exactly what was about to happen. 'Dimitris.' He turned, searching the crowd. The big Greek was nowhere in sight. 'Dimitris.'

Passengers behind him started to surge forward like a cresting wave that threatened to wash him overboard. Caldwell found he had little choice. He strong-armed his way towards the outer side of the deck and grabbed hold of the railing. Panicking feet stampeded down the ramp. Caldwell watched in horror as people in front stumbled and fell. He knew some would be crushed to death as that human tsunami cascaded over them.

❧

Zahar moved quickly in the chaos. He closed in on the courier, pressed the muzzle of his gun against the man's head and pulled the trigger. In the aftermath of the bomb, the silencer Zahar had fitted was probably redundant. He snatched the case from the dead man's grasp and disappeared into the crowd.

❧

Like everyone else, the eyes of Dimitris's second-in-command had switched in the direction of the explosion. When he looked back, the decoy courier was nowhere to be seen. His first thought was that the momentum of the crowd had forced the man in the baseball cap further down the ramp. Then, through a gap in the rushing legs, he saw a motionless shape in a brown jacket slumped against the superstructure. His gut lurched. Obscenities poured from him as he shoved passengers out of his path. When he reached his fallen comrade, he knew he needn't check for a pulse. The hole in the side of the man's head told him everything.

⁊

Caldwell watched Dimitris standing over the body, shaking his head. Red-faced, Dimitris turned and delivered a resounding slap to the face of his second-in-command.

'Fools.' He turned to Caldwell and pulled a GPS tracker out of his pocket. 'They can't have got far. We still have this. I will seal off the area. We will find the bastards.'

Caldwell looked over Dimitris's shoulder at the local map on the display on the GPS tracker. The Greek turned a half-circle as he followed a flashing red dot.

'We've got them.' But his shoulders suddenly drooped. 'Oh no. It can't be.'

'Why? What's wrong?'

'The signal's moving towards the mouth of the harbour. Not along the streets. They must have a motor launch. I will try to contact the navy.'

He dragged out a mobile and began punching digits into it.

With all kinds of unhappy sentiments now crowding his breast, Caldwell looked out over the moonlit bay. In despair, he observed the chaos of dinghies powered by small outboards that were motoring across each other's wakes as would-be rescuers sought to haul victims to safety.

'Don't waste your time, Dimitris. They've gone.'

'But we can track them.'

'If they have any sense, the case with the device will be in the water within the next few minutes.'

Head shaking, Dimitris continued to watch the GPS screen glowing in his hand.

Caldwell looked out towards the dock gates. Excited and frightened tourists mingled with locals to rubberneck at the unfolding fiasco. Amongst them village women dressed in black had already begun their traditional wailing. Sirens and flashing lights heralded the arrival of the island's meagre ambulance and police contingent. Caldwell knew straight away that the local services would never cope. He suspected emergency helicopters would soon be on their way from the mainland.

He picked his way down the ramp. Dimitris followed. Injured and dying people lay everywhere. Moans and occasional screams filled the air. Pleading eyes looked his way. Beseeching arms extended towards him. He had to shut them out. There was work to do. He checked his watch. His helicopter would be waiting. He leaned into Dimitris.

'We need to have a serious talk with that courier from Kosovo. You agree?'

'I will take pleasure in that, my friend. Tonight I lost a good man. We will get the information we need.'

❧

In the cabin, the wide eyes of Halam and Zahar stared at the opened suitcase.

'Newspapers.' Zahar's voice came forced and hoarse. 'Nothing but newspapers. The sons of dogs tricked us.'

Hands shaking and knuckles gleaming white, he clutched on to the beam above the door and scanned the lights of fishing boats and distant taverns twinkling astern. The Greek boatman maintained speed, running-lights off. He had promised the brothers he had navigated these waters with his father from before he was out of nappies. For the money they had paid him he would get them safely to the mainland. After he rounded the southern tip of Syros he cruised into the calmer waters of the fishing anchorage. Zahar continued to look down on the useless pile of paper. The breath rasped in his throat. When at last he could engage with his brother again, Zahar saw the face of a depleted man. Depleted in the way he himself felt depleted.

'Of course they tricked us.' A slow shake of Halam's head. 'We knew this was a possibility when you saw the tail. It means they must have captured the real courier. The man you killed must have been a cop.' An alarmed expression crossed his face. 'Throw the case into the sea, Zahar. It will have a tracking device. Go. Go.'

Zahar jumped like a man shot. Paper fluttered free as he grabbed the suitcase and leaped out to the deck. When he returned he found Halam thumping the table top with a clenched fist. He took up a position on the vinyl squab alongside him.

'What are we going to do, Halam? We need that money. How can we go to Iran with nothing?'

Halam rested elbows on knees. His head went into his hands. 'Quiet, brother. I need to think.'

Zahar sat back with a deep sigh. Halam would think of something. He always did.

After a few minutes Halam's head rose. Dark eyes fixed on his brother's face.

'We did not receive our payment. Kosovo still owes us money. Make us some tea, Zahar, and we will discuss how to collect what we are due.'

20.

Agim Morina complied without question when the message came from Osman Gashi to meet him at the usual place in an hour. Morina – six-foot tall, blond-haired and solidly built – easily passed for Scandinavian, a physical attribute that often worked in his favour. It allowed him to move discreetly about the city. Fellow Kosovons who bothered to look his way assumed he was UN personnel, just as UN staff did. This was all to the good when it came to clandestine meetings which a year earlier he would never have even contemplated.

As a captain in the newly formed Kosovon police force, he had a bright future. Paid a better than average income, life for Morina should have been comfortable. But apartment rents driven up by an influx of better-paid internationals, and a sickly son needing expensive medications, had sent his life into a tailspin.

Then came the morning everything changed.

He was on a break and sitting in the cafe opposite the Central Police Station, mulling into his cup over his reduced prospects. A liberal dose of cognac in the coffee had done little to ward off a fit of depression.

It had been a rainy day – or had it been sunny? He could not recall.

Uninvited, an overweight man in an ill-fitting suit sat down at his table. Morina had been flabbergasted at the arrogance.

'You are Agim Morina,' the man said. His cheerful disposition would have persuaded any onlooker that this was a meeting of friends. 'My name is Osman Gashi. Maybe you've heard of me?'

No movement of Morina's head. Two white crescents appeared above his lower lids as his eyes swivelled upwards to view the intruder.

'Yes. I know who you are.'

'I only need a few minutes to discuss a matter. It could be very important to both of us. I wouldn't have bothered you otherwise.'

Morina spooned sugar into his coffee. 'This morning I have no patience. I'll ask you to leave just the once. If you don't, I'll march you across the road and you can spend the next few days in jail. Your choice.'

To Morina's great surprise, Gashi seemed unmoved by his threat. Worse, the broadened smile gave no inclination at all that he intended doing as Morina ordered. Morina's head squared up. Indignation rose as the unflinching gaze of this disrespectful low-life met that of a Kosovon police captain. The sentiment became even more acute as Gashi continued talking as if he'd not even heard Morina.

'The son of a friend is in your station arrested on a charge of car theft. But he wasn't driving the car. He was merely an innocent passenger.'

Morina felt his jaw tighten. So that was what this was all about. The man needed a favour. As a senior police officer he was not altogether unfamiliar with this kind of approach. Usually it came with a bag of money. But declining such requests had been a matter of pride for Morina. In his mind he was incorruptible. An honest man, just like the internationals. He knew others in the force routinely accepted bribes as a necessary means of supplementing their meagre incomes. However, even though he might not take bribes himself, he turned a blind eye to the activities of his colleagues. A crusader had no future in the Kosovon police force. The truth was that, incorruptible or not, he needed his job.

'A friend of the boy picked him up and took him for a joyride. He didn't know his friend had stolen the car. He's innocent. But you know how it is in Kosovo, Captain.'

'Do I, Mr Gashi?'

'I think yes, officer. Citizens are thrown into Kosovon prisons on the flimsiest of evidence and held for months without trial. They serve their sentences before they get to court, guilty or not guilty. Surely you don't agree with that?'

'It's not my place to comment on the rights or wrongs of the judicial process. I'm a police officer, nothing else.'

'Look. You and I both know it's crazy and unfair. This boy is only eighteen. He comes from a good family. A conviction will ruin his family's reputation. And the trauma of prison could scar him for life.'

Morina expelled a deep breath. 'Mr Gashi. Even if I was to agree with you, and I am not saying I do, why me? Why aren't you talking to the arresting officer or the investigating officer?'

'The paperwork has begun. The decision is no longer in the hands of the arresting officers. Only you can stop it. The documentation can't be allowed to get to the prosecutor's office.'

Morina fixed Gashi with a stare. What he said was true. Once the paper trail began, there could be no stopping a case going to trial. Of course, bribing the judge to manipulate the trial would be easy enough. And a prosecutor could always destroy evidence. But getting to trial took months. And the longer it took the more people in the loop to pay off. It was practical economics to stop things now. His brow furrowed.

'I have an idea where this conversation might be going, Mr Gashi. And I warn you. Do not take it there. I strongly recommend you leave.'

Gashi remained seated. An envelope appeared out of his pocket and found its way onto the table. It slid across to where Morina's hands sat curved around his coffee cup. Morina was dumbfounded. He looked about. No one was watching.

Gashi leaned forward.

'You have a son who needs medical treatment. Your living conditions are not what you wish. Your wife is unhappy.'

Morina's body jerked like he'd been shot. 'What? You've been spying on me? Spying on my family?'

Gashi's voice dropped. Despite himself, Morina found himself leaning forward to hear.

'In that envelope is five thousand euros. On the first of each month you will receive two thousand euros.'

Morina straightened. The veins in his forehead felt like they were about to burst. Never had he been insulted like this. And in public. He should arrest Gashi for trying to bribe a police officer. 'I'm an honest man. You disgust me. Now leave. This is your last warning.'

Morina pushed the envelope back across the table. Gashi made no move to pick it up.

'Honesty is not always the best policy in Kosovo, Captain. I don't work alone. I represent people who have the power to ensure your life becomes a lot worse than it is now. Your job is not as secure as you might think.'

There it was: the stick beyond the carrot.

Morina reassessed the man in front of him. He had misinterpreted Gashi's relaxed manner as bravado, an error in judgment. This was not mere bravado; this man radiated absolute confidence. Other approaches, mostly from worried parents or friends, had been easy to brush aside. They were people who were powerless to threaten him or his family. With Gashi it was different. He was a thug, a gangster. No doubt he knew powerful people, possibly powerful enough to oust him from his job.

Morina made a lightning reassessment. He eyed the envelope. Life would be easier, wouldn't it? His wife happier? And what of his son? Wasn't it a man's greater moral duty to protect and provide for his family? Could he really afford to turn down this money?

Taking the money, he knew, would change his life for ever.

But what life?

He reached for the envelope.

Barely a whisper. 'Give me the boy's name.'

A year and a dozen or so more jobs for Gashi later, and the brief for yet another job was approaching Morina's table.

'Gashi. There you are. Cognac?'

A waiter nodded at Morina's signal. A chair creaked in protest. Gashi planted his forearms on the table and leaned on them. 'There's a situation in the Prishtina Detention Centre. I'm sure you remember Arben Shala. Yes?'

Of course Morina knew of Arben Shala. Shala's arrest had already earned him a generous bonus. But he'd been furious when he discovered Shala was a New Zealand citizen. A foreign national could attract the interest of the international police. The only reason it hadn't was because Shala had been using his Serbian passport. The sooner Shala was gone from prison and out of the country the better.

'Don't worry. He'll be released within the next two weeks.'

'I'm afraid I can't wait that long.'

'Wait a minute. I have no powers to release him earlier.'

'Yes, I know this, Captain.'

Gashi's eyes held Morina's. It took a moment before Morina understood. Once again in this man's company he discovered an unpleasant knot forming in his stomach.

'You can't be serious. You're not asking what I think you're asking?'

'Relax, Captain. Someone else will be doing the dirty work. It is afterwards I need your help. It won't be difficult. I merely want you to act like the good police officer you are. When the investigation takes place, I want a finding of self-defence.'

'But. The UN police . . . ?'

'They won't interfere with an internal investigation. You know that. There'll be witnesses to support the finding. Leave that to me. The UN police will accept whatever you tell them, as long as everything's neat and tidy and in its place.'

An expiration of breath whistled through Morina's teeth. 'Look. These arrests on pretty flimsy grounds have become too damn frequent. Always they come through the central police station and always my name's connected. A pattern's emerging. Something like you're now suggesting could motivate somebody to take a closer look.'

Gashi placed a morning newspaper on the table and pushed it towards Morina. 'Five thousand euros is pinned on page five next to an article on police budget cuts. There'll be another five thousand when the job's done.'

As Gashi walked away, Morina searched through the pages until he found the envelope.

21.

'How much longer do you think?'

Jeff nudged Sulla.

A huge yawn expelled a billow of condensation. Sulla's eyes blinked open.

'Mm? Oh. The last bus to Gjakova leaves in twenty minutes. Do not worry, they will come. They must catch that bus to get home.'

For three hours they'd been parked outside the entrance to the central bus terminal. Sulla insisted it was the best spot. Anyone entering from the city centre would need to walk past his car. Streetlights, vehicle lights and light beaming through apartment windows and from the bus terminal gave more than enough illumination. If the Xhiha brothers came, they would be identifiable quite a long way off. But it was the 'if' that most concerned Jeff.

'I'm bloody cold, Sulla. The inside of a freezer would be warmer than the inside of your damn car.'

Jeff pushed his frozen hands between his thighs. It did little good. There was no escaping the cold. He only had himself to blame. Tomorrow, for certain, he would buy gloves and a decent winter coat. Sulla, wrapped in a wool-lined jacket, gloves and woollen hat, had been able to doze off resting his head against the window.

'I am sorry. I would give you my coat but then I would be cold. So I think maybe it is not such a good idea.'

Jeff chuckled and breathed into his hands.

'You're a very funny man, Sulla.'

Sulla laughed. 'Yes, it is not only you who thinks so. My father, he says this to me all the time.'

'You know. We might be suffering all this for nothing. These fellows might not show at all.'

'Jeff. You worry too much. This is the way they must come to get home. There is only one entrance. Each hour, the buses leave for all over Kosovo.' He shrugged. 'We are a small country. In any direction, it is less than three hours to a border.'

'They have a car. Why not drive back?'

'They are peasants. Buses are cheaper than petrol. They could, of course, climb over that grassy bank bordering the highway, but it is not likely. They will have drunk cognac all afternoon. They won't be climbing anything, never mind driving a car. It is the peasant mentality. Believe me. But if you are too cold . . . ?'

Jeff gritted his teeth. 'We wait, Sulla. We wait.'

Suddenly everything around them plunged into darkness.

'A power cut.' Sulla checked his watch. 'Right on time.'

'Oh, just great. I can't see anything at all out of these windows. When was the last time you cleaned them?'

'When was the last time it rained?'

Jeff sensed Sulla grinning at him. He cracked a smile himself. He knew he became grumpy when it was cold.

'Just wait a minute,' Sulla said. 'It will be okay. You will see.'

Before Jeff's eyes flickering lights began to appear in apartment windows as candles and gas lanterns were lit. Then the bus terminal lights flashed twice. A third time and they stayed on. Jeff caught the rumble of a generator on the night air.

'There, now we can see again,' Sulla said. 'Not as good, but enough I think.'

Jeff blew into his hands.

Sulla drummed his knuckles on the window, filling the car with a staccato rhythm. A soft, tuneless hum vibrated in his throat. After five minutes, just as Jeff contemplated clipping Sulla's ear to halt the irritable sound, it stopped.

'You know, my father could confirm that Arben's family lived on that land and would never sell it. He is held in high regard. His word would be taken as truth.'

'Would your father be prepared to stand up in court?'

'I would need to ask him. But I do not see why not.'

'I'm sure Benny would be grateful. If we ever find him. Is it possible the Xhiha brothers are smarter than we think?'

'No, you must not believe this. They really are as stupid as they look.' Sulla leaned forward to scan the darkness afresh. 'No, Jeff. Whatever is going on, the Xhihas are not behind it. They are just pigeons. I think that is the saying?'

'Close enough.'

Sulla stiffened. A hand landed on Jeff's arm. 'Look. There they are.'

A hard squint. Jeff could just discern two figures emerging from the darkness. The shapes certainly looked promising to him. Sulla reached across and pulled a bundle of rags from the glove compartment. He unwrapped a German Luger. Jeff's eyes widened when Sulla thrust it into his lap.

'You might need this.'

'Where the hell did you get this from? Does it even work?'

'My grandfather stole it from the Germans during the big war. My father has kept it in good order. The magazine is loaded but I cannot guarantee it will fire. But it will scare the brothers. That's all that counts.'

'Let's hope so.'

Jeff glanced up. The brothers had closed to within thirty metres. Their gait looked uncertain and wobbly. Sulla started the car.

'Now remember. Only Ahmed. He is the one that speaks English.'

Jeff gave the surroundings a quick scan. No pedestrians. Anyone in the bus depot would be too far away to notice a disturbance outside.

Jeff flung the door open and raced across the road. The brothers stopped and stared quizzically at the man standing in front of them pointing a pistol. Slow and cow-like, two sets of eyes settled on the barrel of the Luger. Ahmed licked his lips and glanced towards the bus depot. Jeff knew exactly what he was thinking. If they decided to run for it he could never stop them.

Stepping closer he snapped his fingers to grab their attention.

'Hi, Ahmed. Remember me?' Jeff said, slowly and clearly. Ahmed peered to get a better look at Jeff's face. He nodded. A drunken smile displayed a row of tobacco-stained rotting teeth. 'Sure you do. You're coming for a ride. Tell your brother to lie on the ground.'

Ahmed glanced at his brother then back to Jeff. The smile persisted, but Jeff saw a new edge of cunning in it. And he could read the message. This was a case of two against one. And these guys were too drunk to be intimidated by a relic from the Second World War.

Jeff had to catch them both off-guard. A lightning step. A cry split the air as the pistol backhanded the side of Ahmed's head. Grabbing a handful of jacket Jeff pulled the dazed man towards him, the pistol barrel pressed into Ahmed's cheek. His eyes dilated. Unintelligible sounds came from his mouth. At this proximity Jeff almost gagged from the reek of his breath.

'Ahmed. I will shoot you if your brother does not lie on the ground. Do you understand?'

Ahmed's head nodded twice. A brief babble in Albanian followed, loud enough for the brother to hear. Skender crumpled to the ground. Jeff shoved Ahmed to the car. He pulled open the rear door.

'Get inside.'

Ahmed fell in, Jeff close behind. Sulla revved the motor and pulled away. Jeff glanced through the rear window. Skender was a diminishing shadow on the road.

'No one is following.'

'Don't worry,' Sulla laughed. 'No one has noticed what has happened and if anyone did, they wouldn't care. This is Kosovo.'

'So everyone keeps telling me.'

Jeff turned his attention to the man slumped beside him. Ahmed was out to it. Snoring. Jeff just shook his head. He tossed the useless Luger onto the front seat.

༄

'For Christ's sake, Sulla. It's a bloody quagmire.'

As Jeff climbed out of the car his boot had sunk into the sodden ground, mud sliding inside to his socks. Sulla's head popped above his door. 'When the snow melts, the ground goes squishy. It is God's work. I am not to blame.'

'Yeah, right. You owe me a new pair of boots.'

During daytime, the unsealed hectare of land behind the copper-roofed basketball stadium hosted a bevy of trailers and tents. Jeff imagined traders barking out prices on everything from farm produce to electronics. But by night who would know or care what went on here? It would have to be a loud noise indeed that could ever carry to the surrounding apartment buildings. A nod of satisfaction. This was the perfect location for an interrogation. Except for the mud.

Jeff squelched his way around to the rear door. He pulled it open. Ahmed tumbled out. Jeff shook his head.

'Legless drunk.'

Sulla helped Jeff yank Ahmed to his feet. The man's head flopped with little control, mouth slack. A single moan of feeble protest, then silence. A snort of disgust came from Sulla. 'The drunken piece of shit has passed out.'

'Any water in your car?'

'Some bottles in the boot.'

Jeff took firmer hold of Ahmed. 'Could you get them? If we don't wake him up we could be here all night.'

Sulla let go of Ahmed's arm. Jeff managed to keep him upright as far as the front of the car. Ahmed slumped out of Jeff's grip onto the bonnet.

Sulla emptied two bottles of water over the drunk man's head.

With a splutter, Ahmed jolted upright, arms flailing. Sulla leaped back, knocking Jeff off balance. Ahmed continued to shadow box. Finally a wild right cross at Sulla missed, but the momentum of the swing sent Ahmed spinning back into the muck. The scowl on Sulla's face should have burned him to a cinder.

'I really want to kick him.'

Instead Sulla laid hold of him once again and pulled him back onto the bonnet. With a grimace at the soiling of his coat, Sulla grabbed Ahmed's collar to make sure he stayed where he was. A single convulsion and Ahmed's head lifted from his chest. A stupid smile followed. The expression that passed over Sulla's face told Jeff he foresaw what was coming next. But he wasn't quick enough to get out of its way. A gurgle and remnants of undigested food splattered down Sulla's trousers.

Sulla let out a roar. 'You worthless son of a dog.'

In a flash he released his hold of Ahmed and reached into the car, pulling out the Luger. He jammed it hard against Ahmed's temple.

Jeff grabbed his arm. 'Don't . . .'

A loud click.

Silence.

Sulla jerked the weapon before his eyes and glared at it.

'Lump of German shit.'

In some happy world of his own, Ahmed had taken to giggling. Sulla turned from him, mumbled something in Albanian and kicked one of the car tyres. He glared again at the Luger and flung it onto the back seat. Jeff rubbed his hands together. He envisaged a long, cold, miserable night.

22.

'an I intrude, guys?'

Barry looked up with a fork poised between plate and lip to see who else the Kukri bar had attracted for breakfast. Bethany and Morgan, mouths full, offered nods of greeting.

'Huh, Jeff. Take a seat mate. We always have breakfast together on Saturdays. Expat tradition. Anyway, Morgan hates to eat alone.'

A twist of Morgan's eyebrows. 'Barry's a wonderful liar, Jeff. Truth is he's here because he's too lazy to make Bethany breakfast in bed.'

Jeff met her smile then searched around for a waiter. With coffee and a full English breakfast ordered, he sat back and listened to the others chat. After a while Morgan glanced across at him from behind her coffee cup.

'You're quiet this morning. Problem?'

'Uh? Oh. No problem.' Jeff sipped his coffee. Behind the counter the barista banged his metal scoop on the sink bench to loosen a wad of grinds. 'It's just I've come by some information. About Arben Shala.'

Knife and fork clinked to a rest on Morgan's plate. Her eyes fixed on Jeff's.

'Oh yeah?'

'I have reason to believe he's in the Prishtina Detention Centre.' Jeff mentally kicked himself for making this sound like a military briefing. 'Anyway, that's where I think he is.'

'How did you find that out?'

'I, er . . . had a talk with a mutual acquaintance.'

An arch of Morgan's eyebrows. 'A talk, huh?'

'Mm. The information seems pretty reliable. I'm waiting for my driver then I'll go across to the police station and find out.'

Barry's interest perked up. 'Jesus, if that's all your problem is, I'll get it sorted in a jiffy. Here. Write your man's name down on this.'

A notepad and pen slid across the table.

'And you'll do what with it?'

Barry looked around and pointed. 'See the man mountain ogling down the shirtfront of the blonde looker? South African cop. Friend of mine. He'll get us what we want to know.'

The pen did its work. Jeff tore out the page and handed it to Barry.

Morgan's eyes narrowed again at Jeff. 'My, that was a stroke of luck, Jeff. Yesterday there were you and I banging our heads against a brick wall. Today you've found the guy. Just like that. Is there something you'd like to share with me?'

Jeff met her curiosity with a grin. 'Sure there is. My driver and I had a chat with one of the Xhiha brothers last evening. He didn't know much, but he did know where Arben was. I thanked him for his troubles and sent him on his way, and that was that.'

Head tilted to the side, a one-eyebrow arch of scepticism appeared on Morgan's face. 'Really. And in the course of this, shall we say, friendly chat, he proved to be the cooperative type after all. Have I got that right? In direct contrast with our earlier experience of the man? Just goes to show what a poor judge of character I am, doesn't it?'

Jeff squirmed in his chair and cast an eye around for the arrival of his breakfast. 'Er. I guess we Kiwis have a charm all our own.'

'You guess, do you, Jeff?' Morgan turned to Bethany. 'You ever notice any particular charm attached to your countrymen?'

Even though Jeff was pretty certain Morgan was stringing him along for fun, he still shifted again in his seat. Bethany turned wide eyes on Morgan. 'Not a smidgeon, Morgan. Now, if Kiwi women were cans of Steinlager . . .'

Much to Jeff's relief, Barry returned. He looked across and caught sight of the back of the South African disappearing through the door.

'Hansie's going across to the detention centre now. If Arben Shala's in there, we'll know in twenty minutes.'

'Thanks, Barry.'

'It's going to cost you, mate. I told him you'd be buying the drinks tonight.'

Amidst the general bonhomie around the table Jeff was conscious of Morgan's occasional close scrutiny as he ate his breakfast. It came as a welcome relief when Barry's South African mate returned a little more than twenty minutes later. Hansie had an Austrian police officer in tow.

'Everybody, this is Klaus Otto. He works in the Central Police Station as an advisor. I thought you might want to hear his news firsthand. Take it away, Klaus.'

Jeff pushed his plate and coffee mug to one side and rested an elbow on the table. The thickset Klaus looked around the group. A finger brushed across his flare of a moustache. His uniform jacket came in for a quick adjustment. He cleared his throat.

'Arben Shala is in the detention centre.' It sounded like Klaus was filing a report to a superior. Maybe it was just the thick accent. 'He is being held under a fifteen-day holding order. I have no intelligence regarding his well-being. The detention centre is under the control of the UN. Standing orders are that he is to be well fed. All health issues are to be attended to.'

And there had been Jeff fearing that his earlier news delivery sounded like a military briefing. With a suppressed smile he raised a hand.

'What about legal help?'

Klaus appeared to relax a little. Attention switched to Jeff. 'It does not show on his file, but that does not mean he has no lawyer. I think it not likely the proceedings could progress to this point without one. The court may have appointed someone. If it is a court appointee, it could explain why he is still in custody. They are not good, these Kosovon lawyers.'

'Thank you, Klaus. That's good news. It's a relief to know he's alive and well.'

But Klaus maintained eye contact with Jeff. 'I read through the transcript of the charges against him. Shala is accused of knowingly purchasing a stolen mobile phone. This is a serious offence in Kosovo. However, in the original statement given to the court, he said he bought the mobile legitimately from a shop and not off the street as was claimed by the police. He did have a receipt. I thought it unusual that under these circumstances he would still be in custody. I did a bit more digging. He is not being held because of any charges about the phone, but for trying to leave the country while on bail.' Klaus paused. 'If you want my opinion, the whole affair looks most irregular.'

A waiter placed a tray on the table and began loading dirty plates. Something close to a scowl appeared on Klaus's face as he viewed the cause of the clinking and jingling that intruded upon the gravitas of his narrative. Morgan caught his eye. 'You said irregular, Klaus. In what way?'

Klaus glared at the back of the departing waiter. 'If I was the investigating officer,' his eyes scanned the faces focused on him, 'I would be more interested in the man who sold the phone to Mr Shala. He's disappeared and the shop has gone out of business. But Mr Shala had the receipt and purchased the item from a registered store, so I can't see how he could be charged without stronger evidence of illegal behaviour. Without the shopkeeper, this is impossible. In my opinion, it is Mr Shala who is a victim here. Questioned yes, but he should never have been arrested.'

Morgan looked at Jeff, then back at the officer. 'But if this is so obvious to a UN policeman like yourself, surely you can intervene on his behalf? At least have him released from jail?'

'Sadly we are unable to interfere in the judicial process. We are strictly here to observe and advise.'

'Well, why not advise then,' Morgan spat back.

Klaus recoiled at Morgan's accusatory tone. Jeff's hand rose again. 'Is there any way I can get in to see him?'

His neck flexed just the once. A finger ran around the inside of Klaus's collar. 'Normally visitors would need to be family members. But a good lawyer should be able to pull a few strings.'

'I've met the lawyer he used when he first came to Kosovo. I'll go see him.'

Morgan's palms landed in front of her on the table. She eyed Jeff. 'I'm coming with you.'

Jeff's first reaction was to argue. But there was no mistaking the mood of the lady. And it wasn't one which would suffer debate. If Jeff had learned anything in the military, it was how to pick his battles.

'Mm. Good of you to offer, Morgan. Thanks.'

 ❦

Tomi Mema didn't feel aggrieved at all upon hearing Jeff Bradley's request down the line. There was a juicy fee coming his way if the Shala vineyard sold. To meet him on a Saturday when his custom was not to work at all would be part of the investment he'd have to make to earn it. His hands itched at the prospect of such easy money. For the New Zealander to even consider investing in Kosovo showed he had more money than business sense. A ripe plum begging to be picked, no less. He relaxed back in his office chair and pictured summer in Turkey with his family. He would buy the tickets once the cash was in the bank.

A glance at the clock on the wall. Some minutes yet before the agreed meeting time. He set the vineyard file aside and checked through paperwork of cases he'd be taking to court over the coming week. As he perused the pages, he sorted them into the order of presentation. A footstep thudded onto the wooden step outside his office. He placed the cap on the yellow highlighter and put it to one side.

'Mr Bradley, welcome. Oh . . .' The smile became a rictus. 'Ms Delaney, too. How nice. Please come in and take a seat.'

Truth was that Mema had already formed the conviction that 'nice' and this Delaney woman were incompatible notions. Her smile looked to have as little warmth in it as his own. At least he could take her presence as a sign that the Shala property would indeed be the topic of conversation.

Mema settled into his chair, hand resting close to the vineyard file. Business time. 'Now. How might I help you?'

'I have good news, Mr Mema,' Jeff said. 'We've found Arben Shala.'

Solid ground felt as if it had suddenly disappeared from beneath Mema's feet. Acid rose in his stomach. 'Really, that's wonderful.' Shaking hands transported the glass of water on Mema's desk to his mouth. Some spilled. 'Where is he? Safely back home in New Zealand?'

'No. He's still here in Prishtina. In prison. At the detention centre.' Jeff's forehead creased in a frown. 'Are you okay, Mr Mema?'

'Yes. Yes. A little overworked maybe. But tell me. How did you come by this information?'

'I asked one of the international police officers to check the prisons for me. We got lucky. But now I've found him, I need to find out what the hell's going on. I want to retain your services to act as his lawyer.'

'And we would like you to arrange for us to visit,' Morgan added.

'Yes, Mr Mema. As Ms Delaney says.'

The overriding thought in Mema's mind was of Osman Gashi. He needed to contact him. Another shaky sip of water found its way to his lips. He sat back and directed his gaze through the window.

'I must say, I am shocked. Who would have thought that all this time Mr Shala was just over there? Across the road from my office?'

'Will you represent him?'

'Yes, yes, of course I will represent him. As for visits, they allow one per week. But I'm afraid the visitor must be a family member.'

Morgan leaned forward and aimed a hard look into Mema's face. 'I'm sure exceptions are made all the time, Mr Mema.'

An adjustment of position on Mema's chair. 'I will see what I can do. You will need permission from the judge. Monday would be the earliest you could see him. But I must ask you, Mr Bradley. Why so much interest in Mr Shala? There is no legal reason he should be involved in the purchase transaction. And if he has been arrested for some crime it might only complicate matters for you. I was under the impression you barely even know the man.'

With a sideways look at Morgan, Jeff sat back and folded his arms. 'Mm. That. Well, Mr Mema, I have to confess I've not been entirely honest with you about Arben Shala. You see, he's the manager of my vineyard in New Zealand as well as a close friend. And now I know where he is, I want to make sure nothing happens to him. And I want him free as soon as possible.'

Any remaining thoughts Mema may have entertained that he was dealing with a naive amateur vanished in an instant. It took an extreme exercise of will for him to maintain casual eye contact with Jeff.

'If you like,' Morgan added, 'I could ask the USAID officials to intervene. Or, as Mr Shala is a New Zealand citizen, the British Consulate office might have an interest. Would that be helpful?'

Mema's heartbeat was a sickening staccato. His eyes flicked between Jeff and Morgan. 'Let's see what I can do first. I'll check my diary. I only mention prison rules because that is the law. But I am sure I can arrange something.' He pulled a black book on the desk-top towards him. A shuffle of pages followed. An unsteady finger singled out one. 'Ah, here it is. Yes. Be here at nine thirty Monday morning. Visiting hours start at ten. I will take you across.'

Mema forced a smile. He did not like being forced into making knee-jerk decisions like this. Judging from the heat beneath his collar he knew his brow would be beading in perspiration. His hand flipped the diary closed with what he hoped looked like finality.

'Is there anything Jeff or I should bring for Arben?' Morgan asked.

Hands clenched onto Mema's knees beneath the desk to stop himself from thumping a fist on it.

'Oh. Some clothes. I'm sure he would welcome that. A book. Magazines.' Hands pushed onto the desk to assist Mema to his feet. 'Now, can you excuse me? Family, you know? Er . . . A birthday.'

Mema stood in the office doorway and watched until Bradley and the American woman had disappeared from sight. Only when he was certain they were not coming back did he lock the door and clamber back behind his desk. One hand sought the phone, the other flicked through the pages of his diary in search of Osman Gashi's number.

෨

Jeff pulled Morgan to a stop outside the Kukri. 'Thank you for the support today. I won't come in right now. Got to meet up with my driver.'

Morgan stood with hands on hips. Narrowed eyes regarded Jeff. 'This driver of yours. How helpful was he in getting the information on Arben's whereabouts?'

Jeff's eyebrows executed a small rise that he hoped looked like innocence.

'Sulla? He translated for me. Couldn't have done it without him.'

Her eyes narrowed further. 'Really, Jeff? Translated for you? If all you needed was a translator, I speak the language. You know that. And I know more about the vineyard than any taxi driver. You asked for my help, you know? And I went out of my way to give it to you. And now I learn Arben actually works for you. That's a big I-don't-trust-you, don't you reckon? Do I really come across as some kind of flighty tart you can't rely on?'

Jeff embedded his teeth into his lower lip for a second. 'No, of course not.' He tilted his head back as he blew into the air. 'Look, I'm sorry, Morgan. Bad judgement call.'

'Bad judgment call? Not a great answer, is it?' Her green eyes bored into him. 'Don't let it happen again. Okay?'

'No, ma'am. I won't. I promise.'

A half-smile played at the edges of Morgan's mouth. She took a step away. 'Good. I like your attitude, soldier. Now. If you'd like to join up with us here later, the expats gather to watch *Match of the Day*. Afterwards there's usually a disco or karaoke.'

Before Jeff could formulate a response, Morgan spun on her heel and disappeared through the doors. A part of him wanted to chase after her.

But Sulla would be waiting. They had arranged to meet for lunch to discuss what next in the search for Arben. Now he knew where his friend was, he wanted him protected. Sulla might have a contact inside the detention centre. He would catch up with Morgan later.

23.

I'm leaving now, sir.'

The door to Leka's office had opened just wide enough for his secretary's face to show.

Leka's attention switched from his visitor. A wave of acknowledgement and her face disappeared. He turned back to Gashi. The envelope he'd stuffed with euros landed on the table between them.

'Captain Morina should be happy with the extra bonus there. However, he's made a good point. It's been too easy and we've got lazy.'

The smile disappeared from Gashi's face. 'You think it's time to stop?'

'Let's say, I think it wise not to push our luck. When this Shala business is finished with, get rid of the vineyard and the Xhiha brothers. Little games like this? They are peanuts. It is no big loss.' Leka shrugged. 'I have other ways to make money.'

It amused Leka greatly to watch Gashi bristle at the disparaging remark. He knew the big man worked hard at pursuing petty scams such as land grabs like the Shala vineyard. It had been only one of many. Gashi appeared to consider that they somehow elevated him from low-life pimp to sophisticated entrepreneur.

His head dropped. 'You're the boss.'

'The stolen phone ploy has run its course as well.'

Leka needed to consider alternatives. The crimes needed to be petty and carry less than a maximum sentence of two years imprisonment for it to stay in the Municipal Court and under his control. Getting the judge to order that Shala was held in custody a further fifteen days had not been difficult. She would have been delighted to find the envelope pushed under her apartment door. Her task had no great risk attached to it, and didn't even require her to do anything unlawful. That Shala had tried to run had made it easier for her.

'We have another problem,' Gashi said. 'Tomi Mema phoned. Earlier this morning the man from New Zealand and the American woman paid him another visit. They know Shala is in the detention centre.'

Leka's brow crinkled into a knot. 'How the hell did they find that out?'

Gashi picked up a letter opener from the desk and began playing with it. 'It seems the New Zealander was shitting Tomi all along. Shala works for the New Zealander. They're friends. He knew Shala was in trouble and came to Kosovo to search for him. He's teamed up with the international police. They found Shala for him.'

'My God.' Leka's voice was a whisper. He stared without blinking at Gashi.

'They've asked Tomi to organise a visit to see Shala,' Gashi continued. 'They said if he could not organise it for them, they would go to the British office. The American woman said she would talk to the US authorities.'

Leka felt a vein throb in his temple. He'd been warned that giving in to anger could have dangerous effects on his blood pressure. But some insignificant pissant property fraud was now threatening his international money-laundering network. A network worth many millions which had only flourished because he managed to keep it under the radar. Leka found it a struggle to keep his voice calm. 'What did Tomi tell them?'

'That he would organise a visit for Monday. Then he phoned me.'

The retractable pen in Leka's hand clicked open and shut in quick succession. 'If the New Zealander and that American whore meet Shala they will know Tomi has been lying. They'll be yelling for their police friends.' A snap as the plastic pen broke. He hurled the pieces at the wall. 'We can't have the international police talking to Tomi. The man's weak.' Narrowed eyes fixed on Gashi. 'Now listen to me. This has to be taken care of. Right now. You understand me?'

A cursory nod from Gashi.

'I understand. Shala's cell is . . . shall we say, accessible.'

After Gashi left, Leka sat staring at the still-life painting of fruit hanging on the wall above his filing cabinet, without really seeing it. He knew Gashi would get the job done. But he needed a plan in case the international police oversaw the ensuing investigation.

His mobile rang. With a scowl he pulled it from his pocket. 'Yes.'

Halam Akbar's voice. 'This is your man from abroad. We need to talk.'

'What? Now?'

'Yes. Now.'

Leka's jaw clenched for a second. 'Christ. If you must then. But . . . no names.'

'Understood. The courier was followed. The police have him. And the money.'

The throb in Leka's temple started anew. 'The courier doesn't know any of us. There's no way anyone can connect him to you. Or me. We're in the clear. Don't worry.'

'His capture is of no concern to me. You understand, of course, that I never saw any of the money.'

The tone of Halam's voice was too even. There might or might not have been a threat in it. Could Leka take any chances? He knew full well that this assassin would think nothing of blasting his house to kingdom come with him and his family inside it.

'I understand. I shall speak to the client and arrange another payment. No problems.'

Leka was not about to tell Halam the money would come from his own pocket. There was security in letting the terrorist believe he belonged to a much larger organisation.

'Good. But this time I will come to Kosovo and collect it myself.'

The upward jerk of Leka's head sent a twinge through his neck. With a grimace he slapped a hand to the spot.

'No. Absolutely not. The country is crawling with NATO troops. It is far too risky.'

'This is not your concern. Just have the money ready.'

The line went dead.

Leka stared at the phone in his hand for a few seconds. He lowered himself into the armchair Gashi had not long vacated. His head fell back, resting upon the upholstery. Although he didn't want that bomber anywhere near him, Kosovo was probably the last country on earth the authorities would expect him to enter. He decided it was not something he should worry himself with; his bigger concern was the courier. Could he be confident that Gashi had ensured there would be no trail back? After all, the man's land schemes had become sloppy. Was the sloppiness about to contaminate his own business as well? This could not be allowed, not after he had come so far after losing so much.

The need to clear his brain had become pressing. Leka stood and pulled on a coat and made his way into the street. The bite of winter air on his bare head helped to ease the nagging throb. Soon he found the dirt path beneath his feet that led onto Mother Teresa Boulevard. Heavy clouds forming to the west warned him rain was close. He needed to find shelter but instead continued walking, lost in thoughts of the past.

＊

His childhood in Communist Albania had been a happy one. His father, a law professor at Tirana University, enjoyed a better standard of living than most of Albania's citizens and Avni Leka never experienced the harsh existence the dictator, Enver Hoxha, imposed on the majority of his people. Hoxha, fearful of conspiracies to overthrow him, had spies everywhere. Arrests were a common occurrence.

Avni's father, convinced his own arrest was inevitable, fled with his family to his sister in Srebrenica, Bosnia. Avni enrolled in the school of law at the Sarajevo University, his younger brother continuing his studies at a school near Srebrenica. In 1990, Franjo Tudjman decided that, as Tito was dead, Croatia should regain its former statehood.

The Serbian leader, Slobodan Milosevic, had different ideas and determined that he and his Belgrade government would keep Yugoslavia under Serbian rule. In 1991, both Croatia and Slovenia declared independence. War had begun.

Emboldened by the successes of Croatia and Slovenia, the Bosnians declared independence. Avni watched helplessly as the country his family had chosen as their home disintegrated. As the Serbian military moved closer, word of massacres at Zvornik, Lerska and Snagovo quickly spread throughout the region.

Srebrenica became an isolated enclave, the entire region held by Serb forces. There was no escape, and Avni and his family, along with everyone else, became trapped in the town. Avni's younger brother took up a rifle and stood with the other Bosnian troops on the outer defences. Avni stayed back to protect their home and their mother and father.

Finally, when Avni thought all was lost, the UN Security Council declared Srebrenica a safe area and that they were sending international troops to keep the peace. A truce was put in place. The Serbs used the lull in the fighting to build up their forces and when it became obvious that the UN statements were just rhetoric and no troops were to be sent, the Serbs attacked, supported by heavy artillery and tanks.

The Bosnians were no match and within days were completely overrun.

When Serbian soldiers finally arrived on his doorstep, Avni was alone. His father had gone in search of his brother and had not returned. Avni tried to protect his mother but a rifle butt to the head sent him reeling to the ground. A bullet was fired into his chest, collapsing his lung, and he was left for dead. Still conscious, he watched the soldiers as, one after another, they raped his mother, then lifted her unmoving form from the dirt and tossed her into the back of a truck. Lying in a pool of his own blood, laughter caught his attention. Avni watched with deadened eyes as Serbian soldiers and UN troops mingled amiably, sharing jokes and offering each other cigarettes and coffee.

Avni never saw his mother, father or brother again.

On that day he lost all faith in Western justice. The world had turned its back on him, killed his family and declared he was on his own. Well, so be it. Instead, Avni turned to the Islamic community. They nursed him back to health then provided transport back to Albania. When the mullahs called the faithful to prayers, Avni became a regular attendee. His tragic story came to the attention of a visiting Iranian, Hassan Dara. Over coffee, Hassan declared to

Avni he had an interest in working with embittered Islamists to help them find solace through vengeance. To Avni, this offer provided direction to his otherwise purposeless existence.

His law degrees were Yugoslavian and useless in Albania, so he moved to Kosovo and established a law practice. Hassan ensured Avni had the money to bribe his way into a position of authority and grow his influence in the airports, ports and border controls. Hassan began to send him men and women from the Middle East wanting to start a new life in Europe. Under Avni's direction, his henchman Gashi developed corridors for illegal immigration through Montenegro, Croatia and Slovenia into Austria and Italy. He organised boats to smuggle goods and people across the Adriatic.

Soon, Avni was making millions from these illegal activities and needed to hide the money. He established offshore bank accounts, but when the Americans changed the world-banking laws Avni could no longer dump huge amounts into the tax havens. So he began setting up export companies in Western countries. His clients coordinating the illegal immigrations made their payments to Avni by purchasing and importing goods at higher than the normal price. Avni, as a shareholder in all these companies, had the profits paid into his offshore bank accounts. All legal and legitimate with a paper trail to show it. In the end he only received 30 per cent of the original payments, but it was clean and it was plenty.

Hassan, impressed by Avni's ambition and business expertise, proposed another venture. There were many wealthy men and countries around the world who wanted to strike at the heart of Western civilisation, and who were prepared to pay enormous amounts of money as long as the trail never led back to them. Avni hesitated, but then he remembered his mother defiled in the dirt of Srebrenica. When all was in place he hired the Akbar brothers and his reign of terror began.

❧

Tomi Mema sat alone in his office. His secretary had long gone and so should have he. But as much as he loved his family, tonight he did not need the hassle of clambering children and a wife who could be at times over-demanding.

He poured a second cognac and took a sip. Bradley and the American woman were not going away. Of that he was now certain. The tension headache he'd had since meeting them was threatening to become a migraine. Why had Gashi not let Shala do a runner? They already had the vineyard whether Shala signed over the documents or not. But he had experienced before the insatiable need in Gashi for more. It would lead to their undoing.

What if Bradley met with Shala? A shudder ran through him at the thought. But another thought had begun to bother him. Exactly what had Gashi implied when he'd promised to take care of things? Mema couldn't bring himself to articulate his suspicions. Might the day come when Gashi took it into his head that Tomi Mema himself needed some kind of taking care of?

Into Mema's mind once more came the repeated invitation of his cousin to move to Zagreb and start a new life. He recalled how readily he'd told his cousin to stop badgering him. But now the prospect had taken on more appealing dimensions. He had enough money for it.

Mema tossed back the cognac and stared at the empty glass in his hand for a minute. With a bang it went back onto the desktop.

The alcohol was fuelling his resolve, his decision firming. Tonight he would tell his wife they were off to join his cousin. She might hate the idea. Too bad.

But when he pictured her reaction his head drooped.

The cognac bottle came back to hand. Amber liquid trickled into the glass until it spilled over the rim.

24.

A roar erupting in the corner came from a group crowded round an island table, heads turned up and eyes glued to the television. Already covered with spilled beer, empty glasses and ashtrays, the table top was quickly filling with butts which signalled that sports afternoon in the Kukri was underway. Man United had scored.

From their vantage point some distance from the bar, Morgan and Bethany had watched the heated discussion last through two beers, and to the two women it appeared the argument was not going Barry's way. He slammed his empty glass on the counter and yelled for a refill. Neither Morgan nor Bethany recognised the basketball-player-tall man causing Barry so much aggravation. His oval face atop hunched shoulders, and his pencil-thin lips set in a tolerant, sympathetic smile, were spurring Barry into overreaction. He waved his arms about like a drowning man to emphasise his points.

Morgan raised an eyebrow at Bethany. 'What do you reckon? Sports or politics?'

Bethany shrugged. 'I think one more beer and they'll have forgotten whatever it was they were fighting about.'

Morgan cast a glance at her empty glass. Its condition had been the motivation for Barry going to the bar in the first place. Trying not to be too obvious about it, she glanced towards the door. Jeff might or might not show up. And she hadn't quite admitted to herself that the snug skirt, black woollen leggings and emerald-green sweater that displayed her figure so well had been selected with him in mind. She was still a little miffed with the good-looking man from New Zealand.

Barry stomped his way back to the table. He slumped into his seat and glared at the two women.

'Bloody useless UN arseholes. That guy at the bar is Geoffrey Sloan. He works at the justice ministry. He confirmed that everything the lawyer told you is correct. Jeff's mate is stuck in that bloody prison over the weekend. Nothing anyone can do. A court order can have him released but that can't happen until Monday. Even if someone agreed to do it.'

'So that's it?' Morgan said.

Barry presented hands of surrender.

'End of the line. Well . . . maybe not quite. Sloan did say the one man who can help is the Director of Justice. One of your people, Morgan. A Yank. But it's Saturday afternoon. It's doubtful he'll be in his office. And he won't be working tomorrow, that's for sure.'

Morgan's lips pursed. 'Unfortunately, I doubt he'd be very helpful. I've met him before and he spent the entire time patronising me and staring at my chest.'

Morgan shrugged resignedly and for a moment they sat in a defeated silence.

'So what do we do now?' said Barry finally.

'Well, I can think of one thing . . .' said Bethany.

'What?'

'You forgot my drink, darling.'

'Oh, shit. Sorry.' Barry hauled himself out of his chair. Bethany grabbed his arm and pulled him down for a quick kiss.

Morgan sighed and turned to look at the door again. There was still a chance Jeff might turn up.

∽

Avni Leka hung his greatcoat on the cherrywood coat rack near the door. The muffled sounds of a television show filtered through from the next room. Voices babbled away in Spanish. Fatmire must have been watching one of her favourite Mexican soaps. She would not be expecting him. If she had been, the recording of an Italian singer crooning a love song would have accompanied the smell of roasting meat up the hallway to greet him.

He sat on the stool in the hall to remove his shoes. An earlier intention to spend an evening with his children had lost out. After a stressful day what he needed was Fatmire. She alone had the magic touch that could relax him.

A step to the sitting room doorway.

Fatmire lay sprawled asleep across the leather couch in T-shirt and panties. The shirt had ridden up to expose long legs spread in innocent invitation. To look upon her firm young body in this way was as aesthetic as it was erotic for Leka. He barely dared breathe lest he wake her and spoil the moment. This twenty-five-year-old beauty belonged only to him. It had never seemed to matter to her that he was a balding man in his fifties and old enough to be her father.

They had met when Fatmire approached him, looking for work. She had no family, no home. A casualty of ethnic cleansing. But her beauty had captured Leka from the very first. And he still remembered with great joy the surprise he'd felt when she accepted the offer of becoming his mistress. So he'd supplied her with an apartment and income and now, two years later, both were more than happy with the arrangement.

Leka found he could trust Fatmire enough to conduct his covert operations from one of the bedrooms in her apartment. This had the extra advantage of keeping it as far away from his family as he could get it. Fatmire had become his confidante. He discussed and planned his ventures with her. Many a night she would sit up with him as he bounced ideas around. She knew when to hold her silence. Although she did not fully grasp the intricacies of Leka's projects, she understood enough to be a danger to him should the authorities ever come knocking on her door.

His wife knew he no longer loved her, that he had a lover, and had learned to live with it. She had children to love and a bottomless bank account. It was enough. At first he feared his wife might react in the time-honoured way of a woman scorned. But thankfully she had not. He well knew how Albanian women could become irrational and vengeful. But as the wife of a chief prosecutor she was a respected member of her community, her social status being more important to her than becoming acrimonious over her husband's infidelity.

She accepted her circumstances just as Fatmire had accepted hers.

Fatmire's eyes opened. She smiled and reached out a hand. Leka moved forward to grasp it.

⁓

Jeff finally made it to the Kukri by 5 p.m., just in time to watch the second Premier League match of the day. Cheers and groans blended in with the general din of laughter and shouting.

After hearing what Barry had discovered, Jeff said, 'I guess that's it then. We've run out of options.'

He was more disappointed than he was prepared to show. At lunch Sulla had told him he knew no one in the detention centre. Another dead end. The look on Morgan's face told him she could see how he felt. For a second he sensed that she wanted to throw her arms around his neck and tell him things would be all right. He wouldn't have minded that. It would have eased the apprehension lurking inside his brain that things might not be all right at all.

Instead it was Bethany who laid a hand on his arm.

'It must be horrible in that place. I can't begin to imagine what the inside of a Kosovon prison must be like.'

'Me neither,' Barry chipped in. 'What about you, Morgan? Any idea?

A shake of Morgan's red head. 'Not really. I can only guess it can't be good.'

Jeff hoped Morgan was wrong. He had already resolved not to phone Kimie and tell her about Arben being in jail. Not yet. If the fates decreed, the whole affair could be over on Monday and she would never have needed to know.

The waiter came with a tray of drinks and packets of potato crisps. 'Cheer up, mate,' Barry said. He transferred the contents of the tray onto the table. 'You found where he is and you know he's safe. You've hired a lawyer and on Monday you get to see him. It's all going to turn out fine.'

'You're right, Barry. Thanks again to all of you for helping out.'

'No problems, mate. Now, can we watch the match and drink some beer?'

Jeff picked up his beer and tried to relax. Barry was right. Arben was safe for the moment. By Monday it would all be over.

25.

Have I done something to antagonise Sabri?'

It was Sunday afternoon. Courtyard time. Arben walked with Bedri as he did on each visit to the exercise yard.

'Why? What's the little thug done now?'

'Done? Nothing to speak of. It's just that I catch him staring at me sometimes. Not friendly. Then he spits. He doesn't speak any more either. Not that he ever did that much. But now, not at all. It's . . . strange.'

'My friend, Sabri is strange. Don't let it get to you.'

Silence for a minute as the two men stepped out the twenty paces that was the length of the oblong-shaped exercise yard. The ping-ping of a table-tennis ball came from the centre. The laughter of Imer and another inmate occasionally burst into abuse. Arben glanced behind him. Near the entrance gate he spotted Sabri surrounded by a handful of strutting young bucks. Bedri followed Arben's eyes.

'New guys, Arben. Think they own the place. Sabri has them in line in very short order. They all end up terrified of him.'

'How does he do that? He's not that big.'

'How? Let me ask you. Are you scared of him?'

Arben swallowed. He wanted to say no, of course not. But the words refused to come. Bedri's forefinger tapped Arben's chest.

'There's your answer right there, my friend. The guy's a psycho-path. People react without knowing why to all the weird stuff they sense going on in that crazy head of his.' Bedri pulled Arben to a halt. 'Sabri's kind doesn't need a reason to hate. They just hate.'

Arben's gaze turned again towards Sabri. He discovered Sabri looking back. Something in the eyes sent a shiver through Arben. He looked away and turned his attention back to Bedri.

'What was it Sabri did to end up in here?'

Before the question was out of his mouth, Arben wondered if it had been wise even to ask it.

Bedri's mouth tightened. 'You ask? Okay, I'll tell. Sabri and a friend were sitting in a cafe in Prizren. Both out of their brains on drugs. A university student sent to the cafe by his father to collect espressos made the mistake of looking in Sabri's direction. Sabri took it as an insult. He pulled a knife and sliced the kid's stomach open. His guts fell out onto the floor. Sabri was still laughing when the police arrived to take him away.'

Arben felt the blood drain from his face. 'How . . . how long's he in here for?'

'Who knows. His trial keeps getting adjourned. His family's no doubt organising money to pay the bribes. If they drag it out long enough he'll probably get off.'

Arben's eyes widened. 'You're kidding me.'

'This is Kosovo, my friend. So remember. That man is a very crazy person. Crazy people do crazy things. Take the warning.'

'Imer will keep him in order, won't he? That's what he does.'

'Not for much longer. Imer received his release date on Friday afternoon.'

'But he's said nothing about it,' Arben said.

'To me, he has. I'm his friend. It's just that he refuses to get too excited. He says that until the day they let him walk through the gates and do not drag him back, he won't believe he's free. That's Imer.'

But Arben now saw the reason why the dynamic of the cell had in fact changed in the previous two days. Imer had seemed preoccupied. Didn't obsess so much over maintaining order. Now the prospect of losing the man he considered a guardian angel became a horrifying prospect.

That night, Arben sat at the table stirring his coffee. What would he say to Tomi Mema in the morning? Sabri lay in silence on his bunk and was for the moment out of his thoughts. There was a scrape as Bedri pulled up a chair next to him. His mouth came close to Arben's ear.

'Arben, you need to be careful. Sabri has been talking about you to Imer. He said his gang of thugs should beat you up if you don't give them money.'

Arben's stomach lurched. 'But . . . but I don't have any money.'

'He reckons you could pay it on the outside.'

'Why would he do such a thing? I haven't done anything to any of them.'

Bedri's finger pointed at his own temple and performed a circular motion. 'Crazy, remember? Greedy piece of shit too.'

'What did Imer say?'

'Imer said he would beat Sabri to a pulp if he laid a finger on you. He'd do it anyway if it wouldn't affect his release.'

'I understand. Please tell Imer not to do anything.' He gripped Bedri's arm. 'Don't worry, Bedri. I can look after myself. I might be middle-aged but I'm not useless. After the kindness you and Imer have shown me, I would hate it if either of you suffered trying to protect me.'

❦

The need to empty his bladder woke Arben. He'd had a restless night. Trying to sleep with Sabri's radio blaring was hopeless. Arben detected from the chorus of snores that everybody was now asleep. He would turn it off on the way to the toilet. He climbed down from his bunk. Squinting, he studied the line of knobs. Light filtering through cracks in the toilet door gave just enough illumination. He identified the volume controller and reached out.

A hand snapped onto his wrist gripping like a vice.

Arben tried to pull away. The hold tightened. Cold sweat broke out on Arben's forehead as he saw the shadowy form of Sabri rising off his mattress. Arben's mouth opened. No words came. Panic gave him strength. He pulled and managed to shake himself free then shuffled backwards until he hit the cell door. There was no escape. Nowhere to hide. Sabri came after him. Light reflected off something in his hand. Arben knew it had to be a blade.

'Sabri. Don't do this.'

The noise of the radio was covering the gasp that was all the voice Arben could muster. A smile with no humour spread across Sabri's face. Arben threw himself to the side and grabbed the plastic table. With something to keep him separated from Sabri, Arben cast about for a weapon. There was nothing. He reached a hand behind him to hammer on the cell door. The guardroom was some distance away. Would they even hear?

Sabri grabbed the edge of the table, flipped it upwards and dived at Arben's legs. They both fell to the floor. Sabri squirmed and manoeuvred Arben onto his back. Pinned down and facing a mask of hatred within an inch of his face, a surge of adrenaline galvanised Arben's body. A deep breath and he pushed for all he was worth. Sabri tumbled to the floor alongside him. Arben leaped to his feet and kicked the blade from Sabri's hand.

Growling the guttural sound of an animal of the wild, Sabri sprang to his feet. Arben didn't hesitate. All his weight went into a right-hand swing. His fist smashed into the side of Sabri's skull. The psychopath dropped to the floor and lay motionless. Arben stood over him. Breath whistled through his nose. His hand hurt.

But his racing heart was also a triumphant heart. He stood there with eyes closed and a sense of great relief.

From behind, unseen fingers coiled into his hair and tugged. A glint of metal curved through the air. A fountain sprayed from his neck. Incredulous hands grasped. Blood pulsed. Arben backed into the wall and slid to the floor, warm stickiness oozing through the fingers holding his throat. Desperate eyes searched above. Focused on the man standing in front of him.

An apologetic look on Bedri's face? 'I'm so sorry, Arben. I had a job to do.'

Arben watched Bedri step over his outstretched legs, kneel beside the unconscious Sabri and place the blade into his upturned hand.

Lights flashed in Arben's peripheral vision. In his chest a sickening racing of his heart. In his ears buzzing. Loud banging. A voice calling for the guards.

Then the enveloping peace of the dark.

26.

On Sunday afternoon Morgan and Bethany had gone to the street markets and bought tracksuits, T-shirts and other bits and pieces that Mema said Arben might need. Jeff bought magazines and a newspaper from the hotel bookshop. He walked into Morgan's office a few minutes after nine on Monday morning. Her green eyes sparkled a greeting.

He looked over her shoulder as she checked off the list of discussion points he'd jotted down. A whiff of her perfume wafted to his nose. What would it be like to hold her?

She wrote on the list *Health examination*.

'You think that's necessary?'

'He's over fifty, Jeff. I would think the stress from this ordeal has shot his blood pressure through the roof. We might need to organise a doctor.'

'Right now my own blood pressure probably needs checking.'

Morgan's head turned with eyebrows raised. She was treated to a sheepish grin.

'Bit of comic relief. Sorry.'

Jeff could see she was hiding a smile as she addressed herself back to the list. He suspected Morgan quite liked it when he acted the hormonal adolescent. For him, it had been a long time since Rebecca. Not that there had ever been that many women in his life.

It reminded him that he'd not yet contacted Kimie Shala. He would phone her as soon as they were back from meeting with Arben.

～

When Jeff and Morgan entered Tomi Mema's office he insisted they sit. 'First off, good morning to both of you.'

Jeff's instincts leaped to full alert. Something in Tomi Mema's tone was warning him that things were not right. He appeared to be struggling with what he needed to say next.

'What is it?' Jeff asked, alarmed. 'Don't tell me we've been refused permission to visit?' His anger surfaced. 'This is just not good enough, Mema. If we don't get in this morning, I'll go straight to the British office and kick some arse.'

Mema shook his head. 'No, Mr Bradley. It's not that.' Jeff made to stand but Mema's hand went up. 'Please. Just listen. The director of the prison phoned me a few minutes ago. There is no easy way to tell you this. Your friend Arben Shala is dead.'

Jeff opened his mouth to say something but it caught in is throat. He leaned forward. 'What the fuck are you talking about?' he finally growled.

Morgan reached across and put her hand on Jeff's arm. 'Easy, Jeff. Easy.'

Mema gathered himself. 'I'm sorry, Mr Bradley. So sorry. But your friend has died.'

Jeff sat back in his chair. 'I don't believe this. It's not true,' he whispered.

His eyes fixed on Mema. Morgan must have realised he was in shock. She turned to face Mema.

'What happened? Did he have a heart attack?'

'I don't have all the information as yet, Ms Delaney. But it does seem Mr Shala was killed in a fight. With a fellow inmate. I will go across after we finish here and find out exactly what happened.'

Jeff stood. Both fists leaned on Mema's desk. 'Benny in a fight? Not likely. Somebody murdered him.'

'You could be right, Mr Bradley. That could indeed be what has happened.'

Jeff shook his head.

'Arben dead? What kind of alternative universe have I walked into?' His eyes burned into Mema's. 'I want to see the prison director. Now. This morning.'

'I'm sorry, Mr Bradley, but that will not be possible. The prison is in lockdown. There will be an investigation. Only officials can enter. As I represent Arben, I can meet with the director, but that is it. I will make a full report to you when I get back.'

Primal fury swept through Jeff, nearly choking him. 'Report? Fucking report? Fuck the lot of you, Mema. I want inside that prison.' Jeff leaned over Mema's seated form and raised a fist to within an inch of his nose. 'Tell me you understand me, Mema. Tell me.'

The lawyer shrank into his chair. 'Yes. I do understand. But please. Calm down. I am not the responsible one. Please, Mr Bradley.'

The crash of Jeff's chair hitting the floor reverberated within the steel walls of Mema's container office. Three strides took Jeff to the door. He needed to calm down. Get away to think. Mema was right. He was only the lawyer. Harassing him would not bring Arben back. But what was he going to say to Kimie? He pulled the office door open and stared out.

'I need to contact his family and tell them what's happened.'

Morgan stood to go to him, but stopped halfway and turned to face Mema.

'Can you please talk to the director and try to arrange a meeting?'

Her voice was so soft Jeff could barely hear it. When he glanced around he noticed a look on Mema's face close to sadness. This affair was getting to him in a way Jeff wouldn't have expected.

'I will try,' Mema said. 'I will. Please phone me in an hour.'

Morgan joined Jeff at the door. Mema stood and took a pace in their direction.

'There is one more detail we need to discuss. Mr Shala is a Muslim. It is the custom for the burial to take place before the next sunset. If you wish, I shall try to arrange for the release of his body for that.'

Jeff spun on him. 'Before an autopsy? Mema. The man was murdered.'

'This is Kosovo, Mr Bradley, not New Zealand. We do not have much of a morgue. And besides, the cause of death is clear. His cellmate killed him. The killer will already have been isolated and put under special guard. He will not escape a murder charge, this I can promise you. The other cellmates will testify. Don't worry. This man will get what he deserves.'

'No, Mr Mema. Unfortunately the arsehole will not get what he deserves.' Jeff stopped and exhaled a deep sigh. 'Look. I'll have to discuss burial with his family. Where would it take place? They'll want to know.'

'I suggest the village he came from. There is a cemetery and it has a memorial stone to honour those massacred during the war. The bodies of his mother and father will be there. I can arrange for this, if his family would like.'

'I'll tell his wife.'

'When you speak to the family, please pass on my condolences.'

Once outside with the bite of the brisk morning air on their faces, Morgan passed her arm through Jeff's. 'C'mon, Jeff. Let's go back to my apartment.'

27.

Morgan's two-level apartment sat atop a plumbing supplies shop on Rruga Lidhja e Prizrenit. The dirt lane that gave access from the main road, Luan Haradinaj, lay like a bog before them. Jeff ignored Morgan's suggestion to go the long way round and ploughed into the mud. After a few paces he stopped, held out his hand and helped Morgan leap onto the drier spots. At the end of the lane, he pulled a handkerchief from his jacket pocket, squatted and wiped off her shoes.

'Sorry. Wasn't thinking, Morgan.'

'They're just shoes. Really expensive Sergio Rossi shoes, sure. But hey. Italians make plenty of them. Next time I'm in Rome, I'll buy a new pair.'

Jeff smiled an apology. Fleeting.

Inside the apartment he removed his boots and left them by the door then made his way up the stairs to where Morgan waited for him on the landing. She took his hand and led him through to her sitting room. An arrangement of flowers in an emerald vase caught his eye. It sat at the centre of a six-seat dining table pushed up against the farthest wall. Next to the telephone on a writing desk, a laptop, lid up, hummed to itself. Beside it a pile of folders. A three-seater and two two-seater settees formed a U-shape around a sizeable carved Chinese box which looked to serve as a coffee table. Jeff's gaze passed over paintings hanging on the walls. Pot plants placed in strategic positions lent the room a greenness that reminded him of home. The apartment was feminine and unpretentious.

A weariness filled Jeff's body. He allowed it to slump onto the three-seater settee. Morgan walked around behind him and gave his shoulder a light squeeze.

'I'll make coffee.'

Jeff found the movements he could hear in the upstairs kitchen soothing. From where he sat he had a view of the street. A small queue had formed in front of the bakery next to the VW auto shop. Pedestrians dodged motorists as they trudged their way through mud to what appeared to be an unmarked bus stop. A child tugged on her mother's coat and pointed to a red gumboot on the road behind them. The boot had been sucked off her foot in the mire. Three cars ran over it before the mother managed to snatch it up.

Thick beige carpet muffled Morgan's return. A mug of coffee appeared on the Chinese box.

'Here you go. I'll be upstairs if you need me.'

Jeff was grateful Morgan understood his need to be alone.

He picked at a loose thread on the seam of his jeans. His earlier fury having dissipated, he was left feeling devoid of emotion. He held two fingers against an artery in his neck. His attention dropped to the second hand of his watch. Eleven beats in ten seconds. Sixty-six a minute. Normal. How could everything be going as it always had? Continuing as if Benny hadn't passed?

He recalled with a grimace the apprehension he'd felt when he'd promised Kimie he would bring her husband home. That had now transformed into guilt as painful as a white-hot knife plunged through his heart. Who did he think he was to have given such a guarantee? Kimie would hate him forever, and she had every right. She had warned him of the dangers and he'd ignored her. Benny had died in miserable conditions far from home because of some failed harvest on the opposite side of the godforsaken planet. It was unforgivable.

He picked up his coffee. He wanted to hurl the cup against the wall. Maybe his head to follow. Instead the brown liquid laced with cognac came to his lips.

'Benny, Benny, Benny. I'm so sorry.'

Jeff's voice was but a whisper into tiny wraiths of steam.

⁓

'Jesus. What a shit of a thing.' Barry paced like a caged lion. 'That arsehole Yank at the justice ministry needs a rocket up his arse for letting this happen. And those cop mates of mine are gonna get some shit chucked at them. That much I promise.'

Bethany reached out and took his hand. 'Sit down, darling. At least they caught the murderer.'

'There is that, I suppose.' Barry dropped onto the seat alongside Bethany and fixed a look on Jeff. 'So, Jeff. What happens now, mate?'

Jeff shook his head. 'First, I guess the lawyer's organising for me to visit with the prison director. They're making arrangements for a burial sometime tomorrow.'

'Bloody hell, that's a bit quick isn't it? What about his family? They might want the body taken back to New Zealand?'

Jeff raised his eyebrows. 'That's an option? I hadn't thought of it.'

'Well, you should've mate. It's what I'd want done. Not buried in this poxy shithole.'

'Can we do that from here? Send him home?'

'Only one way to find out. Let's go talk to the British office. We should report Arben's death anyway. They'll want to follow up on it.'

Jeff rose to his feet. Purposeful action of any kind would at least take him out of himself.

'Where do we go?'

'Follow me.'

❦

Dragadon Hill was only a short walk from Morgan's apartment. But the road was steep and neither Jeff nor Barry were in the mood for mountain climbing. Forced to go down a series of one-way streets, Barry ended up looping the block before driving his UN vehicle across a disused railway line and beginning the ascent.

'Dragadon Hill. Prishtina's exclusive housing area,' Barry intoned like a tour operator.

Jeff took in the identical two- and three-storey brick homes. Whatever was supposed to have made this particular group of houses exclusive escaped him.

'Not many of the NGOs and consulates have signs outside. And worse, there are no street signs. Makes it bloody impossible to find anyone. But don't worry, mate,' Barry patted Jeff on the knee. 'We'll get there. Dinkum.'

He pulled over to ask a pedestrian for directions. The stocky middle-aged fellow looked thoughtful for a second, then brightened. 'Go to the German office, sir. The British office is one hundred metres past.'

'And the German office is where?'

'Oh. That I do not know. What I hear is the German office is one hundred metres this way of the British office. Good?'

'Fucking wonderful, you useless drongo.' Barry swung back onto the road.

'I thought you knew where we were going?'

Barry grinned. 'Sort of. It's up the hill.'

'So's space, Barry. You've never been there, have you?'

'No, mate. But don't worry, I'll find it.'

Some miracle or other led them to a brick wall that surrounded the three-storey consulate building. A one-man security box sat out the front. The guard, a Kosovon Albanian, glanced up from his newspaper as Jeff and Barry approached. After a cursory glance at their passports he pushed two plastic-covered Visitor ID cards through a gap in the security window. He pressed a button and the adjacent iron gate sprang into life and ground its way sideways.

Jeff and Barry crossed a small courtyard lined with pot plants and wooden benches and stopped in front of a double set of glass doors. The doors allowed passage to only one person at a time. As Jeff stepped through, he noted the thickness of the plate windows. Undoubtedly bulletproof, but they could probably also withstand a small blast. A hand grenade came to mind.

Jeff stood back to let Barry talk to the receptionist. The elderly woman scrutinised the two passports and jotted their names into a book.

'Please take a seat, Mr Briggs, Mr Bradley. The consul, Mr Lyons, will be with you shortly.'

Barry sat. Jeff stood. He looked back through the glass doors into the courtyard. His hands ached from having been bunched into fists so much since the news of Benny's death. He wanted to break somebody's bones. A few minutes alone with the man who murdered Benny would do very well.

A young woman in a dark trouser suit appeared through a side door. 'Mr Bradley, Mr Briggs?'

Barry jumped to his feet. 'That's us.'

'Mr Lyons will see you now. Please follow me.'

Steel filing cabinets, shelves of books and piles of documents filled every square inch of Lyons's office. Papers, files and trays were stacked in an untidy mess on the desk. But Jeff, being a messy administrator himself, had little doubt the man sitting in the wing-backed burgundy leather chair could put his hand on any specific document on the instant if asked.

The fresh-faced Jeremy Lyons looked to Jeff as if he should still be in school – university, at a push. But Barry had told Jeff that Lyons was well into his thirties.

'Take a seat, gentleman.' Jeff thought the British public school accent made Lyons seem even younger. The diplomat remained standing until Jeff and Barry settled. Then he too sat down. 'Now, how I can help?'

Jeff outlined the circumstances surrounding Arben's death. The Consul jotted notes on a yellow pad. At the conclusion of Jeff's narrative, Lyons's brow lowered above baby-blue eyes.

'This is the first I've heard of it. I'll have one of my people contact the prison as soon as you leave. Of course, Mr Shala should have informed us of his arrival, just as you should have of your own, Mr Bradley. We represent all Commonwealth member countries, not just the four Home Nations. Sadly, this is an example of what can happen when rules aren't followed.'

Jeff sat back and glared at the man. 'I don't need a diplomacy lecture, Mr Lyons. Why the hell didn't anyone inform the consulate that Arben was in prison? The bloody UN runs the prison, for Christ's sake. Didn't the prison authorities have a duty to get in touch with someone who could have helped him?'

It was Lyons's turn to look taken aback. 'You're right, of course. Absolutely. I assure you there'll be a full inquiry into why it wasn't done. But for the moment let's put recriminations to one side, shall we? As for the unfortunate Mr Shala, I'm sorry but it's not possible to have the body flown back to New Zealand if this is what you're hoping for.'

'Why the hell not? I'll cover the costs.'

'It's not about costs, Mr Bradley. There are no protocols for the transference of a body out of Kosovo. And there are certainly none to allow trans-shipment through other countries. If Mr Shala had been working for the UN it would be different. But he wasn't, so our hands are tied.'

Barry extended his palms. 'You must be able to do something?'

'In a good amount of time we could. The Home Office could contact the Ministry of Foreign Affairs in New Zealand. They would speak directly to the UN head office then approach the various airlines and transit-countries that would be required to ensure Mr Shala's body made it back to New Zealand. But . . . time.' He grimaced. 'You may or may not be aware that there's a critical lack of morgue facilities here. There just isn't any provision for long-term cold storage.'

Jeff's fist looked about to thump the desk between them. He stalled the move and executed a gentle landing instead. 'Is there any way you could issue a document to at least get the body cleared from Kosovo?'

'That would need permission from the Kosovon courts. It would be difficult. And take about the same amount of time.'

The snort from Barry sounded little less than scornful. 'You must be bloody joking. You have to ask these lying, cheating bastard pricks for permission?'

Lyons appeared impervious to Barry's obscenities. Hands sat folded on top of his desk. 'Yes, I do. Look, I'm not the bad guy here. I'd help you if I could. But what you have to understand is that this office is not an embassy. We only have the powers of a consulate. We may request, we may observe, but we may demand nothing. The best I can suggest is that you have Mr Shala cremated and take his ashes back to the family.'

A stony expression settled on Jeff's face.

'He's Muslim. Cremation is out of the question.' He leaned back and stared through the window. Balancing awkwardly on the roof tiles of the house next to the British office, an old man struggled to secure what looked like an even older television antenna to a chimney. His glance returned to Lyons. 'It seems we've struck a brick wall here, Mr Lyons.'

'I'm afraid you have. I really am sorry.'

Jeff stood and offered the consul his hand. 'Mr Lyons. Thank you for your time. I shall talk to his family. I'll make sure things are done decently.'

⁂

Jeff paced the worn carpet that covered the creaking boards of his hotel room. An untouched glass of whiskey sat on the bedside table. Twice he had reached for it and twice he had decided against it. He wanted a clear head when he spoke to Kimie. He was having difficulty formulating the right words. Alcohol would be no help at all.

Finally he lowered himself onto the bed. The house phone took up residence on his thigh. He lifted the receiver and dialled the number. He counted the number of rings. At five he prepared to hang up. At six the line clicked open.

'Hello.' Marko's voice. He sounded drowsy.

'Marko, it's Jeff.'

'Jeff. Hey, man, you got any idea what time it is? It's bloody early, bro.'

'Marko. Go wake your mother. I need to talk to her.'

'She's asleep.'

Jeff bowed his head with a sigh. He didn't want to spook the kid before he got to the mother. He was too sharp for his own good when he wanted to be.

'Marko, listen to me. I know it's late. Just do as I ask. Please.'

A pause. 'Why? What's happened?' The sleep had gone from Marko's voice. 'You've found Dad? Is he okay?'

'Marko. Go get your mother.'

The order had left Jeff's throat like a military bark. A clatter assaulted his eardrum. He guessed Marko had dropped the phone onto the table. He'd be alarmed and scampering off down the hall to his mother's room. It would take a few minutes for Kimie to compose herself. She would splash water over her face and maybe run a comb through her hair. Arben had once told him of this endearing quirk of hers. That she would not answer the phone until she felt she looked presentable. The image brought a sad smile to his face.

'Hello, Jeff?' The voice sounded guarded.

'Hi, Kimie.'

'You have news? You have found Arben?'

Jeff coughed to clear the lump in his throat. 'Yes, I've found Arben.'

~

The mosque at the cemetery still bore signs of scorching above its windows, although the roof looked as if it had been recently repaired. A dozen pairs of boots tramping in file had left a muddy trail to the graveside. Concrete headstones at various degrees of precarious tilt hunched in protection over mounds of dirt and weeds. Jeff tried to read some of the epitaphs but the Albanian was gibberish to him. Patches of ice the colour of milk chocolate lodged in the shadow of rocky protrusions. Tiny white and blue flowers dotted the uncut grass, adding the only touch of colour to the otherwise bleak surroundings. A bone-chilling wind swept down from the hulking mountains to the west, blustering across the cemetery and the small group of mourners.

Of those who congregated to bid Arben a final farewell, only Jeff, Morgan, Sulla and Tomi Mema had ever met him. Kimie declined Jeff's offer to fly her and the children to Kosovo. She was not prepared to expose her family to the dangers that had taken her husband's life but was adamant the funeral not be delayed. She took comfort in knowing Arben would be reunited with his mother and father. Barry and Bethany had insisted on coming, as had Klaus Otto and Barry's South African police mates. The police contingent stood together avoiding eye contact with anybody. To Jeff they looked more embarrassed than penitent about their role in Arben Shala's death.

Pebbles slipping from the loose soil made hollow thuds on the lid of Arben's casket lying at the bottom of the pit. When informed it was Islamic custom to bury the body in nothing more than a shroud, Jeff would have none of it. He insisted on the casket. His irrationality may have been shaped by Christian values, but he could not bear to think of Arben unprotected from the cold and the wet.

Jeff stood in a fit of gloom throughout the service, Morgan beside him, her arm looped through his. The barrenness, the dampness and the darkening skies all somehow suited the mood. It was fitting the world should be this way on this of all days.

A local imam recited prayers and those present who were followers of the faith extended their hands, palms to the sky. The muddy ridge the party was standing on held many bodies from Arben's family. Casting his eyes out to the valley, Jeff thought he could discern the ancient rows of vines of the Shala family vineyard.

In a few days he would fly home. With Arben dead and the killer behind bars, there was no reason for him to remain in Kosovo. Without Arben to support the claim, any chance of regaining his property for Kimie and Marko was lost. Anyway, he was certain Kimie wouldn't be at all concerned. Kosovo represented nothing but grief for her and her family. Why would she want to retain possession of any part of it?

When the ceremony was over, Jeff asked the others to give him a few minutes alone. The memory of Arben proudly holding up their first bottle of wine made him smile. Then choke with the effort not to weep. He bent and picked up a handful of dirt, rubbing it into his hands, bonding with nature as Arben had taught him. He stretched out his arm and let the dirt fall through his fingers onto the casket.

'Goodbye, Benny.'

28.

offee for you?' Jeff's brain had been miles away. He looked up. Too quickly. 'Ow. Shit.' His hand shot to the side of his skull. Jeff realised too late that the state of his head precluded any sudden movement. 'Yes, coffee. Keep it coming, will you? Breakfast too, please. Bacon and beans and whatever. Okay?'

A nod from the waiter. He poured coffee into the cup on his tray and placed it next to the *Guardian* lying beneath Jeff's hand. The days-old English newspaper had been the only one available in the hotel bookshop. Before unfolding it, Jeff checked the sky. The gloominess of the previous day had departed. If the same clear winter sky he saw now had been around the previous afternoon, maybe his spirits would have revived enough to stop him from drinking his miserable hide into near oblivion.

Jeff drew a deep breath. His decision to sit at one of the Kukri bar's outside tables had been in the hope that the bracing outdoors would help ease the ache in his head. Maybe it had to some small degree.

He opened the newspaper and scanned the headlines. 'Mr Bradley. Mind if I join you?'

A neutral accent. American? This time Jeff looked up with care. Smiling at him was a nondescript, slightly built man in a charcoal-grey suit. Someone's accountant?

'Do we know each other?'

'My name is Lee Caldwell.'

With a tinge of reluctance Jeff gathered in his newspaper and took a quick grip of the offered hand. Without further invitation the man sat and swung his legs over the fixed bench flanking the far side of the wooden table. Something impressed Jeff about the athletic ease of his movements. Despite appearances, this guy was not a desk worker.

'Well, Mr Caldwell. You already seem to know me. So, how can I help you?'

'May I ask what an ex-New Zealand Special Forces officer is doing in Kosovo?'

Jeff stiffened.

'And why would that be any concern of yours?'

'It'll be no news to you that the region from here through to Moscow is, shall we say . . . unstable? Retired Special Forces soldiers are a prime commodity for anyone looking to hire mercenary soldiers.'

Jeff came close to throwing back his head for a laugh, but in deference to its certain painful consequences he stifled the urge. 'You've gotta be kidding. Who the hell are you? CIA?'

Caldwell shrugged. 'Would that surprise you?'

Jeff frowned. 'No, in fact I've spent enough time with you guys to recognise the cut of the cloth. And if you've had me checked out, then you already know I'm not a mercenary. Not interested in becoming one, either. Happy now? If there's nothing else on your mind, I'd like to finish my coffee in peace.'

Jeff's unsubtle attempt at dismissal looked like going nowhere. Caldwell's eyes maintained hold of Jeff's in a way he hadn't experienced in a long time. That time it'd been a hardened Mujahadeen who, at first sign of a falter, would have blown his head off with the

AK-47 pushed up under his jaw. Caldwell looked a lot less scary, but he appeared to possess equal single-mindedness.

The American leaned closer. 'Do you mind telling me what your interest is in Arben Shala?'

Jeff held Caldwell's stare for a long moment. 'Okay. That much is no big mystery.' Jeff paced his words. 'I own a vineyard in New Zealand. Arben was my manager. He came to Kosovo to claim family land and find me some bulk wine. He disappeared. I came to Kosovo to find him. End of story.'

The nod from Caldwell told Jeff he'd told him nothing he didn't already know. 'And did you find him?'

'Yes. In the Prishtina Detention Centre.'

'And now you've found him, what do you plan to do?'

'I don't plan to do anything. I buried him yesterday.'

Caldwell's eyes widened.

Jeff's face creased into a grin. 'You Yanks are not as slick as you think you are, eh? You need to pay your informants better.'

Again Caldwell presented impassivity. 'Hard to find good help these days. So, what now for you?'

'Not that it's any of your business, but the police already have the person who killed my friend. I'm not looking for revenge or to make trouble, if that's your concern. Today I'm booking a ticket home.'

Caldwell's legs swung out from under the table with the same athletic ease Jeff had observed before. 'Then I wish you a pleasant journey. Goodbye, Mr Bradley.'

'Hold on. Not so fast. I think you owe me something.'

A frown fell across Caldwell's face. 'Owe you something? What might that be then?'

'An explanation. About what your interest was in Arben Shala?'

'If he's dead, I no longer have any interest.'

Jeff bounded out from the table and blocked Caldwell's path. 'Wrong answer. You just breeze in knowing more about me than you should. Ask a bunch of questions that are none of your business. And think you can breeze out again and that's it? Well, my friend, let me tell you something you don't know: if you know anything about Arben, like why the fuck he ended up in prison in the first place, then you're not leaving before you tell me what it is.'

Caldwell didn't exactly gape at Jeff but he came close to it. His hands lifted skywards in mock defeat and he sat down again. Jeff returned to his own seat. His head was now throbbing like a drum. He rubbed his forehead and glared at the cause of this renewed agony. Caldwell ran a finger inside his shirt collar and adjusted his tie.

'Since you insist, Mr Bradley, I work for US Trade.'

Jeff snorted. 'Tell that to the Marines. They might even care.'

'It's my job to assess market potential on behalf of US businessmen. There aren't many foreign investors in Kosovo, certainly no Americans. Some Americans do have sense enough to seek the advice of their trade department before they wander into far-off lands looking for deals. If, for example, Mr Shala had been American and if he'd approached me for advice, I could have told him that an organised criminal group were swindling him out of his land.'

Jeff sipped his coffee. It had gone cold. The cup went back onto the table.

'I might also have been able to warn Mr Shala that the gang behind these scams is dangerous, and he should never have come to Kosovo in the first place. Unfortunately, Mr Shala was not an American.'

'So why do you care about an ex-Kosovon getting ripped off?'

Caldwell swung out from the table once again and stood up. He fished a business card from his pocket and dropped it onto the table. 'I'm staying at the Holiday Inn in Skopje. That's just across the border in Macedonia.'

'I know where Skopje is.'

'If you have any difficulties leaving the country, contact me.'

Jeff's eyes narrowed. 'And why would I have any difficulty leaving the country?'

'It happens. Have a safe trip home, Mr Bradley.'

Caldwell turned. After a few strides he had disappeared into the pedestrian traffic. Jeff salvaged the business card. His forefinger stroked along the top edge. 'Now what the hell was that all about?' he muttered.

29.

ill your friend be wanting coffee?'

A tray bearing Jeff's breakfast order was in the process of descending onto the table. 'Friend? Oh. No. Not him. Just fill mine, thanks.'

What kind of magic had that man Caldwell worked on him? Jeff realised his earlier seediness had departed and left him with quite an appetite. He pulled the plate of beans and eggs and bacon towards him and breathed deep of the savoury aromas. Knife and fork attacked the pile.

As Jeff's head was about to come up from his final mouthful, a manila A4 envelope dropped onto the table. 'As promised, a copy of everything that was on Arben's file.'

Jeff looked up to encounter the green of a woodland lake in the eyes of Morgan Delaney. A red, manicured fingernail jabbed at the envelope.

'If Arben's family change their mind and want to reopen the process, they can contact me.' She gave Jeff a quick once-over. 'You look like shit. Did you sleep at all?'

'Some.'

'You shouldn't drink so much.'

Jeff couldn't help but notice the edge in her voice. 'I don't think my head would argue with you.' He tried a boyish smile, but

Morgan showed no signs of taking that particular bait. 'Um. I'm sorry.'

'Mm? About what, Jeff?'

No suitable answer presented itself. He could tell her that at the end of operations soldiers routinely used booze to calm emotions, bond with comrades. But the military was long gone from his life. Maybe he could venture the time-tried tear-jerker that he'd failed his best friend? The maudlin aspects of that option he didn't favour. Of course, there was always the brutal truth that he just got drunk because he bloody well felt like it and it was none of her business. Jeff's better self warned him clear of that one. The male default line it would have to be: eye contact and eyebrows forming an inverted V above nose.

'I dunno. Being a bad boy?'

From the reaction in Morgan's face, cute didn't look like it was ever destined to make the cut. 'Really, Jeff? Well, there's the folder. I wish you a safe journey home and all the best for the future.'

But she didn't leave. Just averted her eyes. A couple with a toddler in a pushchair ambled past. The toddler waved. Morgan waved back.

'Morgan, if you've got something on your mind, spit it out.'

When Morgan turned back the morning sun brought a glow to her face that highlighted her freckles. He hadn't really noticed them before. Now that he had, he thought they added a special touch to her beauty. Like the final dabs on an oil painting.

'I'm not a prude. I just don't like drunks. I saw enough of them in the family pub.'

'I'm not a drunk.'

Jeff's voice had been quiet. Morgan undid the button on her jacket sleeve, then looked up and caught his eye still on her. 'It's not really about that, anyway. I had this crazy idea that you might turn to me. You know? Last night after all that . . . yesterday? But beer and brandy won out. Anyway, what does it matter? You're leaving in a few days. I take it you've booked your flight?'

'I was about to this morning. But I think I might be hanging around a little longer.'

'Oh?'

Morgan placed her bag on the seat opposite Jeff and sat alongside it. Her eyes never left his face. Jeff pushed across Caldwell's business card.

'You recognise this name?'

She squinted at the black on white lettering.

'Mm. No. Not at all. Why?'

Jeff related the details of his meeting with Lee Caldwell. 'Caldwell said the scam that Arben was caught up in was run by an organised gang, which pretty much backs up your theory. What I'm not getting is that even if Arben was being swindled, and let's face it we know that he was, what does that have to do with this guy? Caldwell isn't police. If he's who I think he is, then international espionage is his domain, not chasing a bunch of third-world scam artists.'

By her look of concentration, Jeff could tell the cogs of Morgan's brain had begun to whir. 'Okay, Jeff. Accepting that, where does it lead you?'

'It leads me to believe that whatever trouble Arben was in, it likely had more to do with Caldwell's field of interest than any dispute over the ownership of a vineyard.'

'Which leaves one big question, doesn't it?'

'It does. What's that field of interest? I'm beginning to badly want to know the answer to that. Does that make me crazy or something?'

'I'll reserve my answer to that. Isn't this your driver coming?'

Jeff's head swivelled to see Sulla walk into the courtyard. He signalled the waitress for a coffee then sat on the bench next to Jeff. Sulla's attention centred on Morgan. 'Ms Delaney. Hullo.'

For a split second Jeff suspected Morgan might storm off and leave him to it. With gratitude he noted instead that Sulla had become the recipient of a smile. A smile that may have bordered more on the long-suffering than the affable, but Jeff took it as a good sign.

'Hullo, Sulla.' Morgan directed her attention back at Jeff. 'Why don't you tell Sulla what you've just told me?'

Jeff puzzled at Morgan's solicitous attitude on behalf of Sulla. Then, for once in his life, the machinations of the feminine mind became clear to him. Morgan had one over Sulla by virtue of what Jeff had just told her regarding Caldwell. By guiding Jeff to impart that knowledge to the man she'd hitherto viewed as instrumental in excluding her from Jeff's affairs, the score had evened: fifteen–all. And Morgan held serve. Jeff breathed a prayer of thanks. A concord between these two might not be a bad thing if he intended staying around.

After hearing the details of Jeff's meeting with Caldwell, Sulla rotated his neck. 'I am stiff. Too much sitting in cars. But I too have been thinking there is something else going on.'

'You have? How's that?'

'Nobody just dies in a Kosovon prison. Not the way Arben did. It makes no sense.'

'This is Kosovo.'

Sulla grimaced. 'Yes. Maybe it did happen the way they said. But Arben was not a violent criminal or a drug addict. And he had only been in Kosovo a few weeks, not long enough to make enemies. And now this American appears.' Sulla tapped Caldwell's business card lying on the table. 'Maybe CIA. And this man tells you he has been watching Arben. Why? Because someone is stealing his vineyard?' Sulla shook his head. 'I do not believe this. It must be about something a lot bigger.'

Jeff noticed the look of intrigue on Morgan's face. 'Sulla has something there, Jeff. Our records show there are hundreds of properties in dispute. Put them all together and the value runs into millions.'

'For millions of dollars I myself would kill the entire population of Kosovo,' Sulla said with a grumble of a laugh. 'But it does not make sense to kill Arben. He is the duck who lays an egg of gold. No?'

A sparkle of amusement in Morgan's eye. 'Goose, Sulla. And it's a she-goose too. Men aren't that damn useful. But I agree.'

Thirty–fifteen, Jeff thought. Morgan was clearly de-icing as far as Sulla was concerned.

'Duck, goose, whatever. Arben's murder might have happened this way if he was in a big prison like Dubrave. But in the detention centre so closely monitored by the UN? No. I think it more likely someone ordered him killed.'

Jeff's eyes widened and turned to Morgan.

Two slow nods, her hair now burning like a flame in the morning sun.

'It adds up, Jeff.'

'Okay. Then why? Arben would be useless dead to anyone who still wanted his land despite the Xhihas' phony papers. Why kill him?'

Sulla's fingernail scratched at a coffee ring on the table. 'I hate to say what I am thinking.'

Jeff shot a sharp look at him. 'What? Come on Sulla. Say it.'

'He was your friend, Jeff. It's not good for me to think this.'

'For Christ's sake, Sulla. If you don't tell me, I'll wring that thick Albanian neck of yours.'

Eyes of surprise met Jeff's. 'All right. I think Arben was killed because of you.'

Jeff recoiled. 'Fuck off.'

'Please listen. His arrest over the mobile phone was rubbish. It would never have held up in court. Yet he was kept first in jail. That part I can understand. Someone with power uses the law as leverage to convince him to stop contesting ownership of the vineyard. Then he is released. Maybe whoever is behind this wanted Arben to make an extra payment and his release was so he could arrange the money. I only say this because the documents could have been signed over in the jail. Anyway, when he is released, what does Arben do? He phones you, Jeff, and then he tries to run. The police grab him near the border. Not the border guards. The police. I can only think this was because there are internationals at the border control and the police who took him did not want them asking awkward questions.'

'Corrupt cops?'

'Yes, Jeff. Has to be so.'

'But what does any of that have to do with me? Personally?'

'Whoever is behind this scam did not expect anyone would come looking for Arben. Certainly not anyone from New Zealand. I think that maybe they thought if they squeezed Arben a little harder, scared him more, eventually he would do what they wanted. Then they would let him go. There was no reason to kill him. He can do nothing to defy them. Killing him would only make unnecessary trouble, maybe enough to get the UN police involved. No, they would take his land, take his money, he would go back to New Zealand and that would be the end of it. Then you show up looking for him, asking many questions. Already you have involved the international police. They found him for you. And the night before you are to see him, he is killed.' Sulla shrugged. 'It is too convenient to be coincidence.'

Jeff's frown lines had become ploughed furrows. His eyes remained locked with Sulla's. 'Are you telling me someone murdered Arben because of something he might have told me?'

A nod of affirmation.

The sudden reluctance of his lungs to replenish his air supply had Jeff gripping the edge of the table. The breathlessness departed as rapidly as it had come. But not the guilt.

Morgan's head tilted in query. 'You okay, Jeff?'

'It's okay. I'm just . . . I'm shocked, that's all.'

The words appeared to satisfy Morgan, but her gaze remained on Jeff nonetheless. 'Well. Sulla's just put a theory out there for us to consider. Suggestions of blame or culpability have no place in it. What should interest us more is how it explains the role of this American. Caldwell.'

An exhalation whistled from Sulla's nostrils. 'It is obvious Caldwell did not tell Jeff what is going on because if he is CIA then whatever it is will have international connections. Very serious stuff. And serious enough to get Arben killed. It can be the only reason.'

Jeff found a new focus in the fuzzy lenses he'd been operating with. If Benny's death had been premeditated, a conspiracy, there were culprits out there. That meant he had a mission.

'Then, my friends, I intend to discover two things. What is it that Caldwell knows? And what information was so important that the life of a good man had to be sacrificed to ensure I never got it?' Jeff eyed Sulla. 'Will you drive me to Skopje?'

Something close to a look of indignation crossed Morgan's face. 'Us, Jeff. Will Sulla take us? I'm as involved in wanting to get to the bottom of all this as you are. If this Caldwell has answers about land disputes on a wider scale than has appeared to be the case so far, then it's my job to know what they are.'

Sulla looked to Jeff for some kind of guidance. Jeff resisted the urge to roll his eyes. But his hands did rise in surrender. 'Okay then. Us it is.'

'Very well. I shall drive you both. Let us pay your American agent a visit. Meet me in front of the hotel tomorrow morning at ten thirty. Bring money. Euros.'

30.

At midday the following day Sulla turned off the highway just before the Telecom building and circled Skopje's central business district. They came in behind a shopping mall. The Holiday Inn looked to be more or less annexed onto the end of the complex overlooking the Vardar River. However, the entrance lobby where they had arranged to meet with Caldwell faced away to the city.

It was Caldwell who first spotted Jeff. He approached with hand extended. 'I've been expecting you.'

'Really?' Jeff responded with feigned surprise. 'Meet two friends of mine. Morgan Delaney, a countrywoman of yours, and Sulla Bogdani.'

Caldwell pointed towards the river. 'The Irish pub isn't far. They make good coffee, and the lunch menu is edible. We can talk there.'

He guided them around the sidewalk to the riverside boulevard. An outside table bathed in sun took his fancy. He indicated the group should sit there and signalled for coffees.

Tables in front of the cafes running the entire length of the boulevard were fully occupied, as were the wooden benches dotted along the riverbank. A few hundred metres away a solid stone bridge spanned the river. Caldwell pointed to it. 'It's called the Stony Bridge. Apt, don't you think? Across there is old Skopje.

Tourists flock to the place. And that crumbling mass on the hill is called Kale Fortress.'

Jeff had a fascination for ancient structures, especially forts. He felt a twinge of regret that the timing was all wrong for a closer look.

Caldwell sat back and surveyed his little party. 'Now. How can I help you people?'

'Well, as much as I appreciate the travelogue I haven't come to sightsee. I've come for answers. My friend Sulla here is of the opinion that Arben Shala wasn't killed in some insignificant prison brawl. He's convinced me that someone wanted him dead. And I have a pretty good suspicion you know who. And why.'

'I see.'

'And I'm a little pissed that you made it your business to know where Arben was, knew he was innocent, yet didn't lift a finger to help him.'

Without expression, Caldwell met Jeff's stare for a long moment. Then he nodded. 'Okay. I admit he was being watched, but I really didn't think he was in any particular danger. He should have been about as safe in the detention centre as he would have been in his hotel. His death took me by surprise as much as it did you.'

Nothing in Caldwell's face told Jeff whether he should believe Caldwell or not.

Jeff leaned back in his chair. 'But it still puzzles me why he wasn't out on bail. His lawyer is supposedly one of Kosovo's best. Someone of that ilk should have had little trouble arranging something so simple.'

'That's easy. Arben hired Mema to check over his property, then disappeared. Until I hired him, Mema had no idea Arben was in prison and he couldn't have done anything about it anyway until after the weekend. By then it was too late.'

The smile on Caldwell's face struck Jeff as something closer to a smirk. 'Really, Mr Bradley? My information has Tomi Mema visiting with Mr Shala on any number of occasions while he was in jail. And he was most certainly with him at all his court appearances. He knew exactly where his client was.'

A slap in the face could not have shaken Jeff more. He exchanged glances with the wide eyes of Morgan then turned on Caldwell. 'Bullshit. That's not what Mema told me.'

'Well, one of us is lying. Your call. No pressure.'

Jeff looked away and grasped the handle of his coffee cup. But his hand flexed so hard he feared he might break it. He heard an intake of breath from Morgan as if she was about to say something. But Sulla dropped a hand onto hers with a brief shake of the head. The two of them remained silent watching Jeff.

'Right now, Caldwell, I'm really pissed off. And I'm very sick of being jerked around. So. If you're not lying to me, why don't you stop playing fucking games and tell me why any of this is of interest to you?'

Caldwell leaned forward. 'I've been following a terrorist money trail. That's what brings me to Kosovo. It led me to the name of a local hood. This man's into prostitution, smuggling cigarettes, gambling, even dogfights. But he just didn't come across as having the capabilities to mastermind a terrorist network. But he was the only lead I had. That's when Ms Delaney came to our attention.'

Morgan's mouth dropped open. 'What on earth am I supposed to have done?'

'Don't worry, Ms Delaney. You're not under investigation. If anything at all, I owe you a vote of thanks.'

'And how's that, for God's sake?'

'An alert court-clerk noted your USAID report on the property disputes and your suspicions that an organised crime ring might be behind it. It was referred to various departments and eventually filtered down to me. We followed our suspect to a vineyard owned by two brothers where he picked up several cases of wine. Ordinarily that wouldn't have raised any flags at all. But after I'd read your report, I had one of my men talk to the farm manager. He told us about the dispute with Mr Shala. By the time we'd tracked down Shala, he was already up to his neck in a world of shit. But I saw in him the latest scam victim.'

Jeff couldn't stop himself from pointing an accusing finger at Caldwell. 'And you just left him there, dangling, like bait?'

'Mr Bradley. Please. You should be familiar enough with my line of work to know it's sometimes necessary to risk losing a minnow to catch a shark.' Caldwell's eyes flashed at Sulla in a way that Jeff thought unfriendly, if not outright hostile. 'That shark turned out to be a small-time hood called Osman Gashi. But he wasn't the end of the trail. His nickel-and-dime operations couldn't produce the huge amounts of dirty money flowing in and out of Kosovo like it's the frigging Danube. It was evident that Gashi was moving money for someone else. We were hoping either he or someone connected to Shala might lead us to whoever that someone else is.'

Caldwell's eyes remained fixed on Sulla. Again Jeff noticed the underlying hostility in the look. What the hell was that all about?

'I know this man Gashi,' Sulla said. 'He is very bad. Not so small time.' His face turned with a hard look to Caldwell as if the American had offered him an insult. 'Gashi runs a big gang. Like the Mafia from Italy. If this man is involved then he could have ordered the killing of Arben.'

Caldwell shrugged. 'Have that as you like. The only connection we got from having Shala under surveillance was Mema.'

Jeff's eyebrows rose. 'Tomi Mema's involved in the scam?'

'I can't say for certain. But it's likely.'

Jeff's fingers drummed the table top while he thought. 'Okay then. I know enough about your line of work to know you never suspected me of being a mercenary for hire. So why did you really come to see me in Prishtina?'

'Simple enough. Mr Shala was attracting all sorts of attention out of proportion to a small-time scam. First, there was Gashi. Then you show up looking for Shala. Asking a lot of questions. Making waves. Barging into offices, bothering people who don't like being bothered. I certainly didn't need some ignorant businessman screwing up my operations. So I checked you out and discovered you were not the bumbling wine salesman you pretended to be but a former Special Forces man. Then you take more than a casual interest in a property with ties to a criminal gang. As strange as it might seem, Mr Bradley, even New Zealand harbours its share of criminals, mercenaries and terrorists.'

Jeff snorted. 'What? First you accuse me of being a mercenary. Now I'm a terrorist?'

'Look. You can't blame me for wondering, especially considering the company you keep.'

'The company I keep? What the bloody hell is that supposed to mean?'

Caldwell pulled a file from his briefcase and placed it on the table. Jeff's eyes lit up with shock when he read the name scrawled across the top in bold black letters.

So did Sulla's. 'Why do you have a file on me?'

Caldwell flipped open the folder, turned it with both hands and pushed it across the table towards Sulla. 'Why indeed. Tell me about these explosives, Mr Bogdani. Explosives used in a bombing in Belgium and in Slovenia. You may not be a bomber, but you've supplied one. I'd be interested in knowing where you got this stuff and who you sold it to.'

Jeff saw alarm in the eyes Morgan directed at him. His own alarm was not lessened at the sight of colour draining from Sulla's face.

Sulla turned to Jeff, whites of eyes stark beneath dark brows. 'This is bullshit.'

Caldwell extended a hand to land a sharp rap on the table in front of Jeff. 'I see you didn't realise you were associating with a man with ties to KLA terrorists? The Kosovo Liberation Army, I could accept. After all, they were just freedom fighters. Kosovon Albanians fighting the Serbs to found an independent Kosovo. But that's not what happened here, is it?'

Jeff's head snapped in Sulla's direction. 'Is this true, Sulla? Is it

'I have done nothing wrong. You must believe me.'

'He wouldn't tell you himself, Mr Bradley. So I will. Your Mr Bogdani spent two years in prison.'

The look on Sulla's face showed Jeff a mixture of indignation and rage.

'It is not true. Not . . .'

'Not true? You didn't spend two years in prison for possession of explosives?'

'Yes. I was in prison, Jeff. But it is not how this man is saying. I am no terrorist.' Sulla pointed a shaking finger at Caldwell. 'The explosives I had were old, left behind by the Serbs and turned over to NATO. The CIA knows this. I was never charged with terrorism.'

Caldwell nodded as if he were seriously considering this information. 'I do, Mr Bogdani. There's just one problem with that, isn't there? The explosives handed into NATO were not old. They hadn't been underground for years, and they were certainly not of a type used by the Serbian Forces.'

Sulla's hand dropped back to the table. He sat back and stared at Caldwell. 'This cannot be true. There must be some mistake. I am not lying. The explosives were from an abandoned Serbian stockpile. I have never sold them to anyone. On my honour, I am innocent of that. I swear it.'

Caldwell's head wagged from side to side. 'If I had a dime for every criminal that ever said that to a cop I'd be a rich man. It's all on tape, Bogdani. A BBC docu-drama made in Kosovo had footage that clearly showed an ex-KLA operative, namely you' – Caldwell jabbed a finger in Sulla's direction – 'supplying explosives to someone in the film crew posing as a buyer. The handover of those explosives to NATO was also on film. NATO tested those explosives before destroying them.' He reached to the file and held up a sheet of paper. 'This is a copy of the analysis.' The paper went into Sulla's hands. Caldwell spread some time-stamped video stills across the table. Again he pointed. 'Do you deny this is you?'

Sulla shuffled through the photos. Colour now burned on his cheeks. He looked up at Caldwell.

'It is me. But I am not KLA. I was only acting. Playing a role. The film crew couldn't find a real supplier so I did what the film crew asked me to do and pretended to be one. They promised the film was just for the UK. I wasn't to know they lied about that. So I used the old Serbian explosives I'd found after the war. They were just props. It was make-believe.'

Caldwell stabbed his finger at the analysis sheet. 'Mr Bogdani. All explosives have their own chemical characteristics and reflect the environment where they were made. You would know this, Bradley. Right?'

Jeff looked at Sulla who was now head down, studying the documents from beneath furrowed brows. 'Yes.'

'Then you'll also know there's an easily measurable deterioration process in explosives. These particular explosives showed minimum ageing and they were not Serbian. They were from a batch coincidentally used to blow up a Belgian department store that killed an American ambassador and his family. The same explosives killed eighty-three innocent people in Slovenia. Children. Blown apart. Would you like to see those photographs?'

Jeff noticed Morgan wince and look away to the river.

Sulla wasn't listening. His eyes were studying the explosives analysis before him. A finger pounced at a place on the document.

'Look here. The explosives did not go directly to NATO. It was fifteen days later. Fifteen days.'

Caldwell barely gave the paper a glance. 'That makes no difference. The chain of evidence is clear and documented. The film crew still handed in the explosives that you gave them. Explosives that exactly match the explosives used in the two European bombings.'

Sulla shook his head. 'There is something wrong with your chain of evidence.' He levelled a look at the three sets of eyes on him. 'I can prove it.'

Caldwell had the grace to look surprised. 'Prove it? How?'

'I only gave the film crew enough explosive to look good. I still have all the rest.'

'You kept the stuff? Why on earth would you do that?'

Sulla grimaced like a schoolboy caught with his hand in the cookie jar. 'Albanians do not waste. My neighbour, he had many old trees that had been burned on his land in the war. It is easier to blow up a big stump with explosives than dig it out by shovel.'

Jeff noticed Caldwell's jaw drop. It closed as quickly. The first sign of an honest emotion Jeff had observed in the man.

'There's no mention of that from you in the court transcript.'

'No one ever asked me.'

Caldwell's head tilted to one side. 'I'd have expected your lawyer to make sure somebody did.'

'My lawyer was not so good. He had little interest in my defence. On the first day of the trial he told me he had spoken with the prosecutor about a plea bargain. Because of the time I had already spent in prison, if I pleaded guilty to possession I would be free that day. So I agreed. Three times the Austrian judge asked me if I understood what I was pleading guilty to, and three times my lawyer instructed me to say yes. The judge found me guilty, and sentenced me to five years.'

'Jesus, Sulla. This just goes from bad to worse,' Jeff said.

'This was the lawyer who cheated my father out of our house when the Serbs were slaughtering Albanian Kosovons and stealing all our land in 1998. He is a greedy man. He strong-armed us out of the house for a quarter of its worth and came back after the NATO bombings and demanded a broker's fee. He said he was never paid. Anyway, he said he would defend me for free.'

'Goodness, Bogdani. And this didn't raise your suspicions?' Caldwell asked.

'Of course. But I had gained a reputation as KLA. And an arms dealer. A terrorist. There was a two-page story on me in the *Sunday Times*. My lawyer explained that such a high-profile case would help his law practice. He needed the publicity, and in return I would receive the services of a top-class lawyer. It sounded reasonable to me. More proof I am a stupid man.' Sulla smiled, but it faded quickly. 'So I went off to prison and my father found me a new lawyer. She argued that I had been poorly represented. The police had never actually found me in possession of the explosives, they had only been seen on the film and these had been given to NATO by the British film crew. The new judge agreed and they let me go. The rest you know.'

Sulla's attention dropped back to the photos fanned out on the table. Caldwell studied him for a second. 'The fact still remains, Bogdani. You handed over real explosives to the film crew. The same explosives that did a lot of killing of innocent people.'

Suddenly Sulla tensed. 'See here.' He pushed two photos in front of Caldwell. 'Look closely. The packs I am giving to the journalists? The tops are slightly blackened. But on these photos at the NATO handover, they are not.'

Caldwell squinted at where Sulla was indicating. 'That could just be shadow.' He held the photo to the light. 'But leaving that aside for the minute, where is the rest of the stuff?'

'I have it safely hidden. But I can retrieve it easily enough.'

Caldwell put the photo on top of the rest and returned them to the folder. 'How long would this take?'

'I can have it tomorrow.'

A card appeared out of Caldwell's pocket and went across the table to Sulla.

'Very well. Let me know when you do. I'm after real terrorists, not would-be actors. You can ring me on my mobile. If you ever plan on having a normal life again I suggest you utilise this opportunity to prove your innocence.'

Caldwell sat back and directed a steady look at Jeff. 'There you have it, Bradley. The answer you came here for. Now I'd appreciate it if you would just go home and leave the rest to me. You have my contact details. I promise I'll keep you informed.'

The glare Jeff threw at Caldwell said that he was not given to quietly disappearing on demand. 'Screw you, Caldwell. I'm not leaving. I'm going after the bastards who killed Arben. With or without your help.'

Caldwell smiled. He didn't give the impression of a man easily offended. 'Mm. Once SAS, always SAS? That it?'

'Something like that.'

'I appreciate a noble sentiment as much as the next man. But you're a civilian now. You make wine. I'm sure it's very good wine, but you've been out of the game too long. It shows. And might I say you've caused enough trouble? Why not just leave the intelligence work to people paid to do it? Does that not sound like reasonable advice?'

The amiable insult had Jeff gritting his teeth. But there was no way he wanted Caldwell to see it had affected him. With a half-smile at Jeff, Caldwell shoved Sulla's file back in his briefcase and stood to leave. He picked up the bill the waiter had dropped onto the table for their coffees.

'Now if you'll all excuse me. Ms Delaney, nice to meet you. Goodbye for now, Mr Bogdani. Mr Bradley, have a safe journey home, won't you?'

'Thank you,' Jeff said. 'When I do go home I can assure you I will.'

Jeff watched Caldwell's departing back. But some instinct attracted him to four solid figures in suits that rose from a table some distance away and sauntered in the direction Caldwell had taken. Had it been the heavy shoulders? The athleticism in otherwise relaxed gaits? His eyes homed in on bulges beneath the armpits that would have gone unnoticed to any casual observer. Jeff realised he was taking a grim satisfaction in proving himself not quite as rusty as Caldwell had implied.

And one thing he knew about the CIA's methods. Had Sulla's answers not satisfied Caldwell, even just for the present, all three of them might now be handcuffed with bags over their heads and on their way to a covert American detention facility.

He adjusted his sights on Sulla. 'Any more surprises in the offing?'

Sulla's head shook.

'No Jeff. *Inshallah.*'

31.

Sulla parked down a side street a hundred metres from Tomi Mema's office. Jeff's head twisted to give him a view of the passenger in the back. 'You ready, Morgan?'

'Never readier. Let's go see what the little shit has to say for himself.'

'Hey. Tread carefully there. A feisty in-your-face Yank grabbing him by the family jewels is not what's needed at the moment. We need to scare him, not beat him to death. Not until we know for certain he was complicit in Arben's murder.'

'I didn't club Sulla over the head, did I? And God knows he deserved it.'

Sulla's head shot around to see the look on Morgan's face. Jeff laughed at his expression of shock. Sulla's English may have been excellent, but maybe not his grasp of Yank irony. Jeff's hand extended to pat his shoulder.

'The lady's all bark, Sulla. Now here's the plan. I want you to stay here. Morgan and I won't raise Mema's defences half as much as your hulking great mass of black leather will. We need him relaxed. We won't be that long. Okay?'

'I understand. I will wait.'

Despite the sudden appearance of Jeff and Morgan at his office door, Tomi Mema managed to turn on his polished smile. As he emerged from behind the desk, the hand of the practised professional extended first to Morgan, then to Jeff.

'Mr Bradley. Ms Delaney. So nice to see you both. Please take a seat.' A hand waved to the chairs opposite the desk. He resumed his own. 'Mr Bradley, I thought you might have left Kosovo by now.'

'Not yet. The Shala family has asked me to stay and see if there's any possibility of reclaiming their property. They don't want Arben's death to have been for nothing. How could I say no?'

To Jeff's satisfaction the smile on Mema's face took on a mask-like quality. 'Er . . . I see. And how can I be of service?'

'I want to hire you to dispute the Xhiha brothers' claim. Everyone I've talked to tells me you're the best there is.'

The hook was baited. But Jeff thought the look Mema threw at Morgan held a hint of reticence.

'Of course, anything you need. But we will need to discuss my fee first. And there will be other costs.'

'Money's no object.' Jeff mentally cringed at his use of a Wall Street financier's cliché. But part of his strategy relied on Mema being convinced that he represented rich pickings. 'Name your price. I'll have the money transferred.'

The mention of money appeared to banish any reservations the lawyer may have had for the reasons for Jeff and Morgan's visit. Mema retrieved a sheet of paper from his desk drawer.

'Very well, I'll itemise an estimate for you now.'

Jeff and Morgan watched as he fell to jotting down figures across the page.

'Oh. There is something else, Mema.'

Mema's head lifted. 'Yes?'

'Strange one, this.' Jeff assumed a pose he hoped resembled a look of mild curiosity. 'I've heard you met with Arben a number of times in prison and knew he was there all along.'

A rasp from a quick intake of breath. Jeff had seen wounded soldiers, pale from shock, but none had looked as bad as Mema did right then. A shaky pen found its way back onto the desktop. The lawyer cleared his throat.

'Oh no . . . Mr Bradley. You must be misinformed. I am in the prison all the time. It would be easy enough for someone to jump to the wrong conclusions.'

Wide eyes stayed fixed on Jeff's as a hand wended its way uncertainly for the water bottle on the side of his desk before knocking it over and sending it tumbling to the floor.

'Now, I think we both know that's not true, don't we?' Jeff spoke softly. His tone could even have been mistaken for pleasant. 'I'm not a great fan of people who lie to me.'

Beads of perspiration had broken out on Mema's death-mask of a face. Jeff stood and leaned on the desk, his face inches from Mema's. His voice remained even.

'Whatever games you were playing cost my friend his life.' A gasp from Mema as Jeff's finger lodged hard against his chest. 'So here's the deal. You go get these documents for Arben's vineyard signed off by the court. Don't think for a second of trying any of your dirty tricks on me, you little shit of an arsehole. Or it'll cost you your life. Do you hear what I'm saying?'

Mema appeared incapable of moving, let alone breathing. Jeff pulled away and sat down again with folded arms. He exchanged a glance with Morgan. Her mouth had tightened into a grim smile of satisfaction. She nodded. Jeff focused back on Mema. He looked to be shrinking into his chair.

'You do understand what I've just said to you, Mema?'

Mema's silence and continuing slack-mouthed expression of shock began to dent Jeff's resolve to play it cool with the man. The tightening in his throat warned him his anger was on the rise.

In one move Jeff leaned forward with two fingers poking at Mema's eyes. 'Do you fucking understand me?'

Mema jumped. A frantic nodding of the head ensued.

Jeff's hand dropped. He surveyed the shaking man for a second.

'Good. Good, Tomi.' Jeff stood and gestured to Morgan to do the same. He looked back at Mema. 'Get it done. I'll be back.'

෬෨

Jeff and Sulla proceeded to the Kukri bar without Morgan. She had pleaded the need for a hot shower and an early night.

Barry bought a round of drinks and listened with rapt interest as Jeff described first the meeting in Macedonia with Caldwell, then the encounter with Tomi Mema.

'Bloody hell, mate. Nothing that exciting ever happens to me. Not ever. This is my life. The Kukri, the same people, the same beer and the same sports on the telly. I might as well be back in Sydney watching the Waratahs lose another rugby match. So what happens now?'

'Sulla is going to Peje tomorrow to see his father and get the explosives.'

'And this doesn't worry you, Sulla?' said Barry.

'Is there a problem?' asked Jeff.

'Bloody oath there is,' Barry said. 'You wouldn't know, Jeff, but the whole area is controlled by ex-KLA guys. Mostly they're into smuggling. Back and forth across the mountains into Albania. Other shit as well. From what you guys have just said, Sulla is not exactly one of their favourite sons. If they spot him he might end up with his silly bloody head shot off.'

'I must take that risk to clear my name. If the Americans still believe I am a terrorist, my life will be shit for ever. I'll never get a visa to travel anywhere ever again.'

Barry stared at him. 'I'm thinking a visa would be the least of your problems. If the bloody Yanks suspect you're a terrorist you might end up in a hole in a country that isn't even on the map, mate.' He paused. 'Hey. Here's an idea. Why don't I drive you in my UN vehicle? It could be enough of a cover to get you in and out in one piece.'

Jeff glanced at Sulla. 'Not a bad idea at all. Sulla?'

'No. Thank you for the offer, Barry, but I cannot allow you to become involved.' He turned to Jeff. 'Things could go wrong.'

From further along the bar Hansie's voice called to Barry. He gestured at the rugby match playing on the TV above his head. Barry raised a hand. 'Just a second, mate.' He turned back to Sulla. 'Look, sport, I'll be buggered if I'm going to let you two have all the fun. This is what's going to happen. I'll be outside the Grand Hotel in a UN SUV at eight in the morning. Sharp, mate. Be there.'

Sulla's mouth opened to say something, but Barry had already departed to join Hansie.

32.

It was the third time his mobile had rung in as many minutes. Avni Leka had ignored the first two. 'Damn it.'

Fatmire grabbed his buttocks. Held him. Wouldn't allow him to withdraw. He knew it would make no difference. The moment had passed. Lately, with so much on his mind, attaining an orgasm had proven a hopeless task. Tonight Fatmire had brought him to the precipice twice and each time the blasted phone had broken his concentration.

He rolled onto his back and reached to the side table for his watch. 10.32 p.m. Swinging his legs over the side of the bed, he sat and reached to switch on the lamp. Fatmire rose to her knees and began kneading his shoulders. But Leka bent away to retrieve the ringing mobile buried in his clothes on the floor. He checked the caller ID and frowned. Osman Gashi. Under his breath he muttered a curse. Gashi would not call him at this hour unless there was trouble. And that meant his night was about to be ruined.

He thumbed the answer button. There was no attempt to disguise his irritation. 'Gashi, what do you want?'

'We need to meet. It's urgent.'

'I'm busy. Tell me now.'

Leka had no desire to dress and meet Gashi. Fatmire poured a cognac and placed it on the table next to him. He had no need of the drink. The alcohol would only make his goal more difficult. She lay back and spread-eagled herself across the white satin sheets, gyrating, touching herself, her eyes closed as she thrust her hips in time to imagined music. She was a beautiful, desirable woman, her young body so sculpted, so firm. He felt a sudden wave of sadness and frustration, knowing he could never truly fulfil her sexual needs.

'Not over the phone, Avni. I'll be waiting for you in Edi's Restaurant.'

With a groan Leka dragged his eyes away from Fatmire. 'All right. Give me half an hour.'

He reached for the half-filled glass of cognac next to the lamp and downed it in one gulp.

෨

The taxi dropped Leka outside the Reiffesen Bank. He crossed the road and in the dim light picked his way down the small flight of steps that led to the entrance of Edi's Restaurant. He saw that the smoke-filled cafe and bar was full of locals. No one paid him the slightest attention as he walked between the tables and into the now deserted restaurant section. Gashi sat in the corner.

Leka waved the waiter away. All he wanted was for the meeting to be over quickly and to get back to his bed for a decent night's sleep. He leaned over the table.

'What's so urgent, Osman?'

Gashi displayed no sign of being ruffled at the distinct hostility in Leka's voice. A slow draw of his cigarette. Swirls of smoke aimed at the ceiling. 'Bradley and the American woman and Sulla Bogdani went through to Macedonia today.'

With a sigh, Leka deposited himself on a chair. 'Don't tell me you've dragged me out in the middle of the night to tell me the New

Zealander took a woman on a sight-seeing trip? Are you an imbecile or something?'

Gashi took a handful of peanuts from the bowl. A deliberate pause. He began dropping them one by one into his mouth. Small bits of shell spat out the side of his mouth like shrapnel from a hand grenade. Some fell down his shirt front. Leka knew what Gashi was doing. This was a reminder that he was not a meek secretary to be browbeaten. He intended on wrenching respect out of Leka any way he could.

'All right, Osman. Please tell me why I'm here.' Leka's hands spread in mock defeat. He could permit Gashi these little victories. As long as the idiot did what he was told and carried out his tasks.

Gashi tapped the ash from his cigarette and rested it on the ashtray. 'My men have been following the New Zealander as you requested. He and his companions met someone at the Skopje Holiday Inn. A man in a suit. They went with this man to a cafe where they had discussions for nearly an hour. He showed them several documents. My men could not get close enough to overhear the discussion, but Bogdani seemed to be the centre of attention. He got very upset.'

'Bogdani?' Leka's brows lowered over his eyes. 'Interesting.'

'When the meeting was over, I had one of my men trail the man they met with. He went to the US Embassy. He flashed some sort of ID in his wallet and they let him through without a word. Whoever this man is, he has authority with the Americans.'

'CIA.' It was a whisper more to himself than to Gashi.

Gashi folded his hands on the table. 'With the New Zealander involved, this has got to be about that man Shala. But why would the CIA be interested in an insignificant Kosovon businessman? The vineyard scam was only . . . what was it you called it? Oh, that's right. Peanuts.'

A waiter appeared with an enquiring look at Leka.

'Bring me a cognac.'

Leka's fingers drummed on the table top. It helped him think. His habit was always to assume the worst. Shala was dead and he doubted the Americans were investigating his death. Were they on to him? It wasn't a discussion he wanted to get into with Gashi. The hired thug knew nothing of Avni's terrorist network and the role played in it by his men. As far as Gashi was concerned, the money he smuggled into Greece en route to Europe was simply a matter of laundering. Leka had carefully built terror into a multi-million dollar industry and he was not about to share the profits with Gashi.

The cognac arrived. Leka downed it in one gulp and ordered another. This caused Gashi to raise an eyebrow. But he said nothing. Noticing his reaction, Leka attempted to disguise a flash of indignation. Then he didn't. Fuck Gashi. Let him think what he liked.

'That courier you sent to Greece. Did he know enough to give the police a lead back to you?'

Gashi shrugged.

'Anything is possible, I suppose. Kosovo is a small country. Men gossip like old women. But that would not explain why they would go to Bradley, or what this has to do with Sulla Bogdani.'

'I guess we'll have to wait and see.'

'There's more.'

Leka groaned and downed the second cognac. 'Tomi Mema phoned me tonight. When the three got back to Prishtina, Bradley and the American woman went to see him. They said they had been told Tomi knew Shala had been in prison all along.'

'What did Tomi tell them?'

'He denied it of course. Tried to blame it on a mix-up. But Bradley's not going back to New Zealand. He's demanded Tomi get the family's vineyard back. I told him Bradley should be told to go screw himself.'

Gashi grinned at his personal brashness. Leka refused to join the game. He signalled for yet another cognac.

'Of course you did. You're a tough man.'

Gashi let the snide remark wash over him. 'You know what I think? I think this is all a load of bullshit. I think this so-called CIA agent is more interested in Bogdani than Bradley. It has nothing to do with the vineyard scam. And the truth is there is no connection through Bogdani back to either of us.'

Leka considered enlightening Gashi regarding this miscalculation but decided against it.

'So it doesn't matter if Bradley knows about Tomi,' Gashi continued, 'because now that Shala is dead there is no longer a trail to follow. Eventually it will die away. This New Zealander will grow tired of finding nothing and go home.'

Though Leka nodded in agreement, inwardly he regretted ever having got mixed up with this dumb ox of a man.

33.

arry sighted Sulla sheltering from the rain in the hotel entrance. He sounded his horn and pulled over. Jumping over puddles Sulla crossed the drive and opened the passenger door.

'How ya doing, mate? Hop in. It's gonna be a shitty day with this rain. The traffic will be bloody awful.'

Sulla remained standing outside, hand on the door. 'It's still not too late to change your mind.'

'Come on, Sulla. Get in out of the rain and close the bloody door. And let's get the hell out of here, eh?'

Sulla did as Barry urged. Barry grimaced at the water dripping from Sulla's hair onto the upholstery. He reached under his seat, pulled out a towel and tossed it across, then reversed into the street.

It proved difficult for Barry to contain his excitement at the adventure he found himself embarked upon. He wanted to talk, but Sulla wouldn't cooperate. Several times he tried engaging him in amiable chatter. But Sulla hardly spoke. In the end Barry gave up and concentrated on the road. The rain had reduced to a drizzle, but the potholes had filled, leaving them largely invisible to the eye. Breaking an axle before they made it out of the city loomed as a real possibility. To add to the already difficult driving, great fingers of brownish gunk splashed up onto the windscreen from passing vehicles, which the wiper blades, set to intermittent, struggled to sluice away.

Barry cast another look at Sulla's face. Then at the distant skyline. 'Bloody weather. Rain properly, for God's sake.'

⁓

Avni Leka stood beside his desk double-checking the documents his secretary had prepared the day before. In ten minutes he needed to be in the courtroom. It was a simple case that would only bring a pittance compared with the huge sums of illegal money that passed through his hands from his criminal activities. But he approached modest cases such as this in the same pedantic manner he would a major trial. This kind of devotion to detail had given him the reputation for professionalism that had advanced him from a lowly backwoods lawyer to the city's chief prosecutor. The position allowed him to run his clandestine empire with relative impunity.

When he'd returned to the apartment the previous evening, he saw through the bedroom door that Fatmire was fast asleep. He crept into the spare room and slept in the single bed. If the Americans were coming after him, he needed to be rested and on his toes. Even so, the stimulating mix of coffee, cognac and anxiety decreed he never got the good night's sleep he craved.

Every small detail Gashi had given him turned over and over in his head. And he kept coming up with the same answer. It had to be the damned explosives. He could think of nothing else the Americans would have wanted to discuss with Bogdani. He'd paid well to hide the switch that had implicated Bogdani. Bribes at that level of bureaucracy were always more costly than those to the usually penurious local Kosovon judges and defence solicitors. But it was money well spent. It was vital his clients could supply the bombers with the best quality materials and only leave behind paper trails leading to impenetrable brick walls.

Had the Americans somehow linked the property fraud to the explosives? Damn that stupid Gashi and his petty confidence tricks. Sure, the big man knew nothing of his European operations. But any investigation back from Bogdani might not stop where it should, at Gashi. His stupidity could well allow the trail to carry further. For the first time, Leka considered the desirability of removing Gashi from the equation.

The desk phone rang. Leka checked his watch. Five minutes until court. He hesitated and stared at the phone as it continued to ring. With a 'dammit' under his breath, he plucked up the hand piece. 'Avni Leka.'

'It's me, Gashi.'

'What is it now? Give me some good news for a change.'

'Maybe I can. Bogdani is in a UN vehicle heading west. My men followed. They did not turn off to the airport. They kept straight on.'

'He's going to Peje.'

'So it seems.'

Leka took a moment to think. Why on earth would Sulla risk going back to Peje? Could his father have taken ill? Leka thought it the likeliest reason. It didn't really matter. A heaven-sent opportunity had been presented to him. It was too good to pass up.

'All right, Gashi. It's time to declare open season on Sulla Bogdani. We need to let the KLA know he's on his way.'

Gashi's grunt indicated no enthusiasm. 'I think it better if this information doesn't come directly from me. I have my own problems with the KLA.'

Leka rolled his eyes. But the statement hadn't surprised him. Gashi had a habit of creating enemies.

'Use a second party then. Someone they trust.' An inspiration arrived. 'Tomi Mema. He has kept enough of them out of jail. Assure him that if something happens to Bogdani, the New Zealander will lose his nerve and go home. That should prove motivation enough.'

It was with a minor sense of triumph that Leka rang off. Something might be going his way at last.

◦〜◦

Blerim Basholli lay back and stared heavenwards. Shadows from the branches of the trees outside his window made improbable shapes across the painted ceiling tiles. He imagined them as demon arms from the netherworld beckoning the souls of the dead. Such thoughts always disturbed him, especially when he knew that after his own death he would face a reckoning. Catholics had it easier. For them a few Hail Marys and all was forgiven. For a Muslim like him things were believed to be considerably less promising.

The digital bedside clock read 9.01 a.m. He had an hour. The phone call from Tomi Mema had taken him by surprise. And the reason for his call left him with a queasy knot in his stomach. He had not spoken to Mema in over a year. But out of the blue he delivers him certain news. Why? What was in it for the lawyer? Mema never did anything for nothing.

Basholli's hand felt for the prone body of his wife. Through the bedclothes she radiated soft warmth. She stirred but did not wake. He smiled. She could sleep through anything. He scratched his crotch. His morning erection had lost its strength. It could receive no more encouragement from him. He had work to do. Sulla Bogdani was on his way to Peje. In doing so, he was breaking a long understanding between them: as long as Sulla stayed clear of Peje, Basholli would let matters lie.

Legs slid from beneath the blankets. His wife mumbled a half-protest and rolled over. Basholli's eyes went to her for a moment. But hers stayed closed. He stole away from the bed and found the clothes he had tossed over the back of the chair the previous evening and dressed. Kneeling, he pulled out the bottom drawer of the dresser. Reaching through to the back he withdrew a brown paper package. He took it into the bathroom.

The mirror reflected back at him the hardened face of a man who'd seen much in his life. Had his best friend from the days before the war worn as well? Or as badly? They'd been closer than brothers.

'Sulla, Sulla, Sulla. Why are you doing this to me?'

His attention turned to the package on the edge of the basin. He unwrapped a pistol and two ammunition clips. He slipped the clips into the inside pocket of his jacket and pushed the loaded pistol into his belt. Another glance at the mirror. A hand across an unruly head of hair. He was ready.

Stepping back into the bedroom he paused a moment and looked down once more at the sleeping form of Sulla's sister. He hoped that one day she might forgive him for what he was about to do. He never left the house without kissing her awake. Today he would leave her sleeping.

34.

Captain Agim Morina hurried into his office, closed the door and leaned against it. When he was certain no one would disturb him, a pair of fists punched the air like a triumphant boxer. He opened the thick manila envelope and spilled the stack of surveillance photographs onto the desk – photos his men had taken of Gashi's comings and goings. Useless as straw, most of them, but in their midst was a shiny needle of gold.

A finger ran across the photo of Avni Leka and Osman Gashi in a late night meeting at Edi's Restaurant. The two men were drinking together and deep in conversation. His decision to have Gashi tailed had finally paid off. He'd found Gashi's boss, and now had solid evidence before him that the prominent prosecutor was associating with a known thug and criminal.

In and of itself, the photo was of little importance to him. Certainly his surveillance team expressed no particular interest in it. Criminals and lawyers were much of a muchness in their eyes. Miserable police salaries did little to encourage either curiosity or initiative regarding their occasional connivances.

But for Morina, he finally had in his hands the missing piece of a puzzle.

He pulled out a bottle from the second drawer of his filing cabinet and twirled off the cap. When his coffee mug was half full, he sat on the edge of the desk and relished the bite of cognac down his throat. It was so obvious when he thought about it. Leka as chief prosecutor of the Municipal Court controlled the judges and the courtrooms and made the decisions on whether or not indictments lapsed or proceeded. He raised the mug in a mock salute to the man in the photo.

'A toast to Prishtina's pre-eminent officer of the courts.'

Turning back to the sheaf of photos, he singled out the gem and slipped it into his briefcase. He'd start putting together a dossier, gleaning as much information and connecting as many dots as he could. He would stash the evidence somewhere in his apartment. That would be much safer than leaving it in his office at the police station.

He might never need to use it. He certainly had no desire to jeopardise his secondary source of income. For the time being, he and his family would continue to enjoy the good life in Kosovo.

Maybe in the future he could use this new information to advance his prospects in significant new directions.

He gave a salute to the portrait of a younger uniformed Morina hanging on the wall.

35.

'Arsehole.'

Momentarily blind, Barry decelerated and banged his fist on the dashboard. Another thump, this time onto a control knob and nozzles squirted window washer across the windshield. The offending container truck that had sent a fountain of mud into their path disappeared in the rear-view mirror. The glare from Barry should have singed its tailboard.

The journey had been slow. Trapped behind a KFOR convoy had cost them an hour. The drizzle had become a deluge as if in response to Barry's earlier cursing of God and Mother Nature and any other deity he deemed responsible for the miserable conditions he found himself driving in. Sulla continued to ignore the world and, in particular, Barry's attempts to draw him out.

Finally a gap in the passing lane allowed Barry to accelerate into clear road.

Another ten minutes and the rain eased off and some blue sky began to appear. A rainbow straddled the road ahead, framing the snow-capped peaks of the Albanian Alps in the distance.

The outskirts of Peje drew close.

Sulla came alert. 'Okay, Barry, this is it.'

'Sulla, mate. I thought you were still on walkabout.'

A frown crossed Sulla's face. 'But I have not left the vehicle.'

'No. A walkabout is . . . Forget it. You had better cover up or the whole bloody place will know you're here.'

Sulla leaned against the door, shielding his face with his hand. The huge mountains towering over the town were as picturesque as they were entrapping. The only way out for them now was the way they'd just come in.

'Flies into the fly trap,' Barry muttered.

'What?'

'Never mind. Nothing you don't already know, mate.'

Sulla guided Barry through a labyrinth of back streets until they reached the corner of a cul-de-sac. He pointed to a spot in front of a closed butcher's shop. 'There. Pull in front of the house with the green iron gate.'

'Got it.'

The tendrils of a creeper vine with white and pink flowers covered the two-metre-high red-brick wall. Although the peeling gate was wide enough for a vehicle, thick vines had wound round its cast iron hinges and it appeared not to have opened for some time. Entry was through a small door set into the centre. Through the drooping branches of a willow tree on the other side of the wall, Barry could just make out the upper floor of Sulla's father's house.

'What now?'

'Now we wait and watch.'

'But no one knows we are here.'

'This is Kosovo, Barry. Everyone knows we're here.'

⁓

Basholli had his men in place a good half-hour before Sulla and Barry arrived. When Barry's UN vehicle entered the city a man dressed in a green military jacket and black beret ticked off the plate's number on the paper in front of him.

When this news reached Basholli, he proceeded to his safe house deep in the woods. Surrounding trees shielded the clearing from the morning sun and trails of footsteps criss-crossed the overnight covering of frost. The cold was just as biting inside the house as out. A glance towards the fireplace. One of Basholli's men was using a magazine to fan a flame that fought for life under a pile of damp logs. Displaying little confidence in the likelihood of much warmth from that quarter, the others had opted for the alternative and sipped cognac from glasses held in cupped hands. Coffee bubbled away on the stove. Basholli poured himself a cup.

Word had come through that Sulla had parked not too far from his father's house and he and his driver were now just sitting in the vehicle. The UN vehicle and the UN driver were unwelcome complications. If either came to any harm, Basholli knew Peje would be flooded with international police and he and his men would be first in the firing line. He gave explicit orders to his men that Sulla and his companion were not to be harmed.

∼

Barry's fidgeting was beginning to annoy Sulla. After twenty minutes he'd seen no sign of Basholli's men. They were either not here or so well hidden he was never going to see them.

'Time for me to go in, Barry. You wait here. I will not be longer than ten minutes. Whatever you do, do not leave the vehicle.'

'No way, mate. I'm coming with you.' One of Barry's hands rested on the door handle, the other fingered the UN identification card hanging round his neck. 'See this? Large and easily seen. It's like a bloody bulletproof vest, mate. No one wants to fuck with the UN.'

'This may be so. But I'm not willing to take the risk.' Sulla opened the passenger door. 'I need you to stay here with the car.'

Barry opened his mouth to protest, but Sulla held up his hand. 'Enough. Now. If anything happens, do not come to help me. Drive away and go straight to the police. But Barry, do not leave the vehicle.'

A breath whistled through tightened lips as Barry's raised his hands. 'All right, all right. Don't worry, I've got the message already. Jesus.'

Sulla's eyes narrowed. He was not convinced Barry had really listened to a word he said. He climbed from the vehicle and closed the door. A quick stretch as his eyes scanned the vicinity.

⚬♾⚬

Basholli answered his cell phone on the first ring.

'He's on the move.'

'Good. You know what to do. And remember. No shooting.'

'Understood.'

Basholli snapped his phone shut with a stony expression. In fifteen more minutes, Sulla would be standing before him and it would nearly be all over. The thought of it made him physically ill. But there was no way he could allow his men to discern the distaste he harboured for what the fates had planned for him and the brother of his wife this day.

⚬♾⚬

Sulla planned to get the explosives and leave without disturbing his father. This was not a time for visiting. The longer he was in the area the more he placed his father and Barry at risk. It concerned him that Barry would probably not follow his instructions. The Australian's stubbornness baffled him. And why would a man he barely knew put himself in danger to help him? It was foolishness.

THE FIELD OF BLACKBIRDS

A squeak of complaint and the door in the gate swung open at his push. He was forced to stoop to go through it. As his eyes lifted from the paved courtyard covered with weeds white from morning frost, they settled on the business ends of the barrels of three Kalashnikovs.

36.

'elcome home, Sulla. Please, come in. Stand against the wall. Just there, next to the bench.'

Sulla's earlier decision that he shouldn't upset or involve his father now looked like very poor judgment on his part. He should have asked him to bring the explosives to Prishtina. When he learned of the death of his incompetent son, it would probably kill him anyway. Sulla recognised the speaker waving a rifle at him, but could not remember his name. One of Basholli's lieutenants, he knew that much. The other two he had never seen before.

'Don't do anything stupid. You cannot move faster than a bullet. And you have the old man to consider.'

'Leave my father out of this.'

'Your father is safe. As long as you behave he will not even know we have been here.'

Sulla breathed a little easier. He knew the man spoke the truth. Basholli would never allow anyone to harm his father-in-law. He glanced about the courtyard. His father had been busy. The small vegetable garden looked freshly turned and the fruit trees pruned. Clay pots of varying sizes sat in nooks and crannies. A grape vine was a new addition. He noted that a leg on the small iron table he had bought for his father had rusted.

Three steps and Sulla reached the indicated spot.

'Now, if you will raise your arms please. A quick search. Nothing more.'

Sulla did as instructed. The man to his left moved forward to frisk him.

'He's clean.'

To Sulla's ears came the squeak of a rusty hinge and the shuffle of feet. His gaze flew in the direction of the gate. Barry stumbled into the courtyard with two armed men close behind. Sulla's eyes rolled to the heavens. Yet another poor judgment call.

This was turning into a disaster. He should never have let Barry come.

Barry straightened and held his identification card aloft, waving it like a crusading priest wielding a crucifix to ward off a coven of vampires.

'Are you people stupid? UN, mate.'

The men with the guns exchanged glances then laughed.

Barry tried hard to maintain a brave front. But there could be no disguising his shaking hands, nor the shade of grey his face had gone.

Sulla aimed a hard look at him. 'Barry, just do as they say.'

The spokesman flipped open a mobile phone and moved out of hearing distance. Sulla assumed it would be Basholli on the other end. And he also assumed that the only reason he remained alive was that for some reason Basholli wanted him that way. He couldn't imagine it would be for long. It didn't matter that they were brothers-in-law. Given the belief of senior KLA operatives that Sulla had sold them out to NATO, Basholli had little choice but to kill him.

The phone call over, the headman ordered Sulla and Barry out of the courtyard and into two black Mercedes parked outside: Sulla into the front vehicle, Barry into the second.

It worried Barry that he hadn't been blindfolded. He'd read novels and seen movies. Kidnappers always blindfolded the abducted otherwise they could lead police to the kidnappers' hideouts. He could think of just one reason not to bother with blindfolds. It left his stomach feeling jittery and close to heaving.

With an armed man squeezed either side of him and their rifles across his back for want of room, Barry was forced to lean forward. As the cars drove along the main road out of Peje, his left leg began to cramp. Ten minutes later the vehicles turned onto a mud track and drove into the woods a short way before entering a clearing. The cars stopped outside a single-storey house. Armed men moved forward and surrounded the two vehicles.

This is it, Barry thought. *No one will ever find my body out here.* He now wished he were back in Sydney sunning himself on Manly Beach. This adventure wasn't turning out to be quite as much fun as he'd imagined.

◦∾◦

A dozen pairs of eyes followed Sulla's walk towards the house. He tried to ignore them. He would walk with head high and shoulders back. If this were to be his last day, he would face it like a man.

Sulla knew Basholli had numerous houses like this one, far from prying eyes and listening devices. Such secret lairs were where the planning was done and where his men hid when the heat was on. A small hallway led into an open-plan kitchen-lounge. The stench of cigarette smoke hung in the damp air. It was tempered by the aroma of freshly brewed coffee. Unwashed coffee cups lay on the bench. There were no paintings on the walls, no carpeting cushioned the floors. But Sulla knew the spartan environment would be more than enough for ex-soldiers of the Kosovon Liberation Army.

Blerim Basholli sat behind a circular dining table in the centre of the room, leaning back in his chair with one leg crossed over the other. Two men flanked him. One had a Kalashnikov slung over his shoulder. The other rested the butt of his on his thigh.

Basholli gestured Sulla to sit. 'I wish I could say it was a pleasure to see you, but this is not a pleasure for me. I hope you can believe that.'

'How is my sister?'

'I left her sleeping. She knows nothing of this.'

'The man in the car with me. The international. He is a friend.'

Blerim held up a hand. 'I promise he will not be harmed. Now. To business.' Basholli clasped his fingers together and rested them on his lap. 'I am curious. I heard you had left the country. That pleased me. My first thoughts were *Thank you Sulla, you have spared me the indignity of committing a terrible deed*. But then you come back. Not only do you come back, you come here, to Peje. To my home, Sulla.' Basholli's voice had risen. A vein bulged down his forehead. 'You have slapped me on the face. You have made me very unhappy and now I have to make your family very unhappy. Why? Why have you done this to me?'

'I had no intention of returning here, but I had little choice. I must clear my name to help a friend of your wife's father.'

Basholli shook his head. 'You wish to clear your name to help a friend of your father? How about my name. The names of my men? Are you going to clear these, too?'

'I can explain. But it is a long story.'

Basholli's laugh lacked any discernible humour. 'You were always a good storyteller. This whole mess is because of your damned stories. But . . . we have time. So go ahead. Tell me a story.'

Sulla told his brother-in-law of meeting Jeff, looking for Shala, the scam over the vineyard, the Xhiha brothers. His brother-in-law sat listening without interrupting. When Sulla finished, Basholli scratched the back of his neck then slowly nodded and leaned forward.

'That's all very interesting, Sulla. But it does not explain why you have returned to Pejc.'

'Because of the explosives.'

'The explosives? Always these damned explosives. There were no explosives, Sulla. Just that shit you used for getting rid of stumps. They had nothing to do with us and yet they are still causing trouble. My men are very displeased with your imaginary explosives. Especially those who went to prison because of them.'

'I have felt much guilt for a long time for what I did, and because of what happened to you and your men. My stupidity caused you much grief, but not as much as these explosives will cause you now. The explosives I gave to the television crew were switched before they were handed in to NATO.'

Basholli's head tilted to the side. 'Go on.'

'In Macedonia I met an American. Probably a CIA agent, I think. He told me the explosives NATO received from the television crew were the same used in terrorist bombings in Belgium, and now in Slovenia. They think someone from Kosovo, possibly the KLA, supplied explosives to these bombers. So you and your men are primary suspects.'

A snort came from Basholli. 'Only thanks to you and your idiotic television programme.'

'That may be true. But also thanks to me, I can prove you're innocent.'

'I'm listening.'

'Luckily I still have some of the explosives buried at my house. Once the authorities test them it will confirm the switch and this will clear all of us.'

Basholli sat back and stared at Sulla. 'Even if what you say is true, you could have lived without the clearance of any names.

Started again somewhere else. Clearing your name may be understandable, but it is not as important as staying alive. You knew
what would happen if you ever came back to Peje. You're lucky you
weren't shot on sight. Why risk it?'

'The American agent told me the name of the man they believe
is funding the European terrorists. He has been raising money for
these people through the property scams. He had a friend of my
father murdered. The man I told you about. Arben Shala. Now my
New Zealand friend is going after this criminal and needs my help.'

'And you risked coming back here for this foreigner? He is not
family.' Basholli slapped his chest. 'I am family and what do you
give to me? Nothing but heartache and trouble.'

'I cannot undo the past, Blerim.'

'Even if I believe you, and I think I'm inclined to do so, it
wouldn't matter. Because of you we have suffered. That is still on
your head. It changes nothing.'

'True. What is done cannot be undone, even if it is possible to
clear both our names. But perhaps you might be interested in the
man they are after.'

'Okay Sulla. Last chance. Dazzle me. Who is the man the
Americans are after?'

'Osman Gashi.'

෨৩

'Holy shit. Yahooo! Thank you, God. Thank you, Holy Father
and Mary and Joseph and whoever else. Thank yoooou.' Barry kissed
his hand and bashed the top of the steering wheel. 'Bloody flaming
hell.'

Sulla clung to the strap above the door as the UN vehicle
bounced across potholes and ruts in the road.

'I think you should maybe slow down a little, Barry.'

'Yeah, sure, mate. Just as soon as I pass that last building and we're out of this fucking town. Yeehaaaa.'

'We are safe. I promise. Now please slow down.'

'Okay, okay. But Jesus, mate, I can't get back to Prishtina fast enough. I've been surrounded by guys with Kalashnikovs who wanted to shoot me. How fucking unbelievable is that? Tell you what Sulla, the Kukri is going to get a hammering tonight. Then I'm going to take Bethany to bed and stay there for a week.' He glanced across at Sulla. 'Anyway. What in the hell did you say to get them to let us go?'

Despite a noticeable reduction in speed, Sulla still clung to the door strap. 'I mentioned the name Osman Gashi. It worked as I hoped it might.'

'Really? Why? What's this Gashi guy to them?'

'Gashi murdered Blerim Basholli's father.'

37.

Gasping for breath, Osman Gashi rolled onto his back. The Viagra could keep him as hard as a rock but his lack of physical condition often kept him from crossing the finish line. Perspiration flowed from his pores like floodwaters down the face of a dam. A hand went to his chest. The racing of his heart reminded him of his doctor's warning: too many cigarettes, too much booze, too much food and not enough exercise. 'You are going to have a stroke, Mr Gashi. You must change your lifestyle.'

He'd told the doctor to go screw himself. The old fool received more than enough money from him to import the best medications to keep him healthy and away from impotency's door. He would live the life he wanted.

Gashi rolled his head to the side. The young hooker flashed a smile back at him. He doubted she was warming to him out of any pleasure from their sexual encounter. More likely it was gratitude he was no longer pounding her. What did he care what she thought? Ignoring the smile, he reached out and squeezed a firm, young breast.

The girl ran her hand across his thigh. He pushed it away. He was finished. Any more would most likely kill him.

'Get out of here.'

A flat-hander across her bare arse drew a yelp. Gathering up her clothes she ran from the room.

When his breathing returned to its normal guttural wheeze, he hauled his naked body upright. He reached for a bottle of mineral water lying on the floor and poured the contents over his head then wiped himself off with the bed sheet. Red silk. The men who used his services paid top dollars and expected the surroundings to match the quality of the women he supplied. This was the red room. Red wallpaper, red sheets, red chairs, even the spa bath was red. The shower sported white tiles inlaid with red roses. Gashi enjoyed the erotic effect under dimmed lights. Whenever he banged one of his whores, it was always in the Red Room.

But even the new girl couldn't distract him for long from a new unease in his life. How was it possible that Sulla Bogdani had left Peje alive? Tomi Mema assured him he gave the message to Basholli exactly as instructed. And Mema did not have the balls to lie to him. Sulla could not have entered Peje without Basholli knowing. His men would have been everywhere. What's more, the UN vehicle would be as easy to spot as a lump of coal on a snowfield. What could Sulla have said to make Basholli forgo his long-sworn vengeance?

Gashi spread gobs of imported baby shampoo over the remnants of his hair and stepped under the shower. Soapy water dribbled from his pate and into his eyes. He shut them and purred like an overfed cat as warm water flattened the hairs of his body like waterweeds in a stream. He loved showers. No matter what kinds of human perversions his line of business exposed him to, he was convinced a clean body led to a clear head.

With Sulla still alive, the New Zealander would stay in Kosovo and contest the ownership of Arben Shala's property. Of this he was certain. He needed to close any doors that might lead back to himself. As for the Xhiha brothers, it was long past time that they were reunited with their uncle and the rest of their ancestors.

Where else could he be vulnerable?

He discounted his own men. They would never betray him, greed being enough leverage to ensure loyalty. And death for betrayal was always additional motivation. That left Tomi Mema and Captain Agim Morina. Morina did not know enough about his business activities to be any threat. Certainly he did not know of his connections to Avni Leka.

That left Tomi Mema.

If Basholli had truly let Sulla Bogdani walk, then no doubt Sulla would now know it had been Mema who had warned Basholli of his return to Peje. If Sulla decided to go after Mema the pompous lawyer would squawk like a nest full of baby crows. Mema had handled all the paperwork for the property transactions and represented all the victims. Mema knew everything. On top of that, the New Zealander now knew Mema had lied about knowing Shala.

Avni Leka had orchestrated Mema's courtroom successes and had made the puffed-up charlatan a legend in a country where there were few heroes. In return, Mema had happily done what he was told, leaving Leka the quiet power behind the throne. But lately Mema had displayed a degree of guarded resistance when asked to perform his duties. Because the citizens of Kosovo had come to regard him as the country's most eminent lawyer, he was now making buckets of money from genuine clients with pockets stashed with cash. It seemed that the stuffed envelopes he once greedily grasped without question had lost their appeal. Mema had begun to believe all the media hype, imagining himself to be some sort of Kosovon Perry Mason rather than a bought-and-paid-for third-rate solicitor operating out of a shipping container.

Gashi towelled himself off, downed a cognac and poured another. It was clear what needed to be done. Regrettable, but necessary.

The door opened and a young woman poked her head in. He recognised her as another of the newbies from Moldova. A rare beauty, barely eighteen. She had brought him fresh clothing.

'On the chair.'

The girl did as instructed. Gashi looked down over his paunch. The effects of the Viagra had not worn off. And the shower had rejuvenated him. He held out a hand.

'Wait. Come here.'

⁊

Avni Leka rarely took the chance to visit the few hundred hectares of grassy fields and forest that constituted Germia Park, even though it was only a fifteen-minute drive from the Prishtina business centre. If he felt the need to get away he had always preferred the mountains. Up high he could find an isolated spot to relax and think about nothing. Germia Park in summer could be a little nightmarish. Its lake-sized swimming pool, sports fields and barbeque pits attracted hundreds of Prishtina families to eat and play. He disliked crowds. Each day at the courthouse he was obliged to suffer throngs of citizens. He had no desire to suffer the unwashed masses on his days of rest.

When he entered the park he saw another reason for his staying away: signposts along the forest fringes warning of landmines. Thousands had been laid by the Serbian military but maps showing the location of the deadly anti-personnel bombs had been lost or purposely destroyed. He had once witnessed a stray soccer ball detonate a mine. Deterrent enough to keep his distance. But that pest Gashi had insisted they meet at one of the park's two restaurants.

Gashi had further insisted that they sit outside on the veranda to be as far away from other diners as possible. A light breeze had dropped the temperature below freezing.

'This better be good, Gashi.' Leka pulled his coat collar higher around his neck. 'I'm cold and I'm not happy.'

'What needs to be discussed has to be in private.'

'You have your wish. Now get on with it.'

The black apron of a waiter came into view alongside Gashi. A bottle of cognac and two glasses were placed on the table.

'Make sure we are not disturbed.' The way the waiter turned his back and rubbed his arms through a thin cotton shirt was a clear message to Gashi he needn't worry. 'Wait.' The waiter stopped and glared and rubbed harder. Gashi pulled a wallet from his pocket and passed the waiter a hundred euro note. 'For your trouble.'

The waiter's face broke into a smile. 'No trouble at all, sir.'

He left and closed the doors to the veranda behind him.

Gashi shrugged at Leka's steady stare. 'What? You think me incapable of generosity?'

'I've misjudged you. Accept my apologies. Now can we get to the point before this place freezes my arse off.'

'Blerim let Sulla Bogdani go.'

Leka's mouth dropped to his chin. Brandy sloshed out of his glass onto his coat.

'What? Let him go. Are you certain? Did Blerim not receive Tomi's message?'

'I double-checked with Tomi. He definitely passed on the message exactly as you instructed. Perhaps he had scruples about their family ties?'

'No.' The response was sharp. 'That would have only made killing Sulla more likely, not less. To betray a friend is bad enough. To betray family as Sulla did? Unforgiveable.'

Leka picked up a napkin to wipe droplets of cognac from his trouser leg. The cloth was damp.

'Shit.' He threw it on the table. 'You assured me he would never leave Peje alive, Gashi. Remember?'

Gashi offered a shrug. 'I was wrong. It happens.'

'I think it is happening far too often these days,' Leka snapped.

Gashi was losing his grip. First the debacle with Shala and that damned vineyard, and now Sulla. Halam Akbar would arrive any day now and he did not want any complications while Akbar was in the country.

The thought of Sulla on the loose made him uneasy. That Sulla had been freed from prison so quickly after he had contrived to get rid of him was shock enough; it was some time ago now and that Sulla had not yet come after him was a puzzle, but Basholli not killing him defied belief. What now? Sulla was no killer. Leka did not expect an ambush down a back alley. But Sulla would still want revenge. Leka planned to be long gone before Sulla had a chance to exact it. The timetable had just been stepped up a bit, he decided.

Leka's moment of contemplation must have annoyed Gashi. He lifted the cognac bottle and let it clink against the side of Leka's glass. The ruse worked. Leka inclined back towards him. Gashi topped up his drink before he spoke. 'The New Zealander told Tomi he was staying on in Kosovo to secure the Shala property for his family. But after the meeting with the American, I'm not certain that might be his only reason.'

Leka thought on that. 'Well. Here's a plan. I could arrange for the courts to issue a ruling and have the vineyard returned to the Shala family. That would remove the reason for the New Zealander to extend his stay here in Kosovo.'

To Leka's surprise Gashi looked unruffled by the suggestion. 'You win some, you lose some. At least if the question of the vineyard is removed and he still remains here, we will know I was right.'

'Very well. I'll make arrangements in the morning. Are we done?'

'No. We have another problem: Tomi Mema.'

Leka sat back and tapped his gloves on the table top. 'Mema. What about Mema?'

'If Basholli told Sulla that Tomi Mema warned him about Sulla going to Peje, then Sulla will go after him. Tomi is not a courageous man. He could break. Possibly point him back to us.'

Us? There's no us here. It's just you, *you stupid cretin.*

'Yes, of course. But be careful how you handle it. Tomi is a celebrity. Something happens to him and every police officer in the country will be investigating. Including the internationals. It has to look every inch an unfortunate accident. Are we clear on this?'

'Yes. I understand. Don't worry. Whatever happens the noise will die quickly.'

Leka knew Gashi was mostly right. Kosovo was a land in constant turmoil. A new disaster replaced the old every day. But if Gashi made any mistakes, the international authorities might not be so quick to close off the last chapter on Tomi Mema's life. They did not have quite the same sort of selective memory as Kosovons.

Leka downed his cognac and stood. 'Just remember, Osman: be careful.'

38.

Standing at his desk with the receiver clutched to his ear like a life preserver, Tomi Mema listened to Osman Gashi with growing relief.

'The Municipal Court is to reinstate the title deed of Arben Shala's property to his family. It is to be done first thing in the morning. Are we clear?'

'Yes. I understand. But how do I explain the sudden change of heart to Bradley?'

'You're the lawyer. Think of something. Anyway, what does it matter what you tell him? The family gets the property and Bradley gets to go home. End of story. Just do your job. Prepare the documents and don't screw it up.'

'Yes. And Bogdani? What about him? He will know I warned Basholli.'

'Shit happens, Tomi. I'm doing my best to clean up your mess. So keep your head down and get the paperwork done.'

The line went dead. With a shaking hand Mema sought the cognac bottle. His hands were still shaking when he telephoned Morgan Delaney and asked her to pass on the good news to Jeff Bradley.

༄

'Interesting change of heart, don't you reckon?'

Jeff watched Morgan pace the floor. A pencil tapped across the palm of her hand. Why was it that a bright green sweater could so accentuate the lustrous red of somebody's hair like that? And why was it he found the colour in her fine cheeks and her elegant movements so mesmerising?

'I couldn't get zip out of the courts when Arben was alive,' she said. 'Now they change their minds? I'm a suspicious bitch by nature and I know this place brings out paranoia with red neon lights flashing warnings all over the place, but something doesn't smell right. Maybe you should stall.'

Jeff loved the way she came out fighting on every issue. He also liked the way her hair bounced and her eyes flashed when she became excited.

'I can't really see that I can complain,' Jeff said. 'I sure as hell can't tell Kimie Shala that they offered me the land but I couldn't accept it because a beautiful American had a funny feeling.'

Morgan stopped mid-stride. 'Hang on a minute. Beautiful. Was this a general observation or a compliment?'

'Mm. Maybe I'm leaning towards compliment.'

Morgan grinned and returned to her chair. 'Then the American thanks you. But no, Jeff. Of course you can't turn down the opportunity of getting the property back. Want me to come to court with you?'

'Could I keep you away?'

'Not a chance.'

'I need to get going now. Sulla's waiting outside. We're off to visit Tomi Mema and see if he craps his pinstriped trousers.' Jeff stopped in the doorway. 'Dinner tonight?'

'Is that an order, or an invitation?'

'Which would you prefer?'

'I like my men strong-willed but with manners.'

One eyebrow rose on Jeff's face. 'My men? Okay then, it's an invitation.'

∾

When Jeff walked into Mema's office with Sulla at his shoulder the lawyer cowered behind his desk like a trapped wild animal. His eyes darted back and forth, seeking out a non-existent escape route.

'Hi, Mema. This is Sulla Bogdani, a friend of mine. He's been helping me out while I'm here.'

Mema nodded in Sulla's direction but avoided eye contact. 'Please, gentlemen. Take a seat.'

Jeff remained standing. 'We aren't staying. I've spoken with Arben's family. Are you certain it will be all over tomorrow?'

'With the Kosovon legal system, nothing is ever certain.' Mema's eyes shifted briefly to Sulla then quickly back to Jeff. 'But yes. I believe I can say that Arben's family will be satisfied with the outcome. Of course it's no compensation for their loss. But it is something.'

'And the Xhiha brothers?'

'They must accept the decision of the courts like everyone else. You will have no further problem with the Xhihas. Meet me outside the Municipal Court at nine thirty. I'll try to get it all taken care of as quickly as possible.'

Mema tried to relax after Bradley and Bogdani had left and the immediate threat to his safety appeared to have passed. He retrieved his bottle of cognac from behind the filing cabinet and searched for a glass. There were none. The bottle went straight to his mouth as he flopped back in his chair. How would Gashi react when he found out Bogdani had been to his office?

He put the bottle to his lips again. The burn of alcohol was good.

༄

Light was fading when Lee Caldwell arrived in Prishtina. The traffic lights outside the Grand Hotel were not working and a very youthful-looking Kosovon police officer appeared to be making a hash of directing rush-hour traffic. Caldwell fidgeted with impatience. The car hadn't moved for fifteen minutes.

He pushed open his door. 'Driver. Wait for me in the hotel car park, will you? I'll take it on foot from here.'

Another two minutes and Caldwell was surveying Jeff and Sulla. The two men were standing at the corner of the bar waiting for him. He peeled a pair of kid-leather gloves off his hands as he fixed his attention on Sulla's face. The Kosovon looked anything but relaxed to him.

'Okay, Bogdani. To the point. We tested your explosives and they're not the same as those handed into NATO. I'm satisfied you were telling the truth.'

Tension dropped from the big man's frame. His face creased into an enormous smile. 'Thank you. Thank you, Mr Caldwell. That is very good news. So good.'

Caldwell reached for a handful of peanuts from the bar top. 'Yes. Good news for you, Mr Bogdani. For us it remains bad. There are still explosives out there waiting to be used in other bombings.'

'What I do not understand is why switch the explosives at all?' Sulla asked.

Caldwell shrugged and crunched a couple of peanuts. 'Since you ask, I'll tell you. The protocols for the arms-for-cash programme call for routine analysis of the weapons and explosives handed in. The results are circulated to most international intelligence and crime agencies. Whoever the bad guys are, they obviously knew this and that eventually there would be a match. It's like spraying pepper in the path of a bloodhound. We end up chasing ghosts. Arresting you, for example. Shoving you in jail. Meantime, the real baddies carry on their merry way.'

Jeff was thoughtful. 'Is there any way you can track whoever made the switch through the documentary team?'

'I asked the British police to re-question the film crew and find how the switch could have been made. They say they used a local man working with the UN arms-for-cash programme to hand the explosives over. He was killed during riots over a year ago. Shot through the back of the head.'

'Convenient.'

'Very. And it transpires that his widow is an unusually wealthy woman. He had too much money in the bank, far more than he could have earned at the UN.'

'I have some news for you as well, Caldwell,' Jeff said. 'It seems like you're not the only one who wants me to go home. The title to Arben Shala's property is inexplicably no longer in dispute. Tomorrow I'll be given notarised documents to pass on to Arben's family.'

Caldwell raised an eyebrow. 'Interesting. You have a theory on that?'

Jeff nodded at Sulla. 'Sulla might.'

Caldwell listened as Sulla relayed the events that had taken place in Peje. 'Mr Bogdani, you know these people. Is Tomi Mema smart enough to be our main man?'

'I doubt this. He may have the intelligence for it but he has not the nerve. You think this too, Jeff?'

'I do. Shady lawyer, yes. Criminal mastermind? Unlikely.'

Sulla turned back to Caldwell. 'Gashi and Tomi Mema. No one in Kosovo would believe these two could be working together. In collusion, you say? But for me there is another reason not to believe Mema is the main man. He telephoned my brother-in-law and told him I was going to Peje. He did this knowing Blerim wanted me dead. Fortunately, Blerim did not kill me and he told me Mema had made contact. The point is Mema does not know me well enough to hate me that much. Someone else wanted me dead. Mema was only the messenger.'

Caldwell nodded. Bradley and Bogdani might have been crossing his path more than he would like, but they did seem to stumble over bright, shiny nuggets of truth from time to time. Eventually they might kick over a big one.

Time to turn on the charm. 'Let's celebrate Mr Bogdani's good fortune. Everybody for a round of decent Scotch?'

39.

Tomi Mema staggered into his sitting room and slumped into an armchair. His wife had never seen him in such an inebriated state. She fussed and worried over him. She knelt on the floor to remove his shoes. Mema obliged by lifting his leg. She slipped his shoe off but before she could remove the other, he pushed her aside. 'Where's the television remote?'

His eyes fell upon it lying on a nearby settee. He launched himself from the chair and stumbled across the room. The second shoe clung to his toes. He kicked. It flew over his wife's head and bounced off the wall. The edge of a mat tripped him. Falling backwards in a spin he spread-eagled over the carpet. His wife hurried to his side and tried to help him up.

'Leave me alone. I can do it.'

Mema managed to raise himself enough to crawl into a sitting position on the settee. The anxious face of his wife appeared before him. His mouth gaped twice before words came to his tongue.

'We. Us. Going to Slovenia,' he slurred. Then his world went to blackness.

Morning light filtering into the room caused Mema's eyes to blink open. He stared without comprehension at the ceiling. His head pounded and his mouth was so dry that his tongue had adhered to his back teeth. As he worked at producing a modicum of saliva, he raised his arm. The Rolex attached read a quarter to nine. 'Dammit.'

His wife must be very angry not to have woken him. Somewhere in his memory of the night before he remembered tears and slamming doors.

Right now he had no time to make it up to her. He had to get to court. An unsteady rise to his feet resulted in the sensation of spinning. Only his hand coming to rest on the back of a chair stopped him from crashing onto the coffee table. If he didn't finish the Shala documents in the next few hours, he would be in deep trouble with Gashi. That had to be avoided.

He rummaged through the downstairs bathroom cupboard. A packet of aspirin fell into the basin. He snatched it up and removed two tablets from foil-sealed card. He threw them in his mouth and washed them down with a mouthful of water from the shower head. He shoved his head under the spray. A soaking had him feeling a little better. He stole up the stairs to his dressing room and found a fresh shirt. As he passed the main bedroom he glanced into the darkness and called a timid goodbye.

No reply. He would make it up to her later.

Rain made it impossible to find a taxi. He would have to walk. Hunched under his umbrella he began the twenty-minute trek to his office. Upon his arrival he noticed the cuffs of his suit trousers were damp and splattered with mud. His secretary approached with a cloth but Mema gestured her away. It was almost nine thirty. He had to keep moving.

The Shala file came in for a double-check, followed by the other files he'd need during the day. Satisfied everything he needed was in place, he loaded the lot into his briefcase. If the clerks cooperated he could get the Shala title signed over by ten thirty, hand it to Bradley and still make the start of the new trial on his docket at eleven. After lunch, he'd ring his cousin in Slovenia. With any luck, he'd have his family packed and gone inside a week.

His secretary accepted with good grace the instructions to go to his apartment and bring his other suit to the courthouse. Mema knew she liked his wife and would gossip with her over coffee for an hour. Maybe it would be enough to settle his wife's mood before he made it home.

The rain had eased to drizzle. Using the main road would take too long. He decided to duck down the lane that ran alongside the Thai massage building. It was not sealed, which meant trudging through more mud. But it would save time. Besides, his trousers were already in severe need of cleaning.

A curse sprang to his lips when he spotted the security fence surrounding the supermarket parking lot. He had forgotten the UN had sequestered it. He would need to go the longer way after all.

More mud. But once he was past two kiosks, only a flight of steps and the Statue of Skanderbeg stood between him and the road to the courthouse. In front of the kiosks, a wooden plank supported on two concrete blocks bridged a large puddle. Mema had taken two tentative steps across it when he heard a man calling his name.

With a mutter of annoyance he turned in the direction.

The man in a brown greatcoat and fur busby was not somebody he knew. He pointed to his watch and gestured he had no time. The man raised his arm. Pointed at him.

A gasp left Mema's throat.

Such a blow in his chest. He staggered backwards, almost falling from the plank. Stabs of pain shot through his upper body and into his brain. Was this a heart attack? He thrust a hand inside his shirt and held it to his chest. Something warm and sticky trickled between his fingers. The hand came away with a start. With grow-ing disbelief he found his eyes examining blood. He looked up. The man was coming closer.

And when he saw the gun he understood.

His mouth opened to scream, but no sound came. His brief-case slipped from his grasp and splashed into the water. He barely noticed. What fixated him was the pistol trained on him.

A muzzle flash. Another wallop in the chest. He felt his legs buckling. But his arms wouldn't move. The water parted in a wave as he collapsed into it then surged back, filling his eyes and mouth. He lay, head half submerged, mouth working soundlessly like a goldfish drowning in air. So cold. So very cold. Mema's blurred vision struggled to see as the man bent down and thrust a sheet of paper into fingers that had lost all feeling.

Then nothing.

⌇

Jeff saw Jeremy Lyons from the British consulate talking to a group of people on the steps of the courthouse. The boyish English-man waved an acknowledgement and came across to greet him.

'Mr Bradley. Good morning. Nice to see you again.' The smile was genuine.

'Mr Lyons. Attending court one of your duties?'

'I'm afraid so. But only as an observer.'

'May I introduce Morgan Delaney? Morgan works with the Land Registry Office.'

'I think we may have already met, Ms Delaney. What brings you to court? Are you in need of my assistance?'

'Hopefully not. I'm here to settle a property dispute. We're meeting with Arben Shala's lawyer, Tomi Mema.'

'It's a small world, isn't it? Tomi Mema is the reason I'm here. He's representing a prominent Serbian accused of trying to burn down a mosque. Trial starts at eleven. My colleague from the OSCE and I are to report back on whether or not the Serb receives an enthusiastic defence. She's the one in the red coat over there.'

'And will he, do you think?'

Lyons shrugged. 'We'll have to see. Ah, I see the defendant in question is arriving.'

An unruly crowd had built up in front of the court entrance. Two court officers stood on the steps and kept ordering them to stay back. Murmurings grew louder. A few in the rear hurled abuse and waved fists. A police car cruised up, dropping two wheels through a pothole as it did. Muddy water sloshed over the people in front. This triggered a wave of fury and set the crowd surging towards the car. Two police escorts stood beside the rear door. Uncertain. They looked to Jeff to be assessing whether or not they could safely get their prisoner from the car into the building.

A dozen police armed with batons burst down the courthouse steps. An over-zealous protester pummelling his fists on the passenger window received a blow to the side of his head. With a howl he reeled away, clutching a wound spouting considerable quantities of blood. The sight of an injured comrade managed to dampen the flames of protest a little. The mob backed away. A rock thrown from the rear landed near Jeff. He kept an eye out for more but none came. The escorts pulled the prisoner from the car and rushed him into the building.

'Always fun and games in Kosovo,' Lyons commented.

The OSCE observer and their translator joined Lyons. After the usual introductions, the conversation petered out as they waited for Tomi Mema to show. Morgan tried ringing Mema's cell number. After three attempts and no response, she gave up. At ten thirty

Lyons took his leave of Jeff and asked his translator to accompany him into the courthouse.

He returned almost immediately. 'We seem to have a problem. The judge wants to see me. You too, Mr Bradley.'

'Me?'

'I mentioned you were waiting to see Tomi Mema as well.'

Jeff and Morgan followed Lyons and the OSCE representative inside. Four others were in the courtroom. Lyons pointed out the judge, the court recorder and official translator. He did not know the other man.

The translator said, 'There is no need to sit. This will only take a few minutes.' She nodded to the judge, who proceeded to speak in Albanian. 'I have just received information from the Kosovon police,' the translator interpreted, but not matching the tone of the judge's voice which was as bland as a robot's. 'It is with great regret that I must inform you that Mr Tomi Mema has been shot and killed. The court is closed until further notice. This is a great tragedy for the whole of Kosovo. That is all.'

'Jesus,' Jeff whispered.

❧

'Tomi Mema has been murdered. Shot,' Jeff said.

He made the announcement the minute he joined Barry and Sulla who had been waiting at the cafe on the corner of the court street.

'Holy shit,' Barry blurted. 'Why would someone kill Mema?'

Sulla gripped Jeff's arm. 'Maybe they are sending you a message, Jeff.'

'If that's what it is, then it's a very mixed message. I thought we'd agreed that releasing the property was a none-too-subtle message for me to go home. Why go to all that trouble to arrange a deal and then kill the lawyer before he had a chance to deliver?'

'Good question,' Morgan said. 'First Arben. Now the lawyer. I feel sick to my stomach.'

'What now?' Barry asked.

'The judge gave us the news, then closed the courts. But I assure you it's not over yet. Dammed if I'm leaving Kosovo without something to take back to Arben's family.'

'We will talk to my lawyer, Feime Berisha,' said Sulla. 'She is not as famous as Tomi Mema, but she is very good.'

'She got you out of prison Sulla, which is more than Mema did for Arben,' Jeff said.

'For now we need to keep off the streets,' Sulla warned. 'There will be trouble. Tomi Mema was a popular man. Very famous. After the war he protected KLA soldiers and kept them out of prison for war crimes. Kosovons are proud of him. Now he is murdered. People will blame the Serbs. Maybe the UN as well.'

'Why would they blame the UN?' Barry asked.

'Why not?' Sulla replied. 'People need someone to blame. Kosovo may have a parliament and elections, but the UN is the real government of Kosovo and everyone knows it. People blame governments.'

'Do you think there'll be rioting?' Morgan asked.

Sulla nodded. 'Of course. The nation will mourn in the Albanian way. Something will be destroyed. And then it will be over.'

❧

At seven that evening, Jeff, Morgan, Barry, Bethany and Sulla sat in front of the television set in Morgan's sitting room. Sulla translated as a pretty young blonde reporter standing in the street spoke with pace and much energy into her microphone.

'She is saying crowds have gathered on the streets of all the major Kosovon cities and they are very angry. I think riots will start soon.'

'What surprises me is how quick the reaction has been,' Jeff said. 'The radio and television only just started broadcasting the news of Mema's death.'

'Those people who were near the shooting and saw Mema's body would have had cell phones,' Sulla said. Jeff frowned at him. 'Believe me. It's a small country. Kosovo has ninety per cent unemployment. People are in the cafes with nothing to do but talk. News would have spread across the plains of Kosovo as quickly as fire through a field of sugar cane.'

The television coverage switched to footage from earlier in the day. Cameras zoomed in on Mema's body lying in the mud then panned to the bronze Skanderbeg statue overlooking the scene.

'Now she is saying it is fitting Tomi Mema died beneath the Statue of Skanderbeg. Skanderbeg is an Albanian hero. He fought against the Ottomans. Now she is comparing Mema's fight for the rights of his fellow citizens to Skanderbeg's heroic deeds.'

Barry's head jerked in Sulla's direction. 'You have got to be shitting me. Tomi Mema? This can't be the same back-stabbing, lying toad we've come to know and dislike so much, can it?'

Sulla shrugged. 'Tomi Mema was a celebrity. He was always on television. We Kosovons are very gullible.' He laughed. 'We believe everything we see on the television is the truth. Even that Cola is good for you.'

'With wisecracks like that, Sulla, you might just have some Aussie blood in you.'

Sulla grinned and attended to the next bit of commentary. 'This is very bad. She is suggesting it is an assassination by an organised crime group on the orders of corrupt government officials Tomi Mema was threatening to expose.'

A laugh from Jeff. 'Seriously? '

Sulla turned aside for the screen. 'Tomi would never have exposed a corrupt politician.'

'Not with them paying him so handsomely,' Morgan added.

'But now she is asking why the criminals were not stopped? What was the UN doing in its fight against organised crime? The UN must ultimately accept responsibility for Mema's death.'

The journalist stopped speaking and covered her microphone. She scanned a piece of paper just thrust in front of her and said something to someone off camera. A man stepped into the shot pointing to the paper in her hand and nodding with some agitation. Jeff did not need to understand Albanian to know she had questioned if what was on the paper was for real. The man stepped back out of shot. The blonde journalist brandished the paper before the camera.

'Now she is holding up a photocopy of a document just released to the press. She says it came from the crime scene. Taken directly from Mema's hand. The note claims that his death was because he had recently secured the release of some Kosovon men who murdered Serbs in the war. She is saying his death was Serbian vengeance for the victims' families.'

'Is this true?' Barry asked.

'Better to blame the Serbs than believe us Kosovons could have murdered Tomi Mema.'

'You don't really think the Serbs did this, do you?' Morgan asked.

'Of course not. If Serbs had done such a thing, they would not leave a note.'

Over the next half-hour, Jeff sat beside Morgan as the group watched as the broadcast showed feed snippets on the news from other cities. Mostly the live feed concentrated on central Prishtina. The UN and KFOR commands had moved quickly and established a one-kilometre no-go vehicle zone around the UN headquarters. Roadblocks were set up on all main roads and in all city centres. KFOR-NATO troops in four-wheeled armoured vehicles manned the roadblocks with orders to stop cars, but not to stop the people assembling. Sulla commented that a curfew would have been impossible and useless anyway. With most of its citizens living in central city apartments, the majority of Kosovons were already out of doors inside the cordoned-off no-go zones.

Now the TV cameras returned to the angry crowds gathering in the streets. It also showed shop owners all over town closing up and covering their store fronts with sheets of plywood. One of them was the Kukri bar.

In Prishtina, three hundred Kosovon police officers stood shoulder to shoulder in front of the UN headquarters building. The international police contingent could be seen taking refuge inside the fenced-off compound.

Jeff's head shook, not for the first time that evening. 'You were right, Sulla. It looks like it's going to get nasty.'

'If they've closed the bloody Kukri bar, it must be bad,' Barry said. 'Morgan, I hope you've got plenty of beer in the fridge. It could be a long night.'

Closing on eight thirty the chanting started.

Mee-ma. Mee-ma. Mee-ma.

The juddering picture from some cameraman on foot showed a twenty thousand strong crowd advancing on three hundred police officers at the UN building. The chanting from the street could be heard from Morgan's apartment and when echoed a few seconds later on the live broadcast gave the TV coverage a surreal stereo effect.

Jeff walked to the window and looked down into the street. A few people were drifting by. But they appeared to be the few hardened strollers not prepared to be seduced by the general excitement abroad. Jeff could only hope Morgan's apartment was far enough from the centre of the turmoil to be safe.

He turned back to the group huddled around the small screen.

The chanting appeared to be growing more frenzied as the crowd drew nearer to the UN HQ. The international police could be seen opening the gates and summoning the hopelessly outnumbered Kosovon police force inside the compound with them. Jeff knew what their standing orders would be. The UN troops were not to interfere. They would arrest any rioters scrambling over the walls, but otherwise the upholders of law and order would simply stand back and allow the city to do what cities in chaos are prone to do.

No longer able to vent their anger on the police, the frustrated mob turned their attention to the UN vehicles lining both sides of the main boulevard. The cameras followed young thugs with baseball bats as they went from vehicle to vehicle, smashing windows and battering door panels. Petrol bombs sailed through the broken windows. The crowd cheered as vehicle after vehicle burst into flame.

Impromptu groups of musicians materialised, strumming *lahuta* and *çifteli*, beating on *lodra* drums and *davul*, and blowing riffs on a *zumarë*. Young students, mostly drunk, cavorted around rubbish-bin fires, danced in the streets and sang traditional heroic and epic songs.

By midnight, their frustrations spent, the people began returning to their homes. Tomi Mema's epitaph had been enshrined into folklore. He died in the shadow of Skanderbeg as Prishtina burned.

40.

'Not much damage to the apartment buildings, Sulla.'

'A Kosovon would not destroy another Kosovon's home. We have little enough as it is. The UN has a lot of money. They can always buy new vehicles. In a few days this will be as if nothing has happened.'

Jeff and Sulla carefully picked a path through the burnt-out vehicles and debris strewn across the pavement. Glass crunched beneath their shoes. It was amazing to Jeff how the energetic fervour that had driven the previous evening's violence could so completely dissipate – like it had been nothing more than an early morning mist. He had fully expected to still see groups of protesters. There were none. The acrid stink of rubber and oil from smouldering UN vehicles remained, but that was all.

Citizens were making their way back onto the streets. The cafes were filling.

The city's hawkers were back doing business.

As had been the case with Tomi Mema, Sulla's lawyer also worked out of a converted shipping container, although not quite as austere. The walls were lined with white painted plasterboard. An oil painting of a field of flowers hung above a bookcase. A simple office desk faced them with several filing cabinets to one side.

It looked to Jeff that the three chairs around a glass-topped coffee table at one end were set up for serious conferences.

The woman with greying blonde hair in a ponytail who sat at the desk would have been in her fifties, Jeff guessed. Although apparently engrossed in the contents of a file opened before her, she raised a hand to acknowledge she was aware she had visitors standing in the doorway. She continued to read for another five minutes. With a satisfied pursing of the lips she scrawled a comment on the last page and closed the folder.

The lady's face lifted. It broke into a wide smile as she encountered Sulla. 'Come in,' she said, speaking to Sulla in Albanian.

'Mrs Feime Berisha. I bring you a new client, Jeff Bradley.'

Feime rose and gestured at the chairs in front of the desk. 'Please sit. New clients are always welcome,' Feime said, switching to English. She paused while her visitors settled themselves. Then she sat too. 'How I can help?'

'Tomi Mema was representing Arben Shala. Mr Shala was killed in the detention centre a week ago.'

'Yes, I heard. Very bad business. And now poor Tomi.'

Feime's regret sounded sincere enough to Jeff's ears. But the matter-of-fact expression on her face led him to the assessment that not a lot had got past Mrs Berisha when it came to Tomi Mema.

'Arben Shala's property has been in dispute,' Sulla continued. 'Yesterday the court was set to finalise a ruling in his favour. Tomi Mema was to have the documents notarised and turned over to Jeff on behalf of Mr Shala's family. Unfortunately Tomi Mema was . . . taken to paradise before this could happen.'

Feime threw a quick glance at Sulla and picked up a pen and notepad. 'Ah, yes. Peace be upon him. So. I will need a few details, Mr Bradley. Do you know which court and who it was Tomi was to meet?'

'It was the Municipal Court. But no, I have no idea who he was dealing with.' Jeff passed across the folder Morgan had given him. 'These are the only documents I have. And there's something else. Friends who are in the international police force told me the evidence against Arben was flimsy at best. In their opinion he should never have been detained. I would like to know why he was.'

Feime made a few notes then looked up. 'I will go to the court later today and look over their file on Mr Shala. I will also talk with the chief prosecutor.' Feime shifted in her seat with what looked to Jeff like a touch of embarrassment. 'There is the matter of my fee, Mr Bradley. I'm sorry that you have lost your lawyer and the money you paid him, but I'm sure you understand I cannot work for free.'

'No, of course not.'

Feime's head went down again as she scribbled a figure on a piece of paper. She thrust it at Jeff. She looked relieved when he nodded and pulled out a handful of euro notes from his jacket. He counted several over to her. Feime made out a receipt and handed it to him.

'Good, that is all in order.' She handed Jeff her business card. 'Get Sulla to call me at two this afternoon. I should have some news by then.'

⁓

Once again the events of the last twenty-four hours had Avni Leka mouthing a curse and thumping the desk. For Gashi to have had Tomi Mema shot in broad daylight and in a public place was madness enough. But to kill him before Bradley had taken possession of the documents that would have seen him out of their lives beggared belief. Now Bradley was bound to go find another lawyer. Someone not under his control. And that could only mean trouble. Compounding his problems even further, an international bomber who should never be setting foot in Kosovo was due in Prishtina at any minute. And because of Gashi's stupidity the police and KFOR were on a heightened state of alert. His world was in a mess.

A knock on the door and a head popped around it. 'Feime Berisha wants a quick word.'

Leka hesitated. As chief prosecutor his habit was not to see any lawyer without an appointment. But Feime Berisha's husband had recently been elected into the new parliament. That put them both high on his list of acquaintances worth nurturing.

'Give me a minute and send her in.' Leka quickly tidied his desk, rebuttoned his shirt and adjusted his tie. 'Feime.' He smiled as she entered his office. 'Please take a seat.'

'Thank you for meeting with me at such short notice, Avni. I'll try to be brief.'

'I don't think I'm prosecuting any of your cases, am I?'

Feime shook her head. 'I have a new client. An international. He was a client of Tomi Mema. Mr Jeff Bradley. He's from New Zealand.'

Leka had to suppress the startled exclamation that rose in his throat. Had Gashi been in his office at that moment, Leka swore to himself he would have plunged a knife through his heart. He feigned a fit of coughing.

'Please excuse me. My throat is very sore. I think I might be coming down with something.' He poured water into a glass and gulped a mouthful. 'Let me see. Bradley . . . I seem to know the name, but I can't think why.'

'He is a friend of Arben Shala, the man murdered in the detention centre.'

'Ah, yes. The property dispute. A vineyard. But don't I recall that the court has since decided in favour of Mr Shala?'

'The documents were to be signed on the morning of Tomi's death. Mr Bradley has hired me to take over the file. The formalities still need to be properly concluded.'

'I see. I'm not sure what I can do to help. As you know, since . . . well, since yesterday the courts are closed.'

Feime fixed a steady look fixed upon Leka. 'I would not like to see my client disappointed in this, Avni. It would disappoint me so much as well.'

'Er. Why don't you leave it with me? I'll find out what's needed to complete the process and phone you tomorrow.'

'That would be most appreciated. Thank you. I would also like to look through Mr Shala's court file, if possible? I saw clerks downstairs. Can you authorise that for me now?'

Her eyes betrayed nothing. *This woman's good*, Leka was thinking.

'Is there any need for that? The decision has been made. Only the formalities remain, as you said.'

'Not the property file. I want Mr Shala's criminal file. Mr Bradley asked me to look into the charges against him. His family want to clear his name. Thus I need to see the file.'

Again the steady expressionless look.

Now Leka was convinced there was steel behind the silk. He managed to force a smile. She had every right to ask for the file. He would only be drawing attention to himself should he deny her access. Maybe she would simply skip through it and not delve into too much detail. But Leka knew Feime was far too good a lawyer for such sloppiness.

'Very well. I'll telephone downstairs and tell them to make a copy for you.'

When Feime had gone Leka pulled out his mobile. Gashi created this mess. He could clean it up.

❧

Jeff stood at the window watching a group of small boys kick a battered football around on the patch of bare ground behind the bus stop. The usual Kukri group had gathered at Morgan's apartment for preprandial drinks. Sulla was taking his new friends out for a late lunch at a traditional Albanian place in gratitude for helping to clear his name. Once Jeff had phoned Feime Berisha for news from the courts, they would press on to the restaurant he'd selected in the old part of town.

For the first time since Arben's death, Jeff felt in a lighter mood. He regretted dragging Barry, Bethany and Morgan into his troubles. It had proved a huge relief to him that no one had been harmed. How he would have coped if his actions had caused another person close to him to die did not bear thinking about.

It was time to put the whole dreadful episode behind him and return to New Zealand. Jeff knew he could best serve his friend now by looking out for his family. Caldwell would eventually track down those responsible for Arben's death. There was no point in Jeff hanging about to play detective. Caldwell was right. He lacked the right set of skills and his blundering around might jeopardise Caldwell's investigation. He would instruct Feime Berisha to turn any suspicious details she found in Arben's files over to the American.

A burst of laughter from Morgan cut through his thoughts. He turned to watch her pouring wine for Bethany. They hadn't had a moment alone since the funeral. He had never met anyone quite like her and was experiencing feelings absent from his life since his early days with Rebecca. Not that it mattered. Not that he could let it matter. He was leaving Kosovo and she was staying.

Morgan looked up and caught Jeff's gaze. With a tilt of the head she encouraged him to join the group. He moved across and stood beside her. Their arms brushed. The warmth of her skin through the fabric of his shirt set his heart beating a little faster.

Normality exploded as glass shattered out of the windows and flew across the room.

The sound of gunfire rent the air.

'Get down! Everyone, down!' Jeff shouted.

Five people dropped to the floor as fist-sized pock marks slam-slam-slammed into the ceiling. Clouds of dust and plaster descended.

Barry half-rose with a choking cough. 'What the fuck is that?'

Jeff reached out and pushed down on his head. 'Kalashnikovs. Stay down, for Christ's sake.'

More bursts of fire. Jeff managed to get an arm over Morgan and pull her alongside him. The glass bowl covering the light bulb disintegrated. A frightened Bethany gasped a muffled prayer, her hands over her head, body flinching with every shot. Barry threw his arm across her.

Then the shooting stopped.

The abrupt silence rang in Jeff's ears.

'Stay where you are, guys.'

He rose to a crouch and made a careful approach to the empty window frame. His head poked slowly over the ledge to give him a view of the surroundings below. Small boys were shrieking with excitement and pointing up at the apartment. A crowd of adults gathered around them.

No sign of the gunmen anywhere.

Sulla crept up beside him.

Jeff frowned. 'What the hell was that about?'

'Gashi.' The name from Sulla's lips sounded more like a spit. 'But I think he is only trying to scare us. Otherwise he would have thrown a grenade through the window and we would not be having this conversation.'

'Christ Almighty, Sulla. Bullets do ricochet, you know?'

Jeff stood up and walked across to Morgan with his hand extended. She grasped it and rose from the floor.

'You okay, Morgan?'

'No bullet holes.' She patted her body. 'I'm fine.'

'Bethany? Barry? How about you?'

'I'll be a bloody sight better when someone gives me a flaming beer,' said Barry, helping Bethany to her feet. 'You okay, sweetheart?'

Jeff didn't think Bethany looked okay at all for somebody with the saints in heaven to protect her. She attempted a smile. 'Shaken a bit. I'm good. Look at all this, will you? I can't see you getting your cleaning deposit back, Morgan.'

Barry kissed her nose then hugged her. 'That's my brave girl.'

Jeff caught Sulla's eye. A slow and deliberate nod came back at him.

41.

Jeff studied the name above the menu board. 'The Fushe Kosovo cafe?' he read out loud.

'Fushe Kosovo is the name of this village, also called Kosovo Polje,' Sulla said. 'Rough translation in English – the field of blackbirds. This is the exact site of a battle between twenty-five thousand Serbian soldiers and the might of the Ottoman Empire. Well, that is what the locals say.' Sulla grinned. 'No one is alive to verify it. And who would trust a Serb anyway?'

'Okay, I'll play. Who won?'

'Not the Serbs, my friend, but they fought well. The old people say thousands of blackbirds flew into the bloodied fields and picked over the bones of the fallen and carried away their souls. The rivers ran red for days.'

'Blackbirds? I never thought a blackbird ate flesh.'

'Not blackbirds like you know blackbirds. These were mostly crows, ravens and the like. What the old people should have said was birds that were black. But they didn't, they said blackbirds.'

Jeff nodded. Looking less confused, just.

Sulla turned back to his brother-in-law. A discussion ensued in Albanian. Jeff didn't take exception. He occupied his time watching the late afternoon traffic build up. Diesel fumes spewing out of dozens of generators dotted along the cracked cement footpaths bonded with the octane droplets leaking from rusting car exhausts, and thickened the surrounding atmosphere. Jeff hoped he wasn't about to spend too much time outside, fearful his lungs might become lined with the same black sludge covering the cafe window.

Blerim Basholli had not hesitated when Sulla told him he intended going after Osman Gashi. He arrived in Fushe Kosovo with a dozen men and a small arsenal of weapons hell-bent on bringing Gashi's life to an end. It amused Jeff that only a few days before the two brothers-in-law had been mortal enemies, now they were bickering with each other and slugging back drinks as intimately as any pair of best friends.

Jeff did not share the same level of enthusiasm for Gashi's immediate demise. Not yet, anyway. As much as he agreed the world would be a better place without the criminal gang leader in it, his military experience cast a different light on things. The plain truth was that if Gashi could lead Lee Caldwell to the mastermind behind the bombers, it would save many lives.

An hour earlier, he had gone with Sulla and Basholli to reconnoitre Gashi's house. The first half-mile of road had been sealed. But just before the road ascended a small ridge, it deteriorated into a mud track. Sulla had parked in a small copse of trees and the three had crawled to the top of the ridge. In the distance they saw a concrete block wall surrounding Gashi's three-storey house. Two sentries patrolled the roof. The mile of open ground surrounding the house would make it impossible to approach unseen. It was obvious to Jeff there would be no creeping up on Osman Gashi.

Sulla poured more cognac and turned back to Jeff. 'Getting to Gashi isn't going to be easy,' he said in English. 'Some of Blerin's men are marksmen. They can easily take care of the sentries, even at six hundred metres. But he fears that would only alert the others inside and then these men would not make themselves so visible. I think we all agree that to cross the open ground would be suicidal.

Blerim suggests we could wait for Gashi to leave the compound. Make an ambush.'

Basholli nodded in confirmation. 'Yes. Don't go in like a bull. Wait like the mountain lion,' he said. Sulla grinned at him.

'A sensible option,' Jeff said. 'I agree an attack is out of the question.'

'But this might not happen for days,' Sulla said. 'Gashi has had Tomi Mema murdered, and now attacked us. He will lie low, I am sure of it. If his men do not see you leave Kosovo, Jeff, I think he will try something else. Maybe hurt Morgan or Barry. We cannot wait. Tonight he thinks he is safe because in his stupid fat head he thinks a few bullets will scare us. He will never expect us to come for him.'

'I agree with what Sulla has said,' Basholli said. 'Waiting will give Gashi confidence. But an attack is still not possible. At night is better than day but if the sentry has a night scope . . .'

'We would be like sitting geese,' Sulla said, finishing the sentence for Basholli.

Jeff didn't bother to correct him. 'How many men will he have inside the compound?'

'At a guess, I would say at least eight, maybe ten. But this village is full of Gashi's people. He could have reinforcements within minutes.'

Jeff assessed the men in heavy jackets wandering the street or warming their hands over coal embers. They looked like a mix of peasant farmers and labourers. None looked like soldiers.

Basholli waggled a finger at Sulla and Jeff. 'We must be wary of NATO. We start a war, they come. Armoured vehicles. Helicopters.'

'So, whatever we decide needs to be quick and decisive? Is this what you're saying, Blerim?'

Jeff received a pleased grin in reply. 'I have a rocket launcher. More than twenty rockets. There is no need to go inside the compound to kill him. We blast it to pieces. Shoot the men who run out. Escape before NATO or the police arrive.'

Sulla grinned and slapped Basholli on the shoulder. 'I like this plan. It is a very good plan.'

Jeff disliked dampening such obvious enthusiasm, but he felt the need to persuade them to reconsider. 'Look, guys. I understand your desire for revenge. Gashi ordered Arben's murder, so I'd be more than happy to have you cut his throat.' Jeff drew his finger across his throat. Another smile and another vigorous nod from Basholli. 'But remember. The reason Gashi attacked us and had Benny killed was because we were getting too close to his boss. If we blast the place to smithereens, the trail goes cold and his boss gets away.'

Basholli looked at Jeff with a blank expression. 'I do not care. This is not a concern for me. Gashi killed my father. Now I will have my revenge.'

Cups rattled as Basholli's fist struck the table. Jeff held up his hands, palms facing Basholli. 'I'm not saying don't kill him, Blerim. I'm only saying don't kill him right now. You must have had plenty of opportunities already?'

Basholli appeared to calm down. He offered a shrug. 'Gashi is all the time guarded. Not easy to get to. But I am a patient man. Now my time has come.'

Jeff smiled. 'I'm asking you to be patient a little longer. When we have the information the CIA man needs, you can do what you like. Hell, I'll even help you.' Jeff turned to Sulla. 'Caldwell gave you the chance to clear your name when he could have just arrested you. You owe him.'

Sulla threw a sideways glance at Basholli. His response was another shrug.

Jeff understood their reluctance. This was a big ask. Even if Basholli's men could get close enough, they had neither the resources nor the numbers to storm a heavily armed fortress.

Basholli and Sulla reverted to arguing in Albanian. Jeff turned back to look through the window. It had got darker. Traffic flow had come to a standstill. Impatient drivers sounded horns and yelled at one another.

'Jeff.'

Jeff peered back at the two men.

'Even if we try to do what you ask, it still may not be possible to get to Gashi. The only way into the compound is through a giant reinforced steel gate or over the wall. Many would die this way.'

Jeff swung round in his chair. 'While you guys have been . . . discussing it, I've been thinking. Gashi considers himself to be a businessman, doesn't he?' Sulla nodded. 'And as a businessman, he isn't likely to sacrifice himself needlessly, is he? His fight with us is not about patriotism, or revenge or some higher purpose. It's just about money.'

'What is it you are suggesting?' Sulla asked.

'That I go in and meet with Gashi. Make him an offer he can't refuse, as they say in the movies.'

'He will kill you. What you have got that he would want?'

Jeff's finger pointed at Basholli. 'I tell him Blerim has rocket launchers. I can show him one, and that if he gives me the information I want, he will be left in peace. If he doesn't, then you two will blow us all to bits.'

Basholli sat looking at the floor and shaking his head. Sulla looked close to laughing right in Jeff's face.

'This is a stupid plan. He will not believe you. He will know we will not destroy his house with you in it, and he would be right. Besides, Blerim has only one rocket launcher. Lots of rockets but only the one launcher.'

Jeff lowered his voice. 'I don't think we need to tell Gashi that, do we?'

'I agree with Sulla. Gashi will not believe we will kill you,' Basholli said.

'I could do it,' Sulla said. 'He would believe you would kill me.'

Basholli's eyes bulged out of his head. 'Why would he believe I kill you now when I did not in Peje?'

'Brother of my wife, I will tell him that you let me live because the CIA promised to leave us both alone if I get them the information they want. If I fail, you will gladly blow me to pieces. But if he does give up the information, you and I will renounce our right to revenge and leave him in peace. This is what I will tell him.'

Basholli held Sulla's gaze for a long moment. Then he nodded.

Jeff exhaled a sigh of relief. 'Now. I have a few ideas that might help convince Gashi to be cooperative.'

42.

Sulla wondered if Gashi's compound could be seen from space. Night became day in the glare of the banks of floodlights placed atop the outer wall. He kept his speed under 20 kph and his lights on full beam. He wanted Gashi's sentries to see him coming from a long way off. Basholli and his men were already in position. Whether or not Jeff's plan worked was now in the hands of Allah.

As he drew closer, a small door in the corner of the massive iron gate opened. Two men armed with Kalashnikovs stepped out and waved for Sulla to stop. He pulled over and turned off the engine. This was it. There was no turning back now. He wiped sweating palms on the car seat cover, opened the door and climbed out.

One of the two men held back and covered his comrade who stepped forward. He stopped a few metres short of Sulla. Sulla's assessment was that these men were professionals and not at all what he had expected. Gashi must be paying big bucks.

'What do you want?' the man barked at him.

'My name is Sulla Bogdani. I want to speak to Osman Gashi.'

'Wait here,' the man ordered, then disappeared inside the compound. The second guard said nothing. He kept the Kalashnikov trained at Sulla's chest. Sulla ventured a smile. No response.

After five minutes, the first man returned and waved Sulla into the compound.

'There is something in the trunk I need you to bring. A gift for Gashi.'

Sulla tossed his car keys to the second guard and walked away without looking back.

As he crossed the courtyard he counted at least thirty men. He knew there'd be more inside the house. He and Basholli had badly miscalculated Gashi's fear of retaliation. The house reminded Sulla of the Mexican haciendas he had seen in old Hollywood westerns. Small balconies jutted out above him and vines wound their way through trellises attached to walls that were painted in white, pink and orange. In the foyer an antique coat stand stood beside a black leather two-seater chair. A red-and-black Navajo rug covered most of the terracotta-tiled floor. The guard prodded him through a door and into a spacious lounge furnished in similar manner.

Four men sat round an oak dining table drinking cognac and enjoying the warmth of a log fire. It completed the picture developing in Sulla's head. To him, the whole place looked like a movie set. Gashi had watched too many cowboy films.

The men by the fireplace glared at Sulla. Sulla endeavoured to keep his expression neutral.

Osman Gashi stood with one arm draped across the top of a high-backed leather chair in front of an ornate oak desk.

'Sulla Bogdani. Please, come and sit down.'

He pointed to a second high-backed chair. It looked to Sulla like a studio setting for a one-on-one TV discussion.

Sulla sat as directed.

Gashi lowered himself into his chair. He clasped hands together and rested them on his oversized belly. 'What brings you to my house at this time of night? And, I might add, uninvited.'

'I want the name of a man, Gashi. The man you work for.'

A grin flashed across Gashi's face. It disappeared as quickly.

'Firstly, I am my own boss. I work for no one. Secondly, if there was such a person as you suggest, why would I give his name to you?'

'You and he stole money and property from the man named Arben Shala who you had falsely accused of a crime. You saw that he got arrested and then you had him murdered while he was in the Prishtina Detention Centre. Arben Shala was a friend of the family. Shall I just say you owe me one, Gashi?'

Gashi shook his head with what appeared to Sulla to be a bogus look of disbelief. 'Even if your fairy story were true, I still do not see why any of this leads me to want to help you. Kill, maybe. Help, no.'

Sulla drew a deep breath. He was savouring the prospect of wiping the smile from Gashi's face.

'Recently I was in Macedonia, but I think you already know that.'

Gashi did not respond.

'I met with an American intelligence agent. This agent told me that explosives I gave to NATO were the same explosives used in terrorist bombings in Belgium and Slovenia. Fortunately, I was able to prove they did not come from me. It seems someone switched the explosives and left a trail of blame leading my way. The Americans believe the man who arranged the switch lives here in Kosovo. Imagine my surprise when he told me the man they suspected was Osman Gashi.'

This time when Gashi turned on a laugh, Sulla was sure he detected a shade of anxiety in it. The eyes had become more mobile too.

'Keep talking. This could be amusing.'

'Tomi Mema, Gashi. Killing him was not so clever. And trying to pin it on the Serbs? It may have fooled the average Kosovon, but not me. And not the CIA.'

A tightening of Gashi's mouth. Sulla knew he had struck home. Gashi wiped his brow. Sulla doubted that the heating alone in the room was causing beads of sweat to run down the fat man's neck.

'Then yesterday you went a step too far. Machine-gunning the apartment and nearly killing my friends. It has to stop.'

Gashi leaned forward, all pretence of cordiality gone. 'You come here uninvited. You accuse me of murder. You sit in front of me and insult me in my own home. I should kill you now and be done with it.'

A nod from Gashi now would see Sulla dead and he knew it. That it hadn't happened already meant Jeff was right.

'Fortunately for you, Gashi, I was able to convince the agent that you lacked the wit to organise such an operation. They believed this. And that someone else gave the orders. That is the name I want. They want. Give it to me and I will allow you to live through this night.'

A roar of laughter came out of Gashi. Men at the oak table sniggered in support. 'You have big balls, Sulla. I give you that. Tomi Mema was a fool. You should not waste any sympathy on him. And as for this boss you say I work for, I repeat – I work for no man.'

'I want you to see something.' Sulla made a reach for his pocket. The click of the first tension-release of a trigger sounded close behind his ear. Both Sulla's hands went into the air instead.

'It's only my mobile phone.'

'Get it.'

The guard's hand flew to the pocket Sulla had been aiming for. He pulled out the mobile into Gashi's view. He nodded. The phone was thrust into Sulla's hand. He lifted it and pressed in the speed-dial number of Basholli. The room went still. The line opened and Sulla heard breathing at the other end.

'Go ahead.'

His thumb hit end-call. All eyes remained fixed on Sulla. His gaze lifted and scanned the faces surrounding him.

'So that you can understand how serious your situation is, go up onto your roof and tell me what you see.'

'We're playing games now?'

'Please. Humour me. You'll be grateful that you did.'

❦

The confidence displayed by Sulla rattled Gashi. His instincts told him this was not a bluff.

'Watch him,' he snarled to the men at the table. 'If he moves, shoot him.'

Pistols appeared from belts and jackets.

Gashi left the room and entered the stairwell to the rooftop. After five steps his breathing came in gasps. He stopped for a second clutching the handrail. The journey to the roof would need to be taken in stages.

Emerging into the open air, Gashi found two of his sentries sitting with their backs against a wall, smoking. Cigarettes went flying as both scrambled to their feet and made a grab for their rifles. Gashi walked to the closer man and kicked him in the ankle. A cry of pain was quickly stifled.

'Imbeciles.'

Gashi walked across to the parapet. In the darkness beyond the floodlights he could discern nothing at all. But as his eyes adjusted, he saw them. Lights. Maybe three hundred metres away. Was the fortress illumination playing tricks on his eyes? Several hard blinks and it became clear this was not so. Dozens of lights. His eyes cast further. Lights from all angles.

A sick, panicky feeling hit him in the stomach. No wonder Sulla Bogdani could afford to be so brash with him. He had mustered a small army. He should have guessed Sulla would never have come without a plan to ensure he left alive.

Time for a recalculation. He had forty armed men. And the place was secure in the short term against even quite a sizeable storming. If he kept Sulla prisoner until first light, his snipers could pick off the enemy in the fields and he could summon reinforcements from the village. They would come in behind Sulla's army and destroy them. Sulla had definitely miscalculated.

With a glare at the guards Gashi left to go downstairs.

∞

Sulla watched Gashi return to the room. He noted the confident demeanour. When Gashi sat back behind his desk he did not bother trying to hide a smirk bordering on contempt.

'I see you have brought friends. Just one small flaw. I have you here with me. Your men will do nothing if they think you'll be killed. So what else can they do? Attack me? This is a fortress. You cannot win this way.'

Sulla smiled to himself. Jeff's plan really was working.

'They are not my friends, Gashi. They are Blerim Basholli's soldiers. All KLA. You know Blerim, don't you? Of course you do. You shot his father.'

Colour drained out of Gashi's complexion. 'You . . . you're bluffing. Blerim would never support you.'

'That much is correct. Blerim doesn't give a damn if I live or die. Being expendable makes me the perfect negotiator.'

Gashi's brow creased in confusion. 'Negotiator?'

'I've brought you a gift, Gashi. Just so you know exactly what you're facing.'

Sulla turned to the second man who had escorted him in.

'Please show him, will you?'

The man stepped forward and held up the rocket launcher he had taken from the trunk of Sulla's car.

'There are more than a dozen of these out there, Gashi. Enough, I think you'll agree, to blast this place into oblivion. If I have not left here within thirty minutes, Blerim intends ordering his men to fire.' Sulla made a point of looking at his watch. 'I have already been here fifteen.'

Gashi's eyes flicked around the faces of his men in what looked like panic to Sulla. They in turn were exchanging nervous glances and muttered comments.

Gashi stood and raised a hand. All movement in the room ceased.

'All right. All right. Settle down for God's sake. You.' He delivered a withering glare at Sulla. 'If I tell you what you want to know and you leave, Basholli will do it anyway. So I have nothing to gain except the satisfaction of knowing you will go to hell with me.'

Gashi's stoicism took Sulla by surprise. But he had to gamble that Gashi truly had no desire to die. He raised his voice. 'That is your best plan, Gashi? For you and all these men. What's the point in dying like rats in this hole when there's an alternative? I am authorised to tell you that Blerim will drop his vendetta against you for the death of his father. When I leave, no harm will come to you – or your men.'

As Sulla expected, the mumbles coming from Gashi's men confirmed they favoured the plan now emerging from Sulla's mouth. This didn't go unnoticed by Gashi. He stared at Sulla for a long moment. At last a hand reached down to somewhere below his desk and emerged with a bottle of cognac. It went onto the desktop. Two glasses followed. Sulla watched with growing relief as Gashi filled both glasses and pushed one across to him.

Gashi shrugged. 'I want to hear this directly from Basholli. I want to hear these words from his mouth.'

Sulla took out his mobile phone again and dialled Basholli's number. He passed the phone to Gashi. Gashi took it to the far end of the room. He spoke softly and appeared to listen intently. The conversation lasted nearly two minutes. Gashi was smiling when he passed the phone back to Sulla.

'It seems we both live to see another day.' Gashi held up his glass in a mock salute. '*Gazeur.*' He downed the cognac and poured another. 'Now it is time for me to have a moment of pleasure from this night. I shall enjoy your reaction when I give you the name of the man you seek.'

A harsh chuckle floated in the air.

෩

Barry and Morgan were still awake when Jeff and Sulla returned to Morgan's apartment. Bethany lay asleep on the couch. Barry's two South African policemen mates dozed in armchairs, a dozen empty beer cans on the floor beside them.

'You two look like shit,' Barry said, grinning from ear to ear. 'Morgan and I have spent half the bloody night worrying.'

Jeff appraised the place in a quick glance. 'The apartment looks almost like new again.'

'Yeah. The landlord had the windows replaced quick smart. He dragged the tradesman away from his dinner. The landlord's wife vacuumed up the glass. Thank God we're internationals otherwise it would've taken a month. Morgan's rent is too much income for them to lose. Now, tell us what happened.'

Sulla relayed the events of the evening. 'Jesus, mate. You were bloody lucky. Money on the rank outsider in the Melbourne Cup would be less risky than pulling that rocket launcher stunt. So, who's the guy responsible for all this shit?'

'A man named Avni Leka.'

'Who the hell is Avni Leka?'

'The Municipal Court prosecutor.'

A visible start from Morgan.

'I know that name. Wasn't he your lawyer, Sulla? The man who tricked you and had you sent to jail?'

'That is the man.'

❦

Jeff's gaze out into the darkness had no particular purpose. He didn't even feel trepidation to be standing at the spot where twenty-four hours before a hundred rounds of ammunition had split the air and shattered the window. He listened to the sounds of Morgan following the others down the stairs. Their departing voices floated up to him. Then the distinctive metallic finality of a door being secured.

He strained to hear her gentle footsteps climbing the stairs.

He felt her pause in the doorway. Sensed her watching him. Deciding. He hardly dared breath, or to turn to look at her. The beating of his heart rose a notch. No point straining to hear more. Carpet on the floor prevented tracking her advance any further. But, there it was: a creak of that loose floorboard just a metre behind him. He counted. One – two seconds. With the disturbing effect of little more than a butterfly wing, a hand slid through his arm. His heart rate elevated a few more notches as his shoulder took the pressure of Morgan's head against it.

And the age-old question posed to so many males through so many lives circulated in his head. Was this intimacy or the comforting of an old soldier returned from the front? Jeff's head tilted for a surreptitious investigation. Meeting his gaze were a smile and the greenest eyes in creation. He felt his heart rate go off the scale.

His next actions took on the quality of a dream. Arms drew her close. Lips found her cheek, her neck, then descended on her lips with a hunger that was returned in full.

When Jeff lifted Morgan and carried her towards the bedroom, her arms circled his neck and a whisper brushed into his ear.

It asked him to hurry.

Please.

43.

Jeff mooched through Morgan's kitchen. Six cupboards later, he found a jar of instant coffee and a bowl of sugar. With a mug of the steaming brew in his hand, he pushed open the door onto the third-floor balcony and stepped into a bracing morning. Slender minarets fingered into a clear sky. In the street below, women bundled up against the chill bustled along with shopping baskets and small children in tow. He noted that the police car assigned as protection during the night was gone. Sulla had sounded quite confident that now Gashi had agreed to a truce of sorts, all danger had passed. He was not so sure. He turned indoors.

Morgan appeared wearing a light blue dressing gown and rubbing a towel through her wet hair. She stopped when she saw Jeff watching her. For a second a stupid feeling of shyness held his tongue.

'Um. I helped myself to a coffee.' He held up the cup as if in need of evidence for his claim. 'When I've finished this, I'll use the shower if you don't mind. Then head back to the hotel for a change of clothes.'

Morgan smiled and shook her head. 'You could have joined me if you'd wanted to.'

'The thought did cross my mind.'

Wrapping the towel round her head Morgan tucked in an end at the back to secure it in place then turned her attention to the kitchen. She took a small carton of Columbian coffee from the freezer and scooped three spoons into the cafetière. Boiling water followed. 'That won't take long to draw.' She drew up a chair to the kitchen table. 'You know, I don't mind admitting that all of this violence scares the hell out of me. But you actually seem to revel in it. So I'm curious, Jeff. Why leave the military to go into winemaking of all things?'

Jeff leaned against the doorframe and peered across the top of his coffee. 'It's no big deal. Not really. When I joined the army, I trained at Burnham Military Camp in the South Island of New Zealand, not far from Christchurch. On my second weekend leave after finishing training, I met Rebecca. My ex. I was at a disco with a bunch of the guys and she tapped me on the shoulder and asked me to dance. She was an attractive blonde. How could I say no?'

'Goes without saying,' Morgan said. Jeff couldn't help but notice the wryness in her smile. 'There's absolutely no way a man can turn down a beautiful blonde.'

Jeff pulled a grimace. 'Okay, okay. Smartarse. Anyway we started seeing each other and before I knew it, we were married. We were happy and even talked about starting a family. Then I had a chance to try out for the SAS. I passed the selection course, which meant a transfer to Auckland, New Zealand's biggest city. Way up north. That's where the SAS is based. For a few years all was fine. I loved being in the Squadron, but Rebecca didn't like Auckland at all. She tolerated it for my sake. She was a Christchurch girl and wanted to stay in the South Island. But the army is the army. It owns you and you go where it sends you.'

'You had no choice in the matter?'

Jeff shrugged. 'I could have not applied. But once they accepted me, no. I had no choice. I was away much of the time – overseas, on active duty mostly. The life suited me. But Rebecca became depressed. Complained about the loneliness. Never stopped wanting to go back to Christchurch. At the time I didn't really understand it. There were army wives' support groups for while their men were away. I thought she'd be happy drinking tea and shopping with friends.'

Morgan shook her head. 'Words of a chauvinist, Jeff.'

'You're right. Even my own mother would agree with you, you'll be happy to know. She sat me down and explained what a selfish bastard I was. With a wife came responsibilities; if I'd wanted a career in the SAS, I shouldn't have got married. I think secretly she was using guilt to get me to quit before I got myself killed.'

Morgan stood to pour some coffee. Her head nodded even though her back was for the moment to Jeff. 'Sounds to me like a smart woman, your mother.'

'Anyway, Rebecca finally issued an ultimatum. The army or her. So I resigned from the army.'

Cup steaming in one hand, Morgan paused, eyebrows arched, mid-stride back to the table. 'But you and Rebecca aren't married any more.'

As she sat, Morgan's dressing gown chose that moment to slip aside, exposing a slender pale expanse of thigh. Jeff's eyes developed a will of their own. Morgan broke into a smile and quickly tended to her modesty. Jeff resisted the desire to grin like a schoolboy.

'Sorry. Distracted. Where was I? No, we're not married any more. After I'd left the army, I decided that if I had to be a civilian I was better off in Auckland. By now Rebecca hated Auckland almost as much as she did the army. We fought constantly. Then Rebecca told me she was moving back to Christchurch. And that was that.'

'Have you heard from her since?'

'From Rebecca? Not much. From her lawyers, a great deal. We're still fighting over how to divide the assets. She insists I sell the vineyard. But, see, it belonged to my grandmother. She loved it, but she couldn't look after it properly. When I took it over it was run-down and neglected, more an albatross round my neck than any meaningful sort of asset. I didn't even fully inherit it until after Rebecca had left me. But we weren't divorced then, either. She didn't give a damn about it. It took me the better part of three years breaking my hump to get it productive again. We won awards for our Merlot and Chardonnay. Got some good reviews in a few food magazines so Rebecca thinks the place has become hugely valuable. I offered to buy her out but she wants it to go to auction.'

'You gotta love matrimonial law.' Morgan returned to the kitchen bench for a refill. 'So you're not bitter she made you leave the army?'

Jeff shrugged. 'My father taught me and my brothers that any decision a guy makes, good or bad, it's his choice. Too many people hang onto the past and lose their futures.'

'So you weren't angry?'

'Are you kidding? I was bloody pissed off to hell.' Jeff laughed at his own fit of honesty, but became serious once more. 'Look. She can have anything else she wants from me. But not the vineyard. It's not about the money. My grandmother left me several properties and more than enough cash and investments that I never need worry about working again the rest of my life. For that, I promised her, her vineyard would remain in the family.'

Morgan stirred her coffee, staring at the patterns the spoon made as she added cream. 'I worried about you last night.'

'Now that's interesting, because all I could think of was getting back to you.' Jeff moved from the doorway. A clunk as he placed his mug onto the kitchen bench. Morgan didn't notice him taking up a position behind her chair until his arms fell either side of her with palms flat on the table top. A kiss on top of her head was followed by the caress of lips on her neck. And just as her head twisted to respond – the doorbell decided to do what doorbells do best.

Two grown-ups jumped like teenagers caught necking in Mum and Dad's bedroom.

'Jesus, fucking hell. Oops, sorry, Morgan.'

And two grown-ups found themselves face-to-face trying not to giggle like kids.

The doorbell shrilled again.

'Oh damn. Jeff, you're more decent than me. Go down and get rid of whoever it is, will you? Tell them it's the wrong house or something.'

Part way through the door Jeff drew to a halt. Turned. Went back to Morgan and took her in his arms. Lips met, softly at first, then with more hunger.

'Hmmm. Maybe I won't get dressed just yet.'

The doorbell intruded once more. Jeff held Morgan at arm's length and studied her face.

'Hold that thought while I go chuck the bastards out.'

With Morgan's laugh still in his ears, Jeff bounded down the stairs and flung open the door. His jaw dropped.

Lee Caldwell said, 'You don't look all that pleased to see me.'

'Well, this is kind of an inconvenient moment. I don't suppose I can talk you into coming back later?'

A pursing of the lips. 'Not a chance.'

'Damn. Come on in, then. If you must.'

Morgan had disappeared by the time they made it up to the kitchen. Jeff sat the visitor down and brought the coffee pot to the table with an extra cup. As he poured, he felt Caldwell scrutinising him.

'Well, I guess you're not here to pass the time of day, Caldwell.'

'I hear you had some fun in Fushe Kosovo last night?'

'CIA still following me?' The humourless Caldwell smile met Jeff's frown. 'Last night was mostly Sulla. I stayed in the background.'

'Not by choice, I wouldn't think.'

'Sulla risked his life to get the name of the man you're looking for. Make a note of that for future reference.'

A response looked to be on the tip of Caldwell's tongue. But it died as Morgan walked back into the kitchen. Two pairs of male eyes were treated to the sight of a glowing redhead in navy blue blouse and jeans and just a touch of make-up. Jeff's dearest desire right then was to toss Caldwell off the balcony and whisk Morgan off to the bedroom.

She retrieved her coffee from the bench and joined them at the table.

Caldwell sipped at his cup. 'I'm curious to know why Osman Gashi isn't dead. Or you, Bradley, for that matter.'

'Blerim and Sulla wanted to blow him to hell and be gone, but I persuaded them we needed to break this terrorist gang of yours. Sulla cut Gashi a deal: Give up his boss and the KLA would leave him alone.'

Caldwell looked mildly surprised. 'I appreciate you keeping a clear head. Who is the boss?'

'Avni Leka.'

'Leka. Should I know him? The name isn't ringing any bells.'

'He's the chief prosecutor for the Municipal Court here.'

A slow nod from Caldwell. 'Ah. I suppose it makes sense. He's certainly in a position to manipulate the system. No doubt Gashi will try to warn him, deal or no deal. That sort of snake always manages to slide between both sides of any fence. Anyway, thank you. We'll grab Leka and put an end to him.'

Jeff's forefinger extended upwards in front of his face like he was about to administer a blessing. 'You might want to hold off on that for just a bit.'

'Might I?'

'Gashi also told Sulla that the million euros confiscated in Greece came from Leka and he's been very jumpy. It seems some special visitors are coming to see him about that. Within the next day or so, Gashi thinks.'

This wasn't all Gashi had told Sulla in efforts to save his own skin. But Jeff intended keeping some of it to himself. Information he now possessed was that a man named Bedri Cena slit Arben's throat in the prison cell. Bedri Cena had walked out of the detention centre a free man yesterday. Today Cena would be receiving a visit he never expected.

'No more specific time than just the next day or so?'

'No. But Gashi knew about you, Caldwell. His men saw us talking in Macedonia, and followed you to the embassy. They assumed you're CIA.'

The humourless Caldwell smile again. 'Yes. I made sure they saw us. We weren't sitting outside on a cold day for the fun of it. I hate the cold.'

'Well, it might thrill you to know that when Leka heard about you, our crooked prosecutor almost had a seizure.'

Again the Caldwell smile. 'I've found it always helps move things along a bit faster if the baddies think the CIA's after them.'

Jeff felt heat rising at the back of his neck. Morgan put down her cup.

'Well, your plan worked a treat. They shot up Morgan's apartment two nights ago. We were all here. Go downstairs and take a look at the holes in the ceiling for Christ's sake.'

Caldwell shrugged. 'Unfortunate. But now at least we've got Leka's name.'

'That's not really my point.'

'It's exactly my point.'

Jeff's and Caldwell's eyes locked. Neither blinked. Morgan's chair scraped on the floor as she rose and walked to the spot in the doorway where the sun shone in.

'We Americans, Jeff,' a glare fixed on Caldwell, 'we Americans only preach ethics.'

Caldwell placed his cup on the table. 'These visitors you say Leka has coming. Gashi mention any names?'

'No, but I think we can rule out family and friends.'

'If it was Leka who sent money to Greece to pay off the bombers, the money never got to them. They will still want payment. And frankly, they are of more interest to me than even Avni Leka.'

Jeff stared at Caldwell in disbelief. For the CIA to have only minimal interest in a man who orchestrated and funded terrorism throughout Europe defied logic. Jeff found himself viewing Caldwell through new lenses. Maybe he wasn't CIA after all. A maverick game-player working inside American diplomacy circles with full access to top-secret files? If so, what was the game? His eyes swivelled to Morgan. He sensed from the narrowing of her eyes on Caldwell that she had also picked up that there was something not entirely kosher going on with Caldwell. Caldwell appeared not to notice any change in the atmosphere. Either that, or he was a far better actor than Jeff had imagined.

'My problem is manpower. I have a couple of men nearby, but that's not going to be nearly enough. Besides, I have other work for them. I could use soldiers from Bondsteel, the same guys I've had following you lot. But they don't have the experience for this type of covert operation. Many of the local cops are bound to be on Leka's payroll.'

Jeff thought he could see where this was heading. 'I'm out of the intelligence business and on my way home.'

'You're never out. You know that. You kept your head and did good work last night. No one was killed, and you got valuable information. I'm only going to ask you to help with surveillance.'

'What about me?' Morgan said. 'I know the city and the countryside. And I can speak the language.'

Caldwell shook his head. 'Leka knows who you are, and you haven't the training. He'd be onto you in seconds.'

'I don't need training to watch a door, for Christ's sake. And it's doubtful Leka would even notice me.'

Caldwell and Jeff exchanged glances. Jeff smiled.

'Morgan, I don't think it's possible for any man not to notice you. But she's right in one respect, Caldwell. Anyone can watch a door. Look, snake or not, Gashi isn't likely to warn Leka he's ratted him out. He certainly won't be expecting covert US surveillance on him. Not yet, anyway. Sulla could get a few friends together. Blerim Basholli and his people are locals. They won't stand out. Look. If I do this for you, I do it my way with my people.'

The corners of Caldwell's mouth turned down for a minute as he took time to think this through. 'Okay, I can live with that. But no heroics. Just observe, nothing more. We'll give it a week. If nothing has happened by then, I'll have Leka picked up.'

'I'll need some expense money to pay Sulla and his people.'

'My briefcase is in the car at the Grand Hotel car park. Come with me now and I'll give you enough to get started.'

Caldwell stood and made his way to the stairs.

Jeff turned to Morgan. 'We'll talk later. Okay?'

'You could have a shower here.'

'I can't say that's not tempting, Morgan. But I have to meet up with Sulla. We have some, er . . . business to attend to.'

Caldwell's voice floated up from the floor below. 'Are you coming, Bradley?'

'Right behind you,' he yelled. Then to Morgan he whispered, 'I'll be seeing you soon?'

'I imagine you will.'

❧

On the drive back to Macedonia, Caldwell sent a text message to the Admiral. *Xmas is coming early* – code for *I have a lead*. When he got back to the embassy in Skopje he would give a full report on a secure line. The Admiral would want to know about Leka. There would be no overruling his decision to leave the municipal court prosecutor roaming free for a few days. Getting the bombers was still number one priority.

Bradley and his ad hoc crew had kicked over a good-sized rock. The vermin that lurked beneath had been flushed into the open. But it had been more luck than skill. If only he had the manpower; he would have the New Zealander and his merry men rounded up and kept out of harm's way while the professionals did their job. But the simple truth was that he did not have the men. So he would have to work with amateurs. Caldwell had ordered his own men to stay low, keep an eye on Bradley and wait for instructions while he was out of Kosovo. He would only be gone two days. If there was an emergency, he would have a chopper from Bondsteel bring him to Prishtina.

Either way, according to his judgment, the chase was nearing the end. There was little sense of elation. When it was over, he would simply move on to the next target.

There were always new targets.

44.

Twice Sulla had driven down Agim Ramadani Road. Heavy traffic was making it impossible for him to park close to Prishtina's bazaar and fruit and vegetable markets. He circled the block a third time then gave up. A street vendor selling cigarettes two blocks away offered Sulla space on a patch of council dirt, promising that for five euros he would not steal the car. For another five he would not let anyone else steal it. Sulla unleashed a tirade of outrage. Jeff handed across ten euros.

Standing at the city-side entrance, Jeff estimated that the markets covered four blocks. Display structures varied from rambling lean-tos and converted shipping containers to more soundly constructed stores, warehouses and cafes. Lines of wooden shelving protected by canvas awnings displayed a colourful array of vegetables and fruit.

'If nothing else, you grow good-quality produce in Kosovo, Sulla.'

'For these we can take no credit. They are trucked in from Macedonia and Montenegro daily. Now maize. That is another story.'

Jeff found talking about nothing in particular helped relieve tension. Cleared his head. Sulla was similarly inclined. Walking through the streets, Sulla had pointed out cigarettes, sacks of flour, sugar, rice, home appliances, electronics, glassware, carpentry tools, carpets, cans of paint and even wedding dresses. He declared himself an expert on all products and warned Jeff not to make a purchase unless he was present.

Now the talking was done. It was time. Jeff felt Sulla's hand on his shoulder. The big man leaned into his ear. 'Are you certain you want to do it this way? I can get a rifle from Basholli. You can shoot from the car. It would be over quickly. No hassles.'

'Is he here?'

'Yes, he is. With friends.'

'Which way?'

'This way. Follow me.'

Sulla kept to a cobbled pathway close to a row of small warehouses not much bigger than car garages. Jeff doubted any element of surprise was necessary. However, Sulla wanted to be careful so Jeff obliged.

Sulla pointed to a door behind a stand of peppers, cucumbers and tomatoes.

'That is Bedri Cena's brother's cafe.'

Jeff nodded. A few metres away two sheep in a small pen ran at him. They nudged into the wire netting and bleated. The aromas of kebabs and sides of lamb rotating on spits mingled with the more pungent odours from a display of cheeses on the back of a small horse-drawn trailer. The horse stood still, its head drooped. The straw-thin farmer in attendance sucked in a lungful of nicotine and fell into a spluttering fit of coughing. Jeff mused that he could have been a clone of the Xhiha brothers. Radios hanging from poles played CDs of ethnic music. The discordant sounds reminded Jeff of Turkey.

Even though the temperature was close to freezing Jeff had worn light clothing. His hands ached from the cold. Had he the time, he would have looked for a pair of gloves. Maybe later. He limbered up his arms with circular stretching movements.

When the fight started his joints needed to be loose.

Sulla drew Jeff to a halt outside the cafe entrance. He looked back towards the road.

'Last chance.'

'I'm not changing my mind, Sulla. Let's do it.'

Sulla pushed open the door. A cloud of cigarette smoke and the ubiquitous smells of alcohol, sweat and roasting kebabs sucked out past them into the ravenous open air. The crowded cafe was very hot. Gas heaters turned on high stood in the four corners of the room. The interior was lit only by beams of sunlight struggling through two small windows just beneath the timber roof rafters.

It took a few seconds for Jeff's eyes to adjust.

'That's him,' Sulla whispered in his ear. 'In the corner. The one wearing the red shirt.'

Jeff studied the man sitting with his back to the wall. There were six others seated with him. Two open bottles of cognac sat in the centre of the table. A dead one lay on its side between them. The group was in high spirits. Their conversation loud and animated. Talking over the top of each other. It struck Jeff the mood of the table had a celebratory feel. No doubt a Welcome Home, Bedri party. The man in red yelled something unintelligible. Laughter followed.

Bedri Cena looked not to be a big man to Jeff. But the sleeves of his shirt did draw tight around bulging biceps.

It took four steps to the table.

Jeff bent low. 'You're Bedri Cena?'

Seven heads turned his way.

'Who is asking?'

Good, Jeff thought. If you need someone who speaks English in a foreign country, go looking for street hawkers and criminals.

'We have a mutual acquaintance. Arben Shala, remember him? Arben was a close friend of mine.' Jeff paused. Bedri's face twitched.

'Nice man, Bedri. He has a beautiful wife and two lovely children waiting for him to come home. But poor Arben can't go home and you know why?' Bedri's eyes stood wide and fixed on Jeff's face. 'He can't go home because he's dead, Bedri. And he's dead because you murdered him.'

Bedri's lips pursed. A forefinger rubbed his bottom lip. With deliberation he placed hands on table and pushed himself upright.

'Ah ha. You must be Arben's boss from New Zealand. He told me you might come. I did not believe he had such a good friend, but here you are. Let me give you some advice: go back to your country. I will allow you to walk out of here for Arben's sake. He was a good man. He deserves this much respect.'

A man alongside Bedri also stood. 'Do as he says, foreigner. You are not welcome here.'

Sulla tapped Jeff's shoulder.

'That piece of shit is Bedri's brother.'

The brother glowered at Sulla. Sulla stared back without flinching.

Bedri's friends rose from their chairs and began to spread out. Jeff stood his ground. 'Don't do anything silly,' he said. He took a pace forward. 'I've only come for Bedri.' Jeff turned to the others. 'You cannot help your friend. Leave now.'

Bedri's face closed up to Jeff's. His smirk smacked of extreme confidence, his breath of rotting fish and cognac.

'You are a fool. You cannot beat all of us. Even with your monkey to help you.'

Sulla's arm rose in a signal. Blerim Basholli's plants and a dozen pistols rose as one from amongst the diners.

Sulla turned to Bedri with a laugh.

'Not a bad trick for a monkey, is it?'

Whites of eyes gleamed as the group exchanged cautious glances. Then every one of them sat back down. The sudden movement of the barman caught Jeff's eye. A hand had reached under the counter. In a flash Sulla's pistol was at the man's chest. At a prompt from Sulla's gun he hastened from behind the bar to sit with the others.

A curse cut through the air. The brother launched at Jeff.

'Go, Bedri, go.'

Trapped in a bear hug Jeff staggered backwards. Bedri was still in his sights. A beaded curtain at the rear of the cafe parted as he disappeared. Jeff and his attacker fell against a wall. Jeff found his right hand level with his opponent's testicles. He gripped and twisted.

With a scream the brother released Jeff and grabbed at his crotch.

Jeff arched his torso and pushed forward off his right leg. His body like an uncoiling spring unleashed power through to his shoulder, propelling his right fist with maximum force onto the brother's jaw. The brother flew backwards crashing across the closest tables. Patrons scrambled from his path. Glasses filled with cognac flung across the floor.

Jeff ran for the rear of the cafe. Behind the curtain was a small kitchen. Cigarette frozen in space, the startled eyes of an old man surveyed him. A crude rectangular hole in the wall behind him gave a glimpse of a narrow lane. Jeff turned and bellowed to Sulla.

'Go around the other way. Cut him off.'

Jeff leaped through the gap. When he hit the ground he was quickly into stride. His light clothing and the fact he had swapped his Timberland boots for running shoes now made a difference. He sighted Bedri nearing the end of the lane. If the killer managed to cross the ring road, he would disappear into a labyrinth of alleyways; no chance Jeff would ever catch him then.

When Jeff reached the corner, Bedri was racing up the hill. He put on a spurt of speed. His lungs were sucking hard for air but he was gaining. A glance across his shoulder. Sulla was fifty metres behind. To his surprise Bedri stopped at the kerb. He was bent double catching his breath. Jeff allowed himself a grim smile. Too much cognac inside the man coupled with the weight of heavy boots and winter clothing had sapped his energy. Chest heaving, Bedri placed a hand on the bonnet of a parked car and glanced back. Even from a distance Jeff could see the fear in his eyes. That he would never outrun his pursuer must have been obvious to him. Jeff felt sure he had him. His pace slowed as the distance between them lessened. Bedri threw a look of desperation across the four lanes streaming with vehicles. The only safety for him lay in the myriad alleys on the other side. With a hasty glance at Jeff, now almost within reach, he turned and darted into the traffic.

Car horns blasted. To Jeff's amazement Bedri made it to the third lane. Then Arben's killer looked back to check if Jeff was following. But conscious of the extreme danger, Jeff had stopped at the kerb edge. Fists clenched in frustration he watched as Bedri turned to continue his escape. The truck that struck Bedri flung him into the air like a killer whale tossing a seal. Tortured tyres screamed as the truck braked. Much too late. Bedri bounced onto the bonnet of a red service van and slid into the path of a bus. The bus brakes locked and its tyres smoked as they rolled over Bedri, grinding him into the tar-seal.

Sulla panted up behind Jeff. He took one look at the stalled traffic and horrified faces of motorists and gripped Jeff's arm. 'It is over. Come away now.'

Jeff turned to him with eyes that still saw only the bloody mess of Bedri Cena trapped beneath greasy axles.

'Not quite the way I wanted it, Sulla. But I can live with it.'

'Justice is done and your hands are clean.'

Jeff nodded. 'Take me to the hotel, will you? I need a shower.'

45.

At a touch of a finger, the seat beneath him adjusted to a comfortable reclining position. The voice of the American businessman opposite was asking for smoked salmon with his champagne. A grim smile crossed Halam Akbar's face as he thought how the illusion of wealth and respectability so easily translated into the kind of deference he'd like to stay accustomed to. He and his brother, Zahar, had boarded the Malev Airlines flight from Budapest to Prishtina dressed in the dark suits of successful Saudi businessmen. As expected the first-class cabin crew had been fussing over them like minor royalty. But business was furthest from their thoughts. After the fiasco in Greece he and Zahar were on a quest to get their money. They had a desperate need for that money now, and Kosovo was where it was.

Halam thought again about the one big assumption he was gambling on: that neither the UN nor NATO would be expecting him and his brother to be entering the territory they controlled. He cursed again at the circumstances that were driving him and Zahar to take the risk. But with luck, his care to ensure there were no photos or descriptions in circulation of either of them would pay off. Halam and Zahar should be as ghosts. They would collect the million euros and be on their way to Iran and a new life inside forty-eight hours.

'We are booked into the Prishtina Hotel.'

A smile at Halam from the taxi driver. The boot lid slammed to hide the brothers' suitcase and he hurried to open the rear door.

'It is a very nice hotel. You will enjoy.'

'Is it close to the main centre?'

'A few hundred metres. Not far at all.'

On the journey the driver continued to try to chat with his passengers, but monosyllabic grunts soon discouraged him. Once checked in at the Prishtina Hotel, Zahar insisted they sit in Halam's room to gather their thoughts. 'It makes me very nervous. All the NATO and UN personnel. They're everywhere. And too many police.'

'Relax. They will pay us no attention. There are so many different nationalities here, thousands of them. We will not stand out. Both the UN and the locals will think we are UN staff. We hide in plain sight. The perfect place.'

A doubtful shake of Zahar's head. 'When are you making contact with Avni Leka?'

'Later. I will use a street phone. If there are problems I do not want the hotel name showing up on caller ID. We will meet with him tomorrow. First, we need to walk the city. I want to see Leka's office and reconnoitre the surrounding area. I have been thorough in learning all there is about our man. The Internet is a wonderful invention. We now know Leka is a prosecutor and I have photos.'

'This also makes me nervous. We never meet with the people we work for. It is our best security.'

'Brother, I too dislike that we lose our anonymity. But we must get that money. Now. Make us some tea before we begin and do not worry.'

46.

Even as Bedri Cena's remains were being scraped off the highway, Jeff was turning his mind to the man who ordered Gashi to kill Arben. The team he had assembled might be ragtag by any standards, but he knew he could trust them. Barry had had the courage to drive Sulla to Peje and was still game for whatever was to come. Bethany hadn't fallen apart when Gashi's men strafed the apartment. As for Morgan, she knew the countryside and the language. Jeff smiled as it occurred to him that there was no way she would agree not to be part of all this anyway.

The big plus for Jeff was that he had Sulla and Blerim Basholli. It was time to start surveillance. Jeff had wanted both ends of the street covered. Barry found parking and a good vantage point two hundred metres from the court entrance. Leka couldn't leave without being seen. Morgan and Bethany sat in the cafe on the corner. Barry reached behind the seat and pulled out a plastic Tupperware container with sandwiches Bethany had packed for him. Blerim Basholli shook his head at the food, but accepted a can of soda.

Barry had hardly begun to tuck into his sandwich when the rumble and hissing air-brakes of a truck sounded in his ears. A glance mid-bite and his heart dropped at the sight of the large truck blocking them in. Two men leaped out and began conveying bags of cement onto the adjacent building site. With a grimace at Basholli he put down his sandwich and made to open his window to shout at the men to bugger off.

'Leka,' Basholli hissed.

Barry's eyes flew back to the courthouse. 'Shit. Oh shit.'

～

When Leka appeared Morgan and Bethany exchanged startled glances. As they jumped to their feet, Morgan rummaged through her bag for her mobile.

'He's on the move, Barry. The way he's clinging to his briefcase there's more in it than documents.'

'I know, I know. We've seen him. But we're bloody blocked in.'

Morgan stooped to look through the cafe window. 'Oh Christ, so you are. What're we supposed to do now?'

'Stay on the line and follow him. We'll get to you as soon as we can.'

'Will do.'

Morgan and Bethany dodged a taxi as they dashed across the street.

～

Basholli hurled abuse in Albanian at the driver of the truck. The two men unloading the cement ignored him. One paused to light a cigarette then handed it to his mate. Barry groaned. He continued to hold the mobile close enough to hear if he was called.

'The girls will stay on the line. But what the hell can we do? Those ignorant arseholes could be another ten minutes.'

'I could beat up on them. I would enjoy this.'

'Oh Jesus. Forget that. Look at the police over there in the court entranceway. We can't go getting arrested, for God's sake. Look.

New plan. Bethany and Morgan are following Leka. They know not to get too close. You go after them. I'll stay with the vehicle and follow as soon as I can get the SUV out. I'll phone Jeff and tell him what's happening.'

'Where's Leka now?'

'Just a minute.' Barry put the phone to his ear. 'Morgan, Blerim is coming. Where are you?'

'Mother Teresa Boulevard.'

'Mother Teresa Boulevard, Blerim.'

Basholli left the car and broke into a lope heading back down the courthouse lane. Barry rang off and punched in Jeff's number.

One ring.

'Go ahead, Barry.'

'Leka's on the move. Morgan said from the way he's hanging onto his briefcase it's got more than his lunch in it. I think this might be it.'

'Are you following?'

'No, mate. I'm stuck. Some bloody ignorant truckies have blocked me in. The girls are following Leka on foot. Blerim's gone off after them. I'll call as soon as I can move.'

'You got money on you?'

'Um, yes, mate. Why?'

'Offer them ten euros each. They'll move.'

Finally free, Barry edged his UN SUV out onto the ring road. It proved impossible to cross lanes. He had little option but to go with the flow of traffic. If he turned right at the next two sets of traffic lights, he could loop back and come towards Leka from the opposite direction. At the Grand Hotel intersection he would have little choice but to turn left. Now that his master plan was in place he hoped to hell Leka was either going to the Grand or down the hill.

Morgan was first to spot Basholli closing behind then. She and Bethany had stopped outside the Illyrian Hotel and were feigning interest in a pair of Raybans at a street stall. The hawker, hands in prayerful mode, implored Bethany in Albanian to take advantage of the special winter price. With only half her attention on him, Bethany carried on the pretence of buying. Morgan kept an eye on Leka's movements reflected in a store window.

'What's happening? Where is Leka?'

Basholli glared at the salesman who backed off a few metres. 'Across the street. In front of the bookshop. The man with him just stopped him and won't let him go.'

'You think that this is the man Leka is to meet?'

'No. I've seen this one at the courts. Local lawyer.'

As three sets of eyes scrutinised the two men, the lawyer threw his hands in the air in a gesture of annoyance, turned on his heel and stomped away. Leka watched him for a second, adjusted the briefcase closer to his chest, then strode onwards.

Basholli beckoned Morgan and Bethany into a heads-down huddle.

'Okay. All we can do for now is follow,' Basholli said. 'I think the best thing is for you two to continue after Leka. I will fall back and follow. If you think you are seen, stop and Morgan run your hand through your hair. This will be the signal and I will take over from you.'

Morgan nodded. 'Come on, Bethany. Forget the glasses. We've got our marching orders.' Bethany passed the Raybans to the disgruntled salesman, mouthed an apology and followed after Morgan.

❦

In the SUV Barry reached the Grand Hotel intersection at the same time as the other three. He waved to Morgan and looked down the hill to where she was pointing. No Leka in sight. Drivers behind him blasted horns as he slowed down to find a space to park. None appeared, so he had to keep moving. Then he spotted Leka, just where the road flattened out near the bottom. For motorists the road split into two lanes. Barry had to make a decision – left or right. More horn blasts as he again slowed.

Leka made up his mind for him. He stopped at the left-hand crossing.

Barry swung onto the left lane, cutting in front of an oncoming car. The sound of screeching tyres had Barry bracing for impact. But the offended vehicle slid sideways, missing the SUV by inches. Horn blasts. In his rear-view mirror Barry viewed an angry face and shaking fist.

The traffic lights at the bottom of the hill turned red for vehicles and green for Leka. The prosecutor crossed and disappeared through an opening between an apartment building and a row of shops. Barry checked in the side mirror. Morgan, Bethany and Basholli were on the footpath only halfway down. Leka had got quite a distance ahead of them.

The lights for Barry turned green. He estimated that Leka should have reappeared on the other side of the buildings by now. A hundred metres on, he stopped, blocking cars that wanted to turn into a car park. The driver behind stuck his head out the window and yelled for Barry to move. Then Leka appeared. The commotion caught his attention. He looked directly at Barry. Barry was looking directly at him.

Barry looked away quickly, but it was too late. For an instant Leka had frozen in his tracks, mouth open.

Barry struck the flat of his hand on top of the steering wheel and drove off.

Avni Leka knocked on the hotel room door. The small dark man with the goatee beard who opened the door didn't fit any of his preconceptions at all. He thought he would be bigger. It was on the tip of his tongue to say he must have chosen the wrong room when an impatient gesture signalled he should enter.

'I am Halam Akbar. This is my brother, Zahar. You are late.'

'I was delayed. I ran into a colleague in the street who wanted to discuss a case. I brushed him off as quickly as I could. Please accept my apologies.'

'Accepted.' With the door closed, Halam appeared to relax. 'Sit, my friend. You look nervous. Is something wrong?'

'Er. No. Meeting face-to-face. It's just that it holds . . . dangers.'

'I understand this. But do not worry. We are as anxious to conclude our business and be on our way as you are.'

Leka would very much like to not worry. But the surprise on the face of the man in the UN vehicle had unsettled him. It was the look of a thief caught with his hand in the cash register. He had seen enough of these looks throughout his career. Was this the net closing on him? He dared not think too much on that. His nerve had to hold. He determined he would leave Kosovo this very day.

The minute this meeting was done.

҈

Barry circled the block and returned to where the others had gathered on the pavement opposite the Dance Until Dusk nightclub. At night, when he had driven past, the disco sparkled with pulsating lights. But in the afternoon sun, it looked drab and rundown. An oversized padlock secured a chain threaded through the main entrance's door handles.

He parked. Basholli, Bethany and Morgan climbed in.

'Bad news,' Barry said. 'The bastard looked straight at me. I'm afraid I reacted liked a stunned mullet. I think I gave the game away.'

Basholli shook his head. 'Prishtina is a small town. To bump into the same people all the time, this is normal. Maybe he has seen you before. He will think nothing of it.'

'I hope you're right. Where did he go?'

'Into the hotel with the Albanian flag outside. You see it?'

'I can. We'd better tell this to Jeff. Bethany, you and Morgan get down to the mall and bring Jeff and Sulla to us. Quick smart, eh?'

'Excuse me?' said Bethany.

'Jesus, woman. Okay. Bloody please, then.'

'Better.'

⁊

Leka felt in no mood for the usual etiquette of drinking tea before getting down to business. He placed the briefcase on the table, flicked the catches open and spun it round to show the contents to Halam.

A glance. No change of expression on Halam's face. 'So much money. One million euros. A good day's work.'

'You wish to count it?'

'No, my friend, this will not be necessary. We can trust each other, can we not?'

A snap as the case closed. Leka pushed it across to Halam. Halam passed it to Zahar who dumped it on the bed.

'Now to the future,' said Leka. 'You must wait a few months before I can send you any more projects. Security is tight after Slovenia, but this will pass. Now that our business is done here, I am leaving Kosovo tonight.'

Halam drew back with raised eyebrows. 'Leaving? Why is this?'

313

Zahar placed three cups on the table and poured tea. 'I have pushed the boundaries of one of my enterprises too far. The authorities are asking awkward questions. It is time to re-establish.'

Halam and Zahar exchanged a glance. 'They suspect you have involvement in our activities?'

'No, no, no. Nothing like that.'

Leka realised he had stumbled onto dangerous ground. Both brothers were now sighting him with narrowed eyes. He knew it was absolutely vital to avoid any hint that his own troubles could reflect back onto the Akbars. So he related the events that led to the botched vineyard scam.

'So, you see because of this New Zealander and the American woman, there is bound to be an international investigation. I will simply cut my losses, and turn my attention to more important concerns in my business.'

'I understand.' Halam sounded quite relaxed. 'For me and my brother, always the time comes when we need to move on. But what is different for us is that no one knows our identity . . . until now.'

Halam's steady regard of him made Leka's blood turn to ice.

'This is Kosovo.' Leka's voice barely had the strength of a whisper. He cleared his throat and took a sip of tea. 'Kosovo is not a country. There is no real law here. And there is no proof of any crime on my part. If I leave, the trail stops cold. I think it best not to tempt fate. I have contingency plans in place. My business outside of Kosovo will remain uninterrupted. Nothing needs to change.'

'Yes,' Halam said, and smiled. 'Nothing needs to change.'

'Then if there's nothing else, I will leave you. I must make preparations.'

'By all means.'

Leka stood. The brothers both stood as well. Out the window over Zahar's shoulder, he spied a UN vehicle. It was too far away to make out if anyone was inside it.

When he was safely in the corridor, he collapsed against the wall. Unsteady legs carried him to the top of the stairs. Holding on to the railing he slowly made his way down to the foyer. In response to his nod the receptionist threw him a perfunctory smile then returned to the more important task of filing her nails.

Leka pulled up short of the entrance and peered through the window. He couldn't tell if the UN vehicle parked a few hundred metres away was the same vehicle he had seen earlier. The people inside were just shadowy shapes.

Act calmly, walk calmly. Lose them at the first opportunity. If there is a them.

He stepped out onto the pavement.

∽

Barry nudged Basholli in the ribs. Basholli's head shot up.

'Leka's leaving.'

'Ah ha. No suitcase. The payment has been made.'

'I think you're right, mate. Don't look at him.' Barry averted his face as Avni Leka passed on the opposite side of the street. 'What do we do now? Watch the hotel or follow Leka?'

'The suitcase. We can easily find Leka later.'

'Sounds good to me.'

47.

Leka leaned against the wall in the corridor outside Fatmire's apartment until his hands had stopped shaking. He slid the key into the lock and managed to open the door without making any noise. It closed behind him with a soft click that sounded like cannon fire to his ears. He froze to the spot, heart hammering, and listened for indications he'd been heard. Nothing.

Clutching a hand to his chest Leka sank onto the coat-rack seat and tried to catch his breath. Had he oxygen enough in his lungs he would have breathed a sigh of relief. Here at least was sanctuary. No one knew of this apartment, not even Osman Gashi. Leka's reflection in the hall mirror startled him. He looked nothing like a confident chief prosecutor. More like one of the haunted men he regularly tossed into prison: pale, haggard, exhausted.

He closed his eyes. The unbidden memory flooded back into his mind of another time when things had spun out of control. He had been in Slovenia, driving from the airport to Ljubljana. It had snowed heavily for two days. He was late, irritated and in a hurry. With disregard to the risks he was speeding to make up time lost by his delayed flight. The car hit a patch of black ice.

Out of control and certain he was about to die, Leka experienced an almost spiritual calmness and clarity of mind. He knew enough not to touch the brake and pulled both feet away from the pedals. He drew his hands back from the steering wheel and dropped them to his lap. Whatever was about to happen, he accepted the inevitability of it.

The car spun across three lanes of traffic, miraculously missing oncoming vehicles. He hit the median strip barrier and slid to a stop. And, as now, he sat breathless and feeling dizzy.

So here he was again, but spinning across a different kind of highway. And more than ever he needed the same calmness and clarity of mind. Making the right decisions over the next few hours would be crucial to his escaping Kosovo and remaining alive.

He needed to get to his office. Money and passports were in a safe hidden behind the portrait of Skanderbeg. The twenty thousand euros would be enough to get him safely across the border. His international bank deposit numbers and important files were on a computer memory chip hanging from a chain round his neck. He felt genuine sadness his Kosovon life was over. He would miss the children. But he'd miss his own life more.

He had to move.

First he needed to tie up loose ends.

Fatmire was in bed napping as she often did in the afternoon. She would be naked under the blankets. Leka stood at the door and studied the contours of her body in the dim light of the curtained room. The milky skin of her shoulders. What a marvellous, beautiful creature. The thought of leaving her pained him. She was his confidante, his lover and his friend. She could always make him laugh when his spirits needed lifting. She had made him happier than any woman he'd ever known.

A glance showed him the gentle rise and fall of Fatmire's chest. She often made little sounds when she slept. He had found them endearing. He opened the bottom drawer of the cabinet beside the bed and took out his pistol. As he affixed the silencer he found his sight swimming. Yes, at this of all moments he shed tears of love for her. He placed the gun against her temple. First tension release. His eyes squeezed closed. The pop informed him the second release had engaged and it was over.

He sat in silence, concentrating upon one spot on the wall. A hand rested gently on Fatmire's exposed thigh. He stayed that way until her skin began to cool. When he finally looked at her, blood had soaked into the white pillowcase like wine on the finest table linen.

He stood and whispered a farewell prayer then left the room.

He gathered up documents crucial to his business and put them in the small red bag Fatmire had bought him at New Year. It took barely ten minutes. All other papers he stuffed into the small coal-fired heater and set them alight, poking the burning paper until it had all turned to glowing ash. Satisfied he had taken care of everything, he left the house.

The key he slid back under the locked door.

ᑫᕽ

Jeff, Morgan and Sulla were waiting for Lee Caldwell in front of the shopping mall as arranged by phone. When a Bondsteel helicopter rattled overhead and disappeared somewhere behind the mall, Jeff guessed it'd be Caldwell arriving. Sure enough, within minutes he appeared from a side alley and approached them on foot.

'What the hell's going on?'

'We followed Avni Leka to the Prishtina hotel,' Morgan said. 'He went in with a suitcase and came out empty handed.'

'Where is he now?'

Jeff shrugged. 'Who knows. Barry and Blerim made the decision to stick with the money and let Leka go. They figured you can pick him up later. I agreed with their assessment.'

Jeff knew Caldwell would be pissed at hearing this but would be careful not to show emotion. With satisfaction Jeff observed a small vein engorge on Caldwell's forehead.

'Surveillance on Leka, Bradley. No more. That was the deal. What if Leka takes off?'

'Firstly, the agreement was I do it my way.' Jeff knew his pleasant tone would get up Caldwell's nose. 'Secondly, I thought you said you didn't give a shit about Leka.'

'Well, I don't. Not ultimately. But if he's in the net I might as well pull him in along with the others.'

Jeff's eyes scanned the vicinity. 'Where are your men? Aren't they watching us? Why aren't they trailing Leka?'

'They're assigned elsewhere.' Caldwell pulled out his mobile. 'I'll call them back now.' He stepped out of earshot. Jeff saw him listen and call off then redial at least three times. When he rejoined the three his face wore something close to a scowl. The vein on his forehead stood out still. 'No answer.'

'It looks like you're stuck with just us,' Jeff said.

'For the moment. We need to split up. Keep the hotel under surveillance and find Leka.'

'You want the bombers,' Jeff said. 'And I want Leka. Morgan and I will go check out Leka's office. Morgan, we'll need to use your car.'

'Sure. Let's do it.'

'Just a minute. I take it you don't have a weapon. Have you considered Leka may be armed?'

Jeff displayed empty hands. 'Don't worry, I'll keep it to reconnaissance only. Like you said.'

At last Jeff noted a bending of attitude in Caldwell. Almost a smile on his face. Of exasperation maybe, but a smile nonetheless. 'Be careful.'

'Come on, Morgan. You and I are out of here.'

48.

Caldwell let Bethany lead him and Sulla back to where Barry and Basholli kept watch in the SUV. They climbed into the rear seat. Barry leaned over from the driver's position.

'Rooms Six and Seven. Second floor. Blerim went in and spoke to the receptionist after Avni Leka left. It's a small hotel, no other guests.'

Caldwell delivered a sharp glance at Basholli. 'I hope you were careful. We can't afford to have the receptionist warning them.'

If Basholli took offense at the American's acerbic tone, he gave no sign of it. 'I gave her a hundred euros. It is enough to keep her mouth shut. She does not care about the internationals, only money.'

'Do we know their names then? What these guys look like?'

Basholli's hand rustled in an inside pocket of his jacket. Two folded sheets of paper appeared. 'The receptionist was very helpful. She photocopied their passports for me. Halam and Zahar Akbar, maybe they are brothers. They are both dark-skinned with black hair and Halam has a short beard.'

Raised eyebrows as Caldwell surveyed Basholli. 'Good work Basholli.' He studied the photocopies. 'I don't believe I've ever seen these two before. They must've been operating well below the radar.' The photocopies disappeared into his inside pocket. 'Anything else?'

'These men asked her to make up their bill. They are leaving.'

Caldwell went quiet. Four pairs of eyes studied him. 'We need to keep the situation contained. Trap them in the hotel. If these men make it onto the street, anything could happen. We have to assume they're armed.'

Caldwell's head bobbed and swivelled as he checked out the vicinity. At the same time the options available to him ran through his brain. His two men could not be contacted. Backup from Bondsteel was an hour away. Bradley had the most experience of the people he had in Kosovo. But he was not immediately to hand. Basholli and his two men had combat experience, and no doubt Sulla could handle himself. Barry was the problem.

'Barry. You need to stay out of the way.'

'Like hell, mate. I'm in.'

Caldwell shook his head. 'Now why did I know you were going to say that? All right. I don't have time to argue. Basholli, where are your two men?'

Basholli leaned out the window and made a beckoning motion with his arm. Two men leaning against a battered VW Kombi further down the street tossed away their cigarettes and hurried to the SUV.

'I take it you're all armed?' asked Caldwell.

A nod and a pat of Basholli's breast pocket.

'Very well. Here's what we'll do. Barry, you and Basholli will cover the back. The rest of us will go in the front. Basholli, I want one of your men to cover the street.'

Phrases in Albanian followed. Caldwell's eye landed on Bethany. Her hands rose in surrender. 'I know. I stay with the vehicle.'

Caldwell pulled out his own pistol and checked it. 'Basholli. Don't take any chances. If anyone feels threatened, just shoot. You don't have to worry about what the police might think.'

But even as he spoke, Caldwell was fairly sure from the expressions on their faces that Basholli and his men had not the slightest concern at all for the thoughts of any policeman.

⟋⟍

Halam and Zahar packed up their bag.

'What now?' Zahar asked.

'We will get a taxi to the Macedonian border and walk across. There will be taxis on the other side. We could stop the night in Skopje, but I think it better to move on to Bulgaria.'

Zahar scratched the top of his thigh, a habit he engaged in whenever something troubled him. Halam knew this and bided his time until his brother was ready to say what worried him.

'To me Leka looked nervous.'

'I think we would make anyone who knew us nervous, Zahar.'

'No, Halam. Too nervous.'

Halam knew better than to dismiss his brother's instincts out of hand. It had got them out of many difficulties over the years, even if sometimes it was difficult to distinguish between instinct and paranoia.

'Very well, brother. We shall be cautious.'

Even as Halam spoke, Zahar was sidling up to the window to look into the street. 'Halam, come here.' The urgency in his voice alarmed Halam. In an instant he was behind Zahar peering over his shoulder. 'The UN vehicle on the bend. See it?'

'I see it.'

He viewed a group of men stood chatting next to a UN vehicle some distance away. Nothing unusual in that. Prishtina was full of UN vehicles and people. He kept watching. One of the men looked towards the hotel. Then the others.

'Twice they have looked this way. See. There. See that?'

Halam shook his head. 'I just see people talking in the street.'

'They're coming this way. One has his hand inside his jacket pocket.'

Halam peered more closely. This was no figment of his brother's paranoia. He leaped to the bed.

'Grab the bag. I'll take the briefcase. We will use the fire door.'

The brothers hurried from the room and bounded down the flight of stairs two at a time. In the dimly lit corridor Halam punched the release lever on the safety assembly that secured the door. It didn't budge. Halam uttered a curse.

Both brothers put their weight to the lever.

∾

Barry and Basholli stood at the entrance to the lane that ran down the side of the hotel. Basholli drew his pistol and insisted on going first. With no gun to back any argument, Barry let him proceed. The lane opened onto an unkempt car park encircled by a brick security wall. Faded white lines marked spaces for six cars. They were empty. A bulky metal rubbish bin stood in the left-hand corner. There was no way out other than the lane behind them.

Barry's eyes alighted on the fire-safety door. No handle on the outside. Basholli positioned himself at the corner of the lane.

'We stay here. The best place. We can watch the door and lane at the same time.'

Barry gave the door a push. It didn't move. 'Okay. I don't have any other plans, mate.'

The fire door burst open in his face.

Two figures collided with Barry, knocking him over. They stopped and looked at the man on the ground. Then at the gun in the hands of Basholli.

'Holy shit,' Barry spluttered. He scrambled to his feet and ran towards Basholli pointing back at the two men as he ran. 'Halam Akbar. Stay right where you are.'

Barry saw a look of astonishment on Halam's face. He and his brother exchanged lightning glances.

Basholli pushed Barry aside and brought up his pistol but Halam, following Barry, had closed the gap. The briefcase in his hand arced through the air knocking the pistol from Basholli's hand. It skittered across ground into the fence several metres away. Basholli grunted and swung a punch. He missed Halam, but struck Zahar in the jaw. The smaller man reeled backwards. Basholli leaped on him and wrapped an arm around his neck. They fell to the ground.

Barry stood face-to-face with Halam. Halam growled. The wild animal sound caused an involuntary shiver to run the length of Barry's spine. He twitched. Nervousness. He wiped the sweat from the palms of hands on his thighs. Steadying himself. He already had a fair idea what would happen next. He was ready. Halam ran straight and hard at him. Barry had played rugby all his life and packs of eighteen-stone forwards had run over him more times than he could count. He lowered his shoulders and dived into Halam's legs, dropping him to the ground in a tackle that would have made his junior rugby coach proud.

Barry clung to Halam's legs as if his life depended on it. Halam released hold of the briefcase to punch at the Australian. Barry was strong, but he was no street fighter. He took a blinding punch to the nose. A cry of pain and both hands went to his face.

Halam kicked free.

Out of the corner of his eye Barry saw Basholli drive his elbow into the side of his opponent's head. The man went limp.

Halam saw it as well. An expletive in Arabic stung the air.

Barry scrambled to his knees. A deep breath as he prepared to get upright. But Halam was already standing over him. Barry rolled aside and swung both feet at Halam's ankle. He missed, but connected hard with the suitcase. It slid away. Another roll and he was halfway to his feet.

'Son of a pig.'

A string of Arabic obscenities powered Halam's fist into Barry's face.

Barry slumped back to hands and knees. Blood poured from his nose onto the asphalt. He fought the urge to throw up.

Basholli made a dive for his pistol. Barry saw Halam pause as if weighing his options. There was no way Halam could beat Basholli to the weapon. He turned and ran at the rubbish bin. With the agility of a cat he sprang onto the lid and disappeared over the wall.

Basholli snatched up his pistol and swung it towards Halam.

Too late.

A vicious Albanian curse met Barry's ears. Then a disappointed Basholli made his way over to him.

'He's gone. You okay?'

'Yeah, mate, I'll live.'

Barry's words came thick with blood. He had a good spit. Panting and with no strength to make it to his feet, he remained on hands and knees. Basholli surveyed the unconscious Zahar, then the wall over which Halam had vanished. Barry's head shook.

'No point in chasing after him. Let's just hang on to this one. Besides, I don't feel too good, mate.'

Basholli sat on the ground between Barry and the man he'd left prone and pulled out a pack of cigarettes. A slow roll and Barry was on his back, eyes closed.

Blackness claimed him.

༄

When Barry came round, Lee Caldwell was kneeling beside him. He tried to rise. Caldwell placed a hand on his shoulder.

'Take it easy.'

'Jesus, I'm sorry, mate. I tried to stop him, but I guess I'm not up to this sort of thing after all.'

'Don't worry, we've got one of them and we've got the money. I'm sorry I underestimated you. Good job.'

Barry tried a smile that morphed into a grimace. His mouth hurt and one tooth felt wobbly in its socket. 'Really, Caldwell? You don't think I'm a useless arsehole?'

'Certainly not useless.'

'Thanks. I think. Help me up, will you? I can't lie here all day. Everyone will think I'm a flaming bludger.'

Caldwell extended a hand to help Barry to his feet. He swayed for a few seconds, his knees like jelly. Caldwell pulled one of his arms over his shoulder and helped him stay upright.

'Jesus, I feel like I was hit with a sledgehammer.'

He raised a hand and made a tentative exploration of his forehead where the pain seemed to be centred. What felt like an ostrich egg met his fingertips. His eyes fell on Zahar who had struggled to a sitting position, back against the wall. The bomber's eyes were ignoring the pistols Basholli and Sulla had trained on him.

'I think we keep this to ourselves?' Barry said. 'I'd rather Bethany didn't know I got beaten up. It would just upset her.'

'I don't think you'll be able to hide anything, Barry,' Sulla laughed, but his eyes were concerned. 'Best go see a doctor straight away. You might have a concussion.'

Caldwell's two men arrived a half-hour later in an unmarked four-wheel drive. One of them climbed out and jerked Zahar to his feet. Basholli and Sulla kept their pistols aimed at Zahar's chest until he was handcuffed.

'We'll take it from here,' Caldwell said. 'If we need anything else from you, we'll be in touch.'

With Zahar tossed into the back like a side of beef and covered with a tarpaulin, Caldwell climbed into the passenger seat. A salute and he was gone.

Barry looked from Basholli to Sulla. 'Well, guys, I guess that's Yank for "thank you and now you can all fuck off". I better let Jeff know what's happened.'

49.

Halam bought a razor and shaving cream from a minimarket. In the cafe next to the fried chicken kiosk, he locked himself in the toilet. There was no mirror but the image reflecting off the rear window would suffice. He sprayed foam into his hand and dabbed it over his face. A rip as the plastic covering on the razor came off and he began scraping.

Leka. The name burned in his mind. Zahar had been right. Leka must have betrayed them. Halam rinsed the razor clear of hair then continued attacking the remainder of his goatee. Leka had said he was leaving the country. Tonight. Halam doubted the double-crossing bastard would have left just yet. Certainly not in the last hour.

Halam now needed money more than ever. Leka would have cash on him. Staking out the prosecutor's office for a few hours seemed a sensible move. If Leka did not show in that time he would head for the border. They would meet again, and he swore in his brother's name he would squeeze Leka's throat until his eyeballs burst.

He tried to resist giving any thought to helping his younger brother. The two had long ago agreed that risking the freedom of one in an attempt to rescue the other in the event of capture was off the table. A pointless exercise. The survivor was not to dwell on the other's fate. But words said without pressure are easy. Now the anticipated moment had arrived, Halam was finding it difficult to subdue feelings of outrage and loss. Would he truly never see his brother again?

Halam drew a thumb across his chin. Smooth. Water splashed over his face and he reached for the small towel. The thought of where it might have been struck him. He used the sleeve of his coat instead. The clothes he bought from a store five doors away were not a good match but they changed his appearance and that was all that mattered. Now, any description the authorities might issue of him would be of little use. Beard gone, he looked like any run-of-the-mill store worker.

Halam's old clothes found a new home in a rubbish bin at the rear of the cafe. Out on the street again, he tagged on behind a group of locals heading in the direction of Leka's office. For whatever reason, Avni Leka had cost Zahar his freedom. He would answer for it.

☙

Leka scanned the street. From his office vantage point nothing came into view that should cause him anxiety. Certainly no UN vehicles. The only activity was that of labourers pushing barrow loads of cement up wooden ramps.

Time to leave.

He pushed the pistol into his belt. He had debated leaving it in the car but decided against it. If he was captured by the CIA he well knew what they would do to him. He had no intention of being taken alive. With a small box of documents under his arm, he made his way back down the staircase.

The two court officers were reading the newspapers and chatting behind the glass of the lunchroom. He waved in their direction.

One of them lifted a hand, then returned to their conversation. No one was about to bother a man of Leka's status.

When he reached to the car he threw the carton onto the back seat and climbed in. As the motor roared into life he felt he could relax a little. Nothing but road stood between him and the border. He pushed the automatic lever into drive. But before he could release the brake, the passenger door opened. Leka's heart jumped into his throat. The hostile, piercing eyes of the man sliding into the seat beside him were those of Halam Akbar. The end of a knife pricked at his jugular.

'We meet again, Mr Prosecutor. As you can see I am alone. And I am not happy.'

As Leka gasped for air, a hand patted around his chest then moved down stopping on the bulge just above his groin. A swift movement. With a grim smile Halam brandished Leka's pistol before his face.

'Mine, I think. Now we can go. Drive.'

෬∕৩

Jeff and Morgan sat talking but navigated clear of the topic Jeff most wanted to discuss. Rod Stewart's husky voice sung his songs of love at a low volume on Morgan's car stereo. The rattle of a concrete mixer came from across the street. Men waiting for the mix to blend smoked and stared through the window at the couple in the four-wheel drive. Jeff tried to ignore the way they ogled Morgan. And the remarks and jerky hand movements at crotches that brought toothy grins. Morgan appeared not to notice.

A deep breath and Jeff decided he would have to take the initiative.

'Um. The other day, you know? I wanted to stay. I should have stayed.'

Even as he said it, Jeff cringed. His words sounded whiny and not at all as he'd intended. But in retrospect, to have left with

Caldwell the morning after they had made love for the first time was bad behaviour. And the more he looked at it the more the dimensions of badness grew. And not returning later in the day made it all the more inexcusable. What could he say to her? That he preferred to kill a man rather than spend the day in bed with her.

The lightness of Morgan's laugh unnerved him. 'I'm a big girl, Jeff. You had your priorities. I just wasn't top of the list.'

Jeff winced. He'd rather she punched him in the stomach. 'Oh Christ. You've got it all wrong. Look, I'm not that great an operator. With women, you know? I'm all bloody thumbs and I know it. Christ, Morgan. I . . . I don't want us to end.'

Morgan regarded him with an innocent arch of the eyebrows. 'Well. You're not all thumbs.'

He knew she was teasing him. He wanted to taste her lips, to smell her hair, feel her against him. He leaned towards her, so close he could feel her breath against his skin. She opened her mouth with a whisper.

'Jeff.'

'Yes.'

'I think that's Leka leaving.'

Jeff's head shot around to face Leka's building. 'Bloody hell.'

Despite their nervous tension, Morgan allowed a laugh as Jeff started the motor. She touched his arm. Not the same, but it would do Jeff for now.

❧

Barry picked up the phone on the second ring.

'Barry, it's Morgan. Leka came out of the building and walked to the end of the street. He had a car parked there. Another man got in with him. We're following.'

'The other man. About five foot ten, suit, black hair, dark skin, goatee beard?'

'Yes, all that except for the clothes and the goatee.'

Sulla and Basholli must have picked up the gist of the conversation. They gathered close with heads down listening.

'Okay, so he's changed his clothes and shaved. Don't play games with these blokes, Morgan. They're most likely packing.'

'We've turned onto the main road to Prizren. Passing the bus station now.'

'They're doing a runner. I guarantee they'll take the left-hand fork at the Italian shopping complex and head for the border. I'm going to contact Caldwell. I'll call back in a few minutes. Save your battery. You may be needing it.'

Barry rang off and met Sulla's excited look. 'Leka picked up a passenger and I'll bet all the beer this side of the black stump that it's the bastard who escaped us at the hotel. They're scarpering for the border. Jeff and Morgan are following.'

Sulla rattled off some Albanian to Basholli. He nodded. Sulla turned back to Barry. 'Blerim will alert his men in the border area to watch for Morgan's Range Rover, then he and I will head out after Jeff and Morgan. They have a ten-minute start but with a bit of luck and a few traffic hold ups we might catch up.'

'Good idea. Hand me your mobile please, Bethany.' Barry checked the digital display and wrote the number on a piece of paper. He handed it to Sulla. 'Only call me on that number. I'll keep my line free for Morgan and Jeff.' Barry turned a wide grin on Sulla. 'And Sulla . . . be bloody careful out there, mate. Huh. I've always wanted to say that.'

Sulla frowned at him. 'Why?'

'Oh. It's an Aussie thing. Forget it.'

As the downstairs door slammed behind Sulla and Basholli, Barry was dialling Lee Caldwell's mobile.

50.

Lee Caldwell, his team and Zahar Akbar bounced about as the four-wheel drive crossed over the unused rail line and onto the potholed dirt road that ran through the Prishtina industrial area. The brow of Dragadon Hill brooded above. The remnants of factories and warehouses now lying in piles of rubble bore testament to NATO bombing raids. Some had been cleared enough for use as lumber and construction yards.

The driver stopped in front of one of the few remaining structures that still resembled a building. The tile roof looked unstable and giant slabs of plaster render had fallen from the walls exposing the red brick. But it would do. Caldwell picked his steps across sodden ground, steering clear of puddles that could easily disguise metre-deep holes. The side door, barely attached to its hinges, gave way without the need of the key he had been given.

After a few tugs the rusted chain freed up and the roller door creaked and groaned its way upward. When it was high enough to allow the vehicle to pass beneath, Caldwell signalled the four-wheel drive in. He kept his weight on the chain until it passed, then let go. The door juddered back to the ground, the crash of metal on concrete reverberating throughout the empty warehouse.

Pins of sunlight pierced through holes in the many broken roof tiles. But not quite enough to illuminate the dusty interior. Echoes resounded from the click of Caldwell's leather-soled shoes on the concrete as he walked to a junction box and opened the cover. His peering eyes discovered what looked like a master switch. He flicked it and two naked bulbs hanging from exposed beams came alive. The light was fairly feeble, but it was enough to brighten the interior. Other than some broken wooden pallets against the back wall, the warehouse was empty. Caldwell went into the small office. He pulled on a cord hanging from the ceiling. A fluorescent light flickered into life. A single table and two chairs stood in the centre of the room. It was all he would need. 'Bring him in,' he called out.

Zahar tried to break free from his two escorts but he was no match for the brawny ex-marines. They dumped him into the chair Caldwell had placed against the wall. Then Caldwell pushed the table into his prisoner's gut, effectively immobilising him. Zahar spat in contempt. Caldwell ignored it. Pistol at the ready and aimed at Zahar's head, the driver backed away to stand in the doorway.

Caldwell reached into his jacket pocket and pulled out Zahar's passport. The photo matched, but Caldwell knew the name would be false.

'Zahar Akbar,' Caldwell said, reading the name from the document. 'I won't introduce myself. Who I am does not matter. All that matters is that you have information I want.'

Caldwell slammed the money briefcase on the table. He flicked the catch and the lid sprang open. He drew out a bundle of euros.

'There's a lot of money here, Zahar.' He dropped the money back. 'I'm not the police. I'm not even CIA.' He smiled at the widening of Zahar's eyes. 'I don't have to play by anyone's rules. You will give me the information I want, even if we have to stay here all week. If you are lucky, maybe you will die in the process. Or you could make it easy on yourself. Cooperate. Tell us what we want to know. Then you can sit in a cell somewhere. Eat well, sleep, maybe they will let you read the Koran. It's up to you. You understand what I'm saying here?'

No flicker of emotion. Or even comprehension. Zahar stared ahead in silence.

Caldwell knew this game. The longer the prisoner kept his mouth shut the greater the chances for his companion to escape. His head shook as if in slow sadness.

'Very well. I'm going outside while my friends have a chat with you.'

Caldwell paused in the doorway. A ploy to signify to Zahar it was his last opportunity to cooperate. Zahar said and did nothing. But the sight of wires being removed from a black leather carry bag by one of Caldwell's men caused a momentary widening of his eyes. A mumbled prayer in Arabic and they shut tight.

Caldwell walked away. He felt no sympathy for the man. This was a mass murderer for hire who would keep on killing given the chance. Outside in the factory area he popped a piece of gum in his mouth and leaned against the four-wheel drive. He stopped mid-chew for a fraction of a second when he heard the first muffled scream.

⁓

'I think we are being followed,' Leka said. He checked once more in the rear vision mirror. 'The same green Range Rover has been behind us since we left Prishtina. They have had plenty of opportunity to pass.'

Halam turned to see for himself. 'You are certain?'

Leka shrugged. 'It may be nothing.'

He adjusted the electronic side mirrors, then tapped his brake pedal to slow down. The Range Rover also slowed but had drawn closer. Leka stared in disbelief at what the mirror now revealed.

'Dear God,' he whispered. He accelerated back to normal speed. 'It is the New Zealander and the American woman.'

Halam thought for a second. 'These are the people working with the American spy?'

'Yes. Them.'

The next kilometre passed in silence. Leka stole a quick glance at Halam. His fingers were running back and forth along the barrel of the pistol. He returned steady eye contact.

'You know, Leka. I find it a remarkable coincidence that just after you deliver the money, those people behind us and a CIA agent kick down my door.'

It took very little brain power for Leka to get what Halam was implying. He swallowed hard.

'I've done nothing, Halam. Remember, they're after me as well. It must have been Osman Gashi. The stupid fat shit who works for me. He has made this mess. Maybe he talked to the authorities. Let me make you an offer. I will give you twice our normal fee to kill him.'

Halam's top lip curled. 'I doubt you have that much with you. Perhaps I should cut my losses, kill you now and just take what there is.'

Leka felt the blood drain from his face. 'Of course I don't have that sort of money on me. I have Swiss bank accounts. More in offshore banks elsewhere. Much more. Help get me to safety and I will pay you three times your normal fee.'

Halam said nothing for another kilometre. But Leka felt a distinct sense of relief when he saw Halam had appeared to settle more comfortably in his seat. The bomber's right arm rose to rest along the window ledge. Fingers drummed on the dashboard.

Then stopped.

'First things first, Leka. Other than simply trying to outrun these people, do you have a plan?'

Leka nodded. 'I've been thinking. They're most likely communicating with someone in Prishtina. For the moment they'll believe we're heading for the Blace border and will try to intercept us either there or along the way. In ten minutes we'll be in Ferizaj. There's a turnoff. It leads to another crossing point. It is a winding and difficult road. Somewhere along this road we can stop and rid ourselves of our pursuers.'

Halam took a moment to think this through before nodding an approval. He held up Leka's pistol and checked the mechanism.

⚬∼⚬

Barry had been dialling Caldwell's phone every five minutes. This time was about his fifth attempt at reaching him. 'Where the fuck is he? He always manages to show his ugly bloody mug when you don't need him.'

Bethany placed a beer on the table for Barry just as the line clicked open. 'Jesus Christ, Caldwell. Where the bloody hell have you been?'

'Busy. What do you need?'

'Morgan and Jeff are following Leka. And guess what? He picked up a passenger. Arab-looking guy, exactly like our man from the hotel minus the beard.'

'When?'

'Twenty minutes ago. I've been calling you every five minutes. Sulla and Basholli have gone after them but they're a good ten minutes behind.'

'Damn. Where are they now?'

'Heading for the Macedonian Border. Basholli has his clan watching out for them. At the rate they're going they'll be there in about forty minutes.'

'I'll ring the police and have them alert the border guards. Do you have a licence number and the make of car?'

Barry reeled off the information.

'I'll call you back in a few minutes,' said Caldwell.

⁊

Caldwell dialed the number of the Prishtina Central Police Station. A voice answered in Albanian.

'Do you speak English?' Caldwell asked.

'Yes, I do. How can I help?'

'My name is Lee Caldwell. I'm acting with the full authority of the American Embassy in Skopje. There is a car heading for the Macedonian border. I need it stopped and the men detained. Can you please notify all border crossings?'

'Do you have a licence number and make of car? And the identities of the men you wish us to hold?'

'Yes, I do.'

Caldwell read them out.

'Now the names of the two men?'

Caldwell bit his lip a second. Was the name he was about to relate going to create havoc within the local institutions?

'I have one name only. Avni Leka.'

The line remained silent. Caldwell braced himself.

'Are you there, officer?'

'Yes. Yes. I am here. I'm sorry, Mr Caldwell, but there must be a mistake. Avni Leka? This gentleman is the prosecutor from the Municipal Court. A very respected man.'

'Yes, I know who he is. He's also wanted for questioning by the United States government.' Caldwell hoped he hadn't sounded too terse. It was imperative to have this policeman onside. 'Can you also notify the UN police? My government would be most grateful.'

Another silence. Caldwell held his breath.

'Mr Caldwell?'

'Yes, sir?'

'Leave it with me. I will handle this personally.'

∽

Captain Agim Morina replaced the phone, thankful his men were preoccupied and did not see his face. The beating of his heart was like a jungle tom-tom in his ears. He stood, but had to hold onto the desk to steady himself. Leka was in big trouble. And the man with him he strongly suspected would be Osman Gashi.

If the internationals grabbed these two, surely he'd be next under the blowtorch.

He could buy time by allowing these two to escape over the border; then he would have a chance to work on making things less disastrous for himself. It would not be possible to completely ignore the American's request. But he could delay passing on the information. For a few hours.

He walked slowly back to his office. He needed to destroy all evidence that might lead to him and find a safer hiding place for his dossier. He might need it to bargain for his freedom.

51.

'That's Ferizaj we've passed.' Morgan glanced in the wing mirror. 'Not long to the border now. I'll feel a lot happier when we meet up with Blerim's people.'

Jeff saw that Leka's car was indicating a turn. 'What's he up to now?'

'He's turning onto the overpass.'

Jeff's foot eased off the gas. 'Where the hell does that go to?'

'Turn left at the end of it and you end up at Bondsteel. The American base.'

'I doubt he's going there.'

'You are so clever. But if he goes right after a few back roads and a mountain pass or two, he'll be at the Glloboçice border crossing. It's how you get to Tetovo. That's Macedonia's second largest city. It also has a large ethnic Albanian community. He probably has contacts there.'

'I don't like this. We really are on our own out here.'

'Well, we've come this far we can't lose them now.' Morgan opened her phone. 'I'll call Barry to let Sulla know we're turning off.'

Jeff pulled in to the side of the road. 'What are you doing, Jeff?'

'Dropping you off. Sulla isn't far behind. He'll pick you up.'

Morgan's eyes were like emerald daggers. 'You'll what?'

'I have a bad feeling about this, Morgan. You need to get out.'

'Cut the bullshit and drive.'

'Hey. We've got to consider that they may be on to us. They could be leading us into a trap. I can handle whatever they throw at me. But I may not be able to look out for us both.'

The green eyes bored into Jeff's. 'I can look out for myself. I'm staying right where I am. Now drive. We don't have time to argue.'

Jeff shook his head and engaged the drive lever. 'Okay. But when you're lying in a hospital bed with a bullet in your pretty little arse, don't come whining to me.'

Feeling himself all but truly horsewhipped, Jeff drove across the overpass, turned right and accelerated. Within minutes the surroundings opened to pasturelands. Ahead, the dark of forested slopes approached.

'Pretty little arse?' Morgan muttered.

He glanced across at her. Was that a smug look on her face? He should have stuck to his guns and tossed her out when he had the chance.

'Pretty-ish.'

‍ ‍

'Speed up around the next corner. Stop when I tell you. Brake hard.'

Leka nodded. With his knuckles white on the steering wheel he took the bend at a speed he considered quite dangerous even under normal conditions. Once round the bend he accelerated into the straight.

'Stop!'

The yell in his ear galvanised Leka's response. A slither as the rear of the car swung out. They shuddered to a standstill across the road. Halam leaped out and ran into the centre. Legs astride with the pistol at arm's length, he raised it to shoulder height and steadied.

When the green Range Rover rounded the bend into his sights, three shots went off in quick succession.

⁀

Jeff had barely registered the man in the roadway ahead when his windscreen went opaque. The wheel turned hard right towards the mossy bank. But the bend and the speed caused the SUV to spin a three-sixty and slide towards the chasm the other side. A lurch. The sickening feeling of sudden weightlessness. Sounds of snapping branches. Twisting metal. A horizon gone mad with glimpses of green and rock and grey sky and scattering wings. A plummet seemingly so slow that a man could will it to last for ever.

If he wanted.

⁀

'Good shot, Halam,' Leka yelled. He laughed and struck his fist on the car roof. 'Great shot. Come on, let's get the hell out of here before others come.'

Halam ignored Leka. He made his way to the verge and peered over the edge. His eyes followed the trail of broken branches and trees snapped off at their roots until he saw the shape of the four-wheel drive through the foliage. It had stayed upright and come to rest a hundred meters below, wedged between the trunks of two pines with doors flung wide. He saw no sign of movement. But with the vehicle still the right way up and pointed downwards, Halam knew he needed to assume the passengers had survived.

'We need to go, Halam,' Leka called.

'We have time.'

Halam's eyes surveyed the bank below his feet. Leka saw the set of the man's jaw and threw his hands in the air.

'You cannot be considering going down there. It is folly. They cannot follow us. Not now. They are finished. We need to escape. No one is going to find them. They'll never be seen from the road.'

Halam turned on him. The cold determination Leka saw in that look confirmed his worst fears.

'The Americans will kill my brother. I can do nothing to save him. But Allah has granted me this opportunity to avenge his death.'

Leka felt the pincers of medieval faith and blind justice closing in on him. He wanted to scream at Halam to get a grip. But shades of anxiety at least focused his mind. Maybe a way out of this mess was opening to him.

'Then please hurry up and get on with it. I'll ready the car and wait for you here.'

'Do that, Leka. But don't even think about driving off without me. If you do, I will hunt you down. That is what I do. You know this.'

Leka's eyes widened. Of course he knew it. He knew life would never be safe or happy with an implacable enemy like Halam Akbar on his tail.

He walked off without replying.

Halam edged over the bank.

⁊ひ

Jeff fought for breath. Each inhalation fired bullets of pain into his rib cage. His head throbbed. Pain made him nauseous. He jiggled the safety-belt buckle. The lever gave and the belt released. His sternum fell onto the steering column. He coughed, but the pain of it cut it short. Jeff's only view was of the greenery and branches clinging to the walls of the chasm.

He lifted a hand to his mouth. Fingers explored his bottom lip with care. It felt swollen. Tender too. He spat out blood. It was clear that tree branches must have slowed down the rate of their descent. It was also clear the airbags hadn't deployed because of that. From somewhere he remembered that at under 15 kph – or was it ten – the cartridges would not ignite. Or maybe the Range Rover was just a defective piece of junk and never had any airbags at all. He hoped Morgan had insurance.

Morgan.

It proved an effort to twist his neck. Her head rested on the dashboard, face turned away from him. It looked as if the belt had unbuckled but the straps were still over her shoulders. Shattered windscreen glass dangled in her hair. Sparkling like diamonds. Blood trickled down behind her ear. He tried to reach across to her. A sharp bite of pain ran the length of his arm. He tried again, this time ignoring the pain. Pressing two fingers against Morgan's neck, he searched for a pulse. It took a moment but he found it.

He shook her gently and called her name.

No response.

He needed to get her out of the vehicle.

Arms came to his chest in a weights pull-up position. Pain not too severe. Fingers flexed. Good so far. Jeff tried flexing his leg muscles and rolling his ankles. Nothing appeared broken. Just as he began to formulate his next move, he heard voices.

In the cracked rear-view mirror, as if through a telescope the wrong way around, he made out two men standing on the bank a hundred metres above. With a squint he made out Avni Leka. He did not need many guesses to work out that his companion was the terrorist, Halam Akbar.

'Morgan,' he whispered.

Still no response.

He checked in the mirror again. Halam was scrambling down the bank. Jeff balled his fists.

'What to do, what to do . . . Think.'

A wave of nausea shot through him. A sign of concussion? Little wonder thinking was proving difficult for him. He could attempt to escape but it would mean leaving Morgan behind. He was not about to do that.

He looked back to the mirror.

No Halam.

Jeff figured the man must be rounding on the passenger door. And he could do nothing with Morgan blocking his way. He listened hard. Branches scratched on the paintwork. Halam would be trying to move closer. Jeff heard a muttered curse in Arabic. The way the vehicle had jammed against the tree trunks was hindering him from getting close to Morgan's door. For a sickening second Jeff caught a glimpse of Halam's face through a thicket of branches. He must have managed to climb up to the front wheel. Jeff's heart raced. Halam would almost certainly be trying to aim his gun at him.

Then there was the faintest creak from the steering column as the front suspension supporting Halam's weight revolved a fraction. It took a second for the implications to sink in. Jeff applied both hands to the buckled steering wheel and twisted in the same direction as that movement. A curse then the sound of crashing through the undergrowth. Jeff managed a painful grin as he pictured Halam probably ten feet below, frustrated and angry. Hopefully scratched to hell. It was a fleeting moment of pleasure. He had no doubt Halam was working his way back up to the car.

He moved his legs. His left knee hurt badly. He felt around for anything to use as a weapon. Nothing. But there was a bag of coins in the glove box. He filled his right hand with them.

Light thuds sounded up the panel work. The tops of the branches alongside the vehicle shook suddenly as if blown by a strong breeze. Low guttural mutterings met his ears as Halam manoeuvred his way along the driver's side this time.

Every muscle in Jeff's body tensed. The carpet of dead leaves and twigs crackled and rustled as the killer pulled closer. A head squeezed through the branches and appeared at the edge of the door that hung open. Jeff feigned unconsciousness. He viewed Halam through slit eyes. He had to judge his move with care now. As the pistol rose, Jeff hurled the coins at the face. He leaped out at the would-be assassin. The pistol fired as it flew from Halam's grasp.

Jeff had the man in a bear hug. Bracing his feet on the door-jamb, he pushed himself and Halam clear of Morgan's vehicle. They tumbled further down the bank, thorns tearing at skin and cloth-ing. With a breath-expelling thud they landed in a clearing twenty feet below.

Jeff had managed to hold onto Halam's shirtfront. He pulled Halam to him and delivered a headbutt into Halam's face, shatter-ing his nose. Halam screamed. Blood spurted from his nostrils. Jeff held on grimly. He tried another headbutt, but this time Halam managed to block him with an arm. His right hand worked up under Jeff's chin, forcing his head back.

Jeff sucked in air. Pain assaulted every part of his body. With eyes blurring up and head spinning, he felt himself growing weaker. Probably sensing this, Halam pushed him away. Jeff rolled a few feet further into the clearing and lay on his back panting and looking up at the grey of the sky, now turning charcoal. The concussion caused him to think he was levitating a few millimetres above the ground. The idle thought that followed struck him as perfectly logical for the circumstances: hadn't they had enough bloody rain?

His hand lifted with difficulty. It pained his shoulder. Fingers prodded a little, then stopped. A hole through the jacket. A warm sticky substance oozed across his front.

'Jesus, I've been shot.'

Sounds of movement. A lazy roll of the head and he was looking at Halam crawling towards him. It took Jeff all of his remaining strength to raise himself to his knees.

Both men eyed each other. Halam's face was bloody. The nose swollen and off-centre. Jeff worked up a grin of satisfaction. But even that exertion took its toll. And he could see that Halam was gathering strength. Jeff knew he was going to die in a few moments.

❦

Avni Leka sat in his car, worried that at any moment help for the New Zealander and the American woman would come charging round the corner like the Ottoman cavalry on the Field of Blackbirds. And for him awaited the same fate that befell the Serbs. Minutes had dragged by since that single shot from down the bank. What the hell was Halam up to? Had he injured himself? Maybe the New Zealander had had a gun and killed Halam. He could be climbing up the slope this very minute intent on shooting him.

Leka looked towards the embankment. What was he to do? Sacrifice himself for nothing? He started the engine. He was only thirty minutes from the border. He couldn't wait much longer. Leka pushed the gear lever into drive and stole forward. He glanced into the rear-view mirror. Still nothing.

If Halam survived, he could always deal with the man's desire for revenge later. But to wait any longer could mean disaster for him in the present.

The decision made itself. A depression on the pedal and Leka's car jumped forward leaving a spray of pebbles in its wake.

 ⌒〜⌒

Jeff used his good arm to hold himself steady against the ground. Halam climbed to his feet.

'You are a very determined man. And you have fought well. We children of the Prophet admire this. Such bravery must have its rewards. I promise I will give you a quick death.'

Jeff swayed on his knees. The spinning of his head continued. He managed to maintain eye contact with Halam while he felt across the ground. All he could come up with for a weapon was a handful of dirt. He tossed it with an arm lacking in energy. Halam stopped and smiled as it scattered at his feet.

'Relax, my friend. It will be over quickly.'

Halam's voice sounded almost gentle. He reached down and locked his arm around Jeff's neck. Jeff fought for breath. Then Halam put a hand against the side of Jeff's head. Jeff knew the hold. His neck was about to be snapped.

He had lost.

Crack! Crack!

Jeff fell forward. As he hit the ground, he rolled onto his back and gasped, air ripping into his lungs with icy sharpness along with the realisation he was still alive. Halam fell beside him, sightless eyes staring vacantly into Jeff's own. There was a bullet hole in the side of Halam's head. Blood poured from a second wound in his neck.

Jeff knew from the flashing lights around the periphery of his vision that he was losing consciousness. Through the haze of a darkening world he saw Morgan, fiery hair wild around her face, scratched and bloodied and standing with legs braced, holding Halam's pistol at arm's length. A wisp of smoke threaded from its barrel.

His last thought as he slipped into oblivion was what a woman this would be to love for a lifetime.

༄

Lee Caldwell held his mobile phone in the air. He wanted to throw it against the warehouse wall. Instead he kicked an empty can and sent it clanging into the side of a burnt-out van.

Jeff Bradley and Morgan Delaney were not responding to Barry's calls. He had contacted the Bondsteel military camp and they had a chopper in the air, but he was afraid it would be too little, too late.

One of his men stepped out from the warehouse wiping his huge hands on a rag. 'I think we're done, sir.'

'Tell me then.'

'They're brothers. They use the names Halam and Zahar Akbar. Whether or not these are their real names, well, he isn't saying. They're Palestinians but left many years ago. The Saudi passports are false and they have others. They had never met Avni Leka until today. This Leka gave them the jobs and provided the funding. They came to Kosovo to recover the money they lost in Greece.'

Caldwell smiled. At least Dimitris's man had not died in vain.

'He didn't know how Leka raised the funds or anything else to do with Leka's business. The targets they bombed were always claimed by another organisation.'

'Contract bombers,' Caldwell murmured with a shake of the head.

'He says his brother wanted to retire, marry some girl back home and live happily ever after.' The man smiled as if at a joke. Caldwell didn't join him. 'But our friend wasn't ready to settle down in a tent and herd goats. He said he was negotiating for a new contract on his own, no idea who the target is, or where, only that it's six to nine months from now. That's it. I believe he's told us all he knows.'

'Then he is of no further use to us?' Caldwell asked.

'None at all.'

Caldwell walked back into the warehouse. When he entered the office, Zahar lifted his bloodied head and managed a hollow smile. Caldwell faced the guard.

'So. He thinks he's given his brother time to escape. Well, maybe he has. Take him out to Bondsteel now. They'll want a chat. I'm walking back to town. I need some exercise.'

52.

He felt like he was floating on a raft at sea. The fog dense about him, but in the distance, a light.

'Can you hear me?' The male voice was soft, quiet, American. And unfamiliar.

Jeff nodded but could discern no face anywhere. The light blinded him. Then it disappeared. The fuzzy apparition now emerging into focus at last resembled a human face.

'Mr Bradley. I'm Doctor Joshua Kline. You are in the Bondsteel Military Hospital.'

'Hospital?'

The tang of disinfectant now assaulting his nose convinced him this was true. He rolled his head to one side. Small lights flickered and wavy lines crossed on a green monitor screen. The machine bleeped when he rolled his head back.

'Can you tell me your name?'

'Jeff Bradley.'

'Do you know where you are?'

'Kosovo.'

'Do you know which country you live in?'

'New Zealand. Why am I here?'

'You were in an accident.'

'An accident?'

Jeff's eyes closed. He tried to concentrate. Images came and went like wraiths. He had been following Avni Leka. Then there was a man standing in the middle of the road. Morgan had been in the vehicle. They had crashed.

Jeff opened his eyes. A nurse stood at the end of the bed writing something onto a clipboard. She stepped closer to check the drip line inserted in his arm.

'There was a woman in the vehicle with me. Morgan Delaney.'

'Your companion was discharged the same day. She had a few scratches and bruises, nothing more.'

'Thank God. How long have I been here?'

'Two and half days. You were in a pretty awful state when they brought you in. You'd lost a lot of blood. You had us worried for quite some time.'

'The men I was following. What happened to them?'

'I'm sorry, I have no idea. You'll need to ask someone else for that information.'

When Jeff slept again he dreamed he was fighting in a forest but could not use his arms. A man with his face hidden in shadow was laughing at him. Taunting him. Then the man disappeared and standing in his place was Morgan, holding a gun.

❧

Even with his eyes closed Jeff recognised the perfume and smiled.

'Hi,' he said and opened his eyes.

'Hi, yourself.' Morgan took a chair and pulled it close to the bed. She sat and took his hand. 'I won't ask how you feel because you look awful. So I guess that's the answer.'

'Love your bedside manner. You'd make a lousy nurse.'

'The doctor said you'll be out of here in a few days. I have some important messages for you. Barry wants me to tell you that you owe him a beer, or at least that I'm to get the price of it out of you before you "kark it". I think that means before you go toes up. And Sulla says you owe him for petrol.'

Jeff tried to laugh but winced instead. 'I'm glad they miss me.'

'Barry and his police friends came with me to the hotel. We moved your belongings to my apartment.'

'What about my bill?'

'Caldwell paid it.'

'Morgan. You saved my life.'

She forced a smile. 'You've put me through a lot of grief. Too much for someone I barely know. You owe me an expensive dinner.'

'What about you. Any broken bones?'

'No, but I have a few bruises in places I can't show. And a bump on the head.' She touched her hairline. 'I guess we were lucky.'

He squeezed her hand.

'Thank you for everything.'

Jeff so desperately wanted to keep looking at the beautiful woman, who, in defiance of all logic, seemed to think he was an okay bloke. But his eyelids grew heavy once more. He clung to her hand as if it was a lifeline. And as he drifted off, it comforted him to know she was watching over him.

53.

Jeff tossed his toiletries and other bits and pieces into the small carry bag. Packing with one arm in a sling wasn't easy. His shoulder was stiff and it ached, but it was beginning to free up and the painkillers made it bearable. He would need to put up with the sling for another week or risk nerve damage, the doctor had warned him.

He had been lucky.

The bullet had missed bone and vital organs. The cuts on his face would leave interesting scars. The rest of his body had mostly healed but the inside of his mouth still felt like he had swallowed dirt. He guessed it was the drugs. He stopped short at his reflection in the mirror and nearly laughed. The bruising round his eyes had reduced to black shadows. He looked like a raccoon.

Packing finished, he stood at the window looking out. On the parade ground a hundred metres away, a drill sergeant screamed in red-faced apoplexy as he put a squad of soldiers through a routine. The sun shone and it felt good to be alive. The familiar sounds of the military brought a smile to his face. And yes, if he was honest, he did miss it.

A car was on its way to take him into Prishtina.

When he heard a light tap on the door, he turned expecting to see the driver.

It was Lee Caldwell. 'Bradley. How're you holding up?'

'Been better.'

'I would've come sooner but the doctor said you needed rest.'

'Glad you came. What happened out there? I haven't been able to get anything out of the doctor. And Morgan has been babying me and telling me to wait until I'm stronger. It seems she's uncovered a long lost nurturing streak.'

Caldwell smiled. 'That is one remarkable woman. As I understand it, she came around just as you jumped Halam Akbar. She managed to drag herself out of the vehicle and scramble down the bank after the two of you. She came across Halam's pistol. Then she shot him. Seems her father had problems from time to time in his pub. Bought a gun to protect the daily takings and taught all the family how to use it. Lucky for you, she's a pretty handy shot.'

'I can't argue with that.'

'Morgan did a good job stopping the bleeding. And lucky for you again it was still daylight. When Sulla and the others arrived, they were able to wave down the chopper from Bondsteel and you were brought here. Apart from your well-earned battle scars, you and your friends have come through this little adventure relatively unscathed.'

'And Avni Leka?'

Caldwell sighed. 'He got away. I sent out an alert to the borders but somehow he still managed to slip through. It's a loss, but we now know who we're looking for. We had a stroke of luck when we found one of the officers taking payouts from him – the one who nearly got you killed by failing to pass on my information to the border police. He was keeping a file on Leka and his activities, which has been extremely useful.'

Jeff zipped his bag closed. 'The money for Sulla and Blerim?'

'Taken care of.'

A soldier appeared at the door and reported that Jeff's car was ready. Caldwell picked up Jeff's bag.

'Come on, I'll walk you out.'

Jeff discovered that Caldwell was of the same mind as him as he made to skirt around the top of the parade ground. Only an ex-soldier would know you never walk on the parade ground when a drill sergeant is in the vicinity.

'You're definitely not CIA, are you?'

'No? How do you figure?'

'If you were, there'd have been Navy Seals and black-ops types swarming all over this before us amateurs even knew enough to blink.'

Caldwell said nothing, his pace matching Jeff's.

'You're not with US Trade either.'

Caldwell glanced at him with a half-smile.

'And I'm thinking you're not going to tell me who you're really working for, are you?'

'No. But you, Bradley. You will be going back to New Zealand now, won't you?'

'Oh, yeah. I'm looking forward to going home.'

The driver stood by the open door to assist Jeff. Caldwell waved him away. He threw Jeff's bag onto the back seat. 'Then I guess this is goodbye.' They shook hands. 'Have a good life, Bradley. You deserve it.'

Caldwell helped Jeff into the car then stepped back to close the door. Jeff held up his hand to stop him. 'From an operational point of view, was it a success for you?'

'We broke them up. Captured one terrorist bomber and killed another. Maybe we'll capture Avni Leka before he can regroup and start up somewhere else. Maybe not. In my world this is a success.'

Caldwell slammed the door shut, then tapped the roof of the vehicle.

∞

Jeff asked the driver to drop him at the top of the lane that ran down to the Kukri bar. Morgan had left a message that she would wait for him at the pub. An hour in the back of the Bondsteel vehicle had stiffened his body. It needed a stretch.

Bag in hand, Jeff made his way down the slope. His left knee was troubling him and he walked with a limp. The jolt from each step reverberated across his cracked ribs. But despite the pain and soreness he was happy to be out and about.

The bar owner, Big John, halfway through pouring a pint caught sight of him entering. They exchanged nods. Soldier to soldier. Jeff's pathway to the bar was blocked by patrons crowding around island tables watching *Match of the Day* on the TV. From the bar Big John bellowed for everyone to move aside.

A way opened.

Morgan, Barry, Bethany and Sulla stood at Barry's usual spot. Their faces beamed *Welcome home*, but Jeff could see in their eyes another emotion he had not experienced in a long time. The deep-seated camaraderie that comes from having shared a dangerous mission.

Morgan took a step towards him. Jeff let his bag drop to the floor and reached out with his one good arm. She took his hand and raised her head to brush his lips with hers.

Barry picked up Jeff's bag. 'Enough of that you two. Come on, mate, we've saved you a spot. A lot of bloody beer will be drunk tonight.'

'Barry. What I need most is a table and orange juice.'

'Consider it done, mate.'

After an hour and too many drinks, Sulla took his leave and Barry and Bethany were back arguing with the South Africans.

Morgan and Jeff were at last face-to-face and alone. 'When are you leaving? You are leaving?'

Jeff chuckled.

'This time, yes. In a few days. I have a vineyard to run, remember.'

'And Arben Shala's family? What about them?'

'I'm hoping they'll stay on. Marko knows as much about wine as his father did. The kid'll make a good manager. But Kimie's proud. I'll need to convince her it's not charity. Then there's Arben's vineyard here. I doubt Kimie will ever want to come back so I'll ask Sulla to oversee it until she decides what she wants to do. There's a good man running the place so Sulla doesn't need to know much about the industry. And I'm sure if there's a way to get bulk wine out of Kosovo, Sulla will find it. Having a brother-in-law who is a smuggler might be a big help.'

'What if your ex-wife insists the vineyard goes to auction?'

'I'll find the money from somewhere to keep her paws off it.' Jeff was thoughtful for a few seconds. 'When I think about it, what else can I do? I spread my grandmother's ashes under the jacaranda tree there. And Benny gave his life for that vineyard. How could I let it go now?'

Morgan leaned across the table to kiss Jeff's bruised cheek. She smiled when he winced. 'You're a good man, Jeff Bradley.'

'You know? New Zealand might seem a long way away, but if you can sleep on a plane, it's no distance at all.'

'Is that so? Well, maybe I just might go talk to a travel agent.'

Jeff leaned forward. 'Let's be party poopers. As I recall, Caldwell interrupted us and I believe we have unfinished business.'

'Really?'

'Really.'

She ran her hand down the arm in the sling, then held on to his fingers poking from the end still puffy and blue.

'But what about your poor broken body?'

'Be gentle with me.'

Morgan did not argue when Jeff took her by the hand and led her from the bar.

ACKNOWLEDGEMENTS

I need to thank so many. To my family, extended family, and friends, who readily accepted their role as readers and the others who aided in so many ways, Olivia and Steve Lane, Archie and Hugo Lane, Sandy and Fiona Brown, Trevor and Rosina McGarry, Graham and Valerie Ellis, Julie Brown, Libby Hewitt, John Phillips, Brendon and Angela Madden-Smith, and Craig Flood.

To the many who critiqued my work and helped guide me through the process of arranging my words into legible order, Trisha Hanifin, Sue Gee, Meemee Phipps, Karen Van Eden, David Arrowsmith, Miles Hughes. The many assessors who continuously ripped my manuscript to shreds and left me in absolute despair, Tina Shaw, Graeme Lay, Stephen Stratford, Barbara and Chris Else, James George.

To my military advisors, Captain Martin Knight-Willis Rtd and Ken McKee-Wright.

To Jocelyn Watkin for invaluable marketing advice.

A big thanks to my mentor, Lee N. Wood, an equally big thank-you to Ron Davis, who painstakingly helped craft the final touches. And a special thank-you to the Amazon Publishing team. Emilie Marneur, for finding my book and giving me the opportunity to become a Thomas and Mercer author and to Katie Green and Luke Brown, two truly professional editors who added the final polish.

ABOUT THE AUTHOR

Thomas Ryan has been a soldier in a theatre of war, traded in Eastern Europe, trampled the jungles of Asia and struggled through the trials of love and loss: ideal life experiences for a would-be author. Schooled by professionals who have helped him hone his literary style, Ryan is quickly establishing himself as a skilled writer of riveting thrillers and short stories. He considers himself foremost a storyteller, a creator who has plunged his psyche into the world of imagination and fantasy. Taking readers on a thrilling journey is what motivates Ryan as a writer.